I0668775

THE EMPTY MINT MYSTERY

BLOOD, GUNS, AND GOLD

GORDON PARKER

PUBLICATION
CONSULTANTS
We Believe In The Power Of Authors

PO Box 221974 Anchorage, Alaska 99522-1974
books@publicationconsultants.com—www.publicationconsultants.com

ISBN Number: 978-1-59433-798-7
eBook ISBN Number: 978-1-59433-799-4

Manufactured in the United States of America

Dedication

To Domini

MONDAY, APRIL 19

Betty Anderson stood on the porch of her home, supporting herself with one arm wrapped around a column. She watched the nasty little man drive away, his tires throwing up swirls of dust in the otherwise still Louisiana morning. Claiming to be an agent of the Treasury Department, he had for the second and, he said, final time warned her to cooperate. His agency knew, he said, that she was in possession of valuable property belonging to the United States government.

She tried to make him understand that he was referring to events that had occurred in 1862. Events of which she knew nothing. If she could give him what he sought she would do so.

That only infuriated him more. If she refused to comply with his demands she would suffer for it, he threatened. And, he said, her daughter would suffer. Everything they owned would be jeopardized. His agency would not hesitate to take it all.

Betty Anderson was not a weak person. She was a scion of the Belmonts, a proud family prominent in their parish for generations.

She didn't scare easily.

Today she was scared.

With trembling fingers she dialed her daughter's phone number.

2,000 miles away Darcey Anderson was focused on the document in front of her. It was the final invoice for her design firm's billable hours on a large house now completely remodeled and full of very expensive furniture in San Francisco's elite Pacific Heights. When added to the

[5]

commissions due on the furnishings, it meant a lot of money for her company. It was important.

The ringing of her mobile phone broke her concentration and irritated her. She would have ignored the call but it was her mother.

"Hey, there" she answered. "I didn't expect to hear from you this morning. Are you all right?"

"I don't think so, Darcey." Her voice sounded shaky.

"What's going on, Mom? Tell me."

"Well, a man with the Treasury Department in Washington, D.C., has been coming around here. It concerns that old story about missing Confederate gold. He says it's the property of the U.S. government. He says they have information that it's hidden somewhere here at the Pines and if I don't turn it over the government will seize the farm."

"What? They can't do that. Nobody even knows if that story is anything but a legend. Did you talk to your lawyer? What did he say?"

"He said if the gold exists it is the property of the U.S. government. He said they can make a lot of trouble for us. We can go to court to stop them from taking the farm. He thinks we would probably win but the government could tie us up for years and it would cost a fortune."

"What about the sheriff? Did you talk to him?" Darcey inquired.

"Jack will help us any way he can. But unless this treasury man threatens me physically or breaks a state law there's not much he can do."

"Has he threatened you?" Darcey asked, alarmed.

"No, not directly. He's only talked about taking the farm. But he's a mousy, nervous little man. He's very unpleasant. I'm scared, Darcey. Can you come home for a few days?"

Darcey quickly scanned her calendar for the next three weeks. There was nothing that demanded her presence.

"Of course, Mom. I'll fly down tomorrow. And don't worry. We're not going to lose the farm." She hoped she sounded more confident than she felt.

She took the invoice next door to her executive assistant's office.

"Looks good to me," she said as she handed it to Miles Diaz-Douglas. "Send it. The sooner Mr. Wagner gets the bill the sooner we get our money."

"I am all over that, girl."

"And I'll be gone for a few days. Mom has asked me to come home to help her with a problem. I don't think there's anything on the schedule that you can't handle without me."

"Don't worry about anything here. And tell your mom it's time she paid us another visit."

The Brazilian born Miles was the first employee she had hired when her business began its rapid growth. He was a nice looking man. Two inches taller than her 5' 6", he wore his dark hair cut short and was clean shaven. They were a good team and, when she needed someone to accompany her to an important social event, a handsome couple.

"Why don't you come with me, Miles? I'll teach you to ride a horse," she said, mischievously.

"Are you out of your mind?" Miles responded, pressing his hand to his chest in a gesture of mock horror. "Me? On a farm? Riding a four-legged animal?"

Darcey laughed. "By the way, the Wagners will be holding an open house. I'll need an escort. Will you be available?" she asked.

"Certainly. Has it been scheduled?"

"Not yet. I'll let you know. Are you sure Scott won't mind?" she teased as she left his office.

"Girl, you can have any man you want," the imperturbable Miles replied. "Any man but me. Scott's not worried."

Back in her office, she booked a flight to Shreveport for the following day. Her mother had offered to pick her up but she preferred to rent a car for the drive to the Pines, an hour and a half south of the airport.

That evening Darcey poured a glass of Chardonnay and walked out onto the terrace of her condo. She had purchased it two years ago. It was high in a building on Nob Hill, near Grace Cathedral and Huntington Park. From here she had a view of the entire city. The lights of the Golden Gate and Bay Bridges. She could hear the clang of the street cars on Powell Street.

The evening fog was rolling in. She watched as it closed over the city below her like an oyster protecting its pearl. This pearl of a city.

Her thoughts returned to her family farm in Louisiana. She thought about the conversation with her mother. It was hard to believe that old rumor about an unsubstantiated event in 1862 had come back to haunt them again after all these years. In the past it had been treasure hunters snooping around. The government had never inquired. For that reason her family had decided it was nothing but legend.

APRIL 29, 1862

Shameful. Simply shameful.

From where he stood atop the levee Lieutenant Henry Belmont could see a dozen Union gunboats lying just off New Orleans. Union Flag Officer Farragut had steamed past the fortifications downriver at Forts Jackson and St. Phillip five nights ago losing only one vessel in the process. The pathetically small, under-manned Confederate fleet was no match for Farragut.

The young man in Confederate gray took off his forage cap and ran his hand through his wavy blonde hair. It was a warm spring day. His hair was damp. As he stared out at the victorious Union fleet he was angry. The Union fleet had been met by twelve lightly armed Confederate vessels, two of which were immobile. All because some idiot in Richmond had sent the bulk of the Mississippi River fleet up to Vicksburg, leaving the south's largest port undefended. Eight of the Confederate vessels now lay on the bottom of the river.

Major General Mansfield Lovell commanded an ostensible "army" with which he was expected to defend the city. An army of 3,000 farmers. Few uniforms. No training. Armed only with whatever they had brought from home. Mostly shotguns, and precious little powder and shot for those. The

Union now controlled the lower Mississippi River and New Orleans. Lovell's army couldn't do a thing about it.

He put the cap back on his head, pulling the brim down low over his eyes. They'd have to fight, he reckoned. He was assigned to General Lovell's personal staff. The only action he'd seen was when the general and his staff were riding into New Orleans. Four red-legs fired at them from the trees along the road. The general himself led the five members of his staff in a counter attack. One of the ambushers was killed. The others ran.

Belmont didn't remember much about the fight. He had no idea whose bullet killed the man. It all happened so quickly. When it was over his hand was shaking. He laid his pistol across the leather of his saddle. He didn't trust his trembling hand to get it back into the holster. He remembered what his father had told him.

"Being brave doesn't mean you're not afraid," his father had said. "That's means you're stupid. Being brave is doing what you have to do when you're scared. Just don't let anyone know you're scared."

He didn't think any of the others noticed his shaking hand trying to holster his pistol. What worried him was they had fought four red-legs. Not soldiers. Bandits. How would he react in a battle against well-trained soldiers? That's what worried him.

He looked again at the Union fleet floating just off shore. His father had been right. This war was insanity. The south had no chance to win. No chance at all.

He wished he was at home riding horses through the woods with his brothers, Richard and Benjamin. Richard was with Lee's army in Virginia. Henry didn't know if he was still alive. Benjamin was the youngest. He was home helping their father run the farm.

"Henry," he heard a deep voice calling. A voice with the hard accent of north Louisiana. Neither the musical Cajun nor the diversity-honed New Orleans accent. "Henry Belmont. Over here."

He looked toward the Café du Monde, the coffee house that had opened only weeks prior. His spirits rose as he saw a familiar face from home. He strode quickly down the levee toward the sound.

"Rube, what are you doing here?" Belmont said as he shook hands with the scruffy, laughing man sitting at one of the iron tables in the open air of the coffee house.

"Just brought down a load of freight for a feller. Sit down. They make passable coffee here 'cept they put milk in it," Rube laughed. "But with the war and all it's mostly chicory anyway."

No one knew how old Rube was. Or where he came from. He showed up one day when he was boy. He told folks he was the only one in his family who had survived a tornado that hit their farm. When they asked him where it happened he just pointed northeast. He didn't know for sure. Or how old he was.

The Belmont family took a liking to the orphan boy. They figured he must have been about eight years old. They saw to it that he had a warm place to sleep and plenty to eat. Formal schooling was only a sometimes thing in that part of the country in those days. But Rube was allowed free use of Andrew Belmont's large library. He proved to be a voracious reader. A young man hungry to learn. And even as a boy Rube was not afraid of hard work.

His hair was dark. Almost black. His face was tan and leathery from a lifetime spent working outdoors. He was not a big man, standing three inches below Henry's six feet. But he was known for his great strength. Strength that came from hard work.

As he grew to manhood he developed a special way with mules. He made a decent living doing anything needing a mule. He handled the animals that were used to drag logs out of the tangled forests of the eastern edge of the Big Thicket country. Sometimes he got work hauling freight up to Shreveport or down to Baton Rouge or New Orleans.

When Henry was younger he loved to help Rube tend his mules. The muleskinner treated his animals like babies. Henry asked him one day why he favored the mules over horses.

"Mules are smarter than horses," Rube told him.

That surprised Henry. "I never heard that before."

"Look here," Rube patiently explained "you can work a horse to death. If you push him he'll just keep going until he falls over. A mule won't do that. When a mule gets tired he stops. There ain't a thing you can do to get him moving again. A mule thinks for himself."

Henry sipped the café au lait that had been set before him and bit into the beignet Rube offered him.

"What are you doin' down here anyways?" Rube asked. "I figured you'd be up in Virginia fightin' with old Bobby Lee."

"Richard's up there with Lee. I got assigned as an aide to General Lovell," Belmont said. "Lovell's army is here. Not that it's much of an army."

"Have you heard anything from your brother?" Rube asked.

"Not a word," Henry said, "but the mail isn't exactly reliable these days."

"Richard's a smart man, Henry," Rube said, "and he's tough. He'll do all right."

Henry nodded, hoping Rube was right.

"The Union is taking over New Orleans, Rube," Henry said. "If I were you I'd get out."

"That's exactly what I'm gonna do," Rube said, "just as soon as my wagon's ready. Got me a brand new Newman & Cooper freight wagon. Built up in Iowa. It's a doozy. And I got six of the finest mules you ever saw. I ain't about to hang around here and let'em get drafted into the Union army. But got to finish packing the wheels with grease before I can leave. It was a rough trip comin' down here."

"See many Federals?" Belmont asked.

"They're every place you look up around Baton Rouge," Rube answered. "I had to slip off the road and hide in the woods twice to let Yank horse soldiers go by. They'd have taken my wagon, mules, freight, everything if they'd seen me. Now I guess they'll be all over New Orleans."

"Yeah," Belmont agreed. "New Orleans will be in Union hands by tomorrow."

"Lieutenant Belmont?"

Henry turned to see General Lovell's orderly standing by their table.

"Yes, sergeant?" Belmont said.

"General Lovell wants to see you in his office immediately."

"All right, sergeant," Belmont replied. Rising, he shook hands with Rube. "Be careful going home, Rube. Tell Mother and Father that I'm well."

"I'll do that," Rube said. "See that you stay that way, Henry."

Belmont followed the sergeant to military headquarters where General Lovell waited with his distinctive mutton chop whiskers, which Henry thought made him look a little clownish. In reality he was a fine officer currently handed an impossible assignment. The general motioned Henry into his private office and closed the door behind him.

Half an hour later the door to General Lovell's office opened. The general stepped out, followed by the junior officer.

"Sergeant," Lovell said, "see to it that Lieutenant Belmont gets anything he asks for. Anything. Is that clear?"

Standing to attention, the sergeant replied, "Yes, Sir."

Lovell turned to Belmont. "Good luck, Lieutenant. We're depending on you."

"Thank you, Sir," Belmont replied. He raised his arm in salute. Lovell returned the salute, then turned and strode back into his office, closing the door behind him.

Turning to the sergeant, Belmont asked, "Do you remember the man I was with when you found me earlier today?"

"I think so," the sergeant replied.

"His name is Rube. He has a wagon that he is preparing for travel. Find him," Belmont ordered.

Belmont followed the sergeant out of the office. He didn't think anyone saw his hands trembling.

SUNDAY, APRIL 26

Not everyone liked chicken livers for breakfast. Trent Marshall did. Trent was used to being in the minority.

Marshall was just under six feet tall. His trim body showed evidence of a man who took care of himself. At 45 years his brown hair sported a touch of silver in it. He hadn't shaved in a couple of days, which gave him that popular bad boy look. He was thinking about either shaving or growing a beard. It wasn't that he disliked the stubble. He just didn't like doing the popular thing.

It was Sunday morning. Marshall was at his favorite table in the Coffee Pot, the venerable restaurant that had been serving up breakfast on St. Peter Street in New Orleans' Vieux Carre' since the late 19th century. He had just finished his order of Eggs Conti. Poached eggs resting on a huge, fluffy biscuit, dressed with chicken livers and green onion sautéed in a light wine sauce.

Now his attention was on a bowl containing a rice ball swimming in maple syrup. The calas was a unique New Orleans pastry, once sold by street vendors in years gone by. Most often served with a dusting of powdered sugar, he preferred his with syrup. It wasn't something Marshall would eat every day. Too rich. Too sweet. But it was a treat worth having occasionally. Sunday was always occasionally.

The first bite was the best. The sweet of the deep fried rice ball dripping from its maple syrup bath dueled with the lingering savory of the eggs and chicken livers. A most pleasant duel. No victor. No conquered. Only contentment. Sheer pleasure in a world not always pleasant.

[13]

He had noticed the woman sitting alone as she glanced at him several times, quickly looking away when she thought he might look up. He had not looked up. He was enjoying his favorite Sunday morning ritual and didn't want to be disturbed. His mother worked here as a waitress when he was a boy. When she had to work on Sunday mornings she sat him at this table and brought him the sweet rice ball. Though she had been gone for many years he returned each Sunday. It was a way of holding onto the memory of her.

The woman made it impossible to remain undisturbed as she rose and walked the few steps to his table.

"Excuse me," she said, "are you Trent Marshall?"

He didn't look up. He took another bite of calas. He thought her accent sounded as though it might have started out southern but the drawl had been drained out of it. Probably born southern and moved to one of the coasts. A lot of young people in Louisiana did that. A lot of them came home eventually.

"I don't mean to be rude," she said, "but I'm talking to you. Are you Trent Marshall?"

He sighed. He wiped a bit of syrup from his lips with a white cloth napkin. Finally, he looked up to see the striking blonde standing at his table. It was a warm spring day. She wore a floral sundress and sandals. Her hair was pulled back into a pony tail. He tried not to be swayed but it was difficult. She was stunning.

"Maybe," he replied. "Who are you?"

"My name is Darcey Anderson, Mr. Marshall," she responded to his questions. "I need help. I need an experienced investigator."

"Why come to me?" Marshall asked. "I'm not a cop. Never been one."

"No, but Jack Blake said I should talk to you."

"Now why would old Jack send you to me?" Marshall wondered aloud.

"He said you were the best investigative reporter he's ever known and if anyone could help me you could," Darcey said. "Listen, I'm feeling a little foolish standing here in this restaurant with all these people watching. Would you mind if I sat down?"

Marshall ignored her question. There was a time when he probably was the best investigative reporter in the business. Then he stumbled onto a story involving political corruption. Astonishingly bold theft of the people's money in a state famous for stealing the people's money. He unraveled the scheme thread by thread. The last thread ended at the Toledo Bend Lake fishing camp owned by his best friend, Josh Blair, a legislator representing suburban Baton Rouge. Best friends since they played high school football together.

Marshall had been best man at Blair's wedding. And he was there the night Josh was arrested.

Hands cuffed behind his back, Blair was being led out to Chief Deputy Matt Lorca's vehicle. He stopped in front of Marshall.

"You know my Daddy will have me out of jail by the time you get home," he said, with a smirk.

The smirk disappeared. "Then we'll see about you," Blair said.

"Yeah," Marshall said softly. "Then we'll see."

Marshall watched his friend being led away. He was numb. Emotionally empty. But it was Blair's ten year old son, Johnny, who made the reporter want to vomit.

Johnny threw himself at the man he called Uncle Trent. Striking out at him with his small fists. Crying. Screaming.

"I hate you. I hate you. I hope you die. I wish I could kill you myself."

The boy's mother pulled her son off Marshall, holding him in her arms. She stared at Marshall. No tears. Nothing in her eyes at all. She just stared at him.

It was quiet in the big SUV as Sheriff Jack Blake drove along the dark, narrow road winding through the thick northwest Louisiana woods. He didn't say anything. Nothing at all. He'd been sheriff for a long time. He had been where Marshall was now. There was nothing that could be said that would help. He handed Marshall a bottle of water. He would rather have offered bourbon but it was an election year.

Marshall drove back to New Orleans the next day. He had seen this day coming for a long time. Josh was born into one of the state's wealthiest families. From the day he was born he had anything he wanted. From the time he was born he was told he was the best. The finest. He was admitted to all the best schools. Got all the best jobs. He never had to work for any of it. He had no idea what it meant to have to work for a living.

He believed he was entitled to do anything he wanted. To take whatever he wanted from whomever he wanted to take it. Trent watched Josh humiliate people he considered less than him simply because he could. Trent sometimes felt the sting of Josh's barbs himself.

Marshall knew Josh was a narcissist. He knew it wouldn't end well.

Marshall had known all that for a long time. And yet Josh was his friend. He thought he had to stand by him.

But the price of standing by Josh became too high. Higher than Marshall could pay. He called Jack Blake.

That was ten years ago. Josh died after only three months in prison. Stabbed to death. Marshall hadn't asked why. He didn't want to know.

Trent didn't attend Josh's funeral. He was at the cemetery when they interred the body in the family mausoleum. He stood well back from the crowd. In the trees. Out of sight. He could see Josh's wife and son. He could see her eyes still looked dull. Lifeless. He watched as she tried to comfort her son. He pushed her away. He ran from her. Marshall could hear his grief through the trees. He could feel it in his own chest.

"I thought I might find you here." New Orleans Detective Jordan Baron had walked up quietly to stand beside him. "It wasn't your fault, you know."

"I might have been able to help him before he got out of control," Marshall said.

"No, Trent, you couldn't help him. He was born out of control."

Six months later the story won Trent a Pulitzer Prize. The day he received the certificate and check he laid them on a table. He set a bottle of tequila and a glass on the table beside them. He stared at the certificate. He drank the tequila.

The next morning he tossed the certificate into the trash, cashed the check, and quit his job.

The young woman's voice dragged him back from his thoughts.

"The sheriff said you're the best investigator he ever knew," Darcey said, anger creeping into her voice. "He said you can be quite inconsiderate."

Marshall looked up, suddenly grateful to be pulled from the muddle of bad memories by the woman growing impatient with him. And he owed Jack Blake more than a few favors.

"Well, I guess he's right, Ms. Anderson," he said, "though my mother tried to raise me to be a gentleman." He rose and held a chair for her. "Please join me. Can I get you something?"

Relieved to no longer be the center of attention in the restaurant, Darcey quickly sat. "Maybe a café au lait," she replied.

"Ivy, a café au lait for the lady, please," Trent called out to the cheerful black woman passing their table.

"Coming right up," she replied, her smile disappearing as she cast a glance at the gorgeous blonde now seated at Trent's table.

Moments later, Ivy returned with the cup of coffee laced with chicory, infused with hot milk. She placed the cup on the table in front of the lady. She stared at Trent. Marshall knew Ivy was curious and would pester him until she got the story. He told her a friend of his had asked him to help Darcey with something. That he had just met her.

"Uh huh," Ivy said, rolling her eyes as she walked away.

Darcey smiled. "Seems like she knows you pretty well."

Marshall shook his head. "Yeah, she thinks she's my mother. How did you know where to find me?"

"Sheriff Blake said if it was eleven o'clock on a Sunday morning you'd be in this restaurant at this table."

Marshall nodded. Blake was one of the few people he had ever invited to share his cherished weekend breakfast ritual

"So what is it you think I can help you with?"

"A member of my family has been accused of stealing government gold, Mr. Marshall. A great deal of government gold."

"How much?" Trent asked.

"$483,000," she said.

"Well, that's more than pocket change," Trent said, "but as the theft of government money goes it's not a lot. There's probably a politician here in this city who stole that much before breakfast this morning."

"It was in 1862 gold double eagles, Mr. Marshall," Darcey said. "Today that would be more than $11 million. My uncle was innocent. I want you to help me prove that."

He stared at her.

"Let me see if I understand you correctly," he said, finally. "You want me to help you solve a crime that occurred more than one hundred fifty years ago and prove your relative was innocent."

"That's right," Darcey said, flashing a smile that had convinced other men to do things for her that seemed impossible. Things that seemed ridiculous. But this had to be the nuttiest one of all.

"Lady, that's the goofiest thing I've ever heard," Marshall said, with less sensitivity than he might have shown. "Just plain goofy."

"It is not," Darcey said, in that special voice that made Marshall think she would have stomped her foot if she was standing. Then in a quieter tone, "Besides there's more to it. A Treasury Department man showed up at my mother's house. The government wants its money back."

"This happened a century and a half ago and the government is just now getting around to asking for the money?" Marshall laughed.

"This isn't funny to me, Mr. Marshall," Darcey said. "I'm scared. My mother's scared. We don't know anything about this. Just some old rumors. But the government man threatened to take my mother's home. We'll fight them in court if we have to but it could take years and cost a fortune. Nobody has enough money to fight the federal government if they really want to get you."

The look on the young woman's face told him she was serious. He could see the fear in her eyes.

"This isn't a good place to talk," Marshall said. "Too many people around. Let's get out of here."

Ivy put Darcey's café au lait in a go cup and handed Marshall a cup of his own without being asked. Black with chicory and just a little sugar. She watched Trent walk out of the restaurant with the girl. She was protective of him. She knew how badly he had been hurt. She was worried. She hadn't often seen him with a woman in the past ten years. There was something about this one that made her think she might see her again. She should be feeling happy for him. But she was worried.

He led Darcey out of the restaurant, turning right to guide her the short distance to Jackson Square. They threaded their way through the tourists, musicians, magicians, fortune tellers and artists, both portrait and con, all in the shadow of the magnificent 18th century St. Louis Cathedral.

Darcey pointed out that there were hundreds of people in the square. Far more than had been in the restaurant.

"That's why it's a better place to talk," Marshall said. "Wide open space. People paying no attention whatsoever to us. If you want to go unnoticed put yourself in the middle of a crowd. To quote Sherlock Holmes, 'Hide in plain sight.' If people don't expect to see you, they usually don't."

He guided her through the gate in the iron fence that surrounded the two acres of formal gardens. They passed tourists getting their pictures taken by the fountain at the entrance and on the statue of Andrew Jackson, the hero of New Orleans.

"Was all this here during the War Between the States?" Darcey asked.

That confirmed Marshall's suspicion that she was born southern. Only southerners referred to the war in that way. Elsewhere it was called the Civil War.

"Yeah, and the open air building across the street is the Café du Monde, which started serving beignets and café au lait about the time your uncle was here."

Marshall led her through the gardens until he found a bench that was relatively secluded. They sat and sipped their coffee.

"Tell me your story, Ms. Anderson," Marshall directed. "Tell me everything."

"We really don't know a lot, Mr. Marshall," Darcey began. "I am descended from the Belmont family, a family that has been prominent in northwest Louisiana along the Texas border for several generations. In 1862 my third great uncle was a lieutenant assigned as an aide to the general in command of Confederate forces in New Orleans.

"The Confederates were greatly outmatched by the Union forces so the Confederate general withdrew from the city. But before he left he gave my uncle, Lieutenant Henry Belmont, a special assignment."

"Call me Trent," Marshall said. "What kind of assignment?"

"OK, Trent," she smiled. "And you should call me Darcey. That's so much better than goofy."

Marshall felt himself relaxing in her company. It had been a long time. He wasn't comfortable with it.

"All right, Darcey." he said. "Back to the story."

"Henry's sister, Margaret, was also in New Orleans. Do you know about the Neutral Strip, Trent?"

"Sure," he replied, a twinge of the old guilt running through him. "A strip of land roughly 40 to 50 miles wide between the Sabine River in the west and the Calcasieu River and Arroyo Hondo in the east that Spain and the United States agreed would be governed by neither. That lasted until Spain surrendered claim to all land east of the Sabine by treaty signed in 1819." And also, he thought, it was where he watched Jack Blake arrest his best friend.

"Right. And because there was no law it became a haven for outlaws who preyed on anyone passing through. Grandpa Belmont bought some land there and his wife, Blanche, inherited more when her father died. They built a large, prosperous farm. They called it the Pines. The outlaws stayed well clear of it."

Curious, Marshall asked, "Why is that?"

"Grandpa Belmont was known to be a pretty tough old guy. There's a family story about the time one of Grandpa's hands told him that the leader of one of the outlaw gangs wanted to steal his prize thoroughbred horse. The hand said the outlaw promised to pay him ten dollars if he'd sneak the horse out of the barn that night.

"Grandpa told the man to do it. He said he should get his ten dollars, hand the reins to the thief and then fall flat on the ground. 'Eat dirt,' Grandpa told him.

"The man did as he was told. He got his ten dollars, handed over the reins and fell to the ground. Grandpa was standing behind him with his shotgun. The Strip was less one horse thief, Grandpa kept his horse, and the worker got his ten dollars. Everybody won! Well, except for the horse thief," Darcey laughed.

Marshall smiled. There was something about this woman he liked. That made him nervous.

"After that," Darcey continued, "the outlaws steered well clear of the Pines. They wanted no trouble with Grandpa Belmont."

"Can't say I blame 'em," Marshall said.

"When the war came," Darcey continued, "Grandpa knew there would be more thieves and murderers pouring into the Strip. Deserters from both sides. He sent his daughter, Margaret, to New Orleans to stay with one of Grandma's cousins. They thought she'd be safe here and they were right."

"Interesting," Marshall said, the reporter in him wanting to get to the real story. "But what does all this have to do with your mystery."

"The day the Confederate army left New Orleans Uncle Henry went to see his sister. He said he only had a few minutes. He was off on an important assignment. She tried to get him to tell her what it was. But all he would say was he had been ordered to get a valuable cargo out of the city before the federal troops landed. He was making arrangements to leave that day. Later, when the Union troops discovered all the gold bullion in the mint was gone, Margaret thought that was the cargo that had been entrusted to her brother."

Marshall whistled. "Now that's a story. That much gold delivered to Richmond in 1862 could have made a difference. So what happened next?

"We don't know. Aunt Margaret never saw her brother again. Henry was seriously wounded carrying out his orders. He made it home and died there. Nobody knows where the gold ended up."

Marshall was astonished.

"That's it? That's all we have?"

"Are you going to call me goofy again?" Darcie asked, smiling that smile. The one he saw earlier. To Marshall's irritation he thought it could work on him.

"I'm thinking about it," he said, sounding a little grumpy. "You're trying to find a needle in a haystack. I don't see how this mystery can be solved. I don't think I can help you."

"I think you can, Trent," giving him that smile again. "I know you can."

"You seem pretty sure of yourself," he said, definitely feeling grumpy.

"If it's a matter of money, I can afford…"

"I don't want your money," Marshall cut her off.

"Jack Blake said you'd say that," Darcey laughed. "He said you'll do it because you're bored. He said you need something to do."

Trent looked toward the river. He grimaced, disgusted with himself and with what he knew he was about to do.

"Jack Blake talks too much," he said, standing up. "Come on, let's go."

Dropping their empty go cups into a nearby trash can, Marshall walked briskly to Decatur Street and turned left. Darcey walked fast to match his longer stride.

"Where are we going?" she asked.

"To the Mint."

Marshall led the girl down Decatur Street past the French Market. The old Mint stood overlooking Esplanade Avenue on the edge of the Vieux Carre'. A splendid Greek Revival building from another time. Its dignity intact despite the efforts of man and nature.

"They haven't minted coins here for more than a hundred years. Now it's a museum. I can't think of a better place to start."

Darcey stared up at the six huge columns above them as they ducked into the front door. Just inside a young man whose name tag pegged him as Vinnie asked if he could help them. Marshall explained that they were interested in anything having to do with the gold in the mint in 1862 and what might have happened to it.

"Well, it disappeared. Most people thought it was stolen," Vinnie said, drawing a hostile look from Darcey. "But we don't have any information on that here. Many of our records were lost to mold after Hurricane Katrina. Most of the material that didn't just fall apart when you touched it was taken to Baton Rouge to see if it could be salvaged."

"Looks like a dead end," Marshall said.

"Where do we go from here?" she asked.

"I don't know. We could drive up to Baton Rouge and see what they have there."

"You might not have to go to Baton Rouge," Vinnie offered, trying to make amends to Darcey. "You could talk to Professor Richards."

"Who?" Trent asked.

"Professor Ellen Richards. She was on the faculty of Tulane University and in charge of research here at the museum until she retired a few years ago. I said most of the material went to Baton Rouge after Katrina. The state asked Professor Richards to work on restoring some of the damaged records. If anyone knows about the missing gold it would be her," Vinnie said, glad to be helpful.

Back on the street, Marshall dialed the phone number Vinnie had supplied.

A deep, gravelly voice growled a hello at him. Marshall was taken aback. He was expecting a woman to answer the phone.

"I...uh...I was calling for Professor Richards," he said.

"This is her," the voice growled. "Who's this?"

"This is Trent Marshall, Professor," Marshall started. "You don't know me..."

"I know who you are," the growl interrupted him. "I used to read your stories. You were good. Why'd you quit?"

"Well, uh...it's complicated, Professor," Marshall stammered.

"Why are you calling me?" the growl asked.

Professor Richards seemed to have a talent for keeping you off balance, Marshall thought.

"I'm looking into a story, Professor, about the gold in the mint in 1862. I've been told that if anyone knows about its disappearance it would be you."

"I don't like talking on the phone," the growl continued. "If you want to drive out to my house I'll talk to you."

Trent wrote down the address she gave him. He said they'd be there in half an hour.

"We'll need to walk to my house to get my car," Marshall told Darcey. "Do you mind?"

"I want to solve this mystery," she said. "Let's get your car."

He and Darcey walked the few blocks to Trent's home on Governor Nichols Street just off Royal. He lived in the heart of the Vieux Carre', or French Quarter as it is more popularly known. It suited him. He liked the history. The architecture. The culture. Plenty of characters in the neighborhood. Characters ranging from eccentric to bizarre. Enough to make living there interesting.

Like many French Quarter homes Trent's place looked like nothing much from the outside. A brick wall. Two arched entrances. One a gate large enough for a vehicle. The second a pedestrian entry. Both of faded green wood. He punched a code into the box beside the smaller door. There was a click as the lock released. They stepped inside.

They were in a brick-paved courtyard. A fountain gurgled in the center. Two crape myrtles overflowing with red and purple blossoms dominated that part of the courtyard receiving the most sunlight. A magnolia close to the house offered its snow white blossoms in contrast to the crape myrtles. The inside of the brick wall was a conflagration of plant color. Hydrangeas. Hibiscus. The curly fronds of ferns interspersed among the flowering plants gave the whole courtyard a Caribbean look. To the left rear of the courtyard was another faded green set of double doors. Darcey assumed that was at one time the carriage house.

A large black Jeep was parked in front of the main house, which was as stunning as the courtyard. Columns of iron fretwork decorated the front and supported the second floor. On the first floor were four sets of tall French doors with shutters that could be closed in hurricane season. Now the shutters stood open. On the second floor four matching sets of doors opened onto a balcony from what she assumed were bedrooms.

"Your flowers are beautiful," she said. "It must take a lot of work to keep them up."

"Yeah," Marshall responded, uninterested. "I don't do it. If they had to depend on me they'd all be dead in a week. Ivy's husband, Walter, is the plant man." Marshall clicked the remote in his hand, unlocking the Jeep.

"Climb in," he directed, as he opened the door on the driver's side and got behind the wheel. Darcey had barely closed her door and was still struggling to get her seat belt on when Marshall guided the Jeep out of the courtyard and onto Governor Nichols Street. The faded green gate closed behind them.

They didn't notice the man walking across the street and behind them when they passed through the door into Marshall's courtyard. If they had they would have paid him no mind. He was not memorable. He looked like just another French Quarter character. Brown hair. Shaggy rather than long. Wearing a dark blue shirt with the tail not tucked into his jeans. Running shoes. He stopped to lean against the wall of the market on the corner. No visible tats or piercings. Some might have thought that made him look out of place in the Quarter. Tats and piercings were popular.

They hadn't seen him but he saw them. His heart beat increased. He walked a short distance down Governor Nichols Street. Taking deep breaths. Trying to ease the anxiety just from seeing them. He stopped in a shaded area. He stood in the shadows until the anxiety had passed.

Marshall guided the powerful vehicle out of the Vieux Carre', climbing up onto the interstate. Weaving through the mid-day traffic. Using the six gears of the manual transmission skillfully, he drove aggressively. Darcey was a little frightened. A little thrilled. This man was a mystery to her.

She pointed to the word "Rubicon" written in black letters across the vehicle's hood.

"Your Jeep has an interesting name. Does that mean, like Caesar, we've crossed the river to threaten Rome?" she asked, half joking, half not. "Have we cast the die?"

He turned to look at her. There was no smile. No clue to his thoughts. He just looked at her.

"We'll see," he said. "I'm no Julius Caesar."

"Do you mean you won't lead my army?" Darcey said, doing her best to sound coy.

"No," Marshall replied, working the Jeep's gears. "It means I don't intend to be stabbed in the back."

Darcey felt her temper rising with the rejection.

"If you mean to imply…"

"I don't intend to let you get stabbed in the back either," he interrupted.

With Marshall's aggressive driving it didn't take long to arrive in Metairie, the New Orleans suburb in which Professor Richards lived. Minutes later they were standing at the door of the Tudor style house at the address the professor had given him. It looked like the house a professor would live in. Marshall pressed the doorbell. A full minute, perhaps a few seconds more, went by before they heard the now familiar growl.

"Is that you, Marshall?" said the growl.

"Yes, Ma'am," he replied. "And I have Ms. Anderson with me."

The door was opened by a woman who was old. Very old. Her hair was short and gray. Her face wrinkled. Hands withered. The gnarled fingers of one hand held a half smoked cigarette, a whorl of pungent white vapor curling up. She was wearing an old robe that once might have been red but now could only be described as faded. On her feet were fluffy slippers that looked as though they might fall apart at any minute. As old as the robe. As old as the woman wearing the robe.

"Figured it was you," she said. "Nobody else comes around. But an old woman has to be careful. Y'all come on in."

She turned and shuffled slowly back into the house, leading them through a surprisingly well appointed living room into her office. An office strewn with stacks of books and piles of old papers. Some appeared to be very old. She sat heavily down in the squeaky desk chair and motioned them to the ancient wing back and worn couch, the other available seating in the room.

Marshall took the chair because it was closer to the desk. Darcey sat gently on the edge of the couch, looking nervously around the room.

Professor Richards put her cigarette out in an already overflowing ash tray. She looked at Marshall. Then at Darcey. Back at Marshall, apparently deciding he was the one she should address.

"How can I help you, Mr. Marshall?" she said.

Marshall quickly ran through the story Darcey had told him. He said they didn't know where to start to solve this mystery. According to Vinnie, he told her, she might be their starting place.

The professor laughed. Coughed. Laughed again.

"Vinnie's not much for brains," she said, "but he tries."

She turned toward Darcey. "I'm sure you're aware that for one hundred fifty years it's been assumed that your uncle stole the money."

"I don't believe that, Professor Richards," Darcey said, clearly prepared to be defiant in the face of the old woman's expertise.

The professor was quiet for a moment, just looking at Darcey. Then the laugh. Cough. Laugh again.

"Good for you," Professor Richards said. "I don't believe it either. Never did."

Marshall might have been surprised but he had already decided nothing Professor Richards said would startle him. He'd made the judgment that this was a woman who knew her business. She wasn't afraid to say what she thought. He had the feeling that in her long career whenever she spoke people listened. He would listen, too.

"Why do you think Henry was innocent, Professor?" he asked.

"Everyone else thought he was guilty simply because he died without telling anyone where the gold was and it never showed up anywhere," she replied. "I decided he was innocent for the same reasons."

"Of course," Marshall said. "That makes perfect sense. That was a lot of gold. Why wouldn't he tell someone close to him where he hid it? Had he told anyone some of the treasure would surely have shown up somewhere. Why have a fortune if you don't spend it?"

The laugh. Cough. Laugh again.

"Consider the weight," the professor continued. "It was almost $500,000, mostly in double eagles. Twenty dollar gold pieces. That would be very heavy. And bulky. Hard to hide a load like that when you've been mortally wounded."

"So we agree that Henry Belmont didn't steal the gold," Marshall continued. "How do we figure out what happened to it? Is there anything that might tell us how he took the gold out of New Orleans? Or even if he made it out of the city?"

The professor lit another cigarette, letting the smoke out slowly through her nose as she considered the question.

"Well, it wouldn't have been on the river," the professor said. "The Union controlled the water around New Orleans by then. General Lovell moved his army by train to a camp that had been established about 75 miles north of the city. Maybe Belmont hitched a ride out of town."

"Right," Marshall responded. He was starting to feel the thrill of the chase again. "Why travel slowly in a wagon if you can take advantage of the latest technology for a fast ride?"

"I'll look through some of the old records I have here," Professor Richards offered. "Maybe I can come up with something to point us in the right direction."

"So you're joining our team, Professor?" Darcey asked. "That's terrific. Thank you."

"Oh, I should thank you," the professor growled back. "This is the first interesting problem I've had to think about in a long time. At my age you don't turn down opportunities to have a little fun."

She laughed. Coughed. Laughed again.

"While you're looking, Professor," Marshall requested, "see if you can come up with any ideas on what route they might have taken toward Richmond. They'd have to head generally northeast. But I don't know what the roads in that direction were like then. Or even if there were roads."

"And where Union forces were between here and Richmond," Professor Richards added. "A road wouldn't be much good if there was a Union army blocking it."

"Right," Marshall said.

"I'll dig around in all this mess," she said, waving her arm around the cluttered office, "and see what I can find. Write down your phone number and I'll give you a call if I come up with anything helpful." She handed him a small tablet and pen. He jotted down his name and phone number, handing the tablet back to her.

"While you're doing that," Marshall said, "I'll research load capacities of wagons in 1862. I've been thinking in terms of a wagon but it might have been more than one. Or it might have been a string of mules."

The old woman seemed to move a little faster when she escorted them back to the door. She thanked them for contacting her.

"An old woman doesn't get many requests to work on interesting projects," she said. "This could be my last go around. Even though we're looking for a needle in a haystack."

She laughed. Coughed. Laughed again.

"Told you so," Marshall said as they walked to the car.

They left the old professor standing in her doorway, lighting another cigarette as she watched them drive away. A woman with a job to do. An old woman who felt more alive than she had when she woke up that morning.

Driving back into the city Marshall told Darcey he would drop her at her hotel. He wanted to do the online research he'd mentioned to Professor Richards. He wanted to think about the mystery a bit. He also wanted to talk to Jack Blake. He didn't tell her that.

Darcey was staying at the Hotel Monteleone. Though it was also on Royal Street the system of one way streets in the Vieux Carre' required him to swing out onto Decatur Street and come up on his house from behind. He drove automatically. His mind was focused on missing gold. How could they figure out what happened one hundred fifty years ago?

He drove through the faded green gate into his courtyard, coming to a halt in front of his house. Once in the house he turned right to the library. The room where he spent most of his time.

He sat at the large desk and switched on the laptop. As the computer came on he reached for his phone and dialed Jack Blake's private number. He got Blake's familiar voice. "Can't get to the phone. Leave your number and I'll get back to you."

"Jack, what have you got me into? Call me and tell me about this Belmont thing," he said. "And about this Anderson woman."

In her hotel room, Darcey poured herself a glass of Chardonnay from a bottle she ordered from room service. Then she called Mandy Rillard, her best friend.

Mandy had joined a prestigious San Francisco law firm after graduating third in her class at Harvard Law. She came from a very old and very wealthy Boston family. They had met when Darcey was working out of her small efficiency apartment trying to stretch every dollar to survive as a designer in the highly competitive San Francisco market.

Her big break came when Mandy cajoled her father into hiring her friend as the designer for a building he had purchased in San Francisco. The building was constructed in 1912. The exterior façade was Victorian with only minor updating needed. The interior was a disaster. It had been chopped into twelve small apartments. The plan was to convert it into four large and two very large condos.

The project was a huge success, especially for Darcey. Mandy's father praised her to his San Francisco friends. Mandy saw to it that she was invited to all the right parties. Before she knew it DJA Designs was in demand. DJA for Darcey Jane Anderson. That was when she called Miles, with whom she had worked at her first job, and convinced him to come to work for her. Now she had five designers on her payroll as well.

"Hey there, BFF," Mandy answered. "How're things down on the farm?"

"I'm not on the farm," Darcey said. "I'm in New Orleans working with a very handsome but very irritable investigator."

"Ohhh, a challenge, girlfriend," Mandy said. "A handsome man to be tamed. Hope you brought your spurs down from the farm."

"I never leave home without them," Darcey laughed. "I'm just not sure I want to tame him. There's too much about him I don't know."

"Well, as Miles would say, 'He's a man. He's handsome. What else do you need to know?'"

Trent had spent the last two hours on his laptop. He figured out the weight of a gold eagle. He learned about freight wagons. He read about mules. He had more information about life in 1862 than he ever thought he'd need.

As near as he could figure that much gold would weigh about 1,400 pounds. His research showed there were heavy freight wagons in those days that could haul that load. So Belmont would have needed only one wagon. Six mules to pull it. Six good mules.

His rumbling stomach told him the day was about gone. He crossed to the kitchen at the other end of the house. The refrigerator offered up prosciutto, capicola, and hearts of palm. In the pantry he found jars of artichoke hearts and cornichons. A box of gorgonzola flavored crackers. He quickly put together a charcuterie. A bottle of Napa Valley Merlot would be perfect, he thought.

Back at his desk, he read about the status of recovered government property as he ate the snacks and sipped the wine. He learned that, while the Confederates had held the gold for a brief period, with the end of the war ownership reverted to the United States government. He learned there was no statute of limitations. If the gold was found the government was entitled to it.

By the time the platter was empty his belly and brain were full. Shutting down the laptop, he filled the wine glass nearly to its rim. He used the remote to switch on the television mounted on the wall opposite his desk. The news came on. He watched for a few minutes, glad to be back in the 21st century. But he was tired of thinking. He surfed through the channels until he came across a 1950s black and white western. Excellent. No thinking necessary.

Sometime around midnight he woke up. He had dozed off watching the old movie. The bottle was empty. He dragged himself upstairs to his bedroom. Jack Blake hadn't returned his call.

MONDAY, APRIL 27TH

"When are you coming back, Daddy?" the boy called after the man. The man stopped. He stood still for a moment. Tears were rolling down his cheeks. He didn't speak. He walked on.

"Daddy," the boy called, "Daddy, please come back. I'm scared, Daddy."

A woman reached out to the boy. A woman whose face had become lined with worry. With stress. The woman tried to put her arms around the boy. She couldn't reach him.

Her face changed. She was young and beautiful. Not a care in the world. She laughed and turned. She walked away, too.

Marshall jerked awake. His skin was wet with sweat. The fear made it almost impossible to breathe. The dream. The dreaded dream. Always the same. Terrifying. Merciless. Heart pounding, paralyzing fear.

He forced himself to get out of bed. Stumbled into his bathroom. Splashed cold water on his face. He held onto the sink waiting for his heart to slow down. For the fear to drain away.

Grabbing a towel to dry his face, he walked back into his bedroom. He could smell coffee brewing downstairs. Someone moving around.

He went downstairs to the kitchen in bare feet.

"Well, good morning, sleepy head," Ivy's cheerful voice greeted him. "We thought you might have decided to spend the day in bed." She handed him a mug filled with coffee.

Marshall looked at the clock above the stove.

"7:30 in the morning is hardly all day," Marshall replied.

[30]

"Don't you get sassy with me, young man," Ivy said. "I'd hate to have to come there and slap you."

Marshall grinned. "Thanks for making coffee. Good morning, Walter." He pulled out a stool to join the thin, older black man sitting at the kitchen island with his own cup. "I should say Saint Walter. How do you put up with this woman?"

"Now you hush up, boy," Ivy said. "Don't be putting thoughts in that man's head. He's hard enough to live with as it is."

"Good morning, Trent," Walter said.

Trent had met Ivy many years ago at the Coffee Pot where she was not so much a waitress as she was a New Orleans institution. She had taken a liking to the young man. When he lost first his mother, then his father she was there for him to lean on. She was there through all the troubles that followed.

She was there for him to talk to. To give him advice if he asked for it. More often just to listen.

When he lost his wife she began to stop by his apartment occasionally to clean. Do laundry. Make meals that she would freeze so he could heat them up later. Once he offered to pay her. After she threatened to slap him he never made that mistake again.

It was Ivy who found the Pulitzer Prize certificate in the trash where he had tossed it. She framed it and hung it on the wall. He never mentioned it.

Eventually Trent began to be interested in food. He asked Ivy to teach him about cooking. Ivy was a magician in the kitchen. Trent was a fast learner. Ivy still cooked for him from time to time but he quickly became adept at the kitchen art. When he was able to buy the house they were in now he had a kitchen installed that Ivy called a true wonder.

She bragged on him for the way he furnished the house but scolded him for all the dead and dying plants in the courtyard. The general clutter behind the brick wall.

"This is a beautiful home, Trent," she had said to him. "You have to take care of it."

Marshall had no luck with plants. No interest in them. Cautiously he asked if he could hire Ivy's husband, Walter, to take care of the courtyard and garden. She didn't threaten to slap him.

Marshall's early life had been a struggle. His father left the family when he was four. It was devastating to Trent. He loved his father. He didn't understand why he was gone. He was terrified. It was the source of the nightmare that still haunted him.

Trent's father sent money but it was never enough. His mother worked hard just to put food on the table for her son. Ivy and his mother became friends when they worked together at the Coffee Pot. When one of the cooks tried to force his attentions on Trent's mother Ivy had placed her ample black body between the would-be Romeo and the scared young white woman.

"Nobody better be messing with this girl," Ivy said, "or you'll be messing with me." Nobody messed with Trent's mother.

His father saw him whenever he could but it wasn't the same as having him around. Cub Scout camping trips and summer baseball were torture for Marshall. All the other boys had their fathers with them. Trent was alone. When he thought about his childhood what he remembered most was being alone. Alone and scared.

His mother passed away unexpectedly when he was 14. The woman who had been his world was gone. The one person he was sure would never abandon him, who loved him, who he had loved deeply, would never be back. He would never feel her arms around him again.

To his father's credit, he brought the boy to Baton Rouge to live with him. It was a rocky beginning. Trent had a lot of anger. Anger at his father for leaving the family. Anger at his mother for leaving him, too, though he knew that was unfair. So much sadness beneath the anger. And always the fear. Father and son clashed often and loudly.

Gradually they overcame their conflict. Trent graduated from high school and went on to earn a degree in journalism. His father was at both ceremonies, so proud of his son. He watched Trent begin his career in journalism. Trent later told Ivy those years were the happiest of his life. Those were the only years when he was free from the nightmare. From the fear.

His father passed away 11 years after Trent came to live with him. He remembered holding his father's hand as he lay dying. His father had struggled to speak.

"I'm sorry, son." He gasped. "You deserved better. I always loved you. I just didn't know how to be a father."

Trent was silent, holding his father's hand. He saw his father's eyes close. In that moment Trent understood that his father had done the best he could. That the father had always loved the son even when the son thought he hated the father. That the father felt the hurt as deeply as had the son.

He spoke softly, "I love you, Dad."

Trent felt his father squeeze his hand. And then he was gone.

"Walter, you better get on with what you need to get done," Ivy directed her husband. "I don't want to be here all day. I got things to do."

Walter gulped down the last of his coffee, slid off the stool and headed toward the courtyard.

"See you later, Trent," he said.

"Yeah, later, Walter," the younger man replied.

Ivy poured herself a cup of coffee and balanced herself on the stool Walter had vacated.

"Now tell me about this woman you were with yesterday," she said. "Do you have something for her?"

"I was telling you the truth, Ivy," he answered. "I just met her yesterday. Jack Blake, the sheriff up in Sabine Parish, told her to look me up. She's got a one hundred fifty year old mystery she wants me to help her solve. I never heard anything like it. I don't see how it can be done."

"Uh hunh," she said, disbelieving. "Don't tell me that. You're fascinated with this thing. I can see it in your face. You're bored and you can't wait to get started."

Trent smiled. "Yeah, maybe you're right."

"And you had that dream again, didn't you?"

Marshall looked into his cup, swirling the coffee around.

"Yeah," he said. "First time in quite a while."

"You know you have that dream every time you meet a woman you think might get too close to you," she said.

"Yeah, maybe," he said.

"You know I'm right," Ivy said. "So what about this girl? What's her name? Darcey? You're interested in her, aren't you?"

"I've known her for less than 24 hours, Ivy."

"Well, there's something about this one. I can sense it," Ivy said. "You be careful. I don't want to see you hurt again. But, son, if it feels good, don't you hold back. You can't sit here in this old house all alone forever."

Trent's phone rang. It was Jack Blake.

"Gotta take this," he said, relieved to have an excuse to leave the conversation.

"You took your time getting back to me, Jack," Marshall said, refilling his coffee. He took the mug with him as he headed to his desk in the library.

"Well, good morning to you, too, Trent," came from the phone's speaker. "Aren't you just the measure of good cheer this morning?"

Marshall sat at his desk and sipped his coffee. "Tell me what's going on, Jack," he said. "What do you know about all this? What do you know about the Belmont family and Darcey Anderson?"

"The Belmonts and their descendants have been a prominent family up here since the early 19th century. They're good people, Trent," Blake answered.

"And Darcey? What about her? Is she on the level? It's a strange story she's telling me," Marshall said.

"It's a well-known story up here," Blake said. "I don't know what people thought at the time. I've heard there was a rash of treasure hunters wandering around the state after the war. Dug holes all over. These days most people think there was never any gold to begin with. And there's nobody left who could say for sure either way."

"It happened, Jack," Marshall said. "We talked to a retired professor yesterday who confirmed almost half a million in gold pieces were smuggled out of New Orleans before the Union took the city. She doesn't believe the Belmont boy stole it though. She's doing some research for us right now."

Marshall heard Blake's laughter. "I knew it. I told Darcey you couldn't resist it. Told her you'd figure this thing out."

"Why didn't you call me?" Trent asked. "Or give her my phone number? Why tell her how to find me?"

"Because you might tell me no. And you might not answer the phone if you didn't know who was calling. I knew there was no way you'd say no to her if you saw her in person," the sheriff laughed.

"Jack, it's impossible," Marshall complained. "How do you figure out what happened to a wagon load of gold that disappeared one hundred fifty years ago?"

"Beats me," Blake said. "I'm just an old country sheriff. You'll figure it out."

"Wish I was that confidant," Marshall said.

"Ah, quit your whining," Blake admonished him. "Call me if you need anything from this end. Gotta go."

The line went dead. Marshall tossed the phone onto his desk.

An hour later Ivy and Walter were gone. Marshall had showered, decided to leave the stubble on his face, dressed in khakis and a black pullover. Down in the kitchen he breakfasted on a banana and a glass of milk. He did all that without giving it much thought. He was focused on the impossible task. The seductively impossible task.

The phone rang for the second time. He grabbed for it when he recognized Professor Richards' number.

"Good morning, Professor," he said, considerably more pleasant than he'd greeted Jack Blake. "Do you have news for us?"

"I think maybe so," came the familiar growl. "Can you drive out this afternoon?"

"You bet we can," Marshall said. "Two o'clock be ok?"

"That would be ideal," Richards growled. "See you then."

He dialed Darcey's number. She answered on the second ring.

"The professor wants to see us this afternoon," Marshall told her.

Darcey could hardly contain her excitement. "That's great," she said. "Do you think she found something?"

"Maybe. She thinks so," he replied. He paused for a moment. "If you're not doing anything, I'll buy you lunch before we drive out to her house. Have you been to the Carousel Bar?"

"No," she said. "I peeked into it when I checked in to the hotel but that's all."

"Their lunch menu is limited but the food is good and the Bloody Marys are better."

Darcey thought that sounded great.

"I'll meet you there at noon," Marshall promised.

Marshall stepped into the elegant lobby of the Monteleone Hotel just as Darcey came around the corner from the elevators. He escorted her into the Carousel Bar.

Like thousands before her, Darcey's face lit up when she saw the bar itself. Built like a circus carousel with bright lights and mirrors, the bar turned slowly, making one revolution every fifteen minutes. Marshall guided her to two empty seats at the bar. He thought she'd enjoy that more on her first visit than sitting at a table.

He ordered a Bloody Mary for each of them. They both opted for fried shrimp and oyster po' boys.

"Now this bar couldn't have been here when my ancient aunt and uncle were in the city," Darcey said.

"No," Marshall agreed, "but many famous people have hung out here. Ernest Hemingway, William Faulkner, Tennessee Williams, Truman Capote. Capote even claimed to have been born here in the hotel."

"Was he really?" she asked.

"No," Marshall said. "He was born in a hospital though his mother was staying here at the time. But he was Truman Capote. That was close enough for him."

Darcey laughed. Marshall liked the sound of her laughter.

By two o'clock they were pulling into Professor Richards' driveway. The professor greeted them, cigarette in hand. There was a gleam in her eye that hadn't been there before.

"You've been busy, haven't you?" Marshall inquired, knowing the answer.

The now familiar laugh. Cough. Laugh.

"You know it, Trent," the old professor said. "Haven't had a decent research project in years. Nice to have something to keep me busy. Come on in the house."

She led them back to her office and seated herself at the cluttered desk. Snuffing her cigarette out in the overflowing ash tray, she handed him an old, battered ledger. Lighting another cigarette, she spoke through the smoke.

"General Lovell's staff sergeant was a very thorough man," she said. "He used that ledger to keep track of everything the general ordered. Every move made by every man in Lovell's army. Every gun. Every bullet. Every sack of beans. He wrote it all down."

Marshall handled the old ledger carefully. The pages were brittle and yellow with age. The writing was sporadic. Sometimes clear. Easily legible. Other times cramped and wriggling. Marshall thought some of the journal might have been written while the sergeant was on the move. On horseback. Or in the swaying car of a 19th century train.

Her eyes squinting from the smoke curling up from the cigarette in the corner of her mouth, the professor told him to look at the page where she had placed the bookmark. The page dated April 30, 1862.

"It says General Lovell commandeered a train from the New Orleans Jackson & Great Northern Railroad to transport his army to Camp Moore up near the Mississippi border," Trent read aloud for Darcey's benefit. "It goes on to list each company that was boarded, the names of their officers along with whatever weapons and supplies the company brought with them."

The professor nodded. "Now look at the last page. The last entry in that section."

"Freight car 83," Marshall read. "One wagon, six mules, one officer, one civilian teamster."

He looked at the professor. "No names. No mention of what was in the wagon."

"I think the sergeant was thorough. Very good at his job," Professor Richards said. "I don't think he was dense. He knew what was in the wagon and who the men were. But there was a war on. There was no way he was going to write that down where it might be found by the wrong side."

"Yeah, that makes sense," Marshall agreed. "So this tells us that Lieutenant Belmont had a civilian teamster with him leaving New Orleans. Nobody else. And they probably made it at least as far as Camp Moore with their cargo intact."

"It would seem so," the professor said as she snubbed out her cigarette.

"But where we do we go from there?" Marshall asked. "I think we lucked out that you found this ledger. We can't count on finding more written records."

"You might be surprised, Trent," the professor corrected. "I found this in some of the material the museum at the mint asked me to sort through. I have piles of written records from those days I'm supposed to be going through." She waved her hand around the cluttered room for emphasis.

"People didn't have much to do in their free time in those days," Richards pointed out. "No television. No video games. No movies. They could talk. They could play cards or a few board games, like chess or checkers. They could read. And they could write in journals. They did all those things in what little free time they had. And oh, they also had very large families. That was something they could do after it was too dark to read and write."

The laugh. Cough. Laugh again.

Darcey laughed out loud. Marshall smiled, a bit embarrassed. A little taken aback at the professor's ribald comment.

"I have a few more documents here that I want to sort through," the professor replied.

"OK," Marshall said. "Then I think a road trip would be in order."

"A road trip to where?" Darcey asked.

"To the next stop on the New Orleans Jackson & Great Northern," Marshall said, "which we now know was Camp Moore. Is there anything left of it, Professor?

"Oh yes. There's a museum. I know the woman who runs it. It's not very big and way underfunded. But you might find something helpful. I'll call her and let her know you're coming."

"Great," Marshall said. "Thanks."

"As I said the museum is seriously underfunded," the professor said with a sly smile. "She'd probably be a lot more cooperative if I could tell her she could expect a decent contribution."

Marshall laughed. "Tell her I'll bring my checkbook."

"And remember to look for journals," the professor advised as she saw them out.

They left the old professor shortly after four o'clock. I-10 would soon be backed up with cars carrying people getting off work and anxious to get home. Most of them would spend the next hour cursing as traffic crawled to a near stop. Marshall guided the Rubicon skillfully through the New Orleans road system, avoiding the bottlenecks.

Pulling up in front of the Monteleone, he sat in the car, staring straight ahead for long seconds. He seemed to be trying to make a decision. Darcey began to feel uncomfortable.

Finally he turned to her.

"Dinner tonight?" he asked. "Or have you had enough New Orleans food for one day?"

"Dinner would be nice," she said.

"Dress down or up?" he asked.

"Oh down," she pleaded, climbing down from the big vehicle. "Don't make me dress up."

"Good answer," Marshall said. "Meet me in the lobby at 6:30."

The Rubicon's engine roared as he wheeled away from curb, turning toward Decatur Street and the winding route home.

Trent was in the lobby at 6:30 sharp. Five minutes later Darcey came around the corner from the elevator. She was wearing a form fitting black tee and slacks. Her hair was down. Her bouncing blonde hair brought out the fine features of her face. The bright lights of the old hotel's glamorous lobby made her green eyes sparkle.

They didn't notice the man watching when they came out of the hotel. He followed a block behind them and on the other side of the street. Strolling in what he thought was a nonchalant manner. He thought people he passed would see nothing unusual. He was just a guy walking down the street.

The man watched them closely. They seemed to be getting along. Maybe too well. He didn't like that. It was a complication. He didn't like complications.

Trent led her onto Iberville Street. They crossed the street to a restaurant with a line of customers on the sidewalk.

"Popular place," Darcey said. "That's a good sign."

"The Acme Oyster House has been here for more than a hundred years," Trent told her. "They've survived hurricanes, floods and competitors. Still going strong." He led her to the end of the line, attracting the notice of the large black doorman.

"Party of two," the doorman called out. "Table for a party of two." Though two other couples in front of them held up their hands he motioned for Trent and Darcey. He led them inside to a small table for two.

"Thanks, Clive," Trent said, bumping fists with the big man. "You doing ok?"

"Doing great, Trent," Clive responded. "Good to see you. Ain't seen you around for a while."

"It's a long walk from Governor Nichols Street, Clive," Trent laughed.

The doorman laughed with him. "I hear that," he said over his shoulder as he headed back to the front door to deal with the growing line.

"Does everyone in the French Quarter know you?" Darcey laughed.

"Only the bad ones," Trent said with a straight face but a glint in his eyes. "I helped Clive out with a little problem a while back. He never forgets. You like beer?"

"What are oysters without beer?" Darcey laughed.

"Two Purple Haze," Marshall told the young waitress who brought their menus "and a dozen raw for each of us."

Darcey studied her menu carefully. Trent never picked his up.

"This all sounds so delicious," Darcey said. "I want it all." She was enjoying herself. Feeling comfortable with Trent for the first time.

The waitress returned with their beers and oysters. Trent began mixing horseradish into the container of seafood sauce set in the middle of the platter. Darcey asked for a bowl of seafood gumbo. Marshall ordered red beans and rice with a side of boo fries.

Darcey asked Marshall what boo fires were.

"French fries covered with brown gravy and a little cheese," he told her. "It's called poutine in French Canada. Considered health food in both places."

Darcey laughed.

"Here's to the secrets of 1862," Trent said, holding up his beer bottle.

"And here's to you, Trent Marshall," Darcey said, clinking the neck of her bottle with his. "I really appreciate your help."

Trent dipped an oyster into the spicy sauce before popping it into his mouth. He watched with approval as Darcey also added horseradish to the seafood sauce on her platter.

"So I know something about your family 150 years ago," he said, "but who are they today? Who are you? Tell me about yourself."

"There's not much to tell," she said. "I was born in northwest Louisiana and grew up on the family farm. We raised everything from cotton to collards. Horses, cattle. The family has always been prominent but never really rich. Not until the 1950s when the parish had an oil and gas boom. We allowed drilling in one section of our land. They hit a big pocket of oil and an even bigger one of natural gas and we made a lot of money. We've just sort of been coasting since then."

"Is it still a working farm?" Trent asked.

"Not really," Darcey replied. "Mom keeps a few horses because she loves horses. Oh, and one donkey." She laughed.

"A donkey?"

"My dad brought it home one day," she said, laughing. "I remember coming home for a visit and he showed it to me. 'Now why do I have this donkey?' he asked me. I said I didn't know. Why did he have the donkey? 'That's what I'm asking you,' he said. 'Why do I have this donkey?'"

Trent laughed.

"Growing up in a rural parish wasn't much fun. I had a good life. Great parents," she went on. "But I couldn't wait to get out. I went to London and graduated from the Interior Design School there, with my parents' support. After graduation I moved to San Francisco and found a job. Seven years ago I went out on my own and I got lucky. I have a respectable list of clients with more money than they can spend and seven employees."

"Impressive," Trent complimented her. "You said your mother still lives on the farm. What about your dad?"

"Dad died 18 months ago," she said, quietly. "I never could have succeeded in my business if my parents hadn't supported me financially when I was struggling. I bought my condo six months before he passed away. He and Mom came out to visit me. He loved sitting on the terrace in the evenings looking at the magnificent view of the city.

"Dad told me he was very proud of me. I told him I could never have done it without his help. 'No, Darcey,' he said. 'Your mother and I were glad to help you a little when we could. But you would have been successful with or without us. You've got the Belmont toughness from your mother and my bullheadedness. You would have made it. You might have had to work a little harder and get a little hungrier but you would have made it.

"Mom took his death pretty hard. She came out and stayed with me for three months. She said she just didn't want to be in the house without him. When she was ready to go home I went with her and stayed on the farm for a month until she was ready to live there without Dad. She's doing pretty well now. Or she was until this Treasury man showed up."

"Yeah," Trent said, "I've been thinking about that. Something isn't right there. She never received anything in the mail before he showed up?"

"Nothing. Not a thing. We'd heard the old stories for years but until now nobody from the government ever said a thing to us."

"Doesn't make sense," Trent said. "One hundred fifty years go by and nobody from the government ever said a word. Then some guy from the Treasury Department shows up threatening to take your mother's farm. With no paperwork. That's what's out of place. The government doesn't do anything without paperwork. Months of paperwork. Sometimes years."

They had both finished the oysters. Their waitress took the trays away and replaced them with their entrees.

"So what about you, Trent?" Darcey asked, taking a bite of gumbo.

"Nothing much to tell about me," Trent said. "I was an investigative reporter for several years. Uncovered some nasty business from time to time. Finally got sick of it and quit."

"Just like that?" she asked. "You quit?"

"Just like that."

She took another bite of gumbo, watching him. She knew he wasn't telling her the whole story.

"What made you sick of your job?" she asked, prodding him.

He looked at her with cold eyes. Looked away. Looked back at her. Eyes still cold.

"I learned that there are two kinds of people in the world," he said. "Those who follow the rules and winners."

"And which one are you, Trent?" she asked.

"One who got lucky," he answered, taking a long pull on his beer.

"You ever been married?" she asked, knowing she was probably pushing too far.

[41]

He gave her another look. The icy one.

"Yeah, I was married once," Trent said. "She quit, too."

"Just like that?" Darcey pressed.

"Just like that," Marshall said.

By the time they finished dinner it was fully dark and they could hear the crowd that had already turned Bourbon Street into a long block party.

"I've never been to Bourbon Street," Darcey said. "Can we go see it?"

Trent ordered two beers in go cups.

Outside the man in the long dark shirt and jeans leaned against a wall across the street. He saw them come out of the restaurant and turn left toward Bourbon Street. He was torn. He wanted to end it. He had waited a long time to carry out his plan. But he had to admit he was getting some pleasure from being the watcher. The watcher unseen.

Bourbon Street was even more crowded than usual. People in town for Jazz Fest. Trent pushed their way through the crowd. He felt her grip his arm just above the elbow. He didn't know how he felt about that. He liked it. He feared it. But he decided she was just holding on so they wouldn't get separated in the crowd.

They heard the crowd roar three blocks down the street.

He felt Darcey flinch at the noise. She turned to look at Trent. He was staring straight ahead, a little embarrassed and at the same time trying not to laugh.

"Is that what I've heard about Bourbon Street?" she asked.

"How do you think the girls get all the beads they're wearing?" Trent responded, uncomfortably.

"So these girls we see with all the beads...."she paused. "They're flashing and the men are throwing beads to them!"

To Trent's relief she was laughing.

"Well, it is Bourbon Street," she said.

"No street like it anywhere," he said.

"What's wrong with me?" she said, with a bit of a pout. "Why isn't anyone asking me to flash?"

He glanced at her. D cup, he guessed.

"No reason that I can see," he said. Honestly. Awkwardly.

"Then why don't they want to see my boobs?" she asked, feeling a little piqued.

"Maybe because you're clinging to my arm like a newlywed," he said. She laughed.

"And I'm not letting go either," she promised.

A block behind them the man in the blue shirt struggled to follow them through the crowd. At least, he thought, it was harder for them to spot him in the midst of so many people. But the crowd made him nervous. He didn't like being in such a mob. He could feel the throng pressing in on him. Hemming him in.

At last they turned off Bourbon Street and walked toward the river. Darcey wanted to see it at night. The man stayed a block behind them. On the other side of the street. In the shadows as much as possible. He was feeling better.

He didn't like it that she was holding onto Marshall's arm and they were laughing. Didn't like it at all. They had no right to be enjoying themselves. He smiled a cruel smile. It didn't matter. They didn't have much time left.

Darcey was still trying to figure Trent Marshall out. He could be so distant. So serious. Even, she suspected, dangerous. On Bourbon Street he was as shy as a school boy. Now he seemed at ease. She was enjoying spending the evening with him. She thought she could feel him relaxing. Tension draining from him.

They stopped to look into some of the shop windows as they walked. Darcey spotted a pair of antique silver ear rings she thought she might want to get for her mother. A flicker of movement caught Marshall's eye. While Darcey admired the ear rings Marshall was looking at the reflection in the window glass. He saw a man in a long dark shirt across the street behind them. He was sure he'd seen the same man when they came out of the Acme. He had the feeling there was something familiar about him.

Maybe a coincidence.

Marshall didn't believe in coincidence.

They crossed Jackson Square and Decatur Street as Trent led Darcey up onto the levee. She was fascinated by the Mississippi River. All muddy water and commerce during the day. A beautiful canvas painted by moonlight at night. And always the soothing sound of water touching land. Touching that primordial something within people. A reminder of the beginning of life. Of the first creatures crawling up from the depths. Dripping water. Shaking off algae and diatoms. Breathing air for the first time.

The silence was interrupted by the ring tone of Trent's phone. Darcey wondered who might be calling at this hour. She told herself it was no business of hers. He answered and heard the familiar growl coming across the line.

"Hold on a minute, Professor Richards," he said.

He looked around. They were toward the end of the lighted area known as the Moonwalk. There was only one person anywhere near them. A tall woman with dark hair and horn rimmed glasses wearing a long gray skirt. She didn't seem to be paying them any attention. He didn't think she could hear their conversation from where she was. He pulled Darcey a little farther into the darkness.

"I'm putting you on speaker," he said. "Find anything new?"

"Just more questions," she said. "Why don't you stop by here on your way out of town tomorrow? And think about this. Why would General Lovell have turned over such an important assignment to a young, junior officer who had never been east of New Orleans? Who had never been out of Louisiana? Who was from the western part of the state? You might also think about what Richard Taylor was up to around the same time."

"You're teasing us with riddles, Professor," Marshall protested.

He heard the laugh. Cough. Laugh.

Marshall told her they would see her around ten o'clock the next morning and ended the call.

The man in the blue shirt pulled a baseball cap from his hip pocket. He pulled it low over his face. Watching. Waiting in the dark. His hand clutching cold steel.

The dark surrounded them now. They had wandered too far down the levee. Trent thought they should turn back. It wasn't safe away from the crowd at night.

"Look out!" came the woman's cry.

Marshall felt rather than heard movement to his left. He shoved Darcey behind him and turned to face whatever was coming at them.

The man in the long dark shirt, the black baseball cap pulled low over his face, rushed at them. Moonlight glinted off the knife in his hand. Marshall raised his left arm to deflect the blow. He felt the pain as the sharp blade slashed across his forearm. Curling his right hand into a fist he brought it around aiming for the assailant's nose. But the man was quick and turned to catch the blow on his shoulder.

Still it was enough to knock the would-be assassin to the ground. Marshall leaped at the man but he rolled away. He kicked out with his foot connecting with Marshall's slashed arm. The pain brought Trent's counter attack to an end. The man in the dark shirt got to his feet and ran into the darkness.

He shouted as he ran. "I'll find you, woman. I'll find you and I'll kill you."

Marshall tried to get to his feet. The pain was near unbearable. Blood was gushing from his slashed forearm. The knife had come close to clipping the bone. He fell back to the ground. Tried to get back on his feet. Darcey was at his side now. Holding him. There was someone else. A woman. Perhaps the woman who had warned them.

The woman handed Darcey a scarf.

"Use this to make a tourniquet," she said, dialing her own phone. "I'll call for help."

Marshall tried to pull away. "Got to get that guy."

Darcey was firm. Holding him down. "You're not going anywhere, Trent. You'd never find him in the dark. And you're bleeding so much you wouldn't make it ten feet. You might be tough but you're not immortal."

Marshall didn't like it. She was right. He laid back on the grass. She tied the scarf tightly above the cut on his arm. The bleeding slowed some. Not enough.

They heard the sirens. Ambulance. Police.

The medics took over from Darcey.

"We're taking you to the emergency room," one of them told him.

Marshall was irritated. He didn't want to go to the hospital and said so.

"We have to get the bleeding stopped and get this cut sewed up. That means a hospital. We'll take you there or we'll find you a good funeral home. Your choice."

Marshall was stubborn. He wasn't foolish. He let them load him into the ambulance. Darcey climbed in with him.

Three hours later, Marshall lay in a bed in the hospital emergency room. His wounded arm had been cleaned and tended. The cut had been sutured. His arm was still numb from the local anesthetic. He felt drowsy from the morphine shot he had been given to ease the pain.

Darcey was just outside his room. He could hear her talking to someone. A woman. Then he heard a man's voice. A familiar voice. Darcey stepped into his room accompanied by a familiar face.

Detective Jordan Baron and Marshall had known each other since Trent's days as an investigative reporter. In the beginning each of them distrusted the other. Eventually each came to understand that the other was reliable. Trustworthy. Each had the other's back on more than one occasion as they worked their way through cases involving theft and corruption. Even murder.

"What did you do this time to make someone want to kill you?"

"He wasn't after me, Jordan," Trent said. "He was after Darcey."

Baron reached into his pocket for a pen and a small notebook.

"What makes you think he was trying to kill Ms. Anderson?"

"Because he said 'I'll find you, woman. I'll find you and I'll kill you.' That's what."

"Yeah, I see what you mean," Baron said, writing in the notebook. Turning to Darcey, he asked, "Do you have any idea who this guy is, Ms. Anderson? Or why he might want to kill you?"

"None at all," Darcey responded. "Attempted murder isn't really something I'm used to."

"What brings you to New Orleans?" the detective continued. "Business or fun?"

"Well, kind of business I guess..." Darcey began.

"I'm trying to help her clear up an old mystery, Jordan," Trent interrupted.

"Is money involved?"

"Maybe. But I doubt it," Trent said. "I mean it was one hundred fifty years ago. Chances of solving the mystery are slim."

"How much money, Trent?" Baron insisted.

"Almost $500,000 in 1862 gold," Trent surrendered.

Baron whistled. "That's a lot of money in today's dollars. What's the story?"

"It's the gold that went missing from the mint when the Union army took New Orleans," Marshall explained.

Baron chuckled. "Oh yeah. So that old treasure hunt has started up again. What's your connection with the story, Ms. Anderson?" he asked Darcey.

"One of my family was the Confederate officer assigned to get the gold out of New Orleans, Detective Baron," she explained.

"Well, I wish you luck," Baron said. "But frankly I wouldn't be optimistic. Over the years treasure hunters have dug up half this state looking for that gold."

"It's a matter of family honor for us," Darcey said. "That and the Treasury Department has contacted us demanding that we repay the government for its loss."

"Have they now?" Baron said. "Interesting. I haven't heard anything about that." He wrote in the notebook again.

"What about this other woman out in the hall?" Baron questioned, looking at his notes. "Valerie Martin? Is that her name?"

"I don't know her," Darcey said. "She was walking on the levee this evening and I guess she saw the man with the knife running toward us. She shouted a warning. Without her we might both be dead."

"Is she here?" Trent asked. "She came to the hospital with us?"

"One of the officers brought her at my request," Baron said. "I wanted her available in case I had more questions for her after I talked to y'all. She already confirmed your stories that she had never met either of you before tonight."

Stepping into the hallway Baron asked the woman in the long dress to join them in the room.

"Valerie, this is Trent Marshall," Darcey said. "The other life you saved tonight."

"How do you do, Mr. Marshall?" the woman said. Marshall noted that her voice was low pitched. She was tall with long, straight dark hair and dark eyes behind her glasses. He thought she could be attractive but didn't seem to put much effort into it.

"I'm alive, Ms. Martin," Marshall responded. "And I have you to thank for that."

The woman smiled.

"One more thing," Baron said, turning back to Trent. "What were y'all doing earlier today?"

"I was home until around noon when I met Darcey for lunch at the Monteleone where she's staying," Trent responded. "Then we drove out to Metairie and spent the afternoon with Professor Ellen Richards at her home. She's helping us with some research. We got back to the Vieux Carre' just before five o'clock. I dropped Darcey at her hotel and went home. At 6:30 I met her in the hotel lobby and we walked to the Acme for dinner. After dinner she wanted to see the river at night so we were out for a stroll along the levee."

"Ms. Anderson?" Baron questioned.

"I'm afraid I spent a lazy morning, detective," Darcey said. "I had coffee in my room. I talked to my mother on the phone for a while. I called my office and talked to my executive assistant about a few business issues. The rest of the day I was with Trent."

"Except for the hour and a half after he dropped you at your hotel and before you met him for dinner," Baron noted.

"I was in my room," she said, a bit embarrassed, "freshening up and trying to make myself look presentable before Trent got back." She didn't look at Marshall.

He did look at her.

"And Ms. Martin?" Baron asked. "Just for the record. How did you spend the day?"

"I'm afraid I was a bit lazy today also," Valerie replied. "I'm down here to treat myself to a break after a nasty divorce. I slept in. Had a late breakfast in my room at the Smith-Daly Guest House on Magazine Street. In the afternoon I went for a swim in the small pool there and laid in the sun. I had dinner alone at a restaurant in the next block from the guest house. After dinner I took a taxi to the French Quarter just to walk around for a while before going to bed."

The doctor who had sutured Marshall's arm agreed that there was no need for him to stay in the hospital overnight. An hour later he paid the taxi driver and let himself into his house after promising Darcey that he would go straight to bed. He had dropped the women off at the Monteleone after making Darcey pledge she wouldn't leave it until he picked her up the next day. Darcey and Valerie agreed they both could use a strong drink before either could sleep.

Tuesday, April 28th

Marshall was awakened by the pain in his arm. It was eight o'clock. He was in no shape to travel.

He called Darcey to tell her he wanted to postpone the drive up to the Camp Moore museum for a day. He called Professor Richards but there was no answer. He left her a voice mail message. He took two more pain pills and went back to sleep.

His phone rang at eleven o'clock. Groggy from the pain pills. His arm still aching. It was not a good time. He ignored it. The ringing stopped.

It started up again immediately. He reached for the phone.

"What?" he said into the receiver.

"Well, good morning to you, too, sunshine," came Jordan Baron's voice over the line. "Get your happy self out of bed. We need to talk. I'm coming in."

"Can't this wait, Jordan?" Marshall pleaded. "I feel like terrible."

"No, it can't wait. It's serious."

Marshall dragged himself out of bed and stumbled down the stairs to the kitchen. He needed coffee.

Baron knew the code for the gate and the front door. He drove into the courtyard and let himself into the house. He followed the sound into the kitchen.

"What's so serious it couldn't wait, Jordan?" Trent asked. Then he saw the man trailing Baron. "And what is Burgess doing here?"

"Wasn't my idea, Mr. smart investigator," replied the detective following Baron into the room. "If it was up to me we'd be taking you to the precinct in cuffs."

Steve Burgess and Marshall didn't get along. Several years earlier Marshall had published a story on corruption in the ranks of the New Orleans police department that resulted in three officers going to prison and six others losing their jobs. Burgess had been one of the lucky ones. Marshall had no proof that he had committed a crime. But the story brought enough heat to get Burgess demoted.

Burgess and Baron were exact opposites. Baron was physically fit. His clothes weren't the most expensive but he dressed as well as he could on a detective's salary. His shoes were always shined. He was well read with a refined vocabulary. Likeable.

Burgess was overweight and sloppy. His clothes looked like he slept in them. He probably did. He was vulgar. Hard to like. Even those he called friends didn't like him. Most were people who frequented the same low life bars he did. The ones where the owners gave him free booze because they were afraid not to.

Marshall poured two mugs of coffee, sliding one to Baron and sipping from the other himself.

"Come on, Trent," Jordan said. "Be civil."

Marshall frowned but poured a third mug and slid it toward Burgess.

"I don't want none of your coffee," Burgess said. "Don't want you claiming I take free stuff."

"Pay for it then," Marshall laughed. "Coffee's a buck."

Burgess turned red in the face, but he reached for the mug.

"You still haven't told me what's so serious you had to see me now, Jordan," Trent asked.

"Professor Richards is dead, Trent," Baron said. "Murdered."

Silence. Trent was stunned.

"Murdered?" he questioned. "That poor old woman? Why would anybody want to kill her?"

"We figure you know more about that than we do," Burgess chimed in.

Baron's patience was at an end. He glared at his partner. "Shut up, Steve, or go wait in the car."

Burgess found something interesting to stare at in his coffee cup.

"How did it happen, Jordan?" Trent asked.

"Stabbed in the back," Baron answered. "Didn't look like there was a struggle. As small and frail as she was she couldn't have put up much of a fight if she had tried. She was sitting at her desk. No sign of forced entry."

"Any idea when it happened?" Trent asked.

"Can't be sure until the autopsy but the parish medical examiner is guessing around two or three o'clock this morning," Baron replied. "According to her phone you were the last person she talked to."

"Yeah, she called around nine o'clock while we were walking on the levee," Trent said. "In fact, It had been only a couple of minutes before the guy with the knife hit us."

"Could he have overheard your conversation?" Baron asked

"I put it on speaker phone so Darcey could hear it," Trent said, trying to recall the events on the levee. "I'm not sure if he was close enough to hear. I never saw him until he was right on top of us. Who found her?"

"Her neighbor," Baron said. "They had coffee and read the paper together every morning. This morning she didn't answer the door. He called. She didn't answer the phone. He had a key to her house so he let himself in. Found her face down on her desk."

"Is he a suspect?" Trent asked.

"Doubtful," Baron said. "He's older than she was. Uses a cane. Probably wouldn't have the strength to put a knife in her if she'd asked him to. I think they were just a couple of old folks who enjoyed having someone to talk to in the morning."

"She was a very nice person," Trent said. "It's hard to believe someone would want to kill her. Stab her to death. And on the same night that someone tried to use a knife on Darcey."

"Could be coincidence," Baron offered.

"There's no such thing as coincidence in crime, corruption and politics," Trent responded.

"There was a voice mail message on her phone from you, Trent," Baron continued. "When did you make that call?"

"This morning," Trent said. "Around eight o'clock, I think. Darcey and I were supposed to stop by her house on our way out of town but I postponed the trip. Felt awful when I woke up and needed to sleep."

"Could have been a smart thing to do if you'd killed her, Marshall," Burgess piped up. "Do the job then call and leave a message to show how innocent you are."

"Burgess, you really are an idiot!" Marshall said. "I didn't get home from the hospital until midnight. The hospital where, by the way, a doctor sewed up a gash in my arm caused by a guy with a knife. And you think I popped a few pain pills, found a knife of my own, drove to

Metairie and killed a woman who has been helping us with our research? That's dull-witted even for you."

"Don't you call me dull-witted, Marshall" the fat detective shouted.

"Well, somebody needs to," Marshall shouted back.

"That's enough," Baron said. "Both of you knock it off. Steve, go wait for me in the car."

Burgess slammed his mug down on the kitchen island and turned to leave the room.

"Hey, you're forgetting something," Marshall called after him.

Burgess stopped and turned. "What?"

"The buck for the coffee."

Burgess' face turned bright red again. He pulled a few crumpled bills from his pocket and tossed one down next to the mug.

"There'll be another time, Marshall," he said as he left. "Another time."

"What did Professor Richards say when she called you last night?"

"Not much. She was having a little fun playing riddles with us."

"Riddles?"

"Yeah, riddles," Trent said. "She said we should consider why a Confederate general would entrust a junior officer from northwest Louisiana who had never been out of the state with delivering a wagon load of gold to Richmond."

"You said you had planned to stop by her house on your way out of town. Mind if I ask where you're going?"

"Not at all. Darcey and I are driving up near the Mississippi border to the Camp Moore museum. The professor found evidence that was the first stop for the gold on its way out of New Orleans."

"Are you spending the night there or driving up and back? Baron asked.

"Up and back. Are we suspects, Jordan?" Trent smiled.

"Let's say you're persons of interest," Baron chuckled, "because I'm interested in being invited to dinner again. I need you alive for that."

"Well, you know how to get into the house," Trent said, "and where the refrigerator is. If anything happens to me just feel free to help yourself."

Baron drained his mug and set it on the island.

"I'm serious, Trent," he said. "Watch yourself."

Marshall dialed Darcey's number as he watched Baron leave the courtyard, the faded green gate closing behind him. He filled her in on Professor Richards' death.

"Oh, that poor, sweet lady," Darcey said, feeling the tears welling up in her eyes.

Trent told her he was coming to pick her up for lunch. He didn't want her alone with a lunatic on the loose.

"Bad idea, Trent," she responded, wiping her eyes. "You're injured. You need to rest. I'll take a cab to your house and fix you something to eat. Do you have any food on hand or do I need to stop at a grocery store on the way?"

Her tone of voice made it clear she would tolerate no argument from him. Truthfully he still felt lousy and appreciated her offer. He assured her his kitchen was fully stocked. He gave her the security codes so she could let herself in. He went to his library and stretched out on the couch, covering himself with a throw his aunt had knitted for him before her death. He reached for the television remote. Found a reality show about cops chasing bad guys in remote Alaska. He closed his eyes and listened to the narration.

He was dozing an hour later when Darcey approached the front door. It was flanked on either side by antique stone planters, each holding a boxwood topiary. She entered into a foyer. There was a coat rack and umbrella stand on one side. A huge mirror dominated the opposing wall.

Passing through the foyer Darcey found herself in a living room. A tan sectional sofa surrounded two sides of what appeared to be an original 19th century fireplace. A matching chair completed the frame. The furnishings were sparse but of good quality. It looked comfortable. And neat. Surprising, Darcey thought. She knew Trent wasn't married. She naturally assumed his house would be messy. Maybe not messy. But she hadn't expected neat.

She heard the television in the room to her right. She stepped into a room that served as library and office. The room was all dark wood and leather. Two walls were floor to ceiling shelves filled with books. The wall closest to the door was dominated by a large flat screen television. An overstuffed recliner was empty. The matching couch was occupied by Marshall, his eyes closed. On the screen Alaska State Troopers were protecting campers from an overly curious bear.

A huge desk was placed at an angle across the far corner of the room. Darcey recognized it as a partners' table desk. Made for two people to work together. Mahogany with a light brown leather top. She guessed it was made in the early 19th century. It probably cost more than $20,000. Two leather wing back chairs faced the desk.

On the wall above the desk was a black and gold fleur de lis. On the adjoining wall was a framed football jersey. Number nine. The name "Brees" at the top. Even 49er fans knew Drew Brees, the quarterback who took the Saints to their first Super Bowl win. His autograph was scrawled across the white jersey.

A framed certificate set in among the books drew her attention. She looked closer. To her amazement it was a Pulitzer Prize.

Football memorabilia looking down on a $20,000 desk. A Pulitzer Prize almost hidden from view. Who is this guy?

Trent stirred. He opened his eyes.

"You don't look so good," Darcey told him.

"You should see me from in here," Trent said, pointing to his head with a pained smile. He used the remote to turn off the television.

"I would have been here sooner but Detective Baron came to the hotel to ask me some questions about poor Professor Richards."

"What did he want to know?" Trent inquired.

"Oh, what I did after leaving the hospital. I told him that Valerie joined me at the hotel for a drink. She didn't stay long. She took a taxi to the guest house she's staying in. And I was in bed by one o'clock. Are we suspects, Trent?"

"No. Jordan's a good cop. He's covering all the bases to make sure we're not suspects."

"That's a relief. Can I bring you anything? Are you hungry?"

"Starving," he said.

"OK, you stay right where you are. I'll find the kitchen and see what I can do. Anything sound good?"

"Anything sounds great."

She gave him an amused look and turned toward the other end of the house where she guessed she would find the kitchen. She walked past a large dining table, letting her fingers trail along the edge. Rustic. She recognized it as reclaimed cypress. A hundred years ago it was part of a barn. Or a piece of a house. Now it was just beautiful. And expensive.

If she had been impressed by the dining table the kitchen stopped her dead still. She had known chefs in five star restaurants who dreamed of such kitchens. The stainless steel of the Wolf six burner range with the large hood hanging above. The Viking side by side refrigerator-freezer. The apron front Shaw sink. The white Carrera marble counter tops. The marble continued on the island in the center of the room. Above the island several pots, pans, skillets, a basket filled with potatoes, shallots, onions, and garlic hung from a rack attached to the ceiling.

Who is this man? Cold as ice one minute. Warm as toast the next. Driving a high powered off road vehicle through city traffic like a madman. A skilled madman. But a madman nonetheless. Tough enough to turn unarmed to face a maniac with a knife. Cultured enough to furnish this house. To see to the courtyard and gardens. A $20,000 desk. This kitchen! Who is this guy?

Darcey opened the refrigerator door and found it well stocked. The usual bachelor fare. Hot dogs and thinly sliced ham. But also peppers and celery. Prosciutto and lox. An assortment of cheeses, including a tub of cream cheese. She found a bag of jalapeno-cheese bagels in the freezer. The produce basket hanging over the island provided a red onion. Among the many condiments in the refrigerator was a jar of capers. Lox and bagels. Perfect. Easy and substantial and delicious.

Within minutes she was back in the library setting a tray onto a table near the couch where Marshall was settled. The plate on the tray held a split and toasted bagel. Each half smeared with cream cheese, covered in turn by lox, the thin slices of salmon draping over the sides. Chopped onion and capers sprinkled over it all completed the picture.

"You said anything," she pointed out.

"And anything really looks terrific," Trent said with more enthusiasm than she had heard from him today. "Thank you."

He sat up and reached for a bagel, leaning over the tray as he bit into it to catch any wayward capers before they hit the floor.

"How do you like your coffee?" Darcey asked as she moved back toward the kitchen.

"Black with one sugar," Trent answered.

She returned with two cups of coffee. Placing one for him on the tray, she sat on the edge of the recliner sipping from her own cup.

"You're not eating?" Marshall asked.

"I had a huge room service breakfast after you called earlier this morning," Darcey said. "That's a beautiful desk. It's a partners' desk, isn't it? Made for two people working together?"

Marshall looked over at the desk, then back at Darcey. She was surprised to see his cold look again.

"Yes," he said, "but there's only one person using it."

She sipped her coffee and watched him eat. He was a mystery. Hot and cold. He didn't reveal much about himself.

When he had finished eating he lay back on the couch. He said his arm was hurting but he didn't want to take any more pain pills. He closed his eyes. Darcey carried the tray back to the kitchen and tended to the dishes. When she returned to the library Trent was asleep again.

It was late afternoon when he awoke. He sat up and carefully moved his arm.

"Feeling better?" Darcey asked.

"Much," he replied. "Arm still aches but not as much as earlier."

"My dad always said sleep was the best medicine for anything that ails you," Darcey said.

"My mother said the same thing," he said, smiling at the memory. Darcey liked the warm look better than the cold one.

"Have you been sitting in that chair all afternoon?" he asked.

"Pretty much," she said. "I watched one of my favorite old movies so the afternoon wasn't a total waste. And Valerie called to check on us. Besides you needed someone here with you."

"To watch me sleep?" he asked.

"To make sure you didn't fall off the couch," she laughed.

"You probably should have kicked me off the couch," he said. "We have work to do. We need to get ready to drive up to Camp Moore tomorrow."

"Do you think you'll be up to it?"

"I'll be up to it," he said. "I've been thinking about our last conversation with Professor Richards. She said we should ask ourselves why General Lovell would have entrusted such an important mission to a junior officer from northwest Louisiana. A young man who had never been out of the state. Your uncle was completely ill equipped to transport that gold through Mississippi, Alabama and Tennessee and on to Richmond."

"You're right. I never thought about that."

"He was, however, intimately familiar with the land northwest of here. Especially the land between the Red and Sabine rivers."

"It doesn't make sense, does it?" Darcey asked, puzzled.

"It does if you turn it around. Look at it from a different direction."

"It does?" Darcey looked more puzzled. Then she got it. "Of course it does. General Lovell never intended to send that gold to Richmond. He wanted it to go northwest, not northeast."

"That's the only thing that makes sense."

"But why?"

"Don't know that yet," Marshall said.

Trent didn't want her going back to her hotel alone. He suggested they walk down the street a couple of blocks to a neighborhood tavern that served good bar food.

"Are you sure you feel up to that?" she asked, still worried about him.

"I can't lie around here forever. A little walk this evening would feel good."

He went upstairs and got dressed. Minutes later they were stepping out of the faded green door.

The sound of the shot came suddenly. Unexpectedly. Followed by the thump of lead hitting the door frame, inches from both of them.

Darcey screamed. Marshall jerked her back inside and closed the door, pulling her to the side. Pushing her to the ground. Covering her body with his. A brick wall between them and the unknown shooter. Just in time. Another shot. Another thump of lead sinking into wood.

From the sound of the shots Marshall thought it was a relatively small caliber hand gun. He was certain it couldn't penetrate the brick walls. He was pretty sure about the door. Not certain.

Darcey was screaming. Crying hysterically. Her shoulders shaking as she sobbed. He put his mouth close to her ear.

"Listen to me," he said. "We're going to run for the house. Stay low and close to me. And run as hard as you can."

Darcey was too hysterical to understand what he was saying. He pushed her in front of him. Made her run. Keeping himself between her and the shooter.

Inside the house he pulled her to the side. Another brick wall protecting them. He pushed her onto the floor. Under the dining table.

"Stay there," he shouted. That she heard. She curled into a fetal position. Her knees near her chin. Hands over her ears. Sobbing.

Marshall ran into the library. He found the Springfield Model 1911 semiautomatic hand gun in a desk drawer. He checked the custom 13 round magazine. It was fully loaded. He jacked a .45 ACP into the chamber and ran back to Darcey.

He knelt near her, reaching out to lay his hand on her shaking shoulders, keeping an eye on the entrances to the courtyard.

"Oh my god," she called out. "Why? Who's doing this to me?"

Reaching for his phone he dialed Jordan Baron's number.

The detective answered after two rings.

[57]

"Jordan," Marshall shouted into the phone, "get your guys to my house. Somebody just took a couple of shots at us."

"On my way," Baron responded. The line went dead.

He reached out with one arm to try to hold her. To reassure her. Darcey moved closer to him. Folded herself into his free arm. He held her as her sobbing began to subside. His face in her hair. The sweet smell of her.

"I can't do this, Trent," she said between sobs. "I had no right to get you involved in this."

Trent held her. Gently stroked her hair.

"It's all right, Darcey. It's going to be all right."

"But someone's trying to kill us, Trent, and we don't even know who."

She collapsed, crying, his arm around her. He let her cry. He was still holding her when the faded green gate opened. He raised the gun, clicking the safety off, pulling Darcey's face into his chest so she couldn't see the movement. He relaxed when he saw Jordan Baron wheel his sedan into the courtyard. Baron leaped out of his car, the Herstal semiautomatic police shotgun he favored in hand, and ran to the front door. He let himself in. Marshall stayed where he was until he saw the gate close. No one tried to sneak in behind Baron.

The detective pressed himself against the brick wall on the other side of the front door, looking out the window.

Satisfied that the immediate danger was over, Trent pressed the safety button again and stuck the 1911 into his belt. Baron put the safety on his own weapon and leaned it against the wall.

Trent helped the still sobbing Darcey to the couch and let her sit. While Baron spoke into his mobile phone, Trent stepped into the downstairs bathroom and returned with a box of tissue. Darcey nodded her thanks.

Trent motioned for Baron to follow him into the library. He walked to the bar across from the desk. Reaching beneath it he found what he was looking for. Tequila. He picked up two glasses and took them to his desk. He motioned for Jordan to sit in one of the wing back chairs across from the desk. He filled a glass with the fiery liquor. He offered it to Baron who declined it. Marshall tossed it back.

Then he told Baron what had happened. It was a short story.

Trent filled his glass a second time.

"If no one's using that other glass, I'll have what you're having."

It was Darcey. Shaky. Frightened. Trying to get herself under control.

Trent poured tequila into the second glass and handed it to her as she joined them.

"I've got two uniform cars circling the area," Baron said, "and two plain clothes checking bars and other businesses. Looking for anything someone might have seen that seems out of place."

"Thanks, Jordan," Trent said, sincerely. "We both know catching this guy would be just a stroke of luck."

"We'll do our best, Trent. It's late in the day and the light isn't good. But it's not dark. You never know. We might get lucky. Someone might have seen something. But if this keeps up I'm going to have to ask for a budget increase just to protect the two of you."

Trent frowned as he picked up the tequila and guided Darcey back to the living room, Baron following along.

"This is nuts, Jordan," he said, as he and Darcey sat together on the couch. "A knife last night that nearly took my arm off. Two shots this evening that missed our heads by inches. A poor old woman who never harmed anyone stabbed to death. And we have no clue who or why. Could it really be about something that happened one hundred fifty years ago?"

"It wouldn't seem likely except there's a lot of gold involved," Baron said. "And we've got nothing else. We'll dig the slugs out of your door and run 'em through ballistics."

Trent held the bottle up. Darcey nodded. He poured each of them another shot and set the bottle on an end table.

"So where do we go from here, Jordan?"

"'I'm not sure," the detective said. "You know the old saying about police work. Hours of boredom followed by a few minutes of sheer terror. You've pulled us out of our boredom but I fear the two of you have had the terror mostly to yourselves. I think y'all need to lie low for a while."

"Darcey will have to make up her own mind," Trent said. "As for me, no way. I think it would be a mistake to let this maniac force us into hiding. We'll never get him if we do that. And if he really wants one or both of us dead he'll get us anyway."

"So you're still planning on driving up north tomorrow?" Baron asked.

Marshall looked at Darcey. She nodded. "Yep, we're going."

"And what about tonight?" the detective continued.

"What about it?" Marshall asked.

"I'm concerned about Darcey's safety," the detective said. "I was thinking about putting a couple of uniforms outside her room at the hotel. But I have a better idea. Not sure if either one of you will go for it."

He looked at Darcey.

"Look, I don't want you to be uncomfortable but this place is a fortress," he said. "It's virtually impossible for anyone to get in unless Trent wants them here. Plus he has an armory here. He has guns stashed around this house that I don't even want to know about. There are four bedrooms. And I promise you'll be safe. Trent is nothing if not a gentleman."

"You're renting out rooms in my house, Jordan?" was Trent's immediate reaction. "Didn't know I was in the B&B business."

"No, Trent," Jordan replied. "I'm trying to keep Darcey alive. Your house is the safest place I can think of."

"Well, I don't know," Darcey said. "It does feel safe here. But Trent doesn't seem to like the idea. I'd rather take my chances."

Trent looked from Darcey to Baron and back again.

"No," he said. "Jordan's right. It makes sense. This is the safest place for you. I'm not used to having company. That's all. You should stay here."

"Are you sure?"

"I'm sure. Somebody's trying to kill one or both of us. The smart thing to do is to fort up for the night."

"Good," Baron said. "Do you want me to take you to the hotel to get your things and check out?"

"Not a chance," Darcey shuddered. "I don't want to go outside these brick walls tonight if I don't have to."

"Understandable," Baron agreed. "I can have a police woman pack your clothes and I'll bring them to you. You can settle your bill with the hotel later. I'll talk to the manager. And Trent, don't say I told you this but I'd keep that hand cannon in your belt close by until we get a handle on this thing."

After Baron left Trent asked Darcey if she knew how to use a gun.

"I grew up on a farm in northwest Louisiana, Trent," she said. "I used to go hunting with my dad."

"Well, unlike Jordan you can't carry a shotgun around with you." He went back into the library and returned a moment later with a small silver plated revolver.

"This is a .38 caliber single action revolver," he said. "That means you have to cock it every time you want to fire. It's one of the simplest firearms made and one of the most effective. At close range it can do a lot of damage. If you have to use it, it'll be at close range."

She took the weapon from him, gently wrapping her hand around the polished walnut grip.

"Keep it with you everywhere you go until we get this mess cleared up," he said. "Everywhere."

It was late. Darcey was settled into a guest bedroom. It was quiet in the old house.

Trent stood at the French doors leading from his bedroom onto the gallery. Staring out into the dark. Remembering the feel of Darcey in his arms. He had only meant to keep her safe. But it was the scent of her hair that lingered in his memory.

WEDNESDAY, APRIL 29TH

The sun was shining through the bedroom window when she awoke the next morning. By the time Jordan had returned with her bags it was late. She thought she wouldn't be able to sleep. She was wrong. She fell asleep almost immediately.

She heard noises coming from the courtyard. Nervously, she reached for the small revolver lying on the table near her pillow. She slipped out of bed and moved quietly to the window. Being careful to move the curtain as little as possible she peeked out. She saw an older black man working with the plants. It was the sound of his trowel striking brick that she had heard.

She took a few minutes to brush her teeth and her hair, tying it back in a ponytail. Pulling on her robe and, sliding her feet into a pair of slippers, she started for the door. She dropped the weapon into the pocket of her robe and headed downstairs toward the smell of coffee.

Before she got to the kitchen she heard the voices. One was Marshall. The other sounded vaguely familiar.

She stopped in the doorway. Trent was already dressed in jeans. His black pullover shirt wasn't tucked in. She suspected that was to cover the bulge of the handgun still tucked into his belt. He was sitting on a stool at the kitchen island with a coffee mug in his hand, talking to an older black woman who looked familiar.

"Good morning," Darcey said.

Trent turned to her. "Good morning. How are you feeling today?"

"Surprisingly pretty good," she replied. "I keep wondering if this is all just a dream. Well, more like a nightmare. How's your arm?"

[62]

"Feels fine. Ivy just changed the bandage for me. You remember Ivy, don't you?" Marshall asked.

"Oh, of course," Darcey said. "You're the lady from the restaurant."

Ivy was leaning on the kitchen island across from Trent with her own mug.

"Good morning, Ms. Anderson," Ivy said. "Can I get you a cup of coffee?"

"Well, no to the Ms. Anderson. Please call me Darcey. But a definite yes to the coffee." Darcey sat on a stool next to Marshall.

Ivy poured another mug of coffee and set it in front of Darcey along with a small pitcher of cream and a sugar bowl. Darcey smiled her thanks.

"For a girl who hasn't been in town for long, Darcey," Ivy said, "you sure know how to find the action."

"I've already told her the story of our adventures," Trent explained.

"I'm starting to feel like a jinx, Ivy," Darcey said. "You probably should stay away from me. I wouldn't want you to get hurt."

"Hunh," the older woman said. "Somebody want to point a gun at me they just might wind up eating it."

"Now I need to figure out exactly how to get to where we're going today. There's no rush. We can leave whenever you're ready," Trent said. He took his coffee with him to the library.

Ivy refilled her mug. She looked at Darcey.

"You like that young man, don't you?" she asked.

"Well, we've only known each for a few days but yes, I like him," she said. "I don't really know what that means. He has saved my life twice. That sort of thing does tend to encourage bonding. He doesn't seem to like me though."

Ivy's steady gaze bored into Darcey's eyes.

"I wouldn't say that. I can say that you're the first woman who has spent the night in this house since he's owned it."

"That's surprising," Darcey said. "I would never have thought that."

"I think mighty highly of that boy," the older woman said. "I'd hate for him to be hurt."

"Tell me about him, Ivy," Darcey pleaded. "He's such a mystery. This house. The furnishings alone are worth a fortune. He's got football memorabilia hanging over an outrageously expensive desk. A Pulitzer Prize hidden among a collection of books."

"Trent's daddy left home when he was a small boy," Ivy said. "He adored his daddy and it about broke his heart. His momma died when he was a teenager. He went to live with his daddy then. The only good thing was they got to be father and son again. Then his daddy died right after Trent graduated from college. He didn't have near enough time with either of them. And for sure not with all three of them together."

Darcey looked down into her coffee.

"That football stuff ain't nothing special," Ivy said. "This is New Orleans. I bet you couldn't find a dozen houses that don't have some kind of Saints gear in it. By the way, I don't know how you feel about football and the Saints but if he asks you to go to the Super Dome, don't argue. Just go."

Darcey laughed and nodded as Ivy refilled her mug.

"He got this house thanks to his mother's aunt, his last living relative," Ivy continued. "When she died she left Trent everything she had. She and her husband had a sugar plantation across the river from Baton Rouge. The old house was falling down and the fields hadn't been worked in years. But it was a thousand acres of good land. He formed a partnership with a builder and they put up a slew of million dollar houses around a golf course. Let's just say he doesn't have to work anymore. Ever."

Darcey sipped her coffee and listened.

"And that Pulitzer Prize? I got it out of the trash where he had thrown it. I framed it and put it on the wall."

"Why wouldn't he be proud of that?" Darcey wondered.

"Because he won it for a story he wrote that sent his best friend to prison. He didn't last but three months in the pen. Somebody knifed him. I never understood what Trent saw in that man. He'd lie when the truth would do him better. He surely deserved what he got. But still he was Trent's best friend."

"That's what Trent was talking about when he told me he just up and quit his job," Darcey realized.

"Yep, that's what he meant," Ivy agreed. "He just didn't have the heart for it anymore."

"And his wife? Is that when she left?"

"Hunh, that hussy," Ivy said with disdain. "She was all over him when he was a big shot reporter. Didn't last long when things changed. Trent had a hard time for two or three years. Tried to make a living writing feature articles. But he didn't have a dime to his name until his aunt died. I don't know where his no good ex-wife got herself off to but I sure would have loved to see her face when she heard about Trent's inheritance."

Ivy took a sip of her coffee. She fixed her gaze on Darcey again.

"Now, do I have to worry about you?"

Darcey smiled. "No, Ivy, you don't have to worry about me. At least not as far as money is concerned. I have my own successful business in San Francisco. I don't need Trent's money. You might want to worry about both of us getting shot or stabbed or something."

"Hunh, I'm not much worried about that," Ivy said. "Trent can take care of himself and you both. And that weight in your pocket tells me you might be able to take of yourself."

"I have to admit I sort of lost it when that guy shot at us yesterday, but I'm ok now. And I'm a country girl. I know how to use a gun if I have to."

"Well, that old man out there and I got to go," Ivy said. "I brought some collards and onions from our garden. A country girl can figure out what to do with those. And if you can't Trent can."

"He can cook, too?"

"He had the best teacher in New Orleans, girl," Ivy laughed. "Me."

After Ivy left Darcey went back upstairs. She called her mother to check in. Valerie called while she was getting dressed. Darcey told her new friend about their plans for the day. Valerie said that sounded interesting but Darcey thought she probably didn't mean it. Valerie wondered if they could have dinner together, or at least a drink, when Darcey and Trent got back to town. Darcey told her she would call when they returned.

Two hours later they were in the big off road vehicle roaring out of the city on I-10 West. A few miles out of Metairie they turned due north onto I-55.

Darcey was carrying a shoulder bag large enough to camouflage the revolver and the extra cartridges Trent had provided her. Before they left the courtyard Marshall had placed his larger weapon in the console.

"Hurts my back riding in the car," he explained.

"The one in my bag is heavy for such a small gun."

"Yeah, if you can't get to the gun hit 'em with the bag," he laughed.

"Trent, are we supposed to have permits for these things?" she asked.

He paused for a moment before answering. "Only if we want to carry them concealed."

"But we are carrying them concealed," she said.

"Not yet. Right now we have them in the car. I don't think that's a problem."

"Do you have a permit?" she pursued the question.

"Sort of."

She thought about that vague answer. She thought about the revolver in her purse. She thought about what Detective Baron had said last night. She decided not to ask the next question.

The highway took them across the western edge of Lake Pontchartrain and the eastern edge of Lake Maurepas. The swamp land they were driving through was fascinating to her. She knew there were alligators down there. And snakes. She shivered. She hated snakes. She focused on the water. The small islets scattered about. Fishing shacks. Grasses and plants that thrived in the brackish water.

The part of the state in which she grew up was much different. Thick, almost impenetrable forests of pine and hardwood. Rolling hills. Her dad called it the Louisiana hill country.

She glanced at the speedometer. She was surprised to see how fast Marshall was pushing the heavy vehicle down the highway.

"Get many speeding tickets?"

"A few," he answered. He looked at her and chuckled. "Just the price of having fun."

They drove the fifty miles to Hammond in under forty minutes. Twenty five miles later they exited the Interstate onto a rural road that took them directly to Camp Moore. Marshall drove through the gates and pulled up in front of the museum. It was built in the style of a raised plantation home. The ground floor was brick with four arches. The double entry staircase led up to the second floor. Wood painted white.

Inside they found themselves hurled back a century and a half. Glass cases filled with uniforms, both blue and gray. Rifles. Revolvers. Sabers. Medical implements that were scarier than the weapons.

Darcey was silent as she looked at the exhibits. "How awful it must have been for those men."

"It was a war fought up close and personal," he said quietly.

At the far end of the room an older woman with carefully coifed silver hair looked up from the desk at which she sat.

"May I help you?" she inquired, in the pleasingly sugary feminine accent of another era.

"I hope so," Marshall replied. "Are you Mrs. Hampton?"

"Yes, I'm Anne Hampton."

"I'm Trent Marshall, Mrs. Hampton, and this is Darcey Anderson."

"Oh yes, Ellen said y'all would be visiting our little museum. How nice to meet you," she said, smiling radiantly.

At the mention of Professor Richards, Marshall and Darcey looked at each other.

"I'm afraid we have some bad news, Mrs. Hampton," Darcey said, moving closer to the older woman's desk.

"Oh my, I hope nothing has happened to Ellen. Is she all right?"

"I'm afraid not," Darcey said. "I'm sorry to tell you that she was killed Monday night."

"Oh no. Oh, dear me, no. What happened?"

They told her all that had happened in the past two days.

Mrs. Hampton dabbed at her eyes with a delicate handkerchief. "Poor Ellen. Why would someone want to harm that sweet lady? She never hurt anyone in her life. Who would do such a thing?"

"There are some good cops working on it, Ma'am," Marshall said. "They'll catch whoever did it. Meanwhile we could use your help."

Mrs. Hampton's back visibly stiffened. "Anything I can do, Mr. Marshall. Ellen and I talked about what y'all are looking into. She was a good friend. I'll help however I can."

"We started out thinking that Lieutenant Belmont's instructions were to get the gold to Richmond," Marshall explained. "But something Professor Richards said in our last conversation made us reconsider. I don't think that makes sense at all now."

"Well, where would he have wanted to send it if not to Richmond?" the museum curator asked.

"To safety, Mrs. Hampton," Marshall said. "I think he wanted to send it some place where it could be held safe until other arrangements could be made."

"That does seem reasonable, I suppose."

"I'm interested in any maps or information you have on where Union forces were concentrated in April and May, 1862," Marshall said. "Specifically in Louisiana, Mississippi, northern Alabama and east Tennessee."

Mrs. Hampton thought for a moment. "I think we have some material in our research room that might help you. But off the top of my head I can tell you that many residents of northern Alabama and east Tennessee were unionists. People in those areas never supported secession. It would not have been friendly territory."

She opened a drawer on her desk and took out a key ring. She led them to a door at the rear of the large room. Unlocking the door, she led them into a smaller room. A library table with two chairs sat in the middle of the room. Shelving covered every wall, filled with books, notebooks and file boxes. She ran her finger over several of the file boxes until she found what she was looking for.

"I think you might find what you need regarding the placement of Union forces in here, Mr. Marshall. Take as much time as you need. I'm here until three o'clock this afternoon."

"Thank you, Mrs. Hampton," Darcey said as she followed Marshall to the table.

They spent the next two hours going through the maps and documents in the file box. Marshall made notes to combine the information each of them found.

"I think we can draw a pretty good picture here, Darcey," he said, "and I think it supports our theory that Lovell wanted to send the gold to the northwest."

He stretched a map out on the table.

"Look at this map. They were surrounded. New Orleans had been taken. Baton Rouge would fall in a matter of days. There were 120,000 Union troops up in Mississippi. And Union forces wandering through north Alabama whose only job was to stop movement between east and west."

"There wasn't a chance of getting the gold out to the northeast," Darcey agreed.

"Getting the gold to someplace it could be hidden until they were in a position to take possession and protect it was their only option."

"But if Baton Rouge was in Union hands, how could they get away?" Darcey asked.

"They had a sliver of a route and a small window of time," Marshall said. He pointed to a town on the Mississippi River just north of Baton Rouge. "Their only chance was to get to Bayou Sara and find a boat to take them across the river. Bayou Sara was still in Confederate hands, at least until late in the summer. That was their only chance."

"So are we off to Bayou Sara?"

"We would be," Marshall said, "except it doesn't exist anymore."

"Oh, another dead end?"

"Not necessarily," Marshall said. "Bayou Sara was once a bustling river port. It was wiped out by the war, several years of bad weather and just general poor luck. But St. Francisville was built on the bluff overlooking the old town."

"So we're off to St. Francisville then?" Darcey queried. "What do we do when we get there?"

"I don't know. But I know a guy who might," Marshall replied. "Right now I'm starving. We passed a diner a few miles back. I want a burger and fries."

They thanked Mrs. Hampton for her assistance. Marshall gave her his phone number in case she thought of anything else that might be useful to them. Then he handed her a check. "To support the museum," he explained.

"Oh, that's very generous of you, Mr. Marshall," Mrs. Hampton said when she saw the amount. "Very generous."

"I'd appreciate it if you would report it as an anonymous donation," Marshall requested. "Perhaps you could say it's in memory of Ellen Richards."

"Oh yes. Yes, indeed. Ellen would like that very much."

A few hundred yards from the building the man was walking around the grounds taking pictures. He kept an eye on the door of the museum. When Marshall and Darcey came out of the building, he turned away from them to take a picture of something interesting in the opposite direction.

When they had gone, the man continued walking around the grounds. Taking more pictures. Some time later he watched as Mrs. Hampton locked the museum door, got into her small car and drove away.

A memorial service had been scheduled for Ellen Richards for ten o'clock Friday morning at the Mint. Darcey told Trent she needed to find an appropriate dress to wear. When she packed for the trip she didn't think she would be attending a funeral. Trent would go with her. There was no way he would let her wander around by herself. Not with a killer on her trail.

They still planned to drive to St. Francisville on Thursday. They would try to pick up the trail there.

Valerie called as they drove into the city. At Marshall's suggestion Darcey asked her to meet them at Arnaud's Restaurant. He stopped at the Monteleone and waited while Darcey went inside to settle her bill. While he was waiting, he called the maître d' at Arnauds and asked him to reserve one of the restaurant's private rooms for them.

[69]

They approached Marshall's house cautiously. With the Model 1911 in his lap, he drove slowly down Governor Nichols Street but saw nothing out of the ordinary. He opened the faded green gate and pulled into the courtyard, keeping Darcey low in the vehicle until the gate closed behind them.

The large semiautomatic preceded him as he entered the house and checked all the rooms. Downstairs. Upstairs. Darcey remained by the door, hand inside her bag, fingers wrapped around the grip of the small revolver.

Satisfied that all was well, Trent went back downstairs to reassure Darcey. This was to be a dress up evening. Darcey said she was going upstairs to shower and get dressed. Marshall watched her as she walked away, her jean-clad hips swaying as though rolling in melted butter. He felt himself stirring as he watched her ascend the stairs. He decided a shower was a good idea.

Marshall was already downstairs when Darcey reappeared. He had shaved and changed into a light blue shirt, tan slacks and navy blue blazer. He was opening a bottle of Chardonnay when she stepped into the kitchen. He looked up and felt his breath catch in his throat. She had changed into a black cocktail dress with lace trim and three-quarter length sleeves. The ponytail was gone. Her soft blonde tresses now rested on her shoulders.

He couldn't look away. Didn't want to look away. She was stunning. Beautiful. Breathtaking.

He poured each of them a glass of wine. Still not trusting himself to speak.

She finally broke the silence. "You clean up very well, Mr. Marshall," she said, smiling.

"So do you," Marshall replied, immediately disgusted with himself for such a mundane response. "You're beautiful, Darcey. Really lovely."

"Thank you, sir," Darcey said, pleased with the reaction she had drawn. They clinked glasses and sipped the wine.

They were sitting in the living room when Marshall's phone rang. Jordan was calling to say he was coming in. The faded green gate began to open seconds later. Marshall stepped to the door. Wine glass in his left hand. Right hand under his blazer touching the Model 1911. He recognized the car with Baron behind the wheel. He didn't relax until the gate had closed behind the detective's car.

Baron was off duty. He gladly accepted Marshall's offer of a glass of wine. The three of them sat in the living room while Marshall and Darcey told him what they had learned at Camp Moore.

"Interesting," Baron offered.

"Yeah, but we're still looking for a very small needle in a very big haystack," Marshall said.

Baron sipped his wine, looking at them.

"Darcey, you look very pretty this evening. In fact, you two look like you might be dressed to go out," Baron said with some amount of concern.

"We're meeting Valerie for dinner," Darcey said. "Trent's taking us to Arnaud's. I've heard so much about it."

Baron looked at Marshall. "Someone's trying to kill her, Trent. How are we supposed to protect her with y'all running all over the city? No. Make that all over the state."

"I told you, Jordan, we're not letting this crazy guy, whoever he is, force us into hiding," Marshall said. "Hey, you're off duty. Why don't you join us? You can have a great dinner and protect Darcey at the same time."

"And I was dreaming of going home to a frozen dinner," Baron laughed. "I guess I could substitute Arnaud's if I had to."

They called a cab, which arrived at the gate within minutes.

"Thanks for inviting me, Trent," Baron said as they walked across the courtyard.

"You know Valerie is recently divorced," Marshall said with an impish smile. "Who knows? Maybe the two of you might hook up."

"Yeah, that's just what I need," Baron moaned. "As though the situation isn't complicated enough already."

Darcey tried unsuccessfully to suppress a snicker at Baron's obvious discomfort.

"At least I'll feel better knowing there's a gun protecting you while you're out on the town," the detective said.

"Two guns, Jordan," Marshall said.

"I don't need to hear that."

"Actually three guns," Darcey said.

"Oh, I'm not hearing any of this," the detective said, rolling his eyes.

The taxi delivered them to the restaurant at Bienville and Bourbon a few minutes past seven o'clock. Valerie was waiting in Arnaud's foyer when they arrived.

"There you are," she said as she gave Darcey a hug. "I can't wait to hear about your trip today. You have to tell me everything you found out."

"Let's talk about it when we get seated," Marshall suggested. "Valerie, you remember Detective Jordan Baron, don't you?"

"Yes, of course. How nice to see you again, Detective."

"I'm off duty, Ms. Martin," Baron said. "Please call me Jordan."

"OK. And I'll be Valerie," she responded with a smile.

The maître d' approached them. "Good evening, Mr. Marshall. So nice to see you again. Welcome back to Arnaud's."

"Thank you, James. It's nice to be back. We'll need the table set for four instead of three. My apologies for the lack of notice.

James waggled his fingers at a young waiter who ran immediately to make the requested adjustment.

"Your private room will be prepared as you wish by the time we get there, Mr. Marshall. If you and your guests will follow me."

Marshall looked into the dining room as they passed by. "It's very busy this evening, James."

"Yes, Mr. Marshall, one of our busiest evenings this week."

"Stay alert," Marshall advised his guests as they followed the maître d'. "On evenings like this there have been reports of a ghostly gentleman in evening dress with a remarkable resemblance to Count Arnaud happily watching over his guests."

"How exciting," Valerie exclaimed.

The maître d' led them through the restaurant and up a flight of stairs. Opening a set of tall doors he ushered them into a private dining room consisting of a double parlor. One of the parlors was set for Marshall's small group. When they were seated Marshall asked James to please send up French 75s for everyone.

"It's my favorite cocktail," Marshall explained. "Half liquor and half champagne. It was created at Harry's American Bar in Paris during World War I. They named it after a cannon because it has such a kick."

"Yeah, and one is plenty unless you want to crawl home," Jordan added.

"I hope y'all don't mind but I selected a menu," Marshall added. "Since you two ladies are both new to our city I thought you might enjoy some of our local delicacies. I ordered Shrimp Arnaud, which is shrimp in a remoulade sauce, and smoked pompano for starters. Crawfish in a brandy-infused tomato sauce for an entrée. Brabant potatoes and smothered okra for side dishes. And for dessert, Bananas Foster."

"It sounds wonderful," Darcey said.

"Yes, it does," Valerie added. "Thank you for going to so much trouble."

"Count Arnaud was fond of saying, 'A meal that is only a meal is a lost opportunity.' Besides all I did was make a phone call," Marshall said. "The chef is the one doing the work."

A waiter entered the room with their cocktails.

"This is delicious," Darcey said as she sipped the drink.

"They make theirs with Courvoisier," Marshall explained. "I prefer using a high quality gin. But it's hard to beat Arnaud's version."

"I remember the last time you made French 75s. I wound up sleeping on your couch," Baron said.

"I offered you a guest room," Marshall complained.

"It was too late. By the time you offered I was beyond hearing."

They talked through most of the meal. From time to time the room fell silent as a particularly delectable dish was placed in front of them. By the time the entrée was finished they had discussed the day's activities in detail, answering questions from both Valerie and Baron.

Darcey let Trent do most of the talking. She watched him as he answered his guests' questions. He was a handsome man. More than that there was something about him that drew her to him. He was a complicated man. A man with many layers. His predilection for fine food and drink. His equal fondness of burgers and fries and hot dogs.

His love of fast cars and guns. His vague response when she asked him if he had a concealed carry permit.

His life was one of luxury but he had seen hard times. Very hard times. There was nothing soft about him.

She had seen him show kindness and humility. She had also seen the hard, cold side of him. When they were attacked on the levee he had moved toward the danger. Not away from it. When they were fired on at his house he had protected her with his own body. Led her to safety. She had no doubt he was capable and willing to use the big handgun she knew was hidden beneath his jacket.

"So you're convinced they never planned on sending the gold east?" Valerie asked, rousing Darcey from her thoughts. "Why do you think they went to St. Francisville?"

"I don't think they had any choice but to try to move the gold to the northwest and hide it until there was a large enough force available to take charge of it," Marshall answered. "And with both New Orleans and

Baton Rouge closed to them the next logical place to cross the river was at what we now know as St. Francisville."

The doors to their parlor opened as the maître d' wheeled in a cart with the makings for Bananas Foster. All talk of anything but the show in front of them ceased as the maître d' prepared this most dramatic of New Orleans dishes. There were oohs and ahhs from the ladies as the dark rum ignited and the flames shot up. The spoonful of cinnamon he sprinkled over the flaming banana mixture not only added another layer of flavor but sent colorful crystals shooting up through the flames.

There was no more conversation of missing gold or attempted murder. No conversation at all. How could there be with Bananas Foster on the table?

Jordan got out of the cab to punch in the code that would open the faded green door. The man watching from the shadows across the street felt the anger rising as the three passengers stepped through the door and disappeared into the courtyard. His hand curled around the knife hidden under his shirt. The knife had become a living thing. He knew the knife wanted to get on with it. The knife wanted it as much as did the man. The knife had tasted blood. The knife craved more.

The man and woman had hardly parted since the missed opportunity on the levee. The man didn't see that as a problem. With luck he would take them both. The knife knew that would make the blood taste sweeter. But there had been no opportunity. He had hoped maybe tonight. But there was another man with them. And a cab driver. Witnesses. Too many. He and the knife would have to be patient. He could do it. He wasn't sure if the knife could.

The man came alert when the faded green gate opened and a dark sedan passed through, turning onto Governor Nichols Street. His heart pounded. An opportunity? His hand closed on the knife again. But the gate closed before the car drove away. Another lost opportunity. The man was disappointed. The knife was demanding.

Inside the house Marshall's hand was on the Model 1911 as he watched the gate close behind Baron's car. When he turned Darcey was standing close to him. She put her hand on his arm.

"Thanks for a wonderful evening, Trent," she said, looking up into his eyes. "Everything was splendid. And it was such a relief to escape from all that's been going on."

Trent looked down at her. Her blonde hair was framed by the lights behind her. Her lips slightly parted. Her eyelids looked somehow heavy over her beautiful green eyes. Her breasts rose and fell with her breathing. He felt himself stirring again. He didn't move. He felt frozen.

"Uh, yeah," Marshall stammered. "Yeah, you're right. We needed a break. I uh…I'm glad you enjoyed it." He looked away.

She dropped her eyes. Her hand fell away from his arm

"Well, good night then," she said, as she turned and moved toward the stairs.

"Yeah, good night."

Marshall watched her go upstairs. Disgusted with himself.

"What is wrong with me?" he thought.

Upstairs he paused at his bedroom door for a moment. He looked at the closed door of the room Darcey was in.

"I wish…" he thought, "I wish…I don't know what I wish."

He went into his bedroom.

In her bedroom Darcey was furiously brushing her hair. "Why do you have to be such a gentleman, Trent Marshall?"

In his room, Marshall took off his jacket and tossed it onto a chair. He laid the Model 1911 on the table by his bed. As he unbuttoned his shirt he stepped to the window which looked out over the courtyard. From that window he could also see over the wall to a part of the street beyond. An old pickup truck pulled out of an alley across the street and turned onto Governor Nichols. He thought it was red but the coating of dust made it impossible to be certain.

Curiously the headlights weren't on. He recalled Jordan telling him that when cops were on the lookout for drunk drivers a vehicle at night with no headlights was something they looked for. Probably a drunk trying to make his way home.

Still it was curious.

THURSDAY, APRIL 30

The aroma of coffee wafting up from the kitchen lured her to consciousness rather than awakened her. She lay in bed remembering last evening. It had been a memorable experience. Dinner in a private dining room in one of the world's great restaurants. She was certain Count Arnaud would not have considered the meal a lost opportunity. Had she and Trent been alone it would have been a magical evening.

That thought brought her fully awake. She remembered how attracted she was to Trent the night before. She remembered how distant, how uncomfortable he had been. She knew he found her attractive. He had told her she was beautiful. So why wouldn't he warm up to her? Why did he have to be such a gentleman?

But then what was she thinking? She had met him on Sunday and it was only Thursday. She wasn't accustomed to jumping into bed with someone she'd known for only four days. She didn't think he was either. But she had to be honest. She would have done it with him last night. In bed. On the couch. On the desk in his library. She decided she could do with a shower.

In the kitchen Marshall was also thinking about last night. He was still angry at himself. He wasn't stupid. Darcey had let him know clearly that she was attracted to him. He definitely was attracted to her. Attracted wasn't the word. It was more than mere attraction. She was smart. She was good company. She was gorgeous. He felt himself becoming aroused every time he watched her walk away. Every time she walked toward him. Every time he felt her sitting beside her. So what was wrong with him?

He knew the answer to that. There had been women from time to time after his wife left. But he never let one get close to him. A few one night stands. Fewer that went more than one night. Never one who had spent as much time in his house as Darcey had. He could easily let Darcey get close to him. That thought alone was enough to make him freeze. He had lost so many people he loved. He had sworn to never lose another.

He was standing at the kitchen island working out his frustrations with a large chef's knife and a huge cutting board. He had already chopped an onion and was working on a tomato.

Darcey walked into the kitchen, dressed in jeans and a light pullover. "That coffee smells wonderful," she said. "Did you save any?"

Trent smiled. It was a surprise to him that just the sight of her made him feel better.

"Good morning. Yes, there's plenty. Hope you don't mind a little chicory," he said as he filled a mug for her.

"My dad always liked coffee with chicory. That's the kind I buy now in San Francisco." She was pleased that Trent didn't seem distant or uncomfortable this morning.

He was chopping a triangular shaped dark green pepper. A jalapeno, three cloves of garlic and three small corn tortillas lay on the kitchen island beside the cutting board.

"I hope you're hungry," he said.

"I can't believe it after that wonderful meal last night but I'm starving."

Trent worked the big knife, chopping the pepper into small pieces.

"So what are you creating?" she asked.

"I can't claim to be creating anything," he explained. "I'm making migas. A Tex-Mex version of scrambled eggs. I first ate it in a small café south of the Colorado River in Austin owned by an American family of Mexican heritage.

"What kind of pepper is that?" she asked.

"It's a poblano," he answered, as he used the knife to sweep the small pieces into the bowl with the onions. "Mild with a really nice, deep flavor. And this," he added as he started chopping the jalapeno, "is to add a little heat."

"You don't remove the seeds from hot peppers?" she inquired.

"Never have seen the sense in that," he said. "The heat comes from capcaicin, which is found mostly in the white pith that the seeds are

[77]

attached to. I don't take either the pith or the seeds out because then the pepper wouldn't be hot. And if you don't want your food hot, why use a hot pepper?"

Darcey laughed at his logic. "Can I help?"

"Sure," he said, tossing her the tortillas. "You can tear these into bite-size pieces."

Minutes later he set in front of her a plate piled with fluffy scrambled eggs dotted with bits of onion, peppers, tomato and tortillas, adorned by three slices of avocado and accompanied by more warm tortillas.

Late morning found them on I-10 driving west toward Baton Rouge. Trent had taken Darcey to a popular boutique as soon as it opened. After an hour of trying on various styles of black dresses she had settled on one she though appropriate for Ellen Richards' memorial service. It was in a box in the back seat of the Jeep.

Traffic was light. Marshall's usual heavy foot on the accelerator pushed the big vehicle rapidly forward.

"How much did you say that gold would be worth today?" Trent asked.

The question took her by surprise. He'd never expressed the slightest interest in the value of what they were looking for. She hadn't thought he cared.

"About eleven million dollars," she said.

"You probably just transposed 1862 dollars to current dollars, right?"

"Yes," she said, haltingly. "Isn't that the way to do it?"

'It's one way."

"How would you do it differently?" she said, feeling genuinely puzzled.

"That much gold would be almost eighteen thousand troy ounces," Trent explained. "At today's price for gold that would be more than $20 million."

Darcey looked at him in surprise.

"But the price of gold goes up and down so tomorrow it could be worth less. Or more."

He was amused at the obvious look of consternation on her face.

"It gets better though," he said. "The going price for 1862 gold double eagles for collectors is $3,900 per coin. Given the amount of gold, there would have been 20,927 coins minted."

"20,927 coins?" she repeated, a bit breathlessly. "And collectors are paying $3,900 for one coin?"

"You got it."

"That's....that's..." Darcey stammered, trying to do the math in her head.

"81 million 615 thousand 300 dollars," Trent finished for her.

"That's a lot of money," Darcey said, for lack of a better response.

"Well, if that many coins were dumped on the market the price would drop, but, yeah, now we're talking about real money."

"There are people who would kill us for that much money," Darcey said.

"Darcey, there are people who'd kill us for the change in our pockets," Trent said. "For $81 million they would gut us, skin us and make our teeth into a necklace."

Darcey shivered. "Oh,what have I got us into, Trent?"

Trent glanced at her. He saw the fear in her eyes. Turning his eyes back to the road he laid his hand over hers as it rested on the console.

"Nothing's changed, Darcey," he said, soothingly. "Whoever is after us is still after us. They're not going to stop. I just thought you should know what the stakes are."

"Does $81 million make it more important to you, Trent?" she asked, and immediately regretted it.

He looked at her again, colder this time. His hand went back to the steering wheel.

"I don't need the money, Darcey,"

"Why are you doing this then?" she asked. "You're risking your life and there's nothing in it for you."

He was silent for a long moment.

"Maybe old Jack is right," he said. "Maybe I'm just bored."

Darcey tried to smile.

He looked at her again. She was relieved to see the ice in his eyes had melted a little.

"And maybe I promised you that I wouldn't let anyone stab you in the back," he said

Baton Rouge traffic managed to do what nothing Darcey had seen so far could do. It slowed Marshall down. Hence, it took them almost an hour to get through the capital city and the less than thirty five miles north to St. Francisville.

Except they didn't go to St. Francisville. A little past one o'clock Marshall pulled into a parking lot a few miles south of the old town. He slid to a stop in front of a long, low cinder block building. The heavy

[79]

vehicle's big wheels scattered gravel and raised a cloud of dust almost thick enough to obscure Darcey's view. Almost. She could make out the big electric sign that spelled out "Tony's Lounge." She could read the sign even though half the bulbs were burned out.

As the dust settled Darcey got a better view of the building. She thought Tony got a good deal on blue paint. A really ugly shade of blue paint.

There were three pickup trucks in the parking lot. All seemed well cared for. Working men's vehicles. Parked right at the front door was the longest car Darcey had ever seen. Marshall saw her staring.

"It's a 1976 Cadillac Fleetwood," he explained, "the biggest sedan ever made in the U.S. 20 feet long and it's barely big enough."

She followed Marshall into the bar. It was dark and cool. A deep voice resembling a fog horn boomed out of the darkness causing her to flinch.

"Marshall!" the voice boomed. "Haven't seen you in a year. Where you been?"

"Been busy, Tony," Marshall replied.

"Busy doing what?" the voice boomed again. "Tossing beads at boobs on Bourbon Street?" The man's laugh shook the building.

"That got boring a long time ago, Tony," Marshall said.

"Who's that you got with you?" Tony said, peering to see the woman standing slightly behind Marshall. Darcey edged a little farther into the room. She saw Tony. All four hundred fifty pounds of him. His massive body behind the bar, covering the stool he was balanced on.

"His car?" she asked, sotto voce.

"His car," Marshall answered, also in a whisper.

"Well, I'll be," Tony exclaimed. "You got yourself a looker there, Trent."

Darcey moved closer to Marshall.

"You got enough beads, honey?" the blob of a man asked, as he reached under the counter for a box overflowing with Mardi Gras beads. "Cause I got plenty." He grinned at her.

"Calm down, big fella," Marshall said. "Darcey, meet the one and only Fat Tony."

Darcey reached for Marshall's hand, holding it tightly as she followed him into the room. "You know a lot of weird people, Trent," she said, again in a whisper.

"I know a lot of people who know a lot of people," he responded the same way.

"Y'all come have a seat and let me buy you a drink," Tony said. He noticed Darcey seemed hesitant as Marshall pulled her along behind him.

"Don't worry about Tony, Darcey," Marshall said, good-naturedly. "His bark is worse than his bite. Way worse." Marshall and Tony both laughed.

"Trent's right, young lady," the big man agreed. "You're pretty enough I'd chase you if I could. But you'd be out of here and eight miles down the road before I made it to the end of the bar." He laughed his booming laugh again.

Darcey started to relax. But she still stayed close to Marshall, climbing onto the bar stool he pulled out for her.

Two men sat at one table finishing their lunches; three were at another. Several other tables had yet to be cleared.

All five men were dressed in jeans, work boots and long sleeved shirts. It was a warm day. The sleeves were for protection from sunburn. Both groups rose almost simultaneously and moved to where Tony sat near the cash register to settle their bills. All paid cash.

"See y'all tomorrow," Tony boomed out as the men left. "I do a pretty good lunch business but they're working folk. They gotta eat fast and get back on the job or they come up short on their pay. And lord knows I don't want 'em short on cash because they come in after work, too. That's when they sit at the bar." His laugh rocked the building again.

He set three short glasses in front of them. He reached beneath the bar and came up with the distinctive bottle of Don Julio Blanco. Darcey looked askance at the bottle. She had become a California girl whose drink of choice was Napa Valley Chardonnay. For the second time in a week she was about to swill down a far more potent libation.

"This is fine tequila," he boomed. "I don't pour this for just anyone." He poured a generous shot into each glass.

Tony held up his glass. Marshall and Darcey clinked their glasses to his.

"Down here, young lady, we say, 'Laissez les bon temps rouler.' Let the good times roll!" The big man tossed back his shot. Marshall did the same. Darcey watched, shrugged her shoulders and followed their lead. The liquor was fiery but surprisingly she found she was starting to like tequila.

Darcey had changed the bandage on Marshall's arm before they left New Orleans. The clean, white bandage caught Tony's attention.

"What happened to you?" he demanded. "You throw beads at the wrong boobs?" Again with the booming laugh.

"Some nutcase tried to knife Darcey down on the Moonwalk a few nights ago," Marshall explained. "I got in his way."

"Yeah, you were always good at that," Tony reminisced. "Are y'all hungry? We got a few lunch plates left." Without waiting for them to answer he turned and yelled back to the kitchen. "Hey Deacon, bring us three lunch specials."

Darcey tried to beg off. "We had a pretty big breakfast," she said.

Tony brushed her protest aside. "That was breakfast. This is lunch. And the special today is fried chicken. Deacon makes the best fried chicken in the parish."

Darcey smiled weakly and gave up.

Tony turned his attention back to Marshall. "I think you'd better tell old Fat Tony what's going on, Trent. And don't tell me there's nothing going on. I don't see you for a year. You get one arm what looks like near cut off and show up here with a hot babe on your good arm. There's something stirring. Tell me about it."

Marshall started to talk but stopped as a man who was as thin as Tony was fat appeared from the kitchen, a plate piled with fried chicken, mashed potatoes covered in gravy, and fresh lima beans in each hand with a third plate balanced on one arm. He put a plate in front of each of them and stated clearing tables. All without saying a word.

Tony tore into his meal like it was his last. "Deacon don't talk much," he explained. "He just cooks and cleans up."

Marshall picked up a thigh and took a bite. Darcey nibbled on a drumstick and discovered that Tony had not been hyperbolic. The chicken was as good as she'd ever tasted.

In between bites Marshall spilled the whole story to Tony. The gold. The government man threatening Darcey's mother. The attack on the levee. The shots fired at them. Their visit to Camp Moore. What they had learned there.

"So you think they headed northwest with that gold and maybe they crossed the river here," Tony summarized, his teeth stripping the last bits of meat from a chicken bone.

"It was their only way out," Marshall explained. "There were Union armies in every other direction. They wouldn't have made it a hundred miles if they'd headed for Richmond. We're hoping we could nose around here and find out if anybody knows anything about it."

"That should be easy," Tony said, licking grease off his fingers.

"Easy?" Marshall stammered. "How could it be easy?"

"Cause I've sat at this bar with old Isom about a thousand nights listening to him tell the story of his great grandfather who was a free man of color and owned a boat and how he ferried some Confederates and a wagon across the river one night," Tony said. "And, oh yeah, how there was a shooting involved somehow."

"Isom?" Marshall questioned with considerable surprise. "I never thought about him. I completely forgot he had an ancestor who ran a riverboat out of here. How's he doing? Haven't been out to see him in a while."

"He's 92. Still raises the finest quarter horses in the state. And still rides 'em," Tony said. Turning to Darcey he explained, "Trent's momma and her friend, Ivy, used to bring him up here when he was a boy. They'd have lunch and hang out with me while Isom took Trent out riding horses."

Another conversation was going on in the parking lot.

"Just crawl up under there and do it," the man heard the knife telling him. "Have some guts."

"But it's broad daylight," the man whined. "Somebody might see me."

He knew the knife was growing more impatient. More angry. He knew he was no longer in control. The knife was in control. That frightened the man.

"You make me sick," the man heard the knife say. "You're such a coward. Get down on your back and do what I tell you."

The man laid down on his back and slid himself head first under the big off road vehicle. Cutting wouldn't do. Everything that could be cut was wrapped in stainless steel. But the point of the blade was deadly sharp. The knife couldn't cut. But it could drill. The man applied the sharp tip at what he thought was the most vulnerable point. He was rewarded when an oily liquid began to drip from the hole he had made. One drip. Another. More drips. The man thought the knife would be happy.

He hurriedly pulled himself from under the vehicle. Rising to his feet he brushed himself off as best he could. He moved quickly to the dusty old red pickup and climbed into the driver's seat, laying the knife in the passenger seat. It was where the knife now demanded to ride.

Starting the engine, he eased out of the parking lot onto the highway. He didn't want to leave too quickly and attract attention. He drove a hundred yards down the highway before stopping to back into a turnout that served as entry to a pasture. The gate was locked but there was good brush cover that made it difficult to see his truck from the road.

The knife lay quietly on the passenger seat. The man was relieved. He thought the knife was pleased with him.

"I may never eat again," Darcey complained. "I wasn't even hungry. But that was the best fried chicken I ever ate."

Marshall laughed. "Yeah, and that's why Tony had to find the biggest car ever made. It's the only one he can get into."

They were rolling along a well maintained gravel road that threaded its way between thick forest on one side and green pasture on the other. Occasionally they would pass a small herd of beautiful horses. Grazing. Running. Playing.

Eventually they crossed a cattle guard beneath an arched sign overhead that read "Pierpont Horse Farm."

He stopped the vehicle in front of an old farm house that had been nicely maintained. To the right was the large stable. Three corrals and two outbuildings were scattered around the house and stable.

As they climbed down from the big vehicle an old black man stepped onto the porch. He was wearing overalls with a long sleeved shirt beneath the bib, the kind of boots known as "ropers," and a straw hat, western style. His lower face was covered with a short silver curly beard. He took the pipe out of his mouth, blew out a cloud of smoke, and flashed a big grin.

"Well, boy, I thought you'd forgot about old Isom," he spoke to Marshall in a kindly, soft voice. "It's been a long time. A real long time."

Much to her surprise, Marshall stepped onto the porch and wrapped his arms around the old man, almost lifting him off his feet with the strength of his hug. The gesture brought a throaty laugh and big grin to the old man's face as he wrapped his arms around Trent's waist.

"You don't look any older than you did when you took me out riding your horses."

"Well, that's because I was old then, too. And I'm a lot older now."

"Isom, this is Darcey Anderson," he said. "Darcey, this man is the finest horse raiser, trainer and breaker in Louisiana."

The old man laughed again. When he took off his hat she saw his short silver curly hair matched his whiskers. "I'm very pleased to meet you, miss," he said, "but the boy's exaggerating. Oh, I still raise the finest quarter horses in the state and I'm still the best trainer around. But I'm too old to do the breaking. Had to give that up when I turned eighty. My grandson and his two boys do that work now. Y'all come on in the house and let's have some coffee."

After the tequila at Tony's Darcey thought a cup of coffee sounded good. "I'm honored to meet you, Mr. Pierpont. I've heard a lot about you. I was raised on a farm and learned to ride a horse when I was five. I still have a horse. His name is Prince George."

"That's a good name for a horse. But call me Isom, young lady," the old man said. "I always thought Pierpont sounded too high falutin' for me. It does look good on a sign though." He laughed again, pointing with his pipe to the sign under which they had just driven.

Following the old man into his house, she found a cool, comfortable home. Isom and Trent went into the kitchen. She wandered around the living room, intrigued by the many pictures. Some of them were very old. One, she thought, was what had been called a daguerreotype, the first photograph ever made. It was a process named for its inventor, a man named Daguerre.

The black man in the daguerreotype was dressed in nautical clothes, complete with a captain's peaked cap and a dark jacket with brass buttons. His arm was around a boy who looked to be perhaps six or seven years old.

The kind, soft voice she had heard on the porch came from behind her. "That was my great grandfather and my grandfather," the old man said. He handed her a delicate cup from which the aroma of good coffee emanated. "My great granddaddy was also named Isom. I was named after him."

"It's a beautiful photograph," Darcey said admiringly. "A daguerreotype, isn't it?"

"Yes. It was probably made around 1859 or 1860. My grandfather was born in 1853. He married late and was more than forty when my daddy was born in 1895."

"It's an inspiring photograph."

"That's kind of you to say, miss," he said. "I'm mighty proud of it. It was my great grandfather who got the family started. He was a free man by the 1850s. He managed to get a small riverboat down at Bayou Sara. It was a busy port back in those days. He called his boat the Bayou Queen. He did pretty good ferrying people and goods across the river. Up and down the river. Wherever they wanted to go and could pay for."

He laughed his soft laugh. "He was a smart man. He could read and write. That was unusual for even a free black man in those days. And he was a successful business man. Even more unusual back then."

"My grandfather eventually took over the boat. But by that time Bayou Sara was dying out. He decided to get out of the riverboat business. So he bought this here land and started raising quarter horses. Fine horses. He taught my daddy all about horses and my daddy taught me. So we've done all right. Thanks to my great grandfather getting us started with that riverboat."

Trent was staring up at the daguerreotype. "I remember seeing that picture up there when I was boy. Guess I never thought about who it was."

"You had other things on your mind when you were here back in those days," Isom said, laughing softly. "You loved to get on one of those horses and just ride all day."

"Those were good days," Trent said.

"Yes, they were good days. Special days." the old man agreed. "But now I think you have trouble, Trent. You've got your arm all bandaged up. And I felt the gun out there on the porch. You better tell me about it, boy."

They sat down in the living room and for the second time that day told the story. Isom listened intently, especially when they got to their theory that Belmont had brought the wagon and its cargo to Bayou Sara to cross the river.

"Well, now that just might clear up a mystery I been pondering most of my life," Isom said. "My granddaddy used to tell a story about the night some Confederates showed up looking for somebody to take 'em across the river. There was a sixth man driving a wagon and it was loaded heavy. One of the men was an officer. The man on the wagon wasn't in the army. He was a muleskinner. A white man my great granddaddy had known for a long time. His name was Rube."

"That's it!" Marshall exclaimed. "That's exactly what we're looking for. Do you think you can remember any more?"

"I can do better than that," the old man said. "I've got my great granddaddy's log books."

He walked to a tall, thin bookshelf in a corner of the room. Two shelves were filled with books bound in black leather. Books that appeared to be very old.

Taking a pair of rimless reading glasses from his shirt pocket, Isom peered at the books. "Let's see now. That would be 1862 you said?"

"Yes, 1862," Darcey answered excitedly.

"OK. Here we go," Isom said, extracting a volume from the shelf. "1862. My great granddaddy was very proud of being a riverboat captain. He kept precise ship's logs. An entry for every day. You should find what you're looking for in here."

They followed Isom back into the kitchen and sat at the table to pore through the book while he refilled their coffee cups. Marshall flipped through pages filled with cramped, scratchy, but legible writing. Most pages contained only a few paragraphs describing the day's activities, customers, cargo, etc. The entry for May 3, 1862 was more interesting.

MAY 3, 1862

No business this day. Sent my stoker home.

After dark a squad of Confederates showed up guarding a wagon driven by a man named Rube who I knew. The commander, a Lieutenant Belmont, asked me to take them across the river. Told him I couldn't that night but would do it first thing in the morning.

Rube warned me there would be trouble on the other side.

My stoker showed up early and we were on the river before daylight. Arrived on the west bank just at daybreak. Just as Rube had warned there was a fight.

The lieutenant was badly wounded. I helped Rube bandage his wound and load him onto the wagon.

Returned to Bayou Sara.

Trent closed the ship's log and laid it on the table. He and Darcey were briefly silent.

"Your great grandfather was quite a man," Marshall said.

"He sure was," Darcey agreed.

Isom grinned and lit his pipe. "So that book helps you?"

"It tells us we're right with our theory that Darcey's uncle was under orders to go northwest, not northeast," Marshall said. "And that's probably the key to unraveling the mystery of what happened next."

Darcey reached out and laid her hand over Isom's. "Thank you so much," she said.

"What about this man Rube? Any history on him?" Marshall asked.

"My granddaddy knew him," Isom said. "He was good friends with my great granddaddy."

"I don't know much about him," Darcey added, "except that he worked for the Belmonts and was close to the family. In fact, when Andrew Belmont died his will specified that Rube have a cabin on the farm to live out his old age. And I think he lived into the 20th century. My mom might be able to tell us more."

"Isom, do you recall your grandfather saying anything about Rube after this incident?" Marshall asked.

"Yes, I believe so. I think he showed up from time to time hauling freight on his wagon. But I don't recall ever hearing anything more about what y'all just read."

"This is a valuable clue to what happened in May, 1862, Isom," Trent said, looking concerned. "Somebody's tailing us on this job. We're not sure who it is. He laid my arm open with a knife a few nights ago," he said, holding up the bandaged limb. "That same night he killed a very kind and very old professor whose research pointed us in this direction. Stabbed her to death. He took a couple of shots at us at my house."

"He's not a very nice man. But you don't have to worry about me, boy," the old man said with his soft smile.

"I sure wouldn't want anything to happen to you."

Isom got up and walked to the door. Reaching behind it he retrieved a shotgun with eighteen inch double barrels and exposed hammers.

"Remember this?" he asked.

"Yeah," Marshall said. "You carried it in a scabbard on your saddle when we were riding."

"Yep," the old man said. "I keep it loaded with double ought buckshot magnum shells. If somebody tried to break in this house it would take him out and the wall behind him, too. Most times I wouldn't have to shoot though. There's no scarier sound in the world to a burglar than the sound of cocking those two hammers. That'll usually send any would be bad guys runnin'."

He laughed his soft laugh again. "I wouldn't worry about old Isom, boy. You take care of yourself and this nice young lady here. There are evil people in this world, Trent. There are some who do wrong because they don't know any better. But there are people who are pure evil. Don't ever forget that."

Trent gave him another hug before they left that had the old man complaining. "I'm 92 years old, boy. You can't be crushing me like that.

My old bones won't take it." He grinned at Marshall, before turning to Darcey. "Mighty nice to meet you, young lady. You get that boy to bring you back to see old Isom sometime soon. All three of us will go riding

"I'll do that," she promised. "And you take care of yourself."

Trent threw the big vehicle into gear and drove out of the yard with a final wave. Isom took another drag on his pipe and watched as they receded. He turned to go back into the house. Then something on the ground caught his eye. A large dark stain in the dirt. He knew that hadn't been there earlier in the day. With only a little creaking in his old knees, he knelt down and touched the stain. He found an oily liquid on his fingers. He knew what it was.

Getting up was always harder than getting down at his age. But he managed. He stood puffing on his pipe. Thinking. Watching Marshall's rig getting smaller. He turned and walked back to his house.

"Shut up. Just shut up," the man in the dusty red pickup truck shouted. He had pulled the truck into a grove of trees so it would be difficult to see from the gravel road. "They're coming now. You'll get what you want soon."

The knife wasn't happy. "What do you mean they're coming? You were supposed to fix their car so it would break down. You're pathetic. You can't do anything right."

"I cut the fence," he yelled at the knife. "I got those horses out on the road. He'll have to try to stop or at least slow down. And when he does, his brakes won't work. Then we got 'em."

The man wanted to throw the knife into the woods and run. But he was afraid. The knife wouldn't let him go. The knife wanted blood. The man knew at this point it would be just as satisfied with his blood as with theirs.

For once Marshall wasn't driving in his usual accelerator to the floorboard style. Isom's horse farm was a beautiful place. They were enjoying the view of the pastures. The scattered small herds of sleek quarter horses. Marshall was happily reminiscing. Talking to her about his boyhood days spent here.

He learned a lot about the plants and animals that lived in the woods under Isom's tutelage. The old man showed him the bottle of turpentine he always carried with him. It was for snake bite, he explained. If you get bit, he told Trent, turn the bottle over the bite and it'll draw out the poison.

"I never heard of that," Darcey said. "Does it work?"

"Don't know," Trent said. "I never got bit."

The Rubicon topped a low rise. He was surprised to see several horses milling about the road. He put his foot on the brake to slow the vehicle down. To his surprise the pedal went loosely to the floor. The vehicle didn't slow down. They had no brakes. He down-shifted and that slowed them some but they were still coming up on the horses quickly. He laid on the horn. The horses looked up but were still milling about. There was no way he could avoid hitting at least a few of them on their current path.

He needed room to slow the vehicle as much as possible by manipulating the gears. To the left was fence and pasture. He could see where the fence appeared to be cut but he couldn't go there without hitting the horses.

To the right were woods. Thick woods. Lots of brush. Maybe a gulch. It was a chance. It was the only chance.

He knew if they hit hard enough the vehicle's air bags would deploy. "Tighten your seat belt and cross your arms in front of your face," he shouted to Darcey. He didn't want her to take the full force of the air bags in her unprotected face. She moved quickly to do as he directed.

He swerved the vehicle to the right. Downshifting through the gears he was able to slow the vehicle but was still moving twenty miles an hour when it went into the woods. The vehicle slowed quickly as the thick brush caught it. Fortunately they avoided hitting a tree. But just as Marshall thought they had evaded any additional damage the right front wheel hit a hidden ditch. The vehicle came to a sudden stop. It leaned to the right, bringing the left rear wheel off the ground. The air bags exploded.

The man shifted the dusty red pickup truck into gear and pulled out of his hiding place in the bushes not far from where Marshall's vehicle had come to a stop. Slamming on his brakes he stopped fifty feet from where the Jeep tilted into the gully.

The knife was delirious. "Now we have them," it gloated. "Now I'll taste blood. Blood! Blood!"

The man started to run toward the disabled vehicle. He was terrified by the knife. He had to let the knife taste their blood. He didn't want the knife to taste his blood.

Inside the vehicle Marshall was struggling with the air bag trying to reach the Model 1911, which he had again placed in the console. Darcey was moving, moaning slightly. He felt sure she was not seriously hurt. "Keep down as low as you can," he told her quietly as he drew the big semiautomatic from the console.

Between the air bag, the seat belt and the tilt of the Jeep Marshall wasn't able to move into effective firing position. He could hear the man running toward them screaming about blood. Desperately he aimed his weapon toward the back window and fired off three rounds. The sound of the man's running feet stopped.

"Curse you for a coward," the knife was screaming at the man. "He can't even see to shoot you. He's firing blind."

The man wasn't sure about that. And he wasn't sure which he feared most. Marshall's large caliber pistol or the blood-crazed knife. He hesitated. Then his mind was made up for him.

A shiny black crew cab truck with "Pierpont Horse Farm" painted on the doors was bouncing down the road toward him. Sliding to a stop just a few yards from the dirty red truck, Isom leaned out the window and fired one barrel of his shotgun into the air.

The man with the knife ran for his truck as hard as he could. Congratulating himself that he had the foresight to leave it running he leaped into his seat, tossed the furious knife onto the passenger seat, threw the transmission into gear and, with tires spinning, roared down the road. The knife raged and bellowed at his cowardice.

The black truck did not follow. Isom was more concerned about Marshall and Darcey. The old man climbed down from the cab and, bringing the shotgun with him, made his way to where the big black vehicle lay in the brush, partially in a ravine.

"Are you ok, boy?" the old man asked, concern obvious in his voice. "Young lady! Can you hear me?"

"I'm good, Isom," Marshall said. "Just got to figure how to get out of here." Darcey mumbled something unintelligible, her face still pressed into the air bag.

Marshall managed to get his door open and his seat belt off, struggling to free himself from the now deflated air bag. Darcey wasn't injured but was dazed. The vehicle was slanted down and to the right making it impossible to open Darcey's door. It was not, however, completely on its side so while Marshall's door was higher it was reachable. As her air bag had also deflated, he was able to free her from her seat belt and pull her over the console. Climbing up to sit on the bottom of the door frame, he was able get his hands under her shoulders and pull her up to his level. From there he and Isom helped her out of the vehicle and to the ground.

They both collapsed on the ground from the sheer exertion of extricating themselves.

Still gasping for air, Darcey managed to speak. "Just our luck to draw the lunatic whose mother never told him not to run with sharp objects." She and Marshall lay on the ground laughing. Isom stood over them showing his big grin.

"You've really done it this time, haven't you, Marshall?" the deputy sheriff said as he stepped into the house. He was a big man with a florid face and large nose. A second deputy, tall and thin, stopped in the doorway, leaning against the frame.

"Who did you go after now?" the big nosed deputy asked. "Looks like whoever it was ain't gonna take it lying down. Not like some others I knew pretty well."

Marshall looked up. "Deputy Tibbets. Haven't seen you in a long time."

"Not near long enough for me," the deputy said. "It don't matter anyway. I don't see much to be investigated here. You lost control of your vehicle. Maybe you been drinking. I don't know. I do know I don't see any sign that you were attacked."

Isom took his pipe out of his mouth long enough to ask, "Then how do you explain the pool of brake fluid I found in the yard where Trent's Jeep was parked?"

"I don't have to explain it. No proof it came from his vehicle. Might have been from yours."

Isom tossed a keyring on the table. "Here's my keys. Why don't you take my truck for a spin and see if the brakes work?"

The deputy made no move to take the keys. Isom's soft laugh brought a smile to the second deputy's thin face.

"For all I know he just don't take very good care of his vehicle," the deputy's dislike of Marshall radiating through the room.

"There's also the matter of an eye witness," Marshall pointed out.

"You mean Isom? He's more than ninety. I doubt his eyesight is reliable," the deputy said. "Here's one for you to explain, Mr. hot shot reporter. We found three .45 cartridge casings in your Jeep. Did you fire those rounds?

"I did," Marshall replied honestly.

"Who were you shooting at? Did you hit 'em?" the deputy demanded.

"A mad man who almost sliced through my arm a few days ago, who likely murdered a kindly old woman, and who probably was responsible for draining the brake fluid from the Jeep, was running toward us waving a large knife. With the Jeep tilted into the gully I was unable to aim at him, which I surely would have done otherwise. Had I been in position to aim I would have hit him. Given the situation I just fired three rounds into the air hoping to scare him. Slow him down some."

Marshall laid the large semiautomatic weapon on the table. The deputy grabbed it, a nasty grin on his face. "You got a permit for this?"

Marshall took his wallet from his back pocket and opened it to show Tibbets the deputy sheriff's badge pinned to it.

"That honorary badge is worthless" the deputy blustered. "Every big shot in this state has one of those. Don't mean nothing. It sure as hell don't mean you can carry a gun."

"Can you read, Tibbets? It's not an honorary badge. I'm a special deputy legally sworn by and reporting to Sheriff Jack Blake in Sabine Parish," he explained.

"I don't know nothing about that," Tibbets said loudly. The three people at the table weren't intimidated. Even Tibbets' fellow deputy leaning against the door frame didn't seem impressed. "I'm taking all three of you in for questioning. Maybe a few hours in jail will convince you to be a little more cooperative."

"I don't think so," Marshall said.

As he spoke he dialed a phone number. Thankfully this time the call was answered.

"Well, two calls in one week," the voice of the old sheriff sounded from the speaker. "What's up? Anything new in that case I asked you handle? I had a message from Jordan that you were hurt and an elderly lady murdered. I hope you can wrap it up with no more dead bodies."

Deputy Tibbets turned pale.

"The guy who knifed me and murdered Professor Richards made another run at us this afternoon but we scared him off with the help of an old friend." Isom grinned around his pipe when he heard that. "Now I've got a West Feliciana Parish deputy sheriff named Tibbets here who insists my special deputy's badge is worthless and he's going to take me to jail."

"Is he now?" Blake laughed. "Am I on speaker? Can he hear me?"

"He can hear you."

"Deputy Tibbets, this is Sheriff Jack Blake, Sabine Parish," the voice on the speaker spoke now with authority. "Trent Marshall is, in fact, a special deputy for my office. Duly authorized by the parish and sworn in personally by me. He is now working on a case at my request with, I might point out, considerable risk to himself. I would appreciate any assistance you can give him. If you don't think you can give him assistance I would be happy to call your boss, who is a good friend of mine, and make the request of him. Shall I make that call, Deputy Tibbets?"

"Uh…No, sir," Tibbets said haltingly. "That won't be necessary."

"Do you think you can focus on determining what happened to Mr. Marshall and whoever was with him today so that we might eventually bring a criminal to justice?"

"Yes, sir," Tibbets, now completely subdued, agreed.

"Thank you, Deputy Tibbets. You're dismissed."

"Uh…Yes, sir. Thank you, sir." The deputy started to leave the room.

"Leave the gun on the table, Tibbets," Marshall said without looking at him. The deputy did as he was told. He left the room followed by the other deputy who grinned at Marshall and gave him a thumbs up. Marshall smiled.

Isom took the pipe out of his mouth and spoke as loudly as he ever spoke. "I fired a shell from my shotgun today, Tibbets. You're not interested in that?" There was no reply.

"Don't go taunting him," Marshall warned. "He's been humiliated. You don't want to make him an enemy."

"That man doesn't have a friend in this parish. But his boss keeps two horses in my stable and goes riding with his grandson most every weekend." He laughed his soft laugh again.

"Anything else, Trent? I have more to do than just keep you out of jail, you know," came the voice from the speaker.

"Thanks, Jack," Marshall said. "We're still looking for a needle in a haystack. I'll send you an e-mail with a full report."

After his dressing down Deputy Tibbets called in the Criminal Investigation Division. The CID team arrived quickly and got to work immediately. Marshall, Darcey and Isom were all questioned again. This time around the questioning was professional and respectful. The officer in charge asked Marshall to leave the Jeep where it was until the next day. He agreed the brake line had probably been damaged purposely. The light was beginning to fade. The investigator said he would like to examine the vehicle in full daylight. He said he'd call when they were done so Marshall could arrange for it to be towed.

Isom offered to drive them to the Baton Rouge airport, which was less than half an hour away, where they could charter a flight to New Orleans to avoid arguing with TSA over their guns. Darcey sat in front with the old man. Trent was happy to sit in the back seat holding the box with Darcey's dress. Isom had a fine time telling stories about Trent when he was a boy.

It was almost ten o'clock by the time the taxi from the airport dropped them at Trent's house. Darcey collapsed on the couch.

Marshall, meanwhile, went to the kitchen. He grabbed a bottle of gin from the freezer along with two martini glasses from the freezer. Half filling a martini shaker with ice, he poured in three jiggers of Hendrick's gin, a spoonful of confectioner's sugar and the juice of half a lemon he took from the vegetable basket that hung from the pot rack. Shaking the mixture vigorously, he poured equal amounts into the chilled glasses. From the cooler of the wine rack he took a bottle of Mumm's Napa Brut Prestige. He finished the cocktails with the sparkling wine.

Back in the living room, he handed one of the glasses to Darcey and sat down beside her. Darcey took a healthy taste from the frosted glass.

"Wow! This is your French 75?"

Marshall nodded modestly.

"Jordan was right. This is a great cocktail."

"I won't deny it," Marshall said. "The credit goes to the ingredients. Hendrick's is a small-batch gin infused with roses and cucumber. Just don't forget Jordan's also right about the potency. One is plenty. But I thought it might help you sleep. It's been a stressful day."

"So where do we go from here?" she asked.

"To your family farm."

"What? The farm? Why there?" she wondered.

"Put yourself in Rube's place," he explained. "We know your uncle's orders were to take the gold to the northwest. To someplace where it would be safe. But we don't know where or who he was supposed to deliver it to. We know the state government was abandoning Baton Rouge and moving north. Eventually to Shreveport."

"Right. And my uncle was wounded," Darcey carried on with his train of thought. "Probably seriously. At the very least he would have lost a lot of blood."

"We know Rube was close to your family. If I was him and I had my friend's seriously wounded son to tend and a wagon load of gold to protect I'd take it to the safest place I could think of. The Belmont farm."

"Then we're off to the farm," Darcey said. "I'll call my mother and let her know we're coming."

"Tell her we'll be there Saturday. We need to rest tomorrow and I need some time to make arrangements for the Rubicon. And there's Ellen Richards' memorial service in the morning."

While Darcey was on the phone with her mother Marshall went to the library to check his e-mails. He found only one of importance. From Jack Blake. The sheriff wanted the report Trent had promised.

Darcey ended the call with her mother. She followed Trent into the library.

"When I came down here I never imagined anything like this, Trent," she said. "I thought my mom had a problem with a bureaucrat. I never dreamed there was any truth in those old stories. We're dealing with murderers."

"Yeah, we are," he said, "They killed a kindly old woman who never hurt anybody. They've tried to kill you three times. But, Darcey, our only choice is to fight back. People who do these sorts of things are cowards. When you stand up to them they run away. You've seen that at least twice now."

"I don't know, Trent."

"I do. We are armed and aren't afraid to fire back. That's the big difference. These people are at their best when they are up against old women. Every attack against us has been an ambush. Trying to take us by surprise. To stab us in the back. And I promised you I wouldn't let that happen."

Darcey looked at the chiseled features of his face. He was a handsome man. But more than that he was a strong man. As she listened to him she felt his courage stirring the strength of the Belmonts in her. Trent was right. Together they were a fighting team. They wouldn't be done in by these people who lacked even a modicum of courage.

"Yes, you did promise me that."

"I'll keep that promise, Darcey"

They finished their cocktails. Darcey said good night and started up the stairs. Marshall watched her go. Watched the sway of her hips. Felt the longing.

"Darcey..." he said.

She stopped and turned back to him. "Yes?"

"Uh....rest well," he said, stumbling over his words.

She smiled and went upstairs.

He went back to the library and wrote a report for Sheriff Blake.

FRIDAY, MAY 1

Darcey awoke early even though she was exhausted after the strenuous day they'd had. Trent's power-packed cocktail did the trick as he had promised. She had fallen asleep immediately and slept soundly through the night.

She was wakened by music. A fugue. A song of four notes. High-low-high-low. Then answering notes. High-low-high-low. She awoke smiling. What a beautiful way to start the morning, she thought. Such a contrast to the end of the previous day.

Rising from the bed she slipped into a robe and carefully opened the French doors leading out to the balcony that ran the length of the second floor. The lead singer sang again his four note song. She saw him. A small bird. Round with a broad chest. Its body was white and gray with a black cap and a black-tipped tail. His four notes were the first measure of the fugue. Other winged singers joined in the refrain. She wished she knew more about birds. She knew she was privileged to be enjoying one nature's concerts.

"Carolina Chickadees," Trent's voice came from behind her. She turned to find him offering her a cup of coffee, which she gratefully accepted. He was dressed in shorts, a tee shirt and running shoes.

"They're beautiful," she said. "Are they here all the time or do they migrate?"

"They're not much for travel," Marshall said. "They generally stay in the same area. This particular group might leave the yard when they think they've cleared all the insects. But another group will show up in the fall when the magnolia produces its berries. They like the seeds."

Darcey caught the scent of the magnolia. Vanilla with a hint of lemon.

"This is a perfect morning, Trent," she said, dreamily. "Awakened by a family of chickadees singing their song, the sweet fragrance of magnolia, a cup of coffee on the balcony of a beautiful New Orleans house, a handsome man. What more could a girl want?"

"A gallery," Marshall said.

"A what?"

"Down here it's called a gallery, not a balcony," Marshall said.

"Oh, OK. A gallery then." Once again he was pulling back from her.

"I'm going out to the gym to work out before getting dressed for the memorial service," he said. "You're welcome to join me if you're into that sort of thing."

"I'd love to," she said. "Just let me throw on some clothes and I'll be right there."

"It's over there in the old carriage house," he said, pointing to the faded green double doors.

Yeah, she thought, if I'm into that sort of thing. I'm gonna work your tail off today, Mr. I'm a gentleman Trent Marshall

And she did. An hour later they both were sweating. Breathing hard. She sat on one of the benches with a towel around her neck. Half the room was furnished with a large weight machine hosting several exercises on which Trent spent most of his time. There was both a treadmill and an elliptical. Darcey divided her time between them.

Her attention now was on the other half of the room in which it appeared a vehicle was parked. She couldn't tell what it was because it was covered completely with a soft cloth covering.

"I'm off to the shower," Marshall said.

"OK. What's that?" Darcey asked pointing to the vehicle.

"That's our next ride," Marshall answered as he started across the courtyard.

She watched him go. She had matched him step for step in their work out. And she knew he knew she had matched him. She was anxious to shower also. They were going to stay in the city today so Trent could arrange for the Jeep to be towed. And they needed a down day. Every day since she had met Trent had been full. Excitement. Danger. Murder. It was too much.

They had agreed that she would meet Valerie after the memorial service if she promised to keep the revolver close to her and to stay in well populated public places. She had sent a text message to Valerie before she went to bed the night before. They agreed to meet for lunch at a restaurant on Decatur Street not far from Trent's house.

She started to leave the room but curiosity stopped her. She reached out and lifted the cloth. Just a few inches. All she saw was shiny black metal. Knowing Trent, as she was beginning to, she guessed it would be expensive and fast.

They walked to the Mint for the memorial service, which was well attended. It was obvious Ellen Richards was a respected, even loved, member of the community. As they were leaving they heard someone call their names. They saw Anne Hampton hurrying up to them.

"Thank you so much for coming this morning," Mrs. Hampton said. "Ellen would have appreciated that."

"We didn't know her well or for long," Darcey said, "but we both thought she was a delightful person. And such a wealth of knowledge."

"Oh my, yes. No one knew as much about this state as Ellen did. Besides that she was a good friend. I will miss her." She dabbed at her eyes with the delicate lace trimmed handkerchief.

"But I have something I must tell you," she said. "The morning after y'all were at the museum I came to work and found that someone had broken in."

"Really?" Trent said. "Was there much damage?"

"No. Hardly any. Whoever it was didn't really know what they were doing. They broke into the back room where y'all worked and searched through the files. They made a big mess. I think they were just trying to figure out what y'all were working on."

"I'm very sorry if we brought trouble for you, Mrs. Hampton," Darcey said.

"Don't you give it a thought," the curator said. "Whoever did it is connected to the murder of my friend. If you want to do something for me you catch whoever did that."

"We'll do our very best," Trent promised.

Following the somber morning at Professor Richards' memorial service Darcey and Valerie had a relaxing afternoon. They had a leisurely lunch with probably one Bloody Mary too many. She told Valerie everything that had happened to them. Valerie was fascinated. She asked tons of questions. Wanted to know every detail.

"So what are you doing next?" she wanted to know.

"Today, nothing," Darcey laughed, taking another sip of her third Bloody Mary. "We've been on adrenaline overload. Trent has some business to take care of. And I just wanted to hang with you this afternoon. Oh, and I want to go to this shop on Royal Street. I saw the cutest ear rings there. I want to get them for my mom."

"Are you taking just today off from the case then?" Valerie asked.

"Yes. Over the weekend we're headed north. To my family's farm in Sabine Parish."

"Sabine Parish? For real?" Valerie seemed surprised. "Isn't that where Toledo Bend is? The big lake?"

"That's the one," Darcey said.

"I don't believe this," Valerie was laughing. "I saw a brochure on a beautiful hotel out on the lake and booked a room there. New Orleans has been fun but I decided I want someplace quiet. I can't believe it's the same parish you're going to. What a coincidence."

"Oh, what fun," Darcey said. "You'll have to come visit the farm."

While Darcey and Valerie were enjoying their afternoon together Trent was in his library with a peanut butter sandwich and a glass of cold milk. He was reading everything he could find about Richard Taylor, the son of President Zachary Taylor, who cast his fate with the Confederacy. The young Taylor was a successful planter with a large farm in Louisiana. Though he lacked extensive military experience he was considerably knowledgeable in the logistics of war. When hostilities began he was asked to take charge of training Confederate troops in the southeast. In quick succession he was appointed colonel in command of the 9th Louisiana Regiment and then raised to brigadier general, commanding a brigade in several early battles in Virginia. In 1862 he was promoted to major general and ordered to Opelousas to form what would be called the Army of West Louisiana.

Interesting timing, Trent thought.

Then his mind wandered back to the present. Back to Darcey. He was coming around to facing his growing desire for her. He had once promised himself he'd never again let a woman get close to him. He didn't want the pain that could result from commitment. But this was Darcey. He'd known her for less than a week. Even so there was no doubt in his mind that she was different from other women. She was special.

As feminine, as beautiful, as sexy as any woman he'd ever known. Smart and capable. A successful business woman. Courageous. Comfortable with guns. Even now she was going around town armed like Clyde's Bonnie. And the work out this morning. He didn't think she could keep up with him but she did. If he was completely honest she might have bested him. It wasn't a competition. But he knew better. It was a competition. He also knew she had out worked him. Far from being angry he was impressed.

He told himself to calm down. It was clear they enjoyed each other's company. They had been through some dangerous situations together. That sort of thing created a bond that can come from no other source. The smart thing to do was just go along. Don't try to make anything happen. Or not happen. Don't spend a lot of time thinking about it. Let things happen as they would.

His thoughts were interrupted by the ringing of the phone.

"Trent?" came the booming voice of Fat Tony. "Where are you?"

"I'm at home, Tony. What's up?"

"Isom was in here last night telling us about what happened up at his place after you left here," Tony said. "A couple of my lunch regulars were here, too. They said when they left there was a truck they'd never seen before in the parking lot."

"Could they see who was in it?" Trent asked, suddenly interested.

"No. He had a cap pulled low over his face. He might have been young but they couldn't really tell. Looked like he was talking to someone but they didn't see anyone else in the truck. They said he pointed to your Jeep a couple of times."

"Did they get a description of the truck? License plate?" Trent asked hopefully.

"No to the license plate. At the time they didn't pay much attention to it. The truck was dirty, red and old. A Ford," Tony concluded. "When I opened up this morning I noticed a spot on the ground. You know Fat Tony's not gonna bend over to get a close look but it could have been brake fluid. Don't know if that helps much but thought you'd better know about it."

A dirty red truck. The man who charged them the day before was driving a dirty red truck. A dirty red truck had driven by his house after dark with its lights off Wednesday night. Marshall didn't believe in coincidence.

"Everything helps, Tony," Trent said. "Thanks, man. I owe you one."

"Then get back up here and spend some money," Fat Tony guffawed. "And bring that fine honey with you."

Marshall ended the call. He looked out the window. So while they were in Tony's Lounge drinking tequila and eating fried chicken that guy was in the parking lot drilling a hole in the brake line. If they'd gone outside five minutes earlier they might have caught him.

Marshall was in the library when Darcey and Valerie came in. They were carrying two bags of groceries and giggling like school girls. Darcey showed him the ear rings she had bought for her mother. He told her they were nice. He was sure her mother would like them. That brought another round of giggles from them. He thought liquor might have been involved. He gave them a broad smile.

Darcey told him that Valerie had booked a room at the hotel on Toledo Bend, not knowing that they were headed to the same parish over the weekend. "Isn't that a coincidence?" Darcey asked.

"Yes," Marshall said, thoughtfully. "Yes, it is." He watched Valerie. She didn't seem to be giggling as much as Darcey was. He tried to keep the smile on his face.

That word again. Coincidence.

"Now we're going to make dinner for you, Mr. Trent Marshall," Darcey said, slurring her words only slightly. "I hope you like spicy chicken tacos."

"Sounds great," he said.

Off they went giggling, taking their groceries to the kitchen.

Once they were at the far end of the house, he placed a phone call. He sent an e-mail to Jack Blake asking him to make some inquiries. Within minutes he got a message back from a grouchy sheriff pointing out that it was Friday night.

He sat for a while staring out the window at the courtyard. He went through the events of the past week. Too many things had happened. The walk on the levee. The attack by the crazed man with a knife who would surely have killed them both but for Valerie's warning. Their brief relationship with Professor Richards and her murder. The shots fired at them as they were entering the courtyard from the street. The break in at the Camp Moore Museum. The third attack on them as he struggled to get the Jeep under control without brakes.

There were too many pieces. None of the pieces fit with any of the others. It was like viewing a kaleidoscope. The pieces kept forming themselves into new pictures. None of them stayed together long enough to form a permanent shape.

A very short time later he heard Darcey's voice calling him to dinner. He found the dining table set with dinner ware, including filled water glasses and empty wine glasses. "We thought we'd let you choose the wine," Darcey said.

Marshall went to the cooler section of the wine closet returning with a long necked bottle of Gewurztraminer. "This will be perfect, I think, with spicy chicken tacos," he said as he poured modest amounts into their glasses.

The girls had concocted a salad and piled a generous helping on each plate. In addition, each plate held three tacos. Nicely charred tortillas filled with a magnificent mixture of chicken sausage, roasted red peppers, jalapeno, green onions, corn and cannellini beans. He could feel the heat of a little cayenne. He tasted chili powder, paprika and a touch of garlic. A squeeze of lime juice, a bit of chopped cilantro and a spoonful of salsa added the final touches. A tasty dinner.

After Valerie left in a taxi Trent and Darcey sipped a final glass of wine. They discussed their plans for driving north the next morning. Darcey told him her mom insisted that he stay with them on the farm.

"There's plenty of room," she said. "I haven't told Mom about all the things that have happened. She would have demanded that I come home if I had. Even so we would both appreciate your protection."

"Ordinarily I wouldn't want to be an imposition, but in this case I think you're right," he agreed. "By the way, have you told Valerie that you have a gun in your purse?"

"You mean have I told her I'm packing heat?" she asked, talking out of the side of her mouth in her best gangster imitation. Trent rolled his eyes, drawing a mock slap on the wrist from Darcey. "No, I haven't told anyone that. I'm afraid I'll get arrested for not having a permit."

"Don't worry about that," he said. "We have friends who will help if it becomes an issue. But I think it's very important that you not tell anyone."

Darcey turned serious. "Trent, we've had some close calls this week. Do you worry about…you know…?

"Death?"

She nodded.

"No," he said, "I don't worry about death."

He was silent for a few moments. Stared out the window into the courtyard.

"The dying part's a little troublesome though," he said, turning back to her with a silly grin on his face.

"Oh, you…" Darcey said, laughing as she tossed one of the pillows on the couch at him.

He was glad he hadn't let her get serious. She had needed this day. They both did. Tomorrow they had to get back on the trail. It was important now. It wasn't just a treasure hunt. It wasn't just about clearing the name of her long dead relative. A good woman had been murdered. Someone wanted to kill Darcey. Maybe someone wanted to kill both of them. He couldn't let that happen. He wouldn't let it happen.

SATURDAY, MAY 2

Darcey's curiosity about the shiny black vehicle under the cloth was satisfied the next morning. She could tell by the emblem it was a Cadillac. It looked brand new. It looked impressive. All black. Exterior and interior. She was right. Expensive and fast.

"Do you always have black cars?" she asked.

"Yes."

"Why?" she asked. "Is it symbolic?"

He thought about that as he loaded their luggage in the trunk.

"Yes," he finally answered.

"What does it mean?"

"It means," he paused for effect, "it means I like black cars," he said.

It was her turn to roll her eyes. But she couldn't help laughing when he winked at her.

Inside the vehicle was the classic interpretation of luxury. She sank back into a seat that was at once comfortable to the point of pampering while giving her the sense that it was built for safety.

"Cadillac CTS-V. This model just came on the market. As fine a juxtaposition of luxury and performance as you'll ever see," he explained with obvious pride. He cranked the engine. "The most powerful vehicle GM ever made. 6.2 liter V-8 that can crank out 640 horsepower."

He pushed the button on the remote control that had been programmed to open the faded green gate. As he steered the sleek sedan into the street he continued the recitation. "Zero to sixty in 3.8 seconds. Eight speed transmission. The men who built it say it'll do two hundred miles an hour. It's only been pushed to one eighty nine on the track but I believe the men who built it."

"One hundred eighty nine miles an hour?" Darcey said, appalled. "And you think it'll do two hundred?"

"Yep. Sure do."

"But you're not going to try to prove it today, are you?" she begged, tightening her seatbelt. Sinking a little deeper into the luxurious seat.

"We'll just have to see who follows us," Marshall assured her. "I don't think we'll have to do two hundred to outrun that old truck we saw up at Isom's place."

Just outside the city I-10 became a causeway for a few miles as it crossed the edge of Lake Pontchartrain. Marshall didn't push the speed limit on the causeway. That would be a brain-dead act likely leading to brain-dead people. Accidents on a causeway are especially deadly because there is no place to go. A causeway has little or no shoulder. It has concrete. It isn't worth the risk.

Once they left the causeway and were on dry land he let the car have its head. When the speedometer passed ninety on its way to a hundred mph he noticed that Darcey's eyes were closed. They had a half day's drive ahead of them. He didn't want her to be miserable. He could always take it out by himself to see what it would do. For now he backed off. A few minutes later he noticed her eyes were open and she seemed to be more relaxed.

Baton Rouge traffic wasn't as bad on a weekend. They crossed the tall bridge with its impressive view of the powerful Mississippi River. A little more than half an hour later they turned north onto I-49 in Lafayette. They followed the interstate for an hour and a half. Marshall pulled off the highway and followed a two lane road through a thick green forest to the small town of Lecompte.

"Why are we stopping here?" Darcey asked.

"Because I'm hungry for a ham sandwich," Marshall explained. "And it would be impolite to meet your mother without bringing her a pie."

"Lea's Lunchroom," she laughed. "I haven't been to this place in years."

He pulled up in front of a 1950s era building. "The best ham sandwich you'll ever eat. And the best pies."

Lea Johnson opened the restaurant in 1928. His idea was to make it as simple as possible. There was no menu. Just a great ham sandwich, a daily plate lunch special and a collection of irresistible pies. Lea's wife, who he always called Miss Georgie, brought her mother's pie recipes to the restaurant. Lea's Lunchroom became a must stop for anyone driving between north and south Louisiana. Lea made his restaurant internationally famous when he wrangled an invitation to be a guest on Johnny Carson's Tonight Show. He became one of Carson's favorite characters.

Lea and Miss Georgie and Carson were all long gone. The interstate highway bypassed Lecompte. But travelers still made the short side trip into the small town for one of Lea's ham sandwiches and a pie or two.

Trent parked the car close to the building. He hadn't seen anyone following them today. But he intended to remain alert. The lunatic chasing them had already damaged one of his cherished vehicles. He didn't want anything to happen to the other one.

Like thousands of visitors before her, Darcey thought the ham sandwich was terrific. When it came to choosing a pie to take to her mother she couldn't decide between chocolate and pecan. Marshall bought one of each.

It had been hard for the man in the red truck to keep up with them today. It was only by shrewd guessing that he crossed the river on the new bridge in Baton Rouge. Another clever speculation led him onto I-49 in Lafayette. He thought he'd get some praise from the knife for being so quick to figure out the route to follow. But no. Nothing but ridicule from that monstrous lump of steel. He would like to throw it out the window but lacked the courage.

It was only by luck that he saw them turn off the interstate at Lecompte. There was but one reason why anyone would drive into Lecompte. They were stopping for lunch. He was hungry, too. He'd love nothing better than one of Lea's ham sandwiches. But not with that miserable knife beside him. He couldn't try an attack at the café. He took the same exit but stopped at one of the ubiquitous fast food joints found hovering around interstate highway exits. He bought a burger, fries, and large drink. He ate in the truck.

The truck was in the parking lot of the fast food restaurant. He didn't think it would be noticeable when Trent and that woman passed by on their way back to the interstate. It was a warm day. He was having difficulty keeping his eyes open. His head fell forward a couple of times as he dozed off. He quickly snapped it back, looking to the passenger seat to make sure the knife hadn't noticed. God only knew what that evil sliver of steel would do if it caught him sleeping when he should be vigilant.

Finally the sleek black vehicle drove past him without slowing. He was certain they hadn't seen him. He started the truck and watched. When he saw them turn north onto the interstate he pulled out of the parking lot to follow.

As he accelerated onto the interstate Marshall looked into his rear view mirror. What he saw surprised him. He handed Darcey his phone and told her to bring the camera function up. Switched to video. He told her what he was going to do and what he wanted her to do. He told her not to worry. The windows were tinted and no one could see them. He reached into the console for the big Model 1911 semiautomatic and laid it in his lap.

He drove at a normal speed for a couple of miles in the left lane. The dirty red truck was following about a quarter of a mile behind them in the same lane. Suddenly Marshall wheeled the vehicle onto the grass of the median and slammed on the brakes. The sleek sedan slid to a stop. He had chosen a grassy area so no dust was raised. He told Darcey to get ready.

Sure enough within seconds the dirty red truck came rolling by. They could see the man inside. The usual cap pulled down over his face, which was now screwed up in frustration.

Darcey began making a video of the rear of the truck. When he was too far away they pulled up the video to see if it was clear enough to read the license plate. Marshall thought it was possible that Jack Blake's people could make it out. Marshall quickly e-mailed it to the sheriff and asked him to run the plates if he could make out the numbers.

Two miles down the road the red truck was stopped on the other side of the highway. The knife was screaming at the man. "How boneheaded can you possibly get?" the steel blade raged. "You let them get behind you. You have all the intelligence of a potato."

"I'm sorry," the man said, his voice quivering. "They tricked me."

"I want blood," the knife said. "I want blood and I'm tired of waiting for it."

"I'll get it for you. I promise I will."

"You'd better do it soon. Or I'll get it myself," the knife said, threateningly.

As the knife raged at the man, the sleek black sedan passed them. Marshall slowed as they went by. He wasn't sure if the man saw them or not. He was still wearing the cap pulled low on his face and now he'd added sunglasses. His head was lowered to the steering wheel. When he raised up it looked like he was crying. He was talking to someone but they could see no one in the car with him.

Marshall considered pulling off the road to end it now. He was well armed. But he wasn't sure what arms the man in the truck had. He had attacked twice with only a knife. But he had also fired a couple of shots at them. If he was alone he would have taken a chance. But there were too many unknowns. Too many things that could happen unexpectedly.

Just at that moment Darcey rolled her window down and made a video of the man using the camera function on her own phone. Fortunately he didn't look up. But that decided it for Marshall. He was unwilling to attack when there were too many unforeseen potential outcomes. Too many factors he couldn't control. He was not eager to risk Darcey's life. Better to see what information they could get about the guy and attack on their own terms. When there were fewer risks involved.

Marshall laid on the speed. Darcey didn't cringe this time when the speedometer's needle touched ninety. She wanted to leave that lunatic as far behind as they could. Within seconds the powerful engine had flung them far down the road. He doubted they would see the dirty red truck again today.

Less than an hour later Marshall guided the vehicle off the interstate once more. This time he turned west onto Highway Six. At one time the two lane road that wound through the thick forests and low rolling hills of this northwest part of the state would have qualified as a genuine highway. In today's world it was only a two lane road winding through thick forests and rolling hills.

Darcey said it was about twenty miles to the Belmont farm. Marshall was looking forward to the drive. He was well satisfied with the way the CTS-V handled on the relatively straight interstate. Though he hadn't gone much above ninety he knew he could get a lot more out of her.

Now he wanted to see how she handled on a narrow road with multiple hooks and bends. Anyone could hang on to a fast car going straight. That was like flying on auto pilot. The fun was in the challenge of guiding a high performance vehicle through the sharp curves that lay ahead of them.

It was a testament to the successful collaboration of car and driver that the Belmont farm came into sight exactly twenty minutes later.

That included meticulously heeding the speed limit while driving through a small town that passed out speeding tickets like candy to kids on Halloween. Speeding tickets were an important source of revenue for small towns in this part of the state.

They turned off the main road onto a long driveway that wound down a hill, skirted a fair sized pond and rose up a slight incline to where the old house sat. Darcey had told him the farm was called the Pines. It was easy to see why. The woods surrounding the farm were thick with the tall evergreens. There were none, Trent noted, close to the house.

Like his own home the Belmont house had been built in the early part of the 19th century. The construction, however, was totally different. While his house reflected the Spanish and French influences in the New Orleans of the day, this house was originally built as a "dog trot" house. It was the common design used in this part of the country by settlers moving in from the young United States. It consisted of one or two rooms on either side of an open-ended hallway. Hence, the "dog trot." The family dog could trot right through the house.

There would have been a porch running the length of both front and back. As the family grew and prospered the "dog trot" would have been closed off to make a proper hallway. Rooms on either side would have been refined. Eventually, if all went well, as it had with the Belmonts, a second floor would be added. What Marshall saw now was the final phase of "dog trot" construction. A two story house with a porch running the length of the front. He would bet inside he would find a living room and perhaps a library or den on one side of the hallway; a dining room and kitchen on the other. Upstairs there would likely be three or four bedrooms.

Darcey leaped out of the car with the pies as soon as he shifted into park. "Mom!" she called out. "We're here!"

Marshall slipped the gun into the holster he was now wearing on his belt in the small of his back. While Darcey ran off to find her mother he opened the trunk to retrieve their luggage. He stopped on the front porch and turned to admire the view.

Darcey had told him her fourth great grandparents, Andrew and Blanche Belmont, built the original house. They chose the site well. It was idyllic. He could imagine Andrew and Blanche spent many evenings sitting on this porch looking out over their farm. The view probably was much the same as what he saw today. A pasture with half a dozen horses in sight. Frolicking. Grazing. Now, as then, there was a barn just a short walk down the hill from the house. It was a place worth fighting for.

The house sat at the north end of a low ridge. At the southern end of the ridge he could see a small log cabin. It looked to be very old. There was no tended yard. The only adornment was a yucca plant often seen in this part of the country. It was close to the far side of the cabin's porch. He thought that was probably Rube's cabin. The one specified in Andrew Belmont's will.

His speculation was interrupted by the voices of the women as they came out of the house behind him. He turned to find Darcey with her arm around an attractive woman in her early sixties. Hair attractively arranged. Nails manicured.

She was a small woman. Shorter than Darcey. Trent thought she couldn't weigh more than one hundred ten pounds.

"You must be the Trent Marshall I've heard so much about," she said, a bright, welcoming smile on her lovely face. "I'm Betty Anderson. Welcome to the Pines."

Marshall held out his hand. "I'm pleased to meet you, Mrs. Anderson."

"Oh, give me a hug," the vibrant woman said as she threw her arms around his shoulders. "And stop with the Mrs. Anderson. Call me Betty."

"All right then. Betty it is," he said as he returned the hug.

"Darcey has told me you're a gentleman. And showing up at my house with two Lea's pies proves it. You were raised right," she laughed. "Now come on in the house where it's cool. I want to hear everything that's been going on. I have a feeling Darcey has been filtering the news." She shot her daughter a look.

Once inside Marshall saw that his guess had been right about the layout. Darcey took the pies to the kitchen as Betty led Trent into the first room on the right off the hallway. A living room. Comfortably furnished. An old fashioned fireplace on the wall closest to the hallway. A couch and chairs positioned to enjoy the fireplace on cooler evenings and the flat screen television at one end of the room every evening.

A long bureau was placed behind the couch. The bureau's main purpose was to show off three large trophies. On closer inspection he saw Darcey had won them for swimming.

"Looks like you're quite the athlete," Trent teased Darcey as she joined them. "You didn't tell me about that."

"I was on a swim team in school," Darcey said, gracefully blushing. "I got lucky in a couple of tournaments. I think the other team's star came down with the flu or something." Trent laughed at her obvious embarrassment.

"Don't you believe it, Trent," Betty said. "Darcey was a good swimmer. She could have made the Olympic team if she would have stuck with it."

"Oh Mom," Darcey said, now visibly blushing.

"Well, it's true," Betty said before turning to Trent. "Now can I get you anything? Something to drink maybe?" Betty asked. "I just got home myself a few minutes ago. I had to run into town for a committee meeting today. But I did put together a casserole earlier for our dinner tonight."

Trent smiled. "No, thanks, Betty. I'm good. We just had lunch not too long ago."

Betty sat on the couch and patted the cushion beside her.

"Then sit down here and tell me what's been going on," she insisted. "And I mean everything. All the details. I might be getting old but I'm not so frail I can't handle the truth."

Trent looked at Darcey. She shrugged.

So Marshall told Betty everything. All the details. True to her word, she didn't flinch. She listened closely as he described it all. He watched her face. She showed the same strength he had seen in Darcey.

"Thank you, Trent, for taking care of my little girl," Betty said when he had finished the narrative. She lightly touched his bandaged arm. "And at some cost to yourself. We must see about changing that bandage."

"Darcey's been taking good care of me, Betty," he responded. "She was raised right, too."

"What a nice thing to say. I think her father and I did a pretty good job," Betty said. "But I'm worried for all of us. This government man has really stirred things up."

"I've been wondering about that guy," Trent said. "His story doesn't add up to me. You never received anything in writing from the Treasury Department?"

"Not a thing. He just showed up here one day and demanded that I surrender the missing gold. I laughed at first. I thought he was joking. But he got kind of mean. Said if I didn't cooperate and tell them where the gold was hidden they would take the farm and find it themselves."

"Did he show you any identification?" Marshall asked.

"Yes, but he flashed it so quickly I didn't really have a chance to see it."

"Is that the only time you've seen him?"

"He came back about a week later and asked if I was ready to cooperate. I told him I still didn't know about any hidden gold. He said I'd regret being so unreasonable."

"That's just not the way the federal government works," Trent said, thoughtfully. "They can certainly be heavy handed. But they seldom do anything without a paper trail extending for months before anyone would show up in person."

"That's what I thought, too. I asked the sheriff about it and he thought it was strange. He thought he would have heard about it if it was legitimate. He promised to look into it through official channels. But he said there's only so much he can do. A lot of times the federal government will try to avoid letting local people know what they're doing. That's when he suggested Darcey look you up. He thought you might be able to accomplish more because you don't have to be bound by the rules like he does."

Trent tried to look innocent.

Darcey laughed. "Our Mr. Marshall has been known to skirt the edges of bureaucratic principles, Mom."

"Only because I have people like Jack Blake who'll get me out of trouble if I need help," he said, preferring to avoid the subject. "But let's talk about what might have happened in 1862. I think we can surmise that this man Rube wasn't sure where to go with his friend's wounded son and a wagon load of gold so he came here. We just don't know what happened next. Can you tell us anything about him? Darcey told me that Andrew Belmont's will left him a cabin to live out his old age in."

"Yes, that's true," Betty confirmed. "That's his cabin at the other end of this ridge we're sitting on. Andrew and Rube built the cabin themselves long before Andrew died. Rube lived there while he still worked hauling freight for the Pines and others. The will specified that Rube could live there for the rest of his life."

"Did any of your older family members ever talk about him?"

"Well, yes, now that you mention it," she recalled. "When I was a girl my grandmother's aunt lived here with us for a while. She was almost a hundred years old. She used to tell us stories about life in this parish when she was a girl. And she mentioned Rube from time to time."

"Do you recall anything she said?"

Betty thought about that for a moment. "I recall her saying that he had a beautiful singing voice. That sometimes in the evening Blanche would take her grandchildren down to his cabin. They would gather around him on his cabin's small front porch and he would sing songs for them."

"Wow!" Darcey exclaimed. "From everything we've heard so far I would never have expected that."

"She also said he was a voracious reader," Betty remembered. "She said he read every book in old Andrew's library."

"Interesting," Trent said, thoughtfully.

"Oh, and she said that he had beautiful handwriting," Betty remembered. "Almost like calligraphy. I remember her saying how surprised she was about his reading and his handwriting because from the way he talked she didn't think he had much education."

"Did she ever mention Henry Belmont?" Trent asked.

"No, she never did. And she never said anything about any missing gold either."

"So we know that at some point Rube showed up here. Maybe with Henry and the gold shipment. Maybe later," Trent summarized.

"Another dead end," Darcey said, sounding frustrated.

"Not necessarily," Trent said. "Let's assume that Rube and Henry did arrive here. Now Andrew Belmont is involved. What would the three of them have done?"

"It was well known that even though Andrew owned a large farm he didn't believe in slavery. He also opposed secession," Betty said. "But he was an honest man. And he believed in loyalty. He wouldn't have betrayed his state and he wouldn't have kept something that didn't belong to him."

"Right. So they would have tried to contact someone in authority," Trent said.

"But who?" Darcey questioned.

"The state government was moving north during that period trying to stay ahead of the Union armies," Trent offered.

Betty shook her head. "Andrew would never agree to make contact with them. He thought they were all a bunch of crooks. There was no way he'd turn over that much gold to them."

"I think Henry was still alive in July," Darcey said. "He's buried here in the family cemetery. The date of his death will be on his tombstone. He would have contacts with Confederate units in the area, but if he was badly wounded he wouldn't be able to travel."

"Maybe," Trent agreed. "But remember the Confederate forces were concentrated to the east and north of Baton Rouge. Most of them were actually in Mississippi preparing to face a hundred thousand Union troops."

"That doesn't sound too safe."

"No, it wasn't," Trent said. "According to my research Major General Richard Taylor arrived in Opelousas in July to organize the Army of West Louisiana. Henry might have been alive then or not. But my guess is either way Andrew would have sent word to Taylor. Andrew and Taylor were both prominent Louisiana farmers. They would have known each other. Meanwhile I think Andrew and Rube would have hidden the gold somewhere here on the farm."

"Oh, then that Treasury Department man might be right," Betty said, alarmed.

"Maybe so, though I don't think he's really from the Treasury Department," Marshall said.

"If it is hidden here how do we find it?" Darcey wondered.

"Good question," Marshall said. "How many acres do you have, Betty?"

"Only a hundred acres now. We sold off most of the land after we stopped farming. I just wanted to keep enough for the horses. But at one time the farm was about two thousand acres."

"I don't think we have to worry about the land that y'all sold," Trent said. "It makes more sense, I think, to focus on land close to the house and the barn. They would have wanted to hide it where they could keep an eye on it until they turned it over to the authorities."

"But apparently they never turned it over to anyone. Why not?" Darcey questioned.

"I can't think of a good answer for that," Trent replied.

Their musings were interrupted by the sound of a vehicle in the driveway. Betty looked out the window and saw a white SUV with the words Sabine Parish Sheriff in gold letters. "It's Jack Blake," she told the others.

Moments later the sheriff followed Betty into the living room, his hat in his hands. He was a big man with close cropped silver hair. While his deputies wore uniforms Blake was always dressed in a dark suit and tie with a white western style hat. He had been sheriff in the parish for more than twenty five years. He was now a very healthy and fit sixty. Trent always thought that, even though he was fifteen years younger, he'd hate to have to take Blake on.

[117]

"I swear, Betty, you look younger every time I see you," the politician in the sheriff sparkled.

"Don't go carrying on, Jack," she laughed. "You see me every Sunday at church and at every Chamber of Commerce meeting during the week."

The sheriff's good nature allowed him to laugh with her. "You're looking well, Darcey," he said as he crossed the room to give the younger Anderson woman a hug, "in spite of the company you keep." He nodded toward Marshall.

"Now you be nice, Jack," Betty said. "Trent has been taking very good care of my daughter."

"I knew he would, Betty, or I never would have suggested she get in touch with him," the sheriff responded as he turned to shake hands with Trent, his other hand clasping Trent's shoulder in a gesture of friendship. "I thought I might find you here. How are you, Trent? From the report you sent me y'all have had some close scrapes."

"My arm's still a little sore, Jack, but other than that we're both in good shape. Were you able to make out that license plate enough to get a read on it?"

Jack sat down heavily in a chair facing the couch. He took a square of paper from his shirt pocket and consulted it. "According to the state DMV records the person who is stalking you, who has attacked you twice with a knife and shot at you once is Clint Field. He's eighty three years old, lives in Lafaette, and drives a 2003 blue Toyota truck."

"What?" Darcey exclaimed.

Trent and Jack both laughed. "It's simple, Darcey," Trent explained. "He switched the license plates. Mr. Field probably hasn't even noticed."

"If he realizes you got a picture of his plate he'll just steal another one," the sheriff said. "And as far as dirty red pickup trucks, well, there's probably a hundred of 'em in this parish alone. Maybe more."

"Say, that reminds me, let's take a look at the video you got of the guy himself when we drove by his truck," Trent said.

Darcey reached for her purse to get her camera. "I had almost forgotten about that."

She pulled the video up and showed it to the sheriff.

"It's a little blurry," the sheriff said. "With the cap pulled down low on his face, the sunglasses and his head down on the steering wheel it's hard to make him out." He passed the phone to Trent.

"Yeah, pretty hard to see his face clearly. But there's something vaguely familiar about him."

"Could be you remember him running at you twice now with a knife in his hand," the sheriff suggested.

"Could be," Trent agreed. He didn't think so.

"Send that video to me, if you don't mind," the sheriff said. "I'll add it to the file."

"Well, I'd better get to the kitchen if we're going to eat this evening," Betty said. "Jack, will you stay for supper?"

"No, thanks, Betty," the sheriff said, rising. "I promised Jennifer I'd be home this evening. Trent, that's a fancy car you're driving."

Marshall knew the sheriff wanted to talk to him alone. "It's brand new, Jack," Trent boasted. "This is the first time I've had it on the road. Come look it over."

The two men went outside. They pretended to look at Trent's car while they spoke in low tones.

"Do you want me to assign a couple of men to stay with y'all?" Blake asked.

"I'd love it," Trent laughed. "That's the honest answer. But the only way to bring this thing to a head is to let this guy think he can try again. He won't do that if he gets even a hint that your guys are hanging around."

"I assume you're armed?"

Trent walked around to be rear of the car as though he was pointing something out to the sheriff. He was. The Model 1911 semiautomatic in its holster in the small of his back.

"Oversized magazine. 13 rounds instead of the usual six or seven."

"That ought to do the job."

"One more thing, Jack," Trent added. "Darcey has a small .38 in her purse. It's one of mine. I gave it to her. Hopefully she won't need to use it. But just in case we might need you to swear her in at some point."

"Consider her sworn," the sheriff said. "I'll take care of the paperwork."

After dinner they sat on the front porch. The evening was warm but not uncomfortably so. It was pleasant to be outdoors. To be in the country. Trees and fences and horses for company instead of streetlights and concrete and tourists. The peaceful sound of the cicadas performing their rhythmic dance.

"That plant down by the cabin is called a Spanish dagger, isn't it, Betty?" Trent inquired.

"It has several names but yes, that's one of them," she said. "Back in the outlaw days…when the parish was part of the Neutral Strip…a Spanish dagger in the yard meant the house was a safe haven. The gangs could get food and fresh horses and even hide out if they needed to. Funny thing is old Andrew Belmont was never a friend of the gangs. And they were scared to death of him. They wouldn't come near the Pines."

"Darcey told me the story of Andrew and the horse thief."

Betty laughed. "So you know about 'Eat dirt' then."

"Sounds like he was quite a character," Trent said. "Since the bandits wanted nothing to do with him and the Pines it's curious that there would be a Spanish dagger so prominently displayed. Has it been there since his time?"

"Yes," Betty said. "The legend is that Andrew planted it as sort of a joke. As though he was daring any of the outlaws to show up. As far as I know none of them ever did."

Trent laughed. "He must have been quite a guy."

"Oh, he was. And that reminds me of something. That old aunt told us kids that Blanche Belmont was especially fond of that plant. In the late spring and summer it has the most beautiful tall sprays of white flowers. The old aunt said late in her life Blanche would just sit and gaze at the flowers."

Valerie called to let them know she had arrived and had checked into the hotel. At Betty's suggestion Darcey invited her to come out to the farm for Sunday dinner. Darcey planned to accompany her mom into town for church but they would be back by early afternoon. She told Valerie she was looking forward to showing her the farm. They could even ride the horses if they wanted to.

Later in the evening Betty showed Trent to a very comfortable guest room. As he had guessed there were four bedrooms on the second floor. Betty and Darcey each had their own bath. The two guest rooms shared what Darcey described as a "Jack and Jill" bathroom with doors entering from each bedroom.

It had been another eventful day and Marshall was tired. Still he lay awake for a while trying to fit all the puzzle pieces together. Especially perplexing was the text message he had received the night before in answer to his inquiry. The most perplexing of all.

As he drifted off to sleep the image of Professor Richards floated into his waning consciousness. He could hear her voice.

"You know people didn't have much to do in their free time in those days. No TV. No video games. No movies. They could talk. Play cards or play a few board games, like chess or checkers. They could read. And they could write in journals. They did all those things in what little free time they had. And oh, they also had very large families. That was something they could do after it was too dark to read and write."

Her familiar laugh. Cough. Laugh.

"Look for journals, Trent," he heard her say as her image faded. "Look for journals."

In Betty's room mother and daughter sat on the bed and talked. Like mothers and daughters do. And like the subjects mothers and daughters talk about Trent's name came up.

"You like him, don't you, Darcey?" It was a statement more than a question.

"Is it that obvious?" Darcey replied, a little embarrassed.

"You've never been able to hide things like that from me, you know," Betty smiled. "I can understand why. He's a handsome man. He seems like a good man. But you've only known him a week."

"I know. I don't want to rush into something we both might wind up regretting," Darcey said. "I just wish he didn't have to be such a gentleman all the time. And I wish he wouldn't pull back every time we start to get close."

The mother in Betty said, "Just be careful, Darcey. Don't be in a hurry."

The woman in her smiled.

The man in the dirty red truck liked traveling at night. He thought it was harder for him to be spotted in the dark. Even so he used back roads to skirt the small town on his way to the lake. He found the house he was looking for.

He let himself in. Even though it was late there was a light on in the bedroom. He tried to be quiet but the woman heard him. She came out of her bedroom. When she saw him she stopped still. She stared at him with her dull, lifeless eyes.

"Why are you here? What do you want?" she demanded to know.

It got bad after that. He tried to explain. She yelled at him. Cursed him. Just like the knife. Both of them yelling at him. Cursing him. Condemning him as a coward.

In the end it was the woman against the knife. She wanted him out of her life forever. The knife wanted blood.

They got what they wanted.

He backed the 12 year old Lincoln out of the garage. He parked the dirty red truck in its place, closing the garage door. From the road no one would be able to tell something unusual happened here tonight.

There were three restaurants and bars catering to fishermen five miles down the road. He pulled into one of the parking lots and found a vehicle at the far end. Well out of the light. With a few quick turns of his screwdriver he switched the license plates. The Lincoln drove off into the night. The knife lay on the front seat beside him.

There was blood on the seat.

The knife was sated. For now.

SUNDAY, MAY 3

Marshall awoke to a light tapping on his door.

"Trent, are you awake," Darcey asked softly.

"Getting there," he replied sleepily. "Come on in."

Darcey entered with a cup of coffee. "Thought you might need this to get your eyes open," she said.

He sat up in bed and accepted the coffee gratefully.

"It's Sunday morning and you're not at the Coffee Pot," she pointed out. "You'd better get in touch with Ivy and let her know you're ok."

Trent took a sip of the coffee. "I have a little time," he said, "but you're right. If I don't show up she'll probably call Jordan and demand he launch a search for me."

"Mom and I will be going into town in a couple of hours. Why don't you come downstairs and have breakfast with us?"

Marshall had begged off going to church the night before. He considered himself a religious man. He had seen too many miracles in his life to be otherwise. But he'd never been big on churches.

"Do I have time to shower and get dressed?"

"You can come as you are. We just won't tell the preacher that Mom had a man in his pajamas in her kitchen this morning."

He took the time to brush his teeth and hair before following the scent of frying bacon down to the kitchen, coffee cup in hand. He was still wearing the long sleeve tee shirt and black cotton pants he usually slept in.

"Good morning, Trent," Betty said cheerily. She was wearing an apron over a robe. But her hair and makeup were done. He felt a moment of melancholy as he recalled his mother on Sunday mornings when he was a boy. If she didn't have to work she would be all ready to go before she woke him up. She would cook while he was getting dressed. After breakfast all she had to do was slip into her dress and drag him off to church.

"Good morning, Betty. Thanks for sending the coffee up," he said, drawing an amused look from Darcey and a smile from Betty.

"I've got Irish steel cut oats cooking, if you like that," Betty said. "Bacon will be ready directly. And I can cook you some eggs if you want 'em."

"Real oatmeal!" Trent exclaimed. "That will be great just with bacon. Thanks, Betty. Do you mind if I wander around the place while y'all are in town? I would especially like to look around Rube's cabin if it's ok with you."

"Look around all you want. Just be careful in that old cabin. I haven't been in it in years. I don't know how solid the floor is."

Two hours later Marshall was showered and dressed in jeans, a short sleeved blue work shirt and brown kangaroo leather boots. Alone on the farm, he stood on the porch and surveyed the scene in front of him. He tried to imagine what it looked like in 1862. Tried to envision Henry Belmont and Rube coming up the long driveway in Rube's wagon. Tried to see Andrew Belmont and Blanche coming out on the porch to meet them.

He walked down the ridge to Rube's cabin. Like the house it was well built. The porch and the posts supporting the roof seemed solid. Betty was right though. It wouldn't pay to be careless wandering around a building that hadn't been inhabited in more than a hundred years.

He stepped carefully onto the bottom step. It held. So did the second step. He eased onto the porch, testing the flooring carefully with each step. It seemed solid. Hickory was plentiful here. It is a dense, hard wood favored especially for floors. Trent thought that explained why the cabin was still dependable after so many years.

The glass in the windows looked original. The lock and knob on the front door were very old. He thought the antique dealers on Royal Street would love to get their hands on all that. He tried the doorknob. It turned. He pushed. The door was a little creaky but it opened.

Stepping inside he felt a rush of something going over him. It was as though there was an energy in the old cabin. Something indefinable. Something waiting to be discovered. Something that had waited for a long time.

He was letting his imagination run away with him.

[124]

There wasn't much in the cabin. Two wooden chairs, one with a broken back, the other lying on its side with only two legs. A table with three legs. At the rear of the cabin he saw an old fashioned wood stove. Another prize for a New Orleans antique dealer. To the right of the stove was a pantry slightly above waist high.

Curious, he thought. He opened the doors and looked inside. Nothing. The wood was still solid. Though it was more than a century old it could have been installed last week. Trent was impressed with old Andrew and Rube. They were first rate carpenters.

To his left sat a rusted metal bedstead and springs. At the foot of what had been Rube's bed was a quaint old leather trunk. Marshall knelt in front of it. He stared at it for a few moments. He lifted the top gently. One of the leather hinges had rotted away. The top fell back and off. Inside Marshall found rags. He rummaged through what he assumed had once been clothing. Now just old, rotting rags.

He checked the trunk for a false bottom. Nothing.

He chided himself for feeling disappointment. It would have been too easy to have found something important in the old trunk. No doubt scores of curious Belmont children had pawed through the contents over the past century.

Out of respect he replaced the contents and put the top back in place. He stood up and walked around the room. On a whim he knelt down and looked under the bed. It was dark under there and he couldn't see much. He pushed on the bed and found it would move a few inches toward the wall. On his hands and knees he looked again under the bed. But when he felt the floor begin to give way under his right hand he backed off. He pulled the bed back into place.

At the door he turned and let his gaze again wander around the cabin. He had found nothing but the feeling he had when he walked through the door lingered. Something he couldn't define. Something he could only feel.

He walked down to the barn and looked around inside. That would be a logical hiding place, he thought. Perhaps too logical.

He stood outside the barn and looked back at the cabin on the ridge. His eyes were drawn to the Spanish dagger. He remembered that Betty had said Spanish dagger was one of several names for the plant. He didn't see what that had to do with anything. It was something to think about.

Darcey and her mother got home just past noon. They rushed upstairs to change clothes.

"Most Sundays after church I go to lunch with my Sunday school lady friends," Betty said as she came back downstairs. She had changed her Sunday dress for jeans and a pull over top. "But today I need to get busy in the kitchen."

Darcey was right behind her. Dressed in the same way. Trent followed her into the kitchen.

"Can I do something to help?" he asked.

"Not a thing," Betty said. "I have it all under control."

"Trent's pretty good in the kitchen, Mom," Darcey said.

"Well, if I ever visit him in New Orleans he can cook for me," Betty said as she whirled around the kitchen. "Today he's at my house and I haven't had anybody to cook for in a long time."

Darcey shrugged. Trent was all smiles as he retreated to the living room to see what was on television.

He saw a car coming up the driveway half an hour later. He assumed it was Valerie and called out to Darcey. She came from the kitchen wiping her hands on a towel. Marshall followed her out the front door.

Valerie parked her rental car next to Marshall's black sedan. Darcey gave her a hug as she got out of the vehicle.

"Welcome to the Pines," Darcey told her friend. "I'm so glad it worked out that you could see where I grew up."

"Thanks for inviting me. I wouldn't miss it for the world," Valerie said. She looked around. "So this is the Pines." She took her time looking around. A thorough look. A 360 degree look. An appraisal, Marshall thought. She closed her eyes and breathed deeply. "Yes. Yes. It's very much as I imagined it."

Marshall stood quietly. Observing.

Darcey laughed nervously. "It seems like you're familiar with the farm, Valerie."

"What? Oh no," Valerie said. "It's just that…well, I've always dreamed of living in a place like this. And since you told me so much about it last week I guess…well, I guess I was letting myself engage in a bit of fantasy. It's such a beautiful place, Darcey. You're very lucky to have grown up here."

"Yes, I think so, too. Even though I love my life in San Francisco I'm always delighted when I can come home for a visit. Now come on in the house and meet my mother."

Betty had gone all out with an old fashioned southern Sunday dinner. Smothered pork chops. Mashed potatoes and gravy. Fresh lima beans.

Ivy's collard greens that Darcey had brought with them. Homemade biscuits. And, she reminded them, Trent had brought chocolate and pecan pies from Lea's.

For the second time that day Marshall felt the melancholy of childhood memories. His mother had seldom had the time to prepare such elaborate meals. She had to work long hours. But sometimes, when she had Sunday off, they would drive up to his great aunt's sugar plantation outside of Baton Rouge. Betty's idea of Sunday dinner reminded him of those days at his aunt's house.

After dinner Betty tried to keep him from helping with the dishes. This time he insisted that she sit down and rest. He tended to cleaning up while Darcey took Valerie outside to see more of the farm.

When he was done, he found Betty in the living room with her feet up.

"I'm not as young as I used to be," she laughed. "I've been so excited about having company to do for I think I wore myself out."

"It was a great meal. Thank you so much."

He walked to the window and looked out at the long winding driveway.

"Betty, as far as you know, did the drive up to the house always follow the path it does now?" he asked.

"Yes, I think so. They called this place the Pines because there were so many trees." she said. "All the ones close to the house were cut down many years ago. Pines are beautiful but they snap like matchsticks in a storm. Better to cut one down than wake up to find it in bed with you. Why? Is it important?"

"I don't know. Just curious. I'm trying to get an image of what it looked like here in 1862."

"Pretty much the same as now. The barn has been repaired but never torn down. There were probably some outbuildings back then that aren't here now. There was a lot more pasture since we used to raise cattle and horses. The cotton fields were beyond that. There would have been several acres of vegetables planted out back of the house where I have my small garden now. People had to grow their own food then. There were four cabins along the tree line on the far side of the garden."

"So someone coming directly up the drive would be seen. But they could pull off into the trees and be out of sight."

"Yes, I guess so."

Valerie and Darcey had entered the room as Betty was telling Trent about the cabins.

"You said four cabins," Valerie queried. "Those would have been slave cabins, right?"

"No," Betty responded. "The Belmonts didn't own slaves. Old Andrew Belmont hired workers. He provided housing for some who needed it. Others had their own homes."

"There were no slaves here?" Valerie expressed with surprise. "That must have been very unusual for the time."

"There were certainly many slaves held in bondage down here," Trent explained. "But there were more people who didn't own slaves and even more who opposed secession. In fact, in the only election the pro-secession side won with only 52 per cent of the vote. There were also three parishes that refused to secede. They remained part of the Union throughout the war and provided 23 military units to the federal army."

"Really?" Valerie said. "I never heard about that."

"Most people haven't. Just like most people don't know that East Tennessee and parts of Alabama remained Unionist. And four slave states, Missouri, Kentucky, Maryland and Delaware, voted not to secede. Ironically the Emancipation Proclamation didn't free slaves in any of the states or regions that remained loyal to the Union."

"It's too nice a day to stay inside talking about things that happened so long ago," Darcey interrupted. "Let's get outside. Who wants to go riding?"

Betty said she just wanted to stay right there with her feet up and rest. But they should enjoy themselves. Marshall said he'd join them. He hadn't been on a horse for years. But his recent visit with Isom had brought back memories of the many hours he had spent riding through the woods with the old man. Good memories.

Darcey gave Marshall and Valerie each a hand full of carrots before she led them down to the barn. She directed them as they prepared bridles and the western-style saddles used at the Pines. She opened the gate leading into the pasture. Immediately a beautiful Tobiano paint trotted to her and nuzzled her neck.

"Hey there, big boy, did you miss me?" she said, as she stroked the brown and white horse's muzzle. She fed him a carrot as she introduced her companions. "This is my horse. Prince George. And he does believe he's a prince," she laughed. She fed him another carrot before slipping the bridle into place. He stood patiently as she laid first the blanket over his back, then the saddle, cinching it firmly.

She swung up into the saddle and Prince George happily loped away with her. Marshall and Valerie hung on the fence, watching Darcey and her horse. She was at home in the saddle. Prince George was glad she was home. Trent was impressed. The more he learned about Darcey the more impressive she seemed.

After she and Prince George had a chance to say hello she bridled two more horses and led them to the fence. The gray, she said was the oldest and gentlest of all their horses. His name was Noah. She saddled Noah for Valerie while Marshall saddled the bay, named Mac, for himself. He stroked Mac's neck and withers, fed him a couple of carrots and talked softly to him. By the time he had the saddle cinched and had swung up into it he and Mac were friends. At least he thought they wouldn't hurt each other.

The three of them rode through the pasture mostly at a walk. Every now and again the horses would begin to trot but Valerie was an inexperienced rider. It wasn't comfortable for her. Trent let Darcey and Valerie ride side by side while he brought up the rear. He was interested in listening to the questions she asked Darcey. She wanted to know every detail of events since they had last seen each other only a couple of days before.

He also wanted to use the opportunity to become more familiar with the Pines the way it must have looked in 1862. Darcey showed him the land that had been sold off. At one point they moved into some thick woods, following a trail that looked as though it had been there for a long time. It looked like an old road. A wagon road. There were plenty of horse tracks in the middle of the trail. But the wheel ruts didn't appear to have been made recently. In places they were barely visible.

Marshall paid close attention to the ruts as they came and went. Deep in places. Barely visible in others. The old road rose slightly until it ended in a circular clearing. Ahead and to the right were thick woods. Nearly impenetrable. To the left was a mound. It was lightly covered with brush but no trees. It didn't look natural. It looked vaguely like a miniature of the mounds that people who lived near here in ancient times had built.

One side of the mound was bare of grass and brush. A couple of small depressions meandered down that side. When it rained they would be rivulets providing the falling water with a path from the highest point of the mound. The runoff would slowly, over time, wash it away. He wondered what might appear as time and water had their effect.

He asked Darcey about the mound. She said it had always been there. She thought it might have been where they dumped garbage at one time. "I found some old brass buttons and once there was the blade of a knife sticking out of it after a hard rain. It was old and rusty," she said.

"Do you still have the buttons and blade?" he asked.

"I don't know. I doubt it. I was pretty young when I found them."

After an hour and a half in the saddle Valerie looked like she had had enough. Darcey led them back to the barn. Marshall unsaddled the gray while Darcey took care of Prince George. She showed Valerie how to rub Noah down while Marshall tended to Mac. They gave each horse a few more carrots before turning them back into the pasture.

Back at the house Betty had chocolate pie, pecan pie and vanilla ice cream ready for them.

"Betty, we found what looks like an old wagon road out in the woods," he said. "Can you tell me anything about that?"

"Not much. It was there long before I was born," Betty said. "We've always used it for riding the horses through the woods. I think there might have been some logging out there at some point. As far as I know it doesn't go anywhere. It just sort of tapers out deeper in the trees."

Monday, May 4th

It had been a lazy morning. Marshall thought it was good he lived in the city. It was too easy to do nothing in the country. The relaxation was welcome, he had to admit. But he knew himself well enough to know he could only stand so much of it. That's why Jack Blake had been sure he would succumb to Darcey's request for help. Jack knew Marshall was easily bored. He'd had nothing interesting to pursue for too long. Marshall knew it, too.

Betty had gone into town for a Woman's Club lunch. Marshall made a few phone calls. Darcey was in her bedroom doing the same once it was late enough for offices to open on the west coast. She also called her friend Mandy. Trent could hear her giggling though he couldn't make out what she was saying.

When they both had completed their calls they walked down to Rube's cabin. Trent told her what he had found there the day before.

"Nothing," he said. "Absolutely nothing."

"What makes you think I'll do any better?"

"You never know. Sometimes one person sees what another misses. Can't hurt."

They were more confident about the soundness of the old cabin since Marshall's exploration the day before. The front door opened a little easier today. Darcey stepped inside. She looked around.

"Wow!" she exclaimed. "I haven't been in here in years. It looks exactly as I remembered it."

"I was here for the first time yesterday," Marshall recalled. "When I entered the room I felt something. Like an energy. I felt as though I was being pulled back to the 19th century. I had the feeling there's something here that needs to be found. Wants to be found. Weird, huh?"

"Yeah, a little creepy," Darcey shivered as she spoke. But she wasn't deterred. She followed a similar path around the cabin as had Marshall the day before. She opened the trunk and, as he had done, rummaged through the old clothes. She went into what had been the kitchen and looked into the old wood stove. He had not done that. She found nothing.

"There's something here," Trent said. "Something waiting for us to find it. I know it."

"If there's something waiting to be found it could be a little more helpful in the finding," Darcey said.

Betty's car came hurtling down the driveway as they walked back up the ridge to the house. Her car skidded to a stop. She waved them to her as she got out of her vehicle. She was agitated. Trent and Darcey began to run.

"Mom, are you ok?" Darcey asked as they ran to her. "What's going on?"

"I don't know what's going on, Darcey," Betty replied, her voice trembling. "I want you to tell me what's going on."

"Come sit down, Betty," Trent said.

Darcey led her mother onto the porch and helped her into a chair. "Now tell us what happened," she said.

"It's your friend Valerie. I saw her in town. She was talking to that man from the Treasury Department!"

Darcey was taken by surprise. Trent less so.

"What? Are you sure?" Darcey asked.

"Positive. I saw them both plain as day. She was in her car. That little gray thing. He was standing beside the car talking to her."

Darcey was alarmed. "What does this mean, Trent? What should we do?"

"I'm not sure what it means. Maybe nothing. There might be a reasonable explanation. What we should do for the moment is nothing. What we definitely should not do is over react."

"But we've taken her into our confidence," Darcey said. "She knows everything that we've learned. What if she's not a friend?"

"What do y'all really know about her?" Betty asked, still disturbed.

"We know she probably saved Darcey's life the night we met her," Trent pointed out. "Other than that we don't know anything about her. But she doesn't know everything we know."

"But I've told her…"

"She doesn't know everything we know, Darcey," Trent interrupted her. "Not everything. Now we have an advantage over her. We know something about her that she doesn't know we know."

"So we just do nothing?" Darcey asked.

"Well, when we see her again you can ask her if she's met any interesting men lately," Trent said.

"Besides you, you mean," Darcey laughed and gave him a punch on the shoulder.

"Ouch," Trent cried out in mock pain.

"Well, y'all can laugh if you want to but I'm scared," Betty said.

Trent laid his hand on Betty's shoulder. "It's going to be ok, Betty."

"I sure hope you're right, Trent," Betty said, reaching up to pat his hand with hers. "No offense but I'm going to start sleeping with my snake killer."

"You have a gun?" he asked.

Darcey laughed. "Mom doesn't like guns. She has an old machete that she uses to decapitate snakes that come around the house."

"And I can use it, too," Betty said, as she rose and walked into the house.

"Your mother sleeps with a machete?" Trent asked Darcey, skeptically.

"You don't want to mess with Belmont women," Darcey warned as she followed her mother into the house.

"You better listen to her," came Betty's voice from inside. "And we're most dangerous when we're scared."

Marshall stared after them. Mutely.

The ringing of his phone broke the silence. Marshall hadn't expected to hear from the sheriff so soon. The sheriff hadn't expected to be calling.

"Trent, we've got a murder on our hands. I think you're going to want to see this."

"Who is it? Where are you?" Trent asked.

The sheriff ignored the first question. "You're not going to like it but you know the way."

Marshall felt the tightness in his chest as he drove through the old town toward the lake. He had told Darcey and Betty to stay in the house with the doors locked. He didn't know if this had to do with the attacks on them or something totally unrelated. It could be a coincidence.

Marshall didn't believe in coincidence.

Half an hour after leaving the farm he pulled into the driveway of the lake house. He hadn't been here since the night Blake's deputy had taken

Josh away in handcuffs. He thought he'd never be here again. He hoped he'd never be here again.

Chief Deputy Matt Lorca was coming out of the house when Marshall arrived.

"Hey, Trent," Lorca said. "Glad to see you, buddy. It's been too long. How you doin'?"

Matt was born and raised in the parish. Like generations of Lorcas before him. His ancestors had lived in the area when it was the capital of Spanish Texas. He was a big man. Six and a half feet tall. More than two hundred fifty pounds. Not many around would want to challenge him. That was probably the reason he'd never had to fire his weapon in all the years he had been a deputy.

They got to know each other when Marshall was working on the story that sent Josh Blair to prison. They became friends. Marshall had spent a lot of time fishing with Lorca. Matt had an eighteen foot bass boat. They'd spend whole days on the lake in that thing. Trent would sit in the bow chair. Matt would take the stern seat. He would operate the trolling motor with his foot.

They would fill a cooler with beer, Prosecco and tequila. Matt was happy with beer. Trent wanted options. They'd take along a couple of sandwiches if they remembered. Maybe some chips and salsa. Later in the day Matt would just let the boat drift. Trent would try not to fall in the lake. Some days they'd even catch a few fish.

A couple of times Matt had come to New Orleans to hang out with Trent. They had some fine times roaming Bourbon Street well supplied with booze and beads. Those long days on the lake and longer nights on Bourbon Street helped Trent recover from losing his best friend and the breakup of his marriage.

"Good to see you, Matt," Trent said as they shook hands. "What happened here?"

"It's Josh Blair's wife, Trent. She's been dead a while so it's not a pretty sight."

He led Trent into the house where the sheriff was talking with the medical examiner. Death was noticeable in the air. The body made it real. Murder.

The woman lay in a large pool of congealed blood in the middle of the living room floor. The coroner was kneeling beside her. Leaning over her.

Her open eyes stared at the ceiling. Dull. Lifeless. Not much different than when he had last seen her, Trent thought. Her throat hadn't been cut then.

"What do you think, Doc?" the sheriff asked.

"Well, all her blood drained out within minutes so no clue from livor mortis. Rigor mortis has come and gone. I'd say it happened between 36 and 48 hours ago," the coroner speculated. "Whoever did it sliced through the trachea, the common carotid artery and the internal jugular vein. Nearly cut her head off. But he was merciful, if it could be called that, by slicing through the trachea. She would have gasped for air but would have been unconscious in seconds as the supply of oxygen to her brain was halted.

"How do you think it happened, Jack?" Trent asked.

"She was wearing a robe over what looks like a nightgown. The light's on in her bedroom and there's a book lying open on her bed. No sign of a struggle. No sign of forced entry. Looks like she was in her bedroom reading when someone she knew came in."

"She didn't have a happy life," Trent said. "She sure didn't deserve this ending. Who found her?"

"Matt did," the sheriff said to Marshall's surprise. "Let me show you something.

He led Marshall through a doorway from the kitchen into the garage. Closest to the door was a late model Buick sedan. On the far side of the garage Marshall was astonished to see the now familiar dirty red pickup truck.

"I got to thinking about red pickup trucks. I told you there were probably hundreds in this parish alone. But then I remembered somebody who drove a truck like that. Somebody who might have a motive for murder. Or think they did. I sent Matt out here to see if he'd been around lately. Didn't expect he would find what you just saw."

"Johnny Blair," Trent said.

"Yep. Johnny Blair," the sheriff said. "He's more than twenty now. In and out of trouble since his early teens. Used every kind of drug you can think of. I'm amazed he didn't OD years ago. Or go to prison. He would have gone to jail if his grandfather hadn't bought his way out of trouble time and again. The old man died a year or so ago. Johnny's been running wild ever since. It was just a matter of time before something like this happened. Didn't think he'd go after his mother though."

"But he would have no reason to kill Darcey," Trent said.

"He isn't trying to kill Darcey. He's trying to kill you. Just like he promised the night I arrested his father."

"But when he slashed my arm on the levee I heard him say 'I'll find you, woman. I'll find you and I'll kill you.' Why would he have said that?" Marshall asked.

"Darcey wasn't the only woman on the scene that night. Valerie Martin was there also. And she warned you in time for you to protect yourself. Maybe the threat was directed at her."

Trent nodded. "Why would he have come back here now to kill his mother? That doesn't fit."

"I don't think that's why he came back here," Blake said. "I think y'all really spooked him Saturday when you got pictures of his truck. I think he came here to get another vehicle."

"But why kill his mother?"

"She kicked him out of the house a couple of years ago. Told him to never come back. The way he has stalked you, attacked you, I think he's lost it. I think he's insane. My guess is he showed up here to trade vehicles. She told him to get out and that was enough to put him over the edge. He's out of control, Trent"

"What is he driving now?"

"The Buick is his mother's car. Josh's old Lincoln was in the garage. It doesn't have current plates but that won't matter to Johnny. By now it's wearing somebody else's plates anyway. I'd say we're looking for a gray Lincoln Town Car. At least ten years old. Maybe a little older. He also went through his mother's purse probably looking for cash."

"This could explain the attacks on me. It might mean that Darcey isn't in danger and never has been. Except that she's been with me. But there are some things that don't fit. The break in at the Camp Moore museum. Why would he have done that? And what about Professor Richards' murder?"

"I don't know," the sheriff admitted. "Doesn't make sense, does it?"

"No, it doesn't. I think there's still something we don't know. There are still missing pieces. By the way, Betty saw Valerie Martin talking to the guy who claims to be from the Treasury Department. I don't know what that means either. Maybe nothing. Did you ever get a response to that inquiry I asked you to make?"

"Nothing yet," the sheriff replied. "But you sent me the message on Friday night. Nobody's going to spend their weekend responding to something like that. I should hear something in a day or so."

It was almost dark when Trent reached the Pines. He joined Darcey and her mother in the living room where he told them about the murder at the lake. He left out the frightful details.

"The gist of it is Darcey isn't the target. Johnny's after me. He blames me for his father going to prison and his subsequent death. I think it's safe to say he's insane. And he's decidedly dangerous. It seems to me y'all would be better off without me around."

"I don't think so at all," Betty said.

Darcey agreed with her mother. "I don't know what good it would do for you to leave now, Trent. He's seen you with me several times. He just killed his mother. If he showed up here and you were gone he'd probably kill us in his fury. You just said he's insane."

"That's true," Trent said.

"And besides what about the missing gold?" Darcey added. "What about the break in at the Camp Moore museum? What about Professor Richards' murder? Those things don't have anything to do with this crazy boy's father."

"Can't argue with you there," Trent said. "Jack and I had the same conversation. There are still pieces to this puzzle that we don't understand. And you're right. They don't have anything to do with Johnny Blair."

Betty was firm. "We're safer with you here, Trent. We want you to stay."

"Well then," Trent responded with a grin, "what's for dinner?"

That got him another slug on the shoulder from Darcey and a laugh from both women.

The young man in the old gray Lincoln Town Car had no idea where Trent was. He had been very clever to follow him as far as Lecompte but that's as far as it went. Now he just drove around aimlessly. He drove along the lake road hoping to find Trent's car at one of the camps. He drove out to the hotel and searched the parking lot. Nothing. After nightfall he drove into the old town. Through the residential areas. Still nothing. He wasn't even sure Trent was in this parish. He could have continued north to Shreveport or stopped at any number of small towns along the way. He might not even be in the state.

The knife lay silently on the passenger seat. The blade's thirst for blood had been satisfied. He felt nothing for his mother. Anyway it wasn't his fault. He hadn't killed her. It was the knife. The knife had demanded her death. The knife had demanded her blood. If the knife hadn't tasted her blood it would have wanted his. In a way he could say his mother had given her life to save his. But her sacrifice wouldn't stay the knife's demands for long. He had to find Trent Marshall.

TUESDAY, MAY 5TH

It was another uneventful day. He walked down to Rube's cabin to look around. Still nothing.

Late in the morning he called Sheriff Blake. In the early afternoon Blake's white SUV came up the winding driveway. He declined Betty's offer of one of the sandwiches left from lunch but accepted a glass of sweet tea.

"You called this meeting, Trent," the sheriff said. "What's on your mind?"

"Something has been bothering me since we were at the lake yesterday. This morning I figured out what it is. It's something you said. 'He's out of control.' You were talking about Johnny being insane."

"Yes, I said that. He is out of control," the sheriff said. "Not only that but he has no heart at all. Packed himself a lunch before he left. Right in sight of his mother's lifeless eyes. Only a truly insane person could be so unemotional."

"I agree he's insane. But in terms of what we've been through in the past week he has been in complete control. We've just been waiting to see what he'll do next. We've been lucky so far. We've been able to see him coming and react quickly enough to back him off. There might be a time when we're not so lucky. One of us could get badly hurt. Or worse. We have to change the paradigm, Jack," Marshall insisted. "We have to take control away from him."

"Got any ideas how we do that?" the sheriff asked.

"Not really. Whatever we decide will involve all of us, which is why I wanted Darcey and Betty to participate in this conversation. Johnny might be after me. But they're in danger, too. And he might be after you, Jack. You were the one who arrested his dad."

"I thought about that when we were at the lake yesterday," Blake said. "I made it a point to clean and reload my gun last night."

"But things have happened that we can't connect back to Johnny. We have a puzzle with a lot of pieces that don't fit together. And those puzzle pieces have pictures of each one of us on 'em."

"What do we know for certain?" Darcey asked.

The sheriff supplied the answer. "We know Johnny Blair killed his mother. We know he has tried to kill Trent. And we can surmise that he's willing to kill you also, Darcey, from what he said after the attack on the levee failed."

"Then doesn't it make sense to focus on what we know?" she continued. "If we can fit together the pieces that pertain to what we know then maybe some of the other pieces will begin to fall into place."

"That's logical," the sheriff said.

"I think so, too," Betty agreed. "And I think I have to say what comes next because none of you will. You're all concerned about what might happen to me. Trent has been holed up here at the Pines because he is trying to protect Darcey and me. Johnny probably doesn't even know where he is. I think we should leave this house and let him see us. The only way to kill a snake is get it to come out in the open."

The others were quiet for a few moments. Finally, Darcey spoke up. "I agree with Mom," she said. "We have to take the initiative."

"All right. I'm in," the sheriff said. "I'll assign two cars to..."

"No, Jack," Trent interrupted. "As much as I'd like to have your guys protecting us it's enough to know you have our backs. If Johnny so much as sniffs a cop he'll dig himself a hole and no telling when he'll come out again. It's enough for us all to have your number on speed dial. If we get in trouble you can get to us in minutes."

"As much as I dislike it, you're right"

"Besides," Trent continued, "we're all armed. You know I have my Model 1911 with an oversized magazine. Thirteen .45 caliber slugs as fast as I can pull the trigger. Darcey has a .38 single action revolver in her purse."

"That reminds me," the sheriff said. "Darcey, you are now officially a special deputy assigned to the Sabine Parish Sheriff's Office. Here's your badge. Be sure to keep it with you." He passed her the badge. The same one Marshall carried.

"Darcey, you're carrying a gun?" Betty exclaimed. "You didn't tell me that."

"I didn't want to worry you, Mother."

"Are you kidding me? I wouldn't have worried nearly as much if I'd known you were armed."

"But what about you, Betty?" the sheriff asked.

"You don't worry about me, Jack. I can take care of myself."

"Mom sleeps with a machete, Sheriff," Darcey said.

"You sleep with a machete, Betty?" the sheriff asked incredulously.

"She sleeps with a machete," Trent confirmed.

"You sleep with a machete," the sheriff repeated. He shook his head. "What I don't know about my constituents is downright frightening."

In keeping with their new strategy Marshall was to drive Darcey and Betty into town in his car. The car that Johnny Blair had seen. They didn't really need anything. They were just going to wander through some of the boutique shops that had opened in the old town. They wanted to be seen.

While they were getting ready Marshall sat on the porch staring down the ridge at Rube's old cabin. He couldn't shake the feeling that it held a secret. The answers they were seeking were there. He could feel it. He peered at the cabin as though through a fog. As though the intensity of his focus on the small building would somehow force it to reveal the unknown.

He parked the sleek black sedan on the main street of the old town. Obligingly he followed Darcey and her mother from shop to shop. Playing the role of the bored man accompanying two women as they shopped their way up one side of the street and down the other wasn't acting. It was stodgy. It was also just the cover he needed to watch for the gray Lincoln. He didn't see it.

Johnny Blair saw him. Johnny wasn't dumb enough to drive down the main street. He stuck to the less traveled side streets when he was driving through the old town. He saw Marshall following the two women into a small jewelry store. Quickly pulling the Lincoln into a parking spot out of sight of the main street, Johnny walked between two buildings. He left the knife in the car covered with a towel even though he could hear it shrieking at him as he locked the car's doors. He hoped no one else would hear it.

Johnny settled into a narrow gap between the two buildings. He could see all of the main street clearly but it would be difficult to see him. He watched as Marshall followed the two women from store to store. He watched as the women gave him the packages to carry when they made their purchases. The women looked like they were having fun. Marshall looked miserable. That made Johnny smile. He enjoyed seeing Marshall looking miserable. He wanted more. He wanted to see Marshall die.

Finally there were no more stores on the street. Marshall loaded the packages into the trunk of his car. Johnny watched to see the black sedan head east out of town before running back to the gray Lincoln. He gunned the big Lincoln motor through the back streets reaching the edge of town just in time to see Marshall's car disappear around the steep curve leaving the old town. He followed, staying well back.

Not far enough back. At the top of the hill Marshall looked into the side mirror. He saw the gray Lincoln pull onto the highway.

"We've got a bite," Marshall said. "Now let's see if we can set the hook."

Darcey picked her purse up from the floorboard of the car. Reaching inside she wrapped her hand around the grip of the revolver. "Do you think he'll attack now?"

"I don't think so. When he's attacked before he's had an edge. The dark of night on the levee. No brakes on the Jeep at Isom's. He doesn't have any kind of edge now. I think we set the hook by letting him see where we're going. When he tries again we'll be ready for him."

Johnny Blair saw Marshall turn off the highway. He had turned into the Pines. Marshall's car disappeared behind the thick stand of trees that blocked the view of the big house from this angle. Johnny slowed and pulled off the road. He didn't want to drive by and take a chance on Marshall seeing him. Blair grinned. Now he was one up on his target. He knew where Marshall was but Marshall didn't know he knew. The knife was raging again. Telling him to go for blood now. But Johnny was too smart for that. He did a U-turn and headed back to town.

Just past the thick stand of trees that gave the Pines its name, he slammed on his brakes. On the south side of the highway was an old building that had once been used as a warehouse during the oil and gas boom more than fifty years ago. It sat empty now. It would make a perfect hideout for Johnny to keep an eye on the comings and goings at the Pines. He turned into the entrance and drove slowly alongside the huge building. Halfway down its length was an opening. There once had been a set of doors but now one hung loosely on broken hinges. The other lay on the ground. He turned the wheel and did a K-turn to back into the building.

He got out of the car, leaving the wailing knife on the seat, to walk around the old building. There wasn't much to see. It was just an old empty building. There was a window at the end of the building closest to the highway. The glass was still intact but so dirty no one could see into the old building.

Even better it was only about a hundred yards through the trees to the old house at the Pines. He could easily watch the house from the trees.

He was very pleased with himself. He had put himself in perfect position to await the next opportunity.

Valarie called to invite them to meet her for dinner at one of the restaurants out at the lake. Darcey told her she would check with her mother to be sure she hadn't made other plans.

Trent talked to the sheriff. They both had concerns about drawing Johnny into the open at a restaurant. But the sheriff pointed out that there were some unknowns about Valerie, too. There was a lot they didn't know about her and how she might fit into the puzzle. They agreed it was risky but if they were trying to flush one bird out of the bushes why not try for more? Assuming there were more.

Darcey called Valerie back to accept her invitation. They agreed to meet at seven o'clock that evening.

In the old warehouse Johnny ate a blackened chicken thigh and drumstick. Leftovers he had found in his mother's refrigerator. After he had eaten he stepped out of the old building. He looked up at the clouds that were beginning to gather. The smell of rain was in the air.

He slipped quietly through the woods toward the house. At the edge of the woods he found the half rotted trunk of a tree that had fallen. The perfect place from which to watch the house less than a hundred yards away. He made himself as comfortable as possible where he couldn't be seen. He watched.

At 6:30 he saw Marshall and the two women come out of the house. They were laughing and talking. He couldn't hear what they were saying. But they were getting into Marshall's car. Johnny eased back deeper into the woods before he turned and ran for the warehouse. He was glad

Marshall was on the move before the rain started. At least he wouldn't be caught lying in the woods when the clouds burst.

He waited until he saw Marshall's black sedan pass the warehouse before he turned the ignition to start the car and switched on the lights. He didn't want any light showing from the old building that would alert Marshall to his presence. Pulling onto the highway, he followed Marshall's car from about a half mile back.

Marshall drove down the main street of the old town. Johnny kept pace with him from one street over. At the edge of town it was clear that Marshall was headed for the lake. That knowledge allowed Johnny to fall back a little farther to avoid being seen.

They reached Toledo Town, the small community of restaurants, convenience stores and bait shops that had grown up to serve sport fishermen. Johnny pulled closer to see where they would stop. When he saw them pull up to a restaurant he quickly turned right onto a road just short of the parking lot. He was pleased to see that Marshall let the two women out and then parked well away from the building and the other cars. He probably didn't want to chance getting a ding in his fancy new car, Johnny thought. He decided he would kick in the side of the car after he killed Marshall. It made him laugh to think of it.

The restaurant was not fancy. But its plain walls were decorated with photographs of Toledo Bend Reservoir that Valerie called "lovely." Other than that there was little ornamentation. Plain tables and chairs. Paper place mats with a map of the huge lake and a drawing of a fisherman landing a whopper of a bass. Paper napkins. Just inside the door sat a man playing a pedal steel guitar. Not something to be expected but pleasant background music.

Trent, Darcey, and Betty ordered fried catfish, fries, hushpuppies, and Cole slaw. It was all new to Valerie, the Colorado girl, but she went along with the group.

While they waited for their food she was as inquisitive as ever. They had little to tell her. She heard that a woman had been killed in a house on the lake. Marshall said they heard the news also but had no information they could pass on to her.

"It's just that it happened so close to the hotel I'm staying in," Valerie said with a shudder. "You never know what's going to happen next these days."

Darcey asked her, girl to girl, if she'd met any interesting men at the hotel. She avoided Trent's eyes when she asked the question. He was trying to appear uninterested.

"No," Valerie said. "Not that I've been looking. I might just need a break from men for a while."

"I thought I saw you talking to a man in town yesterday," Betty said.

"You did?" Valerie was surprised. "Oh, I forgot all about that. Some guy staying at the hotel. I ran into him in town and he tried to hit on me. Wanted me to have dinner with him tonight. I told him I was busy, which wasn't true when I told it to him but thank goodness we made plans so it wasn't like I lied to him." She laughed.

They all laughed with her. No one mentioned they knew he was the man from the Treasury Department.

Fried catfish was one of Marshall's favorite foods. A crispy fried crust encasing snow white fish. The fries were hand cut and nicely browned. The hushpuppies were delightfully fried balls of cornmeal with bits of onion. The crunchy sweetness of the Cole slaw provided a nice counterpoint to a plate of otherwise fried foods. Valerie pronounced the meal "exquisite." Not the usual term for fried catfish but Marshall thought it would do.

They ordered peach cobbler for dessert. Valerie asked more questions. What were they going to do next? Did they think they had managed to lose the crazy man with the knife? Did they have any clues at all about the treasure hunt that had started all this? They had no answers for her.

Marshall asked her what she thought they should do.

"Me?" Valerie asked, taken aback. "I have no idea. I don't really know anything about all this except what Darcey has told me. I'm just so glad none of you have been seriously hurt."

Valerie insisted on picking up the tab. "You've fed me three times now," she pointed out. "It's my turn to treat."

She had parked her car very close to the door. Marshall made sure they all made a fuss getting her on her way. There were hugs all around and promises to talk tomorrow. Finally she pulled the dull gray rental car out of the parking lot and onto the road, quickly disappearing in the darkness.

Marshall told Darcey and Betty to stay at the restaurant's front door. It was well lighted. There were plenty of people moving in and out. He would get the car and pick them up. Darcey looked at him with worry in her eyes but said nothing. Her hand went into the purse hanging from her shoulder. Her fingers wrapped around the grip of the revolver.

Her mother kept up an endless chatter about nothing. They played their roles well.

Marshall walked to the far end of the parking lot where he had left his car. It was part of their plan to draw Johnny out into the open. He was here. Marshall could feel it. He resisted looking over his shoulder. As he left the lighted area around the restaurant he surreptitiously eased the big semiautomatic from its holster in the small of his back. He kept his right hand holding the weapon close to his leg. In the dark it would be hard to see. He kept moving forward. Farther from the light. His eyes on the sleek black sedan. Waiting in the dark.

Marshall's car might have been beyond the reach of the restaurant's lights. But he was back lit by those same lights. Easily seen by anyone hiding in the black night. Johnny was hiding there.

The gray Lincoln was parked on the side road abutting the parking lot. The engine was running. The lights were off. Johnny watched Marshall move closer. He was excited. More excited than he had ever been. Trembling with excitement.

The knife lay on the passenger seat. The knife could smell the blood coming closer. Closer. Johnny giggled. The knife made a noise somewhere between a moan and a laugh. They had waited so long. Now it was going to happen. Tonight it would happen

Now! It would happen now!

Johnny shifted into drive. He turned the wheel as he surged forward. The gray Lincoln's headlights came on.

The headlights blinded Marshall. He could hear the car coming toward him. He couldn't see it.

Before he could react, Johnny slammed his foot on the brake bringing the big car to a sliding stop. The door opened and their stalker got out. He stood beside the open car door.

"I have you now, you murderer," he said. "I promised to kill you when you let them take my dad away. I was only ten years old when I made that promise to you but I meant it. I've never forgotten. Now I'm going to do it."

Marshall stood still in the headlights of the gray Lincoln.

"Johnny, you don't have to do this. I'm sorry about your dad. I was sorry when it happened. I didn't want it to happen. He was my best friend. I loved him like a brother." The men were no more than twenty yards apart.

Johnny was quiet. His head tilted as though he was listening to someone. He listened. Then he spoke. But he wasn't speaking to Marshall. "I know. I know. You don't have to tell me. I know he's lying."

Marshall wasn't sure who Johnny was talking to. He remembered Blake saying the young man was insane. He tried again to talk to Johnny. He didn't get very far.

"Johnny, listen to me…"

Johnny waved the razor sharp knife threateningly. "Liar! You shut up! You didn't love him. You weren't his friend. It's because of you that he's dead. You killed him," Johnny screamed. "Now it's time for you to die."

Johnny moved toward Marshall. He held the knife in front of him. Held it to slash. Not to stab. To slash. As he had slashed Marshall's arm that night on the levee. As he had slashed his mother's throat. He was going for Marshall's throat. Marshall was not his mother. Marshall wouldn't give up his throat so easily.

Johnny began to run toward Marshall. Screaming. Unintelligible sounds. Marshall stood still. He let Johnny get to within ten feet of him before he moved. When he acted he took Johnny totally by surprise.

As Johnny brought his arm around seeking to slash at Marshall's throat the older man dropped and launched himself at his attacker's knees. He upended Johnny like a linebacker hitting a running back. He rolled through the hit and came easily to his feet. As Johnny's feet went over his head in the opposite direction he tried to slash at Marshall. The blade found nothing but air. Empty air.

Johnny raised himself to his knees, the knife still held in his hand. Marshall stepped to his left. He brought his gun down on Johnny's upraised arm. With its oversized magazine the weapon weighed four pounds. The crack of breaking bone reverberated through the parking lot. The ulna bone in his forearm had been broken by the heavy piece of deadly metal. Johnny lost partial ability to control his fingers. He could no longer hold onto the knife. It dropped from his hand. Dropped into the dirt.

Marshall stepped on the blade. He kicked it aside. With the knife out of reach the young man seemed to focus on the pain of his broken arm. He tried to clutch the arm to his body but even that was too painful. He knelt in the dirt and cried.

Marshall thought Johnny was no longer a danger. He wanted to help him. But he was cautious. He remembered the two shots fired at them in New Orleans. Johnny might have a gun on him. He still had one good arm. The broken ulna would put normal people out of action. Marshall wasn't sure about an insane person.

"Trent? Are you ok?" He heard Darcey calling.

"Yes, I'm good," he called out. "But we need an ambulance. Call Jack."

She came running up to him, the revolver in her hand. She stopped well out of reach of the crazed young man on his knees in the dirt. She lowered her gun as she realized he was not a threat. She watched as he rocked back and forth. Crying in his pain and frustration.

"Already done. They're on the way," Darcey replied, watching Johnny with horror.

"One of the bones in his right arm is broken," Marshall said. "I don't think he's a danger now. I've got him covered. You can put your gun away."

Chief Deputy Matt Lorca arrived in three minutes. Apparently Marshall's argument that cops hanging around would scare Johnny away hadn't convinced the sheriff. Lorca was close by. Maybe a coincidence.

Marshall didn't believe in coincidence. But he wasn't unhappy that the sheriff had ignored him this time.

"You OK, Trent?" Lorca asked.

"I'm fine, Matt. Johnny has a broken arm. Other than that he's OK, too. His knife is on the ground there," Trent said, pointing to where the grizzly blade lay.

Lorca had already pulled surgical gloves onto his hands. He put the blade in an evidence bag.

The ambulance had to come from town. It arrived fifteen minutes later. Jack Blake was right behind it as were two other deputies.

The EMTs confirmed that Johnny's injury was painful but not life threatening. Handling him as gently as possible, which was not easy as he was still moving his head talking to some unknown entity, they got him onto a gurney. With his good left arm cuffed to the gurney's railing and a deputy riding with them, the ambulance left for the hospital in town.

Trent told the sheriff that Matt had already bagged Johnny's knife.

"We'll run some tests," Blake said. "I don't have any doubt we'll find traces of blood from you, the professor in New Orleans, and his mother."

"You're right about him being insane, Jack," Trent said. "He kept talking to someone. He would turn his head like he was listening. Then he would talk to whoever it was."

"Well, the hospital here will get him stabilized. But we'll send him to the mental hospital in Shreveport. The most important thing is y'all didn't get hurt and nobody else got killed. Thank God for that."

"Betty, I know you're don't drink but I hope you don't mind if I stop at a liquor store before we leave here. I think I could use a drink tonight," Trent said.

Betty had no objection. "Tonight a drink sounds good even to me," she said.

Trent made a stop at one of the liquor stores that had opened at the lake in recent years. Forty five minutes later Trent poured Rebel Yell into three short wide-mouth glasses. He cut the Kentucky bourbon with a little water for Betty. He and Darcey took theirs on the rocks. They sat on the porch and sipped their drinks in silence.

They were surprised a few minutes later to hear the rumble of a heavy truck engine. Headlights stabbing through the dark. An old brown dually truck lumbered into view and came to a halt. The door opened and Matt Lorca climbed down.

"Hope I'm not interrupting," the chief deputy said. "It's been sort of a stressful night. I thought y'all might need some company. Somebody normal," he added with his usual wide smile.

"Come on up, Matt, and join us," Trent said. "Are you off duty? How about a taste of Rebel Yell?"

"I'm off duty and never been known to turn down bourbon," Matt said. "Evening, Betty. Darcey."

"Good evening, Matt," Betty said. "You're always welcome at the Pines."

"And you're right," Darcey added. "A visit from a normal person is welcome."

Matt accepted a bourbon on the rocks and joined the group on the porch. The silence resumed.

The wind was starting to pick up. The storm would break soon. Darcey said she was going to walk down to see to the horses. If only a light rain fell the horses would ignore it, preferring to continue grazing. There was a shed extending from the side of the barn bordering the pasture that provided protection for them if the rain was hard accompanied by thunder and lightning. The horses really hated hail for whatever reason. They got to stay in the barn if a hail storm hit.

Trent and Matt went with her. Trent was holding his bourbon when Mac came trotting up to him. He was flattered that the horse remembered him so quickly. Not so much when he saw that it was the scent of bourbon that attracted Mac. The bay stuck his nose as far into the glass as he could get it.

Trent laughed. "You gave me a boozer to ride," he told Darcey.

Darcey giggled at the sight. "I've never seen a horse do that before."

Trent thought if Mac liked the smell of bourbon he might really enjoy having a little taste. He dipped his finger in the liquor and rubbed a little on Mac's gums. Not a good idea. Mac made a sound somewhere between a snort and a whinny. He tossed his head from side to side. His lips curled back over his teeth. He shook his head as he backed away from Marshall.

"Amateur drinker," Trent laughed.

Just at that moment a shattering peal of thunder and a flash of lightening warned that the dark clouds hovering over them all day were ready to burst. Trent, Darcey and Matt took off on a dead run back to the house. They had barely made it to the safety of the porch when the rain started. Big drops of water falling hard. Trent's dad would have called it a Louisiana gully washer.

Trent poured them another drink. Betty was still sipping her first one. On any other night the storm would have chased them inside. Tonight they sat sipping bourbon, safe and dry on the porch of the old house. They let the storm dissipate the shock of the violence that had threatened to consume them earlier in the evening.

WEDNESDAY, MAY 6TH

Sheriff Blake called while breakfast was being served at the Pines. He asked Trent to come into town to watch Johnny's questioning. Trent downed the last of his coffee and told the women where he was going.

"Not without me," Darcey said. "Mom, I'm sorry about the dishes but I don't want to miss this."

"Y'all go," Betty said. "I'll take care of things here."

"Keep that machete close by, Betty, and the door locked," Trent called as they left the house. "We're not sure this thing is settled."

"You don't worry about me, Trent Marshall," Betty called back. "Better you worry about somebody prowling around here," she muttered to herself.

The rain had let up after falling through the night. Marshall had heard thunder rolling across the sky from time to time. In spite of that he slept well. Rain falling on the roof of the old house was an effective sleep aid.

They met with the sheriff before the interrogation. He introduced them to Jason Adams, chief of his Criminal Investigation Unit. "I'm going to have Jason conduct the interrogation," Blake explained. "Johnny knows you and me, Trent, from the night his dad was arrested."

"He knows me from far more than that, Jack," Marshall said. "There was a time when he called me Uncle Trent."

The sheriff nodded solemnly.

"I don't think we're going to get much from him," Adams said. "From what I've seen he's completely delusional. At some point I might suggest that one or more of you come into the room. Maybe the shock of seeing you might bring him back to some semblance of reality. I don't think there's much chance of that but it might be worth a try."

"Johnny will be in the interrogation room. His good arm will be cuffed to the chair, which is secured to the floor," the sheriff said. "There will be a male nurse in attendance to assure his injury isn't aggravated in any way. A video camera mounted discreetly on the wall will film the whole thing. The three of us will be watching from the adjoining room but he won't be able to see us."

Trent and Darcey sat with the sheriff in the dark. Matt Lorca came in to join then. They could see Johnny and the nurse in the brightly lighted room on the other side of the one way mirror. Detective Adams entered the room and sat down across the table from Johnny. He introduced himself before asking a few questions intended only to identify Johnny for the record.

"Have you been advised of your rights?" Adams asked.

Johnny nodded his head in the affirmative.

"I'm sorry but I have to ask you to answer the question verbally," Adams said.

Johnny pressed his lips together and made a motion like he was zipping them shut. He threw his head back in laughter.

"I'll ask the nurse in attendance to confirm that the subject has refused to speak but has answered the question in the affirmative," Adams said.

"I can confirm that," the nurse replied.

"So you're aware that anything you say can and will be used against you in a court of law," Adams continued. "You're aware that you're entitled to be represented by an attorney. If you can't afford an attorney one will be provided for you. Do you want an attorney present to represent you?"

Johnny tilted his head giving Adams a quizzical look reminiscent of a puppy. "Why would I need an attorney?" Johnny asked. "I haven't done anything wrong."

"So you're declining the offer of having an attorney present?" Adams clarified.

"Are you stupid or what?" Johnny said. "I told you I haven't done anything wrong."

"You were driving a 12 year old gray Lincoln when you were apprehended," Adams said. "How did you get that vehicle?"

Johnny rolled his head around. He stared at the ceiling. Finally he responded. "I got it from my dad's house."

"You stole it?" Adams asked.

Johnny shouted his response. "I didn't steal anything. That just shows how ignorant you are." The young man giggled.

Adams' voice remained calm. "If you didn't steal it who gave you permission to drive it?"

"My daddy said I could drive it."

"When did he tell you that?" Adams asked.

"Yesterday," Johnny answered angrily. Then he looked around the room. The anger disappeared from his face. He seemed confused. He looked like a little boy. "No, I mean last week."

He was quiet. His eyes on the floor. Forlorn. A pathetic little boy.

"Or maybe it was a long time ago," he said, his voice barely audible.

He laughed. His voice suddenly strengthened. Speaking loudly. Jubilant.

"Yeah, that's it. He always told me I could have it. Sometimes he let me sit on his lap and pretend to drive it."

"OK, thank you," Adams said. "Now let's talk about your mother. Why did you kill your mother?"

Johnny first looked surprised. Then his eyelids lowered until he was staring out through narrow slits. "I didn't kill my mother," he hissed.

"You didn't kill her?"

"No, I didn't kill her," Johnny said. He looked around the room. He leaned over the table as far as he could. His voice was now a whisper. "But I know who did." He leaned back and grinned. He seemed proud to have a secret.

"Can you tell me who it was?"

Johnny's eyes grew big. He looked wildly around the room. "It wanted blood," he hissed as he turned his face back toward the detective. "It wanted someone else's blood but I couldn't get it. So it drank my mother's blood. I couldn't stop it. It would have taken my blood if I tried to stop it."

"Who? Who wanted blood?" Adams pursued.

Johnny seemed to shrink. To draw into himself. "The knife," he said in a whisper so low he could barely be heard. "The knife. I couldn't control it. I tried. I really tried. But I couldn't control it. I would never kill my mother." His face had changed. He was the little boy again. He was crying little boy tears.

"Could you control it when you attacked Trent Marshall in New Orleans?"

The little boy was suddenly gone.

"Yes," Johnny shouted. "Yes, I controlled it then. I wanted to kill him. I still want to kill him."

"And Ms. Anderson," Adams pressed. "Do you want to kill her, too?"

"I don't know any Ms. Anderson," Johnny shouted.

The detective consulted his notes. "On the levee that night you said, 'I'll find you, woman. I'll find you and I'll kill you.' Did you mean Ms. Anderson?"

Johnny looked frustrated. His eyes roamed the room. He seemed to suddenly remember something. "That woman who warned Trent. I'll kill her. Is her name Anderson?"

"No, it's not."

Johnny leaned again across the table and spoke conspiratorially.

"What's her name? Tell me her name. I won't tell anyone you told."

Adams ignored the question.

"Tell me about Ellen Richards," Adams said. "Why did you kill her?"

"Who?" Johnny asked.

"The elderly woman in Metairie. The one you stabbed to death."

"I didn't stab any old woman."

"Did the knife stab her?" Adams asked. "Did you lose control of the knife at her house?"

"I never was at any old woman's house. I don't even know any old woman in Metairie. So how could I have taken the knife there?" Johnny laughed. "You really are stupid."

"You fired two shots that came close to hitting Mr. Marshall," Adams said. "Why did you decide to shoot him instead of using the knife? Had you already lost control of the knife?"

Johnny looked genuinely surprised. "I don't know what you're talking about. I never shot at anybody. I don't even have a gun."

"All right. You don't have a gun," Adams repeated. "One more question. Did you break into the museum at Camp Moore?"

"Camp Moore? What's that?" Johnny asked. "Like Great America or something? My daddy took me to Great America one time."

Adams didn't reply. He looked at his notes. His finger went down the page as though he was reviewing the questions he had intended to ask. "Number two," he said, as though he wasn't aware he was speaking out loud. "OK. Yes, number two."

That was the agreed upon code for Trent to come into the interrogation room alone. Blake was number one; Darcey number three.

In the darkened room Trent rose to his feet. Blake and Darcey both knew how difficult this would be for him. He stepped through the curtains that hung behind them assuring no light would show through the one way mirror when he opened the door.

Adams kept his eyes on Johnny as Marshall stepped into the room. The young man looked at the door. His face changed again. He was the little boy.

"Hello, Johnny," Marshall said softly.

"Uncle Trent," he said in a little boy's voice. "Uncle Trent, tell 'em I didn't do anything wrong. They think I killed my mom. Tell 'em I didn't do that. You know I'd never do that."

"The knife did it," Marshall said. "You tried to stop it but you couldn't control the knife. Is that right, Johnny?"

"Yes. Yes. That's right. I knew you'd tell 'em, Uncle Trent."

"And did you try to stop the knife that night on the levee when it slashed my arm, Johnny?"

Johnny sat up straight in the chair. His face changed again. The little boy was gone. There was nothing but hatred in his eyes. "No!" he shouted. "I did that. I wanted to kill you. I still want to kill you. I been watching you. You never knew it. But I been watching you. In New Orleans I watched you. And I been watching you here, too." He laughed. A maniacal sound.

"I will kill you. I promised I would kill you. I was only ten years old but I promised. And I will, too. I will kill you."

"Did you try to shoot me, Johnny?" Marshall asked, still speaking softly.

"No. What's wrong with you people?" Johnny shouted. "Are you all stupid? I never tried to shoot you. I don't want to shoot you. I'm going to kill you with a knife. Just like you killed my daddy. I want you to feel what my daddy felt when you killed him."

"I didn't kill your dad, Johnny."

Johnny's head lowered between his shoulders. His eyelids lowered again to slits. His head bobbed and turned. He looked much like a snake preparing to strike.

"Yes, you did" he hissed. "You and that sheriff did it. My daddy would still be alive right now if y'all hadn't put him in jail. If he was here he'd fix you. He'd fix you for sure."

"I'm sorry for you, Johnny," Marshall said sincerely.

"You shut up!" the young man shouted, spittle flying from his lips. He jerked against the cuff holding his arm firmly to the chair. "I don't want any apology from you."

Marshall nodded. "I'm not apologizing. I feel sorry for you is all. You're not anyone I ever knew."

"What do you think, Jason?" Blake asked. They were back in the sheriff's office. Arrangements were being made to take Johnny under guard to the hospital in Shreveport that had facilities for the criminally insane. "Any chance he's faking it?"

"I've seen plenty try," Adams responded, "and some of them have been pretty good actors. I've never seen anyone like him. He'll have to be examined by a psychiatrist but I think he has no connection whatsoever to reality. I do think he's about as dangerous a prisoner as we've ever had. It'll be a relief when we get him to Shreveport."

Blake nodded. He looked at Marshall. "You'll be a lot safer with him locked up, Trent."

"As far as he goes, yes," Marshall agreed. "But you heard him. He didn't seem to know anything about Professor Richards' murder or the break in at Camp Moore. He seemed especially believable when he denied shooting at us. Would you agree, detective?"

"Yes, I agree," Adams responded. "He didn't seem to know anything about the lady in Metairie. He thought Camp Moore was an amusement park. He could be faking those things. But I do agree that he was being honest about not shooting at you. He seems determined that you should die as his father did. By the knife."

"There's another point that occurs to me, Jack," Trent continued. "Do you know how Josh Blair was killed?"

"Another prisoner got him with a knife."

"Yes, but do you know if he was stabbed or was it a slashing wound?" Trent asked.

Blake thought for a minute. "It seems to me his throat was cut. I can call the warden and find out for sure."

"Good. Let's assume for the moment that you're correct," Marshall said. "I agree that Johnny seemed most sincere when he denied shooting at us. When he said he wants me to die as his father died. By the knife."

"So where are you going with this, Trent?" the sheriff asked.

"Modus operandi, Jack," Marshall said. "Johnny attacked me twice. He slashed my arm the first time. Last night when he came at me he again was holding the knife to slash. Not to stab. To slash. He killed his mother by slashing her throat. But Professor Richards was stabbed in the back."

Blake nodded slowly. "A different MO. Would you agree, Jason?"

"I think I would," Adams replied. "Though it's another question we should pursue with the psychiatric folks once they've had a chance to evaluate him."

"In the meantime," Darcey spoke up, "wouldn't it make sense to assume that Trent is right?"

"I think so," Blake said. "Johnny's apparent preference for slashing his victims is another piece that doesn't fit with the others in this puzzle. I think we have to assume there's another killer out there."

"And unlike Johnny whoever it is only wants the missing gold. They'll use a knife, a gun, or whatever's handy to get what they want," Marshall added.

As Trent and Darcey were leaving the building Blake called Marshall back. The sheriff was holding some papers in his hand.

"The response to the inquiry you asked me to send to Colorado came in," the sheriff said as he looked over the report. "Martin is her maiden name. Valerie Martin. Born in Denver. She's lived there all her life. She married a fellow named Wayne Erickson. Small time hustler. Looks like he had a series of commission-only sales jobs. Some of them bordering on illegal. Everything from used cars to aluminum siding scams. He tried being a mortgage broker at one point but went broke when the real estate market crashed a few years ago. Investigated for fraud but not charged. Probably because there were so many fraudulent brokers in those days there was no way to prosecute them all. Not much else."

"No record of a divorce?"

"No, not that I see."

"Well, she said the divorce was just granted so it's possible it doesn't show up in the record yet," Marshall said. "No work history on her?"

"Not much. Looks like she worked with him in the mortgage business."

"OK. Thanks, Jack."

Before he caught up to Darcey he placed a phone call.

"I think it's time to go back to New Orleans," Marshall announced.

Darcey and Betty were taken by surprise. Marshall had seemed deep in thought since they returned to the Pines after the painful experience of Johnny Blair's interrogation. They told Betty about his theory that Johnny wasn't the only danger they faced. Their challenge now was to figure a way to flush out whoever else might be stalking them.

"What do we gain by doing that?" Darcey questioned.

"I don't know," Marshall answered honestly. "I do know that we got Johnny put away when we took control. The puzzle isn't solved yet but at least one of the pieces is where it belongs. I think we should do something now to shake things up a bit and see if any other pieces fall into place. Going back to New Orleans seems a better move than just sitting here waiting for something to happen."

"I guess that makes sense," Darcey agreed. "What about Mom?"

"We take her with us. What do you say, Betty? Up for a trip to the Crescent City?"

Betty smiled. "When do we leave?"

"Tomorrow morning will do. We're in no hurry. We'll hit the road whenever we get up and around."

"Should I pack my machete?" she asked. Darcey and Marshall laughed.

"The machete can wait for you here," Darcey said. "Trent's place in New Orleans is a fortress."

Sheriff Blake called late in the afternoon. He had talked to the warden about Josh Blair's death. The warden confirmed that the man's throat had been cut in a particularly vicious way. His head had been almost completely cut off. The warden said he'd never seen so much blood in his entire career.

"Just like Johnny's mother," Marshall said. "And just as Johnny planned for me."

"Yep, I think you called it, Trent. Johnny's MO doesn't fit the Richards woman's murder and the attempt to shoot you. There's somebody else out there."

Marshall told the sheriff about their decision to return to New Orleans and why. Blake agreed. "Smart move," he said. "We got Johnny when you took control and drew him out. It's risky but it might work again."

Marshall told him they would be back in a couple of days.

Darcey called Valerie to tell her they were going back to New Orleans. She asked Valerie if she wanted to go with them.

"Uh…no, I don't think so but thanks," Valerie said, hesitatingly.

Darcey laughed. "You're getting interested in the guy you met at the hotel. You are, aren't you?"

"Oh, I don't know. Maybe."

"So when are you going out with him?" Darcey pressed her friend.

"Tonight," Valerie laughed. "But it's not really a date. We're just going to have a drink in the bar and then dinner here at the hotel."

"Well, you mind your manners," Darcey urged her. "You just got out of one bad marriage. Don't get carried away."

"I do seem to attract bad boys," Valerie said. "But don't worry. I'm in no hurry to get involved with any man."

Darcey told her they would only be gone for two days. Valerie said she would be at the hotel when they got back.

Darcey told Trent about her conversation with Valerie. They still hadn't told her that the man she was seeing was the one claiming to be from the Treasury Department.

"Do you think we should tell her?" she asked.

"No, I don't. I think we should let it play out."

"It is a strange coincidence though, isn't it?" Darcey commented.

There was that word again, Marshall thought. Coincidence.

"We have to be cautious," he said. "We have to watch closely. And we have to be prepared for anything. Absolutely anything."

THURSDAY, MAY 7TH

The drive south was a leisurely one. They left at mid-morning. Darcey let her mother ride in the front passenger seat. Betty was fascinated with all the new technology in the high powered car. For once Trent controlled the lead in his foot. He didn't want to frighten Betty.

He called Jordan to let him know they were en route back to the city. He asked the detective to join them for dinner when he got off work. The detective said he'd see them around seven o'clock.

Ivy was glad to hear he was coming home. He had checked in with her periodically while he was at the Pines. He didn't want her to worry about him.

In typical Ivy fashion she took charge immediately when he told her that Darcey's mother was with them.

"I'm off today so Walter and I will get your house ready. I'll make sure there are clean sheets on the beds. Uh…will you be using three bedrooms?"

He glanced at Betty from the corner of his eye. He hoped she hadn't heard that.

"Yes, that's what we need," he said, conspiratorially.

"And I'll make dinner for y'all. You want to make a good impression on that girl's mother," Ivy continued. Marshall turned his head to the side and rolled his eyes.

"OK," he said. "But you and Walter plan on having dinner with us. And Jordan will be there, too."

"Well, let's hang up this phone and let me get busy," Ivy declared. "I got to get to your house and get to work." She sounded jovial as she said goodbye.

[159]

It was late afternoon when they arrived at the house on Governor Nichols Street at Royal. Betty was wide eyed as they drove through the faded green gate.

"Why, this is beautiful, Trent," she said. "It's like something you'd see in a movie."

"I think some scenes from a movie were shot here at one time. But that was a long time ago. Long before I moved in."

Walter had been watering the plants when they came in. He shut off the water and came to the car. Trent introduced him to Betty. He and Trent unloaded the luggage and took it into the house.

The house was filled with wonderful aromas radiating from the kitchen. Ivy heard them entering and came out to meet them.

"Well, welcome home, young man," she said as she wiped her hands on her apron. Marshall gave her a hug.

"And welcome back to you, Darcey," she said as she turned to hug the younger woman.

"Thanks, Ivy," Darcey said, returning the hug. "And this is my mother, Betty."

"I'm very glad to meet you, Ivy," Betty enthused. "Darcey and Trent have told me so much about you."

"What smells so good in here?" Darcey asked. "What are you cooking up?"

"Oh, we're gonna have a dinner, young lady," Ivy chortled. "I'm making my famous stuffed peppers with mashed potatoes and green beans. And buttermilk pie for dessert."

It was a festive evening. After the violence and tension of the past few days they had learned to grab festive whenever it came within reach.

After dinner Betty insisted on helping Ivy with the cleaning up. Walter made himself comfortable channel surfing in the living room. Trent, Darcey and Jordan retreated to the library.

Marshall briefed the detective on the murder of Johnny's mother and the young man's second attempt on his life. He described the interrogation in detail. Jordan agreed that it was doubtful Johnny would ever stand trial but would spend the rest of his life in a mental institution.

"I remember when he called me Uncle Trent. I used to take him fishing," Marshall said, sounding a bit blue. "Never thought he'd end up like this."

"It wasn't your fault, Trent," Jordan said. "His father made bad choices. Johnny blames you only because he can't bring himself to blame his father. Everyone else in this state knows the truth. Even the boy's mother. That's probably why he killed her."

"Yeah, maybe so. No point in dwelling on it," Marshall said, moving on. "We still have someone out there trying to kill me. Or Darcey. Or both of us."

Jordan was surprised. "How do you figure that?"

Marshall explained the discussion he'd had with Sheriff Blake regarding the differences in the attempts on his life and the two murders. Jordan agreed it could mean there was more than one potential killer.

"The question is," Jordan wondered, "are we looking for one person or two? We have a stabbing in one instance and shots fired in another."

"I don't know," Marshall said. "The one thing that seems certain is that Johnny's a slasher. He slashed me once. Tried to slash me a second time. He slashed his mother's throat. His father died after having his throat slashed. I think using a knife to slash his victim is more than just an MO for him. I think it's important to his twisted state of mind. The stabbing and shooting don't seem to me to have the same kind of psychological relevance."

"So we've caught a slasher," Jordan said. "Now all we have to do is find a stabber and a shooter. Another would be killer. Or maybe two. That should be easy enough." He and Darcey laughed.

Marshall first glared at them. Then he laughed, too.

While murder was the subject in the library the talk in the kitchen was all about romance.

"Ivy, have you noticed the attraction between Darcey and Trent?" Betty ventured.

"I sure have," Ivy said. "But I'm starting to wonder if either one of them will ever do anything about it."

"Well, they haven't known each other very long," Betty pointed out.

"That's true enough. Trent was married once and it turned out he made a bad choice. He hasn't let any woman get close to him since. Darcey's different though. They've been forced to spend a lot of time together. Darcey started staying here for protection. They've been staying in separate bedrooms."

"Same at the Pines," Betty chimed in. "Darcey has never been married. She has been so focused on her career. She hasn't taken the time to get to know any men. She's definitely attracted to Trent though. I think they like each other. That's a good sign."

"Lord, yes. Any fool can fall in love and get married but if you don't like the person whose face you see every morning when you wake up that marriage will not last."

"Isn't that the truth?" Betty agreed. "Darcey's father was my best friend. When he passed away I didn't think I'd survive."

"Oh honey, I know what you mean. I been with that old man sitting out there watching TV for a long time. Sometimes he drives me crazy but I don't know what I'd do without him." They both laughed.

"I get feelings about these things," Ivy said. "I think Darcey might be the one to break through the barriers Trent has built up around himself. I think they'd be good for each other."

"And I think you're right," Betty agreed. "So I think we should just stay out of it."

"Oh, you got that right," Ivy agreed. "Two old women like us trying to push either one of them? Oh no. That's the last thing those two need. But that is one wedding I'll be glad to attend."

FRIDAY, MAY 8TH

Marshall sat at his desk staring out the window at nothing in particular. Crotchety. That was the word. He was crotchety.

They had agreed on the same strategy that worked in Sabine Parish. Marshall would appear outwardly as their guide as they wandered through the Vieux Carre'. In reality he was their first line of defense. They all had Jordan's number on speed dial. If anything happened the detective would be there within minutes with back up.

They spent hours roaming through the shops on Royal Street. Darcey and Betty inspected the merchandise in each store. They bought a few things. More for show than for wanting. Marshall stayed close to the door. Watching everyone going in or out. Everyone passing by.

Nothing.

He took them to the old French Market at the end of Decatur Street. They wandered through scores of stalls. It was a mistake taking them there. Too many people jammed together. He stayed close to the women. Watched everyone. He didn't like it. Too crowded.

They stopped at one stall offering scarves. Silk and wool and cotton. Many colors. He found himself watching Darcey. She draped a scarf over her head and covered her nose and mouth with one end. Only her eyes were showing. She turned her head and looked back over her shoulder at him. Her sparkling green eyes were smiling. She was beautiful. He found it hard to take his eyes off her. He felt his breathing becoming heavier. His pulse speeding up.

He forced himself to look away from her. This wouldn't do. She was in danger. They were in danger. He had to get them out of there. This was not a good place. He led them away from it.

Betty wanted to take some pictures in Jackson Square. That wasn't much safer than the French Market but at least it was open space. Not as many people. Not jammed together. If there was a threat he would have a chance to see it coming. They walked the few blocks to the square. He took pictures of Betty and Darcey sitting on the fountain near the statue of Andrew Jackson. Betty took pictures of the street artists and musicians. He dropped a ten dollar bill in the hat of one man who played a particularly inspired clarinet. He watched everyone.

It was late afternoon. They were beginning to tire. Trent led them up Chartres Street to the Old Napoleon House. Betty was fascinated by the history of the building. Owned originally by Nicholas Girod, an early mayor of the city. He offered the house to Napoleon when the French emperor was sent into exile for the second and final time. It's said that Dominique Youx, the most daring of pirate Jean Lafitte's officers, was to captain the ship that would bring the emperor to New Orleans. Napoleon died before the plot could be carried out. It's a romantic story. A romantic story is good for business.

Trent and Darcey ordered Pimm's Cups, the bar specialty. Betty had a lemonade. On the rocks. Trent had taken them to Galatoire's for lunch. He made sure they tried several of Jean Galatoire's original dishes. Even though they had spent several hours walking after lunch no one was hungry. Trent asked the waiter to prepare a large container of seafood gumbo for them to take home. He would cook some rice. They could eat if they wished. When they wished.

Now Marshall was sitting at his desk staring out the window at nothing in particular. Crotchety. Definitely crochety.

Jordan called to say he was coming in. A few minutes later the lanky detective pulled through the faded green gate and stopped in front of the house. He let himself in and joined Marshall in the library.

"Well, aren't you the cheerful one," he said, taking a look at Marshall.

Marshall said nothing. He frowned and looked out the window again. Then back at Baron.

Darcey came in with a rum and coke for each of them. "I assume you're off duty, Jordan. If not Trent can probably use two of these."

Jordan laughed and took one of the tall, chilled glasses. "If he wants another one he'll have to get it himself."

Just watching her walk across the room made Trent not crotchety. Watching her walk across the room was a delight to him.

"Mother has gone upstairs to freshen up," Darcey said. "I think she's taking a power nap. We wore her out today."

"And I've just been sitting here feeling out of sorts because no one attacked us today," Trent said. "That's really something to regret, isn't it?"

"We should be celebrating that y'all are still alive," Jordan pointed out.

"Yeah, well, I am glad we're all still alive," Marshall said, "but we were trying to draw someone out today. Our strategy worked in Sabine Parish. It's not working here."

"What do we learn from that?" the detective asked.

Marshall looked at him thoughtfully.

"That we're in the wrong place," Marshall said. "I think you have it, Jordan. We did everything but beg someone to attack us today and we got nothing. The same strategy worked in less than twenty four hours in Sabine Parish."

"It could mean that the second would be killer is smarter than the first one," Baron noted.

"But isn't it a matter of playing the odds?" Darcey asked.

"Say, you're starting to get the hang of this detective business," Jordan said.

"I'm with you, Darcey," Marshall said. "Jordan might be right about the second suspect being smarter than the first. But for us the best thing is to play the odds. And the odds are that whoever is after us isn't here. I don't believe they've given up. All that tells me we should head back north."

Marshall's phone rang. A call that would settle the debate.

"Someone broke into the Pines," Sheriff Blake said when Marshall answered the call. He had put the sheriff on speaker.

Darcey gasped, putting her hand to her mouth. "Oh, no!" she gasped.

"I don't think there's any damage," Blake assured her. "But whoever did it was definitely looking for something. They went through every drawer and every closet in every room."

"How did you find out about it, Jack?" Jordan asked.

"One of Betty's neighbors stopped by this afternoon bringing her some fresh eggs. She discovered it. The door was standing wide open. She called me. I got right out there with a couple of my deputies. Poor woman was just sitting in her car trembling when we got there."

"Interesting timing," Marshall noted. "The day after we left."

"They either knew everyone was gone or at least you weren't there, Trent. If they thought Betty was home alone it means they were willing to eliminate her."

"How did they get in without setting off the alarm?" Darcey asked.

"Whoever did it knew enough to bypass the alarm," the sheriff said. "It's pretty easy for someone who knows what they're doing. Y'all have a lot of cleaning up to do but fortunately there's no real harm done. Any luck down there?"

"Not a bit," Marshall said. "We had just about talked ourselves into coming back up there when you called. This settles it for us. We'll head north first thing in the morning."

"I'd say your strategy worked," Jordan said when Trent ended the call. "And I was wrong earlier. You've been in the right place. If you'd stayed up north the break in probably wouldn't have happened. Maybe it wasn't the way you expected but you drew someone out."

Later that night Marshall sent the sheriff an e-mail asking him to make one more inquiry.

SATURDAY, MAY 9TH

There was nothing leisurely about the drive north. They were on the road early. Trent pushed the powerful engine as much as he could without scaring Betty. They turned into the long winding driveway of the Pines a few minutes past noon.

"Oh my," was Betty's only comment when they stepped into the hallway of the old house.

The sheriff had described the scene accurately. Every drawer had been pulled out and emptied. The contents of every closet, every cupboard were scattered about. But there didn't seem to be any damage to the house. Whoever did this wasn't vandalizing the house. They were looking for something.

The three of them went to work. Room by room. Picking up. Putting away. Trent asked repeatedly if they could think of anything missing. They could not.

The work went surprisingly fast. The worst of it was in the kitchen where the intruder, or intruders, had dumped out containers of flour and sugar and corn meal.

Upstairs they found that the laptop computer Darcey had given her mother was missing. "Our intruder is going to try to break your passwords and log into your machine, Betty," Trent said.

"Well, they're going to be awfully bored," Betty said. "They won't find anything but e-mails from Darcey, a couple of cousins and some of my lady friends in town. And a lot of recipes."

"Have you checked to see if anything valuable is missing, Betty? Jewelry or anything like that."

She glanced down at the floor near the bed. "Anything valuable is in the safe. Doesn't look like they found that."

"Where is it?" Trent asked.

"In the floor just under the bed. One of the Belmonts had a false floor put in to hold it. I'm not really sure who or when."

"Show me."

Betty knelt down by the edge of the bed. Looking closely Trent could see a section of the flooring in which there was a barely noticeable gap between the boards. Betty pushed down on that section of flooring and it popped up to reveal a small steel safe with a combination lock. She quickly worked the combination and opened the box. It contained a few pieces of jewelry and some documents.

"Everything's here," she said. "I don't think they found the safe but even if they did they wouldn't be any closer to the missing gold than they are now. They just won't believe that I don't know anything about that."

Watching Betty open the false floor triggered something in Trent's memory. He walked down the hall and looked out the window. Darcey followed him. She was beginning to understand his body language. She could tell when he was so focused that everything and everyone around him was shut out. She stood quietly beside him for a few moments.

Finally she spoke softly. "What are you thinking, Trent?"

"I'm thinking they trashed the wrong house. Come with me," he said, turning to walk quickly down the stairs. "Betty, we're going down to the cabin. We'll lock the door behind us but keep your snake killer handy."

Marshall walked rapidly down the ridge to Rube's cabin. Darcey had to almost run to keep up with him.

"What do you think is in the cabin?" Darcey asked, a bit breathlessly.

"I'm not sure. Seeing your mother pop open that false floor just reminded me of something I noticed the first time I went through the cabin. There was a section of floor that gave way when I leaned on it. At the time I thought it was a century old floor that was rotting. I moved away from it. But maybe I was wrong."

They went up the steps onto the porch and into the cabin. Trent stomped on the floor. It was solid. The cabin might be old but it had been well built. As he had done before, he pushed the bed frame toward the wall. He pressed on the flooring with his hand. It was solid. He moved his hand a few inches and pressed again. Solid. He pressed another section. It gave way. He pushed harder. A section of flooring about twelve inches across sank. As Trent pressed on the front the corresponding rear section about twenty four inches back raised up creating a hole in the floor. There was no safe. Just a metal box. A very old metal box.

Trent carefully lifted the box from its hiding place. It was heavy.

"I think we should take this up to the house to open it," he said softly, in awe of the box. "I think your mother deserves to be present."

They sat in the living room. They were gathered around the metal box. They were quiet. All three of them looked at the box as though it was a religious artifact. From their point of view it was.

"Do you want to do the honors, Betty?" Trent asked. "After all, whatever is in there is most likely part of your family history."

There was no lock. It was a simple metal box with a hinged lid. Betty tried to open it but it wouldn't budge.

"I think I'm going to need some help, Trent," she said. "The hinges are all rusty."

"Well, they didn't have WD-40 in those days. Fortunately we do," Trent. "At least I hope we do."

Darcey ran down the hall to the kitchen where she looked under the sink and found the ever present lubricant. She brought with it a towel to set the box on to protect the table. Trent sprayed the old hinges. They gave the lubricant a few minutes to do its work. When Trent tried it the hinges were still resistant. He gently moved them up and down. Slowly they gave way. Flecks of rusted metal fell onto the towel. The lid of the box was raised for the first time in more than a century.

Three packages lay in the box. Each package was wrapped in leather. Trent lifted one, unwrapping it very gently. It was a large revolver. He didn't know if it was loaded. Chances were that if it was loaded the gunpowder was no longer effective. But there was also a chance the powder could be unstable. It had been heavily oiled before being wrapped. Consequently it was in much the same condition as the day it was laid away.

He carefully pulled the hammer back to half cock. That allowed him to turn the cylinder. There were no loads in the cylinder. No caps on the nipples.

"I think this is a Colt Dragoon. A six shot revolver. Probably .44 caliber. A very effective weapon in 1862. Very popular. I would guess this is Rube's gun."

Trent laid the weapon on the table and reached into the box for the second package. When it was unwrapped they saw a revolver with a very different look to it. It had a second barrel beneath the main one. He went through the same careful process to assure himself that this gun was also not loaded.

"I never thought I'd see one of these outside a museum. This is a LeMat revolver. Designed by a man in New Orleans. The cylinder holds nine bullets. Probably .40 caliber. The second barrel is a 20 gauge shotgun. These guns were very popular with Confederate officers. I think you're looking at your Uncle Henry Belmont's sidearm." He laid the LeMat down beside the colt.

The last package was the most amazing of all. A pair of single shot pistols, each a little smaller than his hand. The wood frames were decorated with silver filigree. The steel barrels short. Each muzzle loading weapon was fired by the hammer falling on a cap covering the nipple.

"This is rarest of all," Trent said reverently. "This is a matched set of original Philadelphia Deringers made by Henry Deringer himself. Probably .41 caliber. Later imitators changed the name to the more familiar Derringer, with two r's. But these two are the real deal. They're in perfect condition. I never thought I'd see a matched pair of these even in a museum."

Betty reached out and ran her hand over the small, deadly weapons. Darcey stared at them. Speechless.

"It's strange, isn't it, to suddenly be presented with such relics," Betty said, her voice barely audible. "It's like we've suddenly been thrown back in time. We're sitting here in this old house where Henry and Rube both once sat. We're looking at the weapons they carried. The weapons we know they used to fight off bandits."

There was something else in bottom of the box. Something flat. Also protected by a leather wrapping. Trent carefully lifted it out and gently unwrapped it. A leather bound book. He could hear Professor Richards' raspy voice again.

Look for journals, Trent. Look for journals.

"It's been lying there for more than a hundred years," Darcey said. "Why didn't it disintegrate?"

"Rube protected it well," Trent said. "The tight seal of the box protected it from water. The darkness inside the box alone would serve to protect it from condensation. So would the leather wrapped around it."

They all three stared at the book Trent had now exposed.

"Well, are you ready for the answers we've been looking for?" he asked. He took the silence for yes. His fingers moving as lightly as possible, he opened the book. The words on the page were beautifully crafted.

"Just as my old aunt said," Betty marveled. "It's like calligraphy."

It was impressive. Beautiful. What it said sent chills through all three of them.

THE JOURNAL OF REUBEN JACKSON
NOVEMBER 1919

I can't say for sure how old I am. I judge that I am nigh onto 85. I was born on a farm in the days when people didn't always record births and deaths but in the family bible. I lost my family and our bible when I was a boy. A tornado killed my whole family. I don't know how I survived. I have no memory of the event.

My earliest memory is of being here in this parish. I believe I was born here but I do not know that for certain. I am thankful that Andrew and Blanche Belmont took me in and cared for me. They became my family. They gave me a room to sleep in. They fed me. Blanche taught all us kids how to read. Andrew had a large library. All the children, including me, were encouraged to use it. I read every book he owned. Blanche taught us all to write. She had such nice handwriting. I tried to copy it as best I could. Andrew and Blanche both taught us arithmetic.

Andrew didn't believe in slavery. The people who worked for him were paid wages. I worked for him and he paid me wages, too. His black workers were paid the same as us whites. But he and Blanche were much more to me than my employers. They became the only family I had.

Now they are gone. Andrew died in 1879 at the age of 80. I have missed him.

Blanche left us in 1905. She was 96 years old and surrounded with grandchildren and great grandchildren as she passed.

These last 14 years have been lonely for me. The Belmont descendants have honored Andrew's wishes and treated me well. But I have outlived my friends. I am ready to join them in the next world.

Andrew and Blanche were strong people. That terrible war cost them dearly. Because of his stand against slavery and secession Andrew was not popular among many of his neighbors. Still he was loyal to his native state. He might not have agreed with his neighbors but he wouldn't fight against them.

Their oldest son, Richard, fought with General Lee in Virginia. He survived the war. He came home to work with his father, taking over the farm when Andrew died.

Benjamin, the youngest, was a disagreeable young man. He did not want to work. He had a surly nature. He quarreled often with his father and brothers.

Henry was the middle son and to my mind the finest of all the children. The way events played out Henry came to be ill thought of by some. The fact is Henry was a hero.

That is why I have taken it upon myself, while I'm still able, to write down here the truth of what happened in 1862.

Henry was a lieutenant serving under Major General Mansfield Lovell in New Orleans in April, 1862, when the federal fleet took the city. I had hauled a load of freight down from Alexandria for a man and was getting ready to come back up here. But a Confederate sergeant came up and said Henry needed me. He gave me a piece of paper with an address written on it.

When I got there Henry told me the general had assigned him a top secret mission and he needed my help. I told him I would do whatever I could to help him. Then I got the biggest shock of my life.

Henry led me into a room with stacks of boxes. All those boxes were filled with gold double eagles. Henry said there were more than 20 thousand of them. He had been assigned to sneak them out of the city before the federals could get them. He asked me if I would help him. Of course I would, I told him.

We loaded those boxes on my wagon. It was a heavy load but my wagon was sturdy and my six mules strong. We could make it just fine.

The general had told him to get the wagon down to the railroad depot just as soon as he could. So off we went. What there was of the Confederate army in New Orleans was being loaded onto a train. Henry and I were assigned to a box car. There were just the two of us with the wagon and mules.

The train took us to a military camp about 75 miles north of New Orleans up near the Mississippi border. Henry left me to tend the animals while he went to report to the general. He told me to keep a sharp eye on the wagon.

Henry was gone about an hour. When he got back I was as surprised by the general's orders as he had been. We thought the general wanted us to take the gold to Richmond. We could not figure out why he selected us for the job since neither one of us had ever been up that way before in our lives. But that was not the general's plan at all.

He said there were federal armies to the east and north. The federals even had Baton Rouge near captured to the southwest of us. The only way out, he said, was to go northwest. He figured Henry knew that part of the state as good as anybody. That is why he gave the job to such a young officer.

He told Henry that Dick Taylor had been promoted to Major General and would be in Opelousas in a few weeks to organize an army with men from the western part of the state. He said he thought the best thing to do was to hide the gold until General Taylor was in position to take possession of it. Knowing that General Taylor and Henry's father were friends, he told Henry to get the gold to his family's farm. When he heard General Taylor was back in the state Henry was to find him and tell him where the gold was.

He said he was assigning a squad to travel with us. It was a small squad because he didn't want to draw attention to us. I didn't like what I saw when those men showed up. One of them was named Hart. I knew him from Fallen Springs not far from here. He hung out with the outlaw bands that holed up there. I told Henry about it. He didn't like it much either. He said we'd just have to keep an eye on them.

He asked me if I was armed. I had already retrieved my Colt Dragoon revolver and stuck it in my belt. I opened my coat just enough to show it to him. He told me to keep it close at hand. He was armed with a LeMat that his father had given him. Together we could fire 16 times without reloading. I figured that gave us pretty fair odds if we stayed alert.

We thought our best chance was to cross the river at Bayou Sara, north of Baton Rouge. I knew a free man of color there who owned a riverboat and owed me a favor. I was sure he'd ferry us over.

We pulled out before daylight. The load was heavy and the going slow. It took us three days to make the 50 miles to Bayou Sara. It was near dark when we got to where the Bayou Queen was tied up. I had Captain Isom Pierpont pegged right. He agreed to take us across the Mississippi the next morning.

We were pretty sure the men riding with us had figured out what our cargo was. They had several whispered conversations when they thought we were not looking. That convinced us they were planning on killing us and taking the gold.

Henry and I took the captain into our confidence after the squad was asleep. We figured they would hit us as soon as we got across the river. We had our two guns and the advantage of surprise. Hart and his mangy crew didn't know we were on to them. Captain Pierpont was also armed. He had a small caliber revolver that would be deadly in a close quarters fight like this one promised to be.

There were still a few hours until daylight when the ship's stoker showed up. Captain Pierpont sent him down to the engine room right off to start building steam. We wanted to be on the water while it was still dark.

The three of us checked the loads in our revolvers. Henry got his squad up and boarded though they complained all the way. Captain Pierpont made the crossing with no lights.

Sure as we figured Hart and his men made their play as soon we got the wagon off the boat. We had expected them to start shooting but they did manage to pull a little surprise on us. They attacked with knives. I reckon they didn't want to alert anybody that might be up and working around the river.

Between the three of us we managed to shoot them all. I shot Hart in the arm but he was able to get back on his horse and escape. Before I shot him he had managed to drive a big Bowie knife into Henry's back. Henry was hurt bad but managed to fight on.

When the fight was over Henry was bleeding something awful. Captain Pierpont came up with some clean white cloths. We got the bleeding stopped and the wound bandaged. We got him into the wagon and made him as comfortable as we could. I tied his horse onto the back of the wagon.

The small community of New Roads was just waking up as we passed through it. They must have heard the shots but nobody paid us much mind. Shots fired during the war didn't attract a lot of attention.

We had about 150 miles to travel to get to the Belmont farm. We were heavily loaded so the going was slow. I wanted to make the trip as easy as possible on Henry. We couldn't make but about 15 miles a day.

I know every road and trail in this country. We were able to travel without attracting attention. We never ran into troops from either side the whole way.

What with having to stop every couple of days to forage for food for Henry and me and the mules, it took us two weeks to make the trip. We got to the Pines just at sundown.

Andrew, Blanche, and I managed to get Henry up to his bedroom and into bed. His mother stayed with him, cleaning his wound and putting a fresh bandage on it.

Andrew and I went downstairs. He poured us each two fingers of bourbon. It was the first drink I had tasted since I left New Orleans. It felt warm in my belly.

I told Andrew about the orders Henry received from General Lovell. When he was wounded Henry gave me the written orders to hold on to. I showed them to Andrew. The general didn't mention the word "gold" in writing. He just said Henry was to get the "cargo" to General Taylor when in Henry's judgement Taylor was prepared to accept it.

Andrew was every bit as shocked as I had been. But we knew we should act quickly. We talked it over and decided to unload the boxes from the wagon and store them in the farm's storm shelter. When the war started Andrew had dug out a secret room down there. He figured it might come in handy if there was fighting around the Pines. It was hidden by a wall of shelves where they kept tomatoes and fig preserves and such that Blanche put up for the winter.

There was just the two of us. We did not think it a good idea to involve any of the hands who worked at the Pines. Not that they were not good people. It was just that so much gold would tempt a saint.

Andrew's youngest son, Benjamin, was not at the farm that night. He had been sent to help a neighbor build a new barn. Andrew decided not to let Benjamin know about the gold. He didn't give his reason but I knew Benjamin to be of less character than his father and brothers. He proved me right a short time later when he took one of the horses and rode off, never to return. He was still very young. Andrew and Blanche tried to find him but were unsuccessful. The family never saw him or heard from him again.

We waited until late that night after everyone else was asleep. It took us the rest of the night to get it done. We were both bone tired. It was all I could do to get my boots off before I was asleep.

The next day Andrew, Blanche, and I sat with Henry in his bedroom. Henry agreed with what we had done with the gold. We decided we could do nothing until Dick Taylor got to Opelousas.

Henry's wound was a bad one. The only doctor nearby had gone to the war. There was nothing to do for it but keep it clean and for him to lie as still as possible so as not to start the bleeding up again. With luck he would not come down with a fever. Blanche did the best job she could nursing her son back to health.

We were all on high alert for the next few weeks. Andrew and I took turns standing guard at night. The hands who worked for Andrew knew only that Henry had been wounded and had come home to recover. Nothing more.

Finally in July we got word that General Taylor had arrived in Opelousas. Henry was still not able to travel. I was to ride south to find the general. Andrew gave me his fastest horse. I didn't stop but to rest the horse and sleep for a few hours myself. I made the trip in just over two days.

I found the camp where Taylor was assembling his army easy enough. When I told the sentry I had a message for the general he took me to a Major Bohmer. This officer was dressed in a fine gray uniform that looked to be tailor made for him. His boots were polished to a high shine and his military spurs glinted in the light. His hat sported a large red plume. He wore a handle bar mustache and a goatee trimmed to a sharp point.

He rose with a smile that showed his teeth. It did not seem genuine to me. Something about the man led me to mistrust him. That put me in a hard place when he told me that General Taylor was ill and could not be disturbed. He told me he was the officer of the day. He said if I had a message for the general I should deliver it to him. I did not care to do that but could not see that I had a choice.

I decided to deliver the message to the major but not deliver it. I told him that Lieutenant Belmont was in possession of cargo important to the Confederate cause. The lieutenant had been seriously injured in a skirmish, I said, without mentioning the fight was with a squad of Confederates. I told him I would return to Lieutenant Belmont with any instructions the general might care to issue.

When I had delivered my message the major flashed that phony smile and told me to wait. He would speak to the general and would return directly. However, he did not move toward the large officers' tents. Instead he walked out of sight in the opposite direction. Something was not right.

I eased into the trees edging the camp and moved as quietly as I could in the direction the major had gone. Soon enough I saw him talking to a rough looking group of men. I recognized one of them as Sergeant Hart, the leader of the ruffians who tried to do us in after we crossed the river. The same who had plunged his blade into Henry's back.

I could not trust Major Bohmer. I knew Sergeant Hart only too well. I had no faith that the general would get my message. I regretted delivering even a vague message to the major. It seemed to me the best course would be to get out of there as fast as I could. That is exactly what I did.

Two days later I arrived back at the Pines. Andrew, Blanche, and I again gathered in Henry's room where he still lay abed. I reported to them what had occurred in Opelousas. We realized that we were in for a difficult time. We had a tough decision before us. No one of us disagreed that the gold was the property of the Confederate government. We fully intended to turn it over to that government. We would not, however, turn it over to men we knew to be ruffians simply because they wore the gray.

What, we asked ourselves, if the war was lost? What then? We thought that ownership would revert to the Union. In that event we would not hesitate to turn it over to them. Meanwhile we were in a bad place.

We also agreed that each of us was to be armed at all times, including Blanche who was no mean shot. Andrew also picked two of his best hands who he would arm.

We waited. Henry did not improve.

Half way through August one of Andrew's hands came running up to the house to report that a squad of Confederates with a wagon were coming our way and only five miles out. That gave us about an hour to prepare for whatever was to come next.

Blanche went to Henry's room. There she sat with his LeMat revolver. She was prepared to defend her injured son if necessary.

Andrew positioned one of his armed hands at the corner of the house out of the view of anyone riding up to the house. The second he positioned behind a large oak tree that would give him a field of fire from the rear of the squad. He and I sat in chairs on the porch. We waited.

The horsemen rode up the long winding drive. The red feather in his hat fluttering, Major Bohmer rode in the lead side by side with a man in a finely cut civilian suit and silk top hat. Behind them rode five men in ragged Confederate gray and butternut. The villainous Sergeant Hart was at the rear driving the wagon. His hat was pulled low over his face in an attempt to disguise himself. Not low enough.

Bohmer approached with his trademark, teeth-baring smile.

"Good day," he said, "Do I have the pleasure of addressing Mr. Andrew Belmont?"

"You do," Andrew replied. "And you are, sir?"

"I am Major Todd Bohmer, aide to Major General Richard Taylor," the officer replied. "And this, sir, is Mr. Jesse Walsh, a representative of the government of the state of Louisiana."

"Please, gentlemen, dismount and join us here on the porch out of the mid-day sun," Andrew said. I had to stop myself from turning to stare at him I was that amazed at his ability to remain civil with this rabble confronting us. I knew we had a fight coming. Andrew seemed to think we were to have a picnic.

The major and the civilian dismounted and stepped up onto the porch.

"Good day, Mr. Jackson," the major addressed me. "I was surprised and disappointed that you did not wait for me as I directed you."

I nodded to him.

"How might I be of service, Major?" Andrew asked.

His direct statement took the major by surprise. He had expected to engage in small talk before getting to the business of his visit. Andrew was too shrewd to allow the major to become comfortable.

"We...uh...we are here with orders from Major General Richard Taylor to take possession of certain cargo that we understand you are holding for him," the major stammered.

"I see," Andrew replied, as cool as he could be. "And what would that cargo be, major?"

Bohmer hesitated. Walsh was impatient.

"You know why we're here, Belmont," he stated. "We're here to take possession of the gold."

Andrew remained calm. He ignored Walsh. "Do you have written orders for my son from General Taylor, Major?"

"Well, not exactly," the major replied. "The general has been unwell as of late."

"We do not need any written orders, Belmont," Walsh said loudly. "You have property of the Confederate government and you are to turn it over to us."

Andrew still remained calm. He stared into the eyes of the pompous politician.

"My son arrived here seriously wounded in carrying out his duty, Mr. Walsh," Andrew said with disdain in his voice. "He carried with him written orders. He will follow those orders. Only written orders from my friend, Dick Taylor, will over ride those orders. If you have no written orders then I suggest you leave this place and return when you do.

"You will regret your obstinance," Walsh sputtered.

"I've been threatened by better men than you, Walsh," Andrew responded. "I suggest you and this popinjay get on your horses and lead your squad of thugs off my property."

"We can take the cargo by force," Walsh shouted.

"I wouldn't try it," Andrew replied calmly.

Walsh and Bohmer stood silently staring at us for a few moments. Walsh then told Bohmer to remount. They would address the issue at another time. Neither Andrew nor I believed him.

The two men mounted their horses. The waiting had come to an end.

It was no surprise to me that Walsh was the aggressor. Bohmer was no soldier. Walsh reached under his coat and brought forth a small caliber revolver. Andrew was not caught unaware. He raised his arm. The Philadelphia Deringer he had cocked and tucked into his sleeve fired its single shot. His aim was true. The ball struck Walsh in the belly. The would-be murderer was not expecting Andrew's reaction. The revolver fell from his hand. He sat in the saddle staring down at the hole in his midsection through which a rapidly increasing flow of blood was spilling. He looked up at Andrew in disbelief as he collapsed, falling heavily from his horse.

Walsh had fired no shot. Andrew's small pistol was hardly more than a soft "pop." For several moments Bohmer and his squad of ruffians did not realize they had lost the first round of the battle. At length Bohmer pulled his horse to the side and ordered his squad to charge. Given the situation it was an order that made little sense but then he was not much of an officer.

His squad spent precious seconds milling round. I rose and drew my trusted Colt Dragoon. The first of the so-called squad drew a sawed off shotgun. I shot him from the saddle, my ball striking him mortally just below the sternum. I looked then for the traitorous Sergeant Hart.

There was no knife for him this time. He drew a pistol from his belt as he stood in the wagon, swinging the barrel toward me. My Dragoon roared again. The ball penetrated a lung as it threw Hart off the wagon. He was not to run from this fight.

A third bandit drew a pistol and fired at Andrew, the lead striking a column just inches from where he stood. He returned fire with his second Deringer, the ball smashing through his opponent's right eye. The man was dead as he sat in the saddle.

Andrew's hands joined the fray at this point. The man Andrew had armed with a small caliber pistol and placed at the corner of the house took out a fourth brigand as he tried to fire at me with a revolver he had drawn from his belt. He died with a bullet through his stomach.

The hand behind the tree, armed with a Colt Dragoon similar to mine, took down the last of the pillagers with a well-placed shot through the heart.

Bohmer had never drawn a weapon. He sat his horse as he watched his small command, such as it was, destroyed. He looked at the bodies lying all around him as though he wondered what he should do. He did as any coward would do. He turned his horse and attempted to escape.

I raised my Colt but Andrew touched my arm. "We shouldn't shoot a man in the back," he said.

I looked at him for only a second. I took aim and shot Bohmer from his saddle. Square between the shoulder blades.

"You're a fine man, Andrew," I said. "And you are certainly right that we should not shoot a man in the back. But that was no man. That was a creature intending to kill us all. Had we let him live you can be sure he would be back with a larger force. I regret having to do it but I'm not sorry for it."

Andrew nodded.

Knowing time was short, as neighbors might have heard the shots, we quickly decided on a plan of action. Two of

Andrew's hands were instructed to take the wagon and horses at least 20 miles north and turn all the horses loose, leaving the wagon in the woods. They were advised to avoid contact with anyone. They took two of Andrew's horses with them for their return.

The four of us who had part in the fight loaded the bodies in my wagon. We took them into the woods bordering the pasture. Deep into the woods on a trail we had made some time back when I did some logging for Andrew. We dug a mass grave and tossed the bodies in. When it was done there was only a mound of dirt, which would soon be concealed by grass and bushes.

It was a crass handling of the dead. But we had no choice. These were not men who deserved much in the way of words that might send them on their way to heaven. That was certainly not the direction toward which their souls would travel.

Two days later Henry died. We buried him in the family cemetery behind the big house. In their grief Andrew and Blanche were not inclined to do anything more to support the Confederate cause. We decided to resume waiting. If a legitimate force arrived with proper orders we would gladly turn over the gold. Until then it would remain hidden where we placed it. But we would take no more risk upon ourselves to see it delivered.

Months went by. We heard that General Taylor's Army of West Louisiana had met with mixed success. It became apparent, however, that the south was losing the war. The only questions remaining, it seemed to me, were how much longer the fighting would continue and how many more would die.

Life continued on at the Pines. I resumed hauling freight though business was slow. The war had sapped the south's economy. There was little freight to be hauled.

We heard of foragers for both armies raiding farms throughout the area taking everything they could lay their hands on. We herded most of the farm's cattle and horses into the woods. Everything of value we hid in those same woods. We kept a guard out there night and day. Andrew and I took our turns on guard duty along with each of the hands.

In the spring of 1865, as the surrender of southern forces began, Union troops rode up to the Pines. None of us were armed but we weren't alarmed. We thought the time had come to rid ourselves of the accursed gold. We were greatly mistaken.

The captain commanding called for all of us to gather in front of the house. Four of Andrew's nine hands were black, the remainder white. The Union captain informed the black men that they were now free and didn't have to work at the farm anymore. One of the black men had fought with us when Confederate brigands tried to take the gold. He told the Union captain now that they had always been free. They said they worked for Andrew because he paid them.

This seemed to enrage the captain. He called for the owner of what he called the "plantation." Andrew stepped forth and identified himself. The captain berated him for so thoroughly frightening the black men as to cause them to lie about their status. Andrew responded that the men were not lying. He said they were not and never had been slaves. They were hired hands.

The captain asked if he had family who fought for the Confederacy. Andrew replied that he did. He told the captain that while he did not hold with slavery and opposed secession he would not turn against his family, friends, and neighbors, nor would he try to stop them from fighting for their beliefs.

The captain cursed Andrew for a liar. He drew forth a short barreled shotgun from a saddle scabbard. He fired a barrel at Andrew. Fortunately the man's horse reared as he fired. Andrew was hit in the left foot. His boot filled with blood but it was not a dangerous wound. The charge in the barrel was not strong enough to penetrate the leather with sufficient power to do significant damage.

Andrew did fall to the ground. Blanche ran to him, cradling him in her arms. For a moment I thought the captain would fire again endangering both Blanche and Andrew. I was prepared to launch myself at the man. But he turned to his reason for being on the farm.

He ordered his men to search the farm and take everything. The soldiers scattered over the fields. They rounded up the few cattle and horses we had left in the open pasture. They rummaged through the house taking all the food they could carry and anything they thought might be of value. While the Union troops stripped the farm Blanche and I, aided by two of the hands' wives, tended to Andrew.

Eventually the piratical troops rode away, herding cattle and horses before them. Andrew watched them go with fire in his eyes.

"The devil take them all," he said. "The Confederates killed my son. The Union just tried to kill me and did rob me. That gold shall remain where it is forever. No government is worth what they have taken from us."

He and I tore down the entrance to the storm cellar where we had hidden the boxes of gold. Together we covered it over.

And thus the affair was ended as far as we were concerned.

Now as the end of my time draws near I am left with memories of my friend Andrew Belmont. Memories of working here at the Pines with him. There were fine times with these good people who gave me a family when I had lost mine. Who gave me a home when I had none.

Andrew said he wanted me to have a home of my own here at the Pines for as long as I lived. He and I built this cabin with our own hands. We'd take a break sometimes to drink lemonade that Blanche brought down to us. We'd lean against the frame near the big green plant at the edge of what would be my porch. Andrew called it a Spanish dagger though it has many names.

Some evenings Blanche would bring her grandchildren down to my cabin. They'd gather around me on the porch. I would sing songs for them and tell them stories. Those were happy memories.

There were sad memories of Blanche sitting here on my porch. She would gaze at that same plant when it was in bloom with its large white flowers as she mourned the loss of her husband and her sons. She called it the Lord's candelabra.

I look now at the long fronds with their sharp points. Doleful memories arise for me. I think of it as Adam's needle. I suspect it will be the last thing I see on this earth. I expect that time will come soon.

And so Rube's story ended.

Tucked into the back of the small book between the last page and the leather cover was a sheet of paper. Yellowed and brittle. Trent very carefully unfolded it and smoothed it out as best he could without breaking it. It appeared hurriedly written in a strong hand.

Lieutenant Henry Belmont is herewith ordered to take possession of a cargo of significant value to the Confederate States of America. He is further ordered to transport that cargo to northwest Louisiana via the shortest and safest route possible in his judgment. There he is to hold the cargo in secrecy and in safety until Major General Richard Taylor has formed the Army of West Louisiana and, in Lieutenant Belmont's judgment, has sufficient strength to take possession. At that time Lieutenant Belmont is to make contact with General Taylor and arrange for the transfer.

So ordered on this 30th day of April 1862.

Mansfield Lovell, Major General, Confederate States of America

It was silent in the room as we finished reading. It was a story that was felt more than read. Felt deep inside.

"Oh, how terrible for those poor people," Darcey said, finally breaking the silence. "They endured such hard times. It's a wonder they survived at all, much less live as long as they did."

"They were very strong," Betty said. "I can see that strength in you, Darcey. It's part of your heritage."

"Now we know what happened here in the spring and summer of 1862," Trent said. "We have written proof that your Uncle Henry was, indeed, following General Lovell's written orders."

"They can all finally rest peacefully," Betty said.

"Part of the mystery is solved. We know that the gold is here and we know why it's here. Betty, do you know where that old storm cellar was located?"

"I have no idea. This is the first I've ever heard that there was a storm cellar."

"And we don't know how to find it," Darcey said. "Not without digging up the whole farm."

"We might be able to figure it out," Trent said. "But it won't be easy."

"It's spooky to think about those bodies buried out in the woods," Betty said "I've ridden horses by that mound since I was a girl and so has Darcey."

"I did find some brass buttons and one time a rusty knife blade out there," Darcey reminded them. "Remember, Mom?"

"That's right. I'd forgotten about that. I didn't think much of it at the time."

"We won't be in any trouble about that, will we, Trent?" Darcey asked.

"I can't imagine that you would be. It happened one hundred fifty years ago. And neither you nor Betty had a hand in it. We will need to let Jack know about it though."

SUNDAY, MAY 10TH

Jack Blake was politician enough go to church before driving out to the Pines. Now he sat with Trent, Darcey and Betty on the front porch in the early afternoon. They had showed him the journal and summarized the contents for him. He sipped on the sweet tea Betty had made and pondered what should happen next.

"When you stir things up, Trent, you do a good job of it," the sheriff said. He took off his hat and ran his fingers through his short silver hair. "You knocked down some powerful hornets' nests back in your newspaper days. But this one tops 'em all. I'm going to have to give some thought to what has to be done."

"I would urge nothing immediately, Jack," Marshall suggested.

"Trent, we have bodies out in the woods. We have gold hidden somewhere on the Pines. A lot of gold. I can't just do nothing."

"I don't expect you to do nothing, Jack," Trent argued. "I'm just saying don't rush into it. Let's think this through. First, the bodies have been there for a century and a half. They're not going anywhere. The last of the people involved in the fight that killed them died a hundred years ago. That situation will wait.

"Second, once this journal becomes public this parish, and the Pines in particular, are going to be overrun with treasure seekers. They'll destroy this place. And some of those treasure seekers won't be very nice people. If we aren't careful how we handle this you're going to have a world class mess on your hands."

"You have a point there," Blake said thoughtfully. "Remind me to thank you for that some time."

"Jack, if we handle this right you're going to be famous. The country sheriff who solved a one hundred fifty year old mystery. Why, those four guns and that journal alone are historic treasures. The Louisiana State Museum will make you a hero. It'll all look mighty good at election time."

"Since you put it that way," Blake grinned, "I'm feeling better about it. So what do we do next?"

"We keep stirring things up," Marshall said with an enigmatic smile.

Later that day Darcey called to tell Valerie that they were giving up.

"Giving up?" Valerie's voice coming over the phone line sounded disbelieving. "You mean you're just going to walk away? But you've made so much progress."

"Not really," Darcey said. "It's true that we got the guy who attacked us. As it turned out he was after Trent for putting his father in prison. He had nothing to do with our efforts at proving my uncle innocent."

"So you're giving up on that?" Valerie protested. "And on finding the gold? That's why you came back to Louisiana."

"But we've hit a dead end, Valerie," Darcey patiently explained. "Other than tracking it to Camp Moore we've made no progress on locating the gold whatsoever. We don't have any leads to follow in any direction. Besides I have a business to run. I've got to get back to San Francisco."

Trent was driving back to New Orleans the next morning, Darcey told Valerie. She said he would take her to Louis Armstrong Airport down there to fly back to San Francisco.

They promised to keep in touch. Darcey invited Valerie to visit her in San Francisco. Valerie promised she would.

Later in the afternoon Darcey and Trent walked down to the pasture. Prince George trotted up to Darcey to nuzzle her and get a couple of carrots. Mac was getting to know Trent. He liked carrots, too. He wasn't far behind Prince George.

They saddled Prince George and Mac. Mounted, they loped across the pasture side by side. Darcey led them away from the trees where the bodies from that long ago fight lay buried. She guided them up another path that curved along the ridge behind Rube's cabin and the big house. A few hundred yards down the path they came out of the trees into a neatly trimmed clearing. There was a knee high, old-fashioned iron fence enclosing several tombstones.

"The family cemetery," Darcey said respectfully.

They sat their horses in reverent silence.

"The largest one in the center against the rear fence is the tombstone of Andrew and Blanche. One marker for the two of them. Together in death as in life," Darcey explained.

Some of the stones had weathered worse than others. The lettering on a few was little more than adumbrated. Barely visible. Others could be read clearly. Next to Andrew he saw the stone of the eldest son, Richard, with a similar one beside it that he assumed was Richard's wife. Next to Blanche he could make out Henry's resting place.

"What a remarkable family, Darcey," Trent said softly. "What an extraordinary life they led."

"There is perhaps the most extraordinary one of them all," Darcey said pointing to a solitary stone that rested alone in front of Andrew and Blanche.

Trent looked at it closely. It was clearly marked.

Reuben Jackson
Loyalty Above All
November 12, 1919

"A simple inscription," Darcey told him.

"What better way to describe him?" Trent concluded.

Darcey dismounted and stepped through the gate. She knelt by her father's grave for a few minutes, reaching out to touch the stone marker.

"I wish you could have known Dad, Trent," she said. "He was a good man. You would have liked him."

She mounted Prince George again. They rode back toward the barn without speaking. Back in the barn they unsaddled and rubbed their mounts down. The horses happily accepted another handful each of carrots before loping off across the pasture.

Trent closed the gate and turned to find Darcey standing behind him. Without thinking he put his arms around her and drew her to him. She folded into him, raising her face to his. He kissed her. Pulled her closer. Feeling her body close against him. She felt good in his arms. He ended the kiss. He held her. He buried his face in her hair. Inhaling the scent of her.

And then the tightness in his chest began again. What was he doing? He couldn't do this. He wanted her. But he couldn't do this.

"Uh…We'd better get up to the house. Betty will be wondering where we are," he mumbled as he released her and started walking up the ridge.

Darcey stood motionless. Watching him go. Stunned.

"Trent Marshall, I hate you," she said, hoping he heard. She went back into the barn and spent twenty minutes throwing hay around with a pitch fork.

"What's wrong with me?" she said out loud, tossing a large fork full of hay from one stall to another.

"Never mind me. What's wrong with you, Trent Marshall?" Another fork full of hay.

"Gentleman. Yeah, you're a gentleman, all right," she cried out, hurling the pitch fork like a lance. Leaving it quivering in a bale of hay.

MONDAY, MAY 11TH

Deputy Beulah Linville stayed inside during the day. She was wearing plain clothes. Her car had been hidden in the barn since before daylight. Her assignment was to stay close to Betty Anderson. Mrs. Anderson's daughter, Darcey, had left that morning with Trent Marshall. Deputy Linville thought the trouble was over when they caught that lunatic Blair boy. But apparently Mrs. Anderson was still in some danger. The sheriff wanted her protected. The deputy didn't know any more than that.

The sheriff himself had received a call that morning from the governor requesting his presence that afternoon at a meeting of, according to the governor, "extreme importance." Blake was not happy. But a call from the governor was a call from the governor. Not to be ignored.

Chief Deputy Lorca had given her the assignment. She had her service revolver in her purse but she wasn't much good with a handgun. The chief deputy had looked the other way the last few years when she failed to qualify with it. She had been with the sheriff's office for more than twenty years. She planned to retire next year. The chief deputy knew that. He covered for her. He's a good man, she thought.

Besides she had brought her Henry .45 Long Colt lever action rifle with her. Her daddy had given her that gun and taught her to shoot it. Taught her well. She could drill a bull's eye at a hundred yards with it. It was leaning against the wall by the front door.

But the deputy wasn't worried. This was easy duty. She would be relieved at sundown. She would be home in time for dinner with her husband. Their children were both out of high school now. Their daughter was in Baton Rouge going to LSU. Their son was working offshore for one of the oil companies. Since it was just the two of them Deputy Linville didn't like to work evening shifts if she could avoid it. She liked to be home with her husband in the evenings.

But meanwhile, the Pines was a beautiful place to spend the day. Mrs. Anderson was good company. Even better, she made them tuna salad and sweet tea for lunch.

As the afternoon sun fell lower in the sky she stood in front of the big windows in the living room. She looked out over the fields. She envied the Anderson family. She couldn't imagine what it must be like to have a place like this in the family for generation after generation. Century after century. They were, she thought, fortunate people. She and her husband had worked hard for what little they had. Every day had been a struggle for them. But she wasn't resentful. That's just the way it was.

The noise startled her. It had been quiet all day. A few infrequent bird songs. The distant sound of a horse snorting from time to time. This was more like the sound of leather scraping on wood. She ignored the service revolver in her purse. She reached for her rifle.

She heard the sound again. It seemed to be coming from the left side of the front porch.

Mrs. Anderson came down the hall. She was about to say something when Deputy Linville held up her hand, motioning for her to be quiet. Mrs. Anderson stopped where she was. Deputy Linville nodded, indicating that Mrs. Anderson should stay put.

The deputy eased the front door open. She raised her rifle to her shoulder. Stepping quickly onto the porch she looked over the barrel of her rifle to her left. She walked to the front of the porch, rifle still at the ready. She saw the vehicle. No one in it. Why would it be here? Strange, she thought.

She heard a soft sound. "Pffht." The last sound she would ever hear. The bullet entered the left side of her forehead. Just above her eye. Penetrating her brain. She was dead when she fell to the floor.

In the house Betty heard the sound. "Pffht." She wasn't sure what it was. It sounded like air rushing through a compressed area. Then she heard a thump. Like someone had dropped a sack of potatoes. She waited for what seemed to her to be a long time.

"Deputy Linville?" Betty said in a tone only slightly louder than a whisper There was no response.

Betty eased back down the hall to the kitchen. She had left her snake killer there. With the long, sharp knife in her hand she tip-toed back down the hall to the front door.

"Deputy Linville?" she whispered again. Again there was no response.

The front door was open. Carefully, cautiously, quietly, Betty stepped through it onto the porch. She saw Deputy Linville. Lying on her back. Her rifle cradled in her arms. Her eyes staring sightlessly at the ceiling.

"Oh my God," Betty called out. "Deputy Linville…Beulah…" She rushed to the fallen woman and knelt beside her. There was nothing she could do.

Had there been something she could do she would not have had time for it. The hand that pressed the cloth over Betty's face came from behind. She instinctively inhaled deeply assisting the drug in doing its duty. She felt a slight burning sensation around her mouth. Within seconds Betty was unconscious.

Trent and Darcey were walking down Front Street in Natchitoches. The brick-paved street of the three hundred year old town followed the Cane River. It was no longer a river but a winding ribbon of a lake created when the Red River changed its course in the early part of the 19th century. A French explorer named St. Denis had built a fort at this spot in 1714. The river still flowed here then. The Spanish had a settlement just a few miles to the west near where the Pines was located.

Trent reached out to take Darcey's hand. He led her across the uneven bricks of the small town's main street. They sat on the grass covering the steep slope leading down to the old Cane River. It was peaceful. A few minutes respite from the tension they had been under for days. The tension that still enveloped them. More so now that they had left Betty alone at the Pines.

They were trusting the sheriff's office to protect Betty. Trent had all the faith in the world in Jack Blake and his staff. But they were involved in a manner of combat. He knew that in combat every plan begins to fall apart as soon as it's put into action. If anything happened to Darcey's mother he would never forgive himself.

They laid back in the grass. She had moved past the anger she felt when he kissed her and then abruptly walked away. Trent was struggling with emotional memories. Bad memories. Crippling memories. She knew that. She knew that he was attracted to her. That he wanted there to be something between them. That he was uncertain what that should be or how to get to it. And she instinctively knew she should not push him. She would be beside him. She would let him slay his demons. Let his emotional scars fade. Then she would see to it they never returned to haunt him again.

For now it was enough to lie beside him in the grass. For now.

Trent's phone rang. He felt his heart sink into his belly when he saw Matt Lorca's name on the screen.

"Hey, Matt," he answered the call. "What's up? Everything OK?"

"No, everything is definitely not OK. We've got big trouble, buddy. Betty's missing and the deputy I assigned to stay with her is dead. Jack's already on the road headed back."

Trent stared at the water. He couldn't look at Darcey.

"Where are you now?" Trent asked.

"At the Pines. I've got men combing the area around here."

"We're on our way," Trent said, ending the call.

Darcey took the news stoically.

"Let's go."

That was all she said.

Trent let all 640 horses under the hood have their heads. They made the twenty five miles from Natchitoches to the Pines in just over fifteen minutes. He ignored the small town speed trap. When they arrived, an ambulance was turning onto the highway. The vehicle carrying away the deputy's body.

Trent pulled the sleek black vehicle off the driveway onto the grass near a deputy's car. If there were any kind of tracks, vehicle or human, near the house he didn't want to roll over them. They walked up to the house, being careful where they stepped.

Chief Deputy Lorca was on the porch talking to another uniformed deputy. He saw Trent and Darcey coming.

"Don't worry about where you step, buddy," he called out. "We've already been over that area. There's nothing you can disturb."

Trent walked up to the porch. Darcey, ashen-faced, kept herself pressed as close to him as she could get.

"What do we know, Matt?" Trent asked.

"Not much so far," the chief deputy said, his normal bubbly personality much subdued. "I called Beulah, the deputy I assigned to Betty today, late this afternoon. She didn't answer so I drove out here. It looks like she stepped onto the porch for some reason. Don't know why. She was shot in the left side of the head with a small caliber bullet. The kind often used in close up professional hits. Death would have been instantaneous."

Lorca walked to the edge of the porch left of the front door. "The shot probably came from here judging from the position of the body. We didn't find a spent cartridge. Another similarity to a professional hit."

"Are you kidding?" Trent asked in a questioning tone. "A professional hit?"

"Just giving you the facts, buddy," Lorca responded. "Not drawing any conclusions."

"Yeah, I know. Sorry, Matt. Go ahead."

"The front door was standing open. No sign of a struggle inside. It looks like Betty followed Beulah out onto the porch. There was a machete lying close to the deputy's body but no blood on it."

"Mom's snake killer," Darcey said quietly from behind Trent.

"Her what?" Lorca asked.

"The machete. She called it her snake killer."

"Anything else, Matt?" Trent asked.

"That's all so far."

"Not much to go on," Trent said, looking around as though he might be able to divine something the deputies had missed. He could see half a dozen deputies moving slowly around the house, down by Rube's cabin and the barn, and in the trees that framed the clearing in which the house stood.

Lorca's phone rang. One of his men reported the dilapidated warehouse located through the trees behind the house.

"I'll be right there," Lorca said, as he ended the call. "This is worth checking out. Can we take your car? Looks like I'm blocked in."

Darcey climbed into the back seat. Lorca flinched slightly as he opened the door to the passenger seat in the front.

"Touched the cowling on my boat motor last weekend. It was a little warm," Lorca said, noticing Trent's questioning look at the slight redness on the palm of his right hand.

"That's not good."

"It's not bad. Just a little tender is all," he shrugged it off. "This is some fine ride, buddy. Brand new?"

"Yeah. These things just came on the market."

"Nice," Lorca said.

It took only seconds to get back to the highway and drive the short distance to the old warehouse. Trent pulled off the highway but didn't drive into the area around the building.

"This is a mess," Lorca said, looking around. "Looks like tire tracks from at least three vehicles that I can see. Probably more. No telling when any of them was made. Did y'all find anything inside?" he asked one of the deputies.

"It's a mess in there, too," the deputy replied. "Just a lot of garbage. Chicken bones. A few old blankets and rags. Some used rubbers. Ummm…Sorry, Ma'am," he said, embarrassed not to have noticed Darcey's presence.

"At least the kids have the good sense to use condoms, deputy," Darcey responded.

"Yes, ma'am."

"Anybody who finds anything bring it directly to me, understand?" Lorca ordered.

There were muttered responses from the men moving slowly about the area.

"OK. Thanks. Lock the door and don't let anyone in. The sheriff will want to take a look before you do any cleaning." Trent ended the call. He nodded to Jack Blake. "Just what we thought."

He accepted the old fashioned glass with bourbon over ice that Darcey offered. The sheriff had arrived from Baton Rouge shortly after Matt and the other deputies left. The three of them were alone with the cicadas. Darcey sat beside Trent, her own glass in hand.

"What you thought about what?" she asked.

"When Valerie told us in New Orleans about the 'coincidence' of her reservation at the hotel out on the lake on the same day we were driving up here I called the manager. She had not made a reservation. I checked with him later. She never made a reservation. She never had a room at the hotel."

The sheriff took it from there. "I made some inquiries in Colorado. Martin is Valerie's maiden name. She married a man named Wayne Erickson. There's no record of a divorce. Erickson is the man who showed up here threatening Betty about the missing gold. And by the way, Trent, your guess was right. He did work briefly at an alarm company. He was fired but the company manager refuses to say why unless we get a court order."

[197]

"That explains who bypassed the house alarm," Trent said.

"Erickson was staying in one of the hotel's condos," Trent said. "When Valerie got here she just moved in with him. And now they're gone."

"So do you think Valerie and her husband have my mother?" Darcey asked.

"Looks that way," the sheriff replied, honestly.

Darcey felt tears welling up in her eyes. "Do you...Do you think they will kill her?"

"No," Trent replied quickly. "No, Darcey, I don't. This is all about the gold. They're going to use her as leverage to get the gold. They think we know where it is. We'll hear from them sooner or later. They have nothing to gain by killing her."

Trent hoped he sounded confident. He didn't feel it though he knew what he was saying was logical. Assuming Valerie and her husband were logical. A potentially dangerous assumption.

"But where could they be?" Darcey worried.

"I have men combing the parish, Darcey," Blake said. "And I've requested assistance from the surrounding parishes and Sabine County in Texas on the other side of the lake. We'll find your mother. And I think we'll hear from the kidnappers soon."

"You can count on that, Darcey," Trent agreed with the sheriff.

When Betty regained consciousness she was in a room that was not familiar to her. She was lying on a cot. It was dark. There was a slight burning sensation around her nose and mouth.

She felt no pain. She felt panic. She fought hard against it. They would find her. She knew they would find her. Meanwhile, she was still alive. She was determined to remain so.

She couldn't see anything. She could hear voices mumbling but couldn't make them out. She thought she heard water moving. Maybe a creek? She could smell something like old motor oil. To help herself fend off the panic she focused on what she could hear and smell.

Tuesday, May 12th

Trent and Darcey met the sheriff at the hotel at eight o'clock in the morning.

The hotel boasted one of Trent's favorite golf courses. He had often met old friends for golf weekends there. He had a casual acquaintance with the manager. Michael Sloan was a thin, friendly man with silver hair and matching mustache. He was in the hospitality business and was good at his job. On most days a smile came easily to his face. Not on this day.

Blake passed out surgical gloves to everyone. He pulled a pair onto his own large hands as well.

Sloan unlocked the door. He was appalled at what he saw.

"Would you look at this mess?"

Sloan had told them that the man and woman staying in the room refused service over the past few days except for requesting fresh towels. The extent of trash was surprising. The small kitchen and living room were littered with piles of fast food containers, some still half full, and empty wine bottles. Mostly reds, Trent noticed. Cheap reds.

The bedroom looked much the same. More fast food containers. More empty bottles of cheap red wine. Piles of used towels on the bathroom floor.

Sloan stayed in the hallway looking in while the other three moved slowly around the condo. Trent stood at the door separating the living room from the bedroom. He looked at the couch. Then back at the bed.

"This is interesting," he said.

"Find something?" the sheriff asked.

"I don't know. But notice the blanket and pillow on the couch. Someone has been sleeping out there."

"A third person sharing the place?" Darcey asked.

"I don't think so," Trent answered. "Look at the bed. It's messy but only on one side. Someone has been sleeping in the bed alone."

"Valerie and Wayne aren't sleeping together," Darcey said. "Maybe they are divorced."

"Maybe," Trent said. He looked closely at the pillows on the bed. Then he went into the living room and looked closely at the single pillow on the couch. "Jack, the picture of Erickson that came with that report showed him with short light brown hair, right?"

"Right."

"We have a few short light brown hairs on the single pillow on the couch. Several long dark hairs on the pile of pillows on the bed."

"What does that tell us?" Darcey asked, puzzled.

"Maybe nothing important," Trent said. "Valerie has been sleeping comfortably in the bed. Wayne has been sleeping not so comfortably on the couch. I think it tells us which of them is in charge."

"Is that important?" Darcey continued.

"Might be. We'll see."

Chief criminal investigator Adams showed up with his forensic crew at nine o'clock. The sheriff shooed Trent, Darcey and Sloan out of the condo so Adams could do his work.

"I'm sorry about this, Michael," Blake said to the hotel manager. "My people will work as quickly and discreetly as possible."

"Don't worry about it, Sheriff," Sloan said. "The hotel will cooperate in any way we can."

Betty had eventually fallen asleep after exhausting all her senses with very little result. When she awoke it was light. There was no artificial light in the room. There was only daylight from a very small window set high on the wall just beneath the roof. She tried to figure a way to get up to that window. There was nothing else in the room but the cot. There was what appeared to be a work bench on the other side of the room but it had been cleared of all tools.

The night before she had heard faint voices. It sounded to her like a man and a woman. But the voices were sufficiently indistinct that she couldn't be sure. It sounded like they were arguing. In the daylight she heard nothing. She could do nothing. She could only listen. Use her sense of smell. Think.

She knew Trent and Darcey would be looking for her. She knew Jack Blake would have his whole department driving the back roads seeking a clue to where she might be. She had noticed her missing ear ring when she first woke up. She didn't know where or when she had lost it. She hoped someone would find it and realize its significance.

Meanwhile she could do nothing. Use her ears. Her nose. Her brain.

Trent pulled to the side of the road when they reached the old warehouse near the Pines. He told Darcey he wanted to take another look. They walked around outside the building. Lorca had said yesterday that there were too many tire tracks to be meaningful. Trent knelt down and looked at the tracks closely.

Matt was probably right, he thought. He saw multiple tracks crisscrossing the dirt. He walked a line closer to the trees separating the warehouse from the Pines. He saw several trails leading into the trees. He wasn't surprised by that. This had been forest for thousands of years. It had never been cut. After the Belmonts established the Pines they built a few cabins along the edge of the trees for some of their hired hands who had no homes of their own. Generations of children had roamed through the thicket.

He picked what looked to be the most used of the trails. With Darcey following close behind him, he followed it in the direction of the house. He spotted nothing unusual. Until he reached the clearing behind the house.

The trunk of a downed pine tree lay rotting at the end of the trail. Looking closely, Trent could see pieces of the soft wood had recently been knocked away. A few feet back from the tree trunk there were two clear indentations in the earth and leaves.

"Look there," he said to Darcey, pointing to the fallen tree where it had been marked not long ago.

"And there," pointing to the indentations.

"Someone rested their elbows on the tree," she agreed with his conclusion. "Their knees made the marks back here. Someone laid here to watch the house."

He snapped several pictures of the spot from different angles with the camera on his phone.

"Do you have a scarf or handkerchief or something like that?" he asked, finding a stick about twelve inches long. Darcey pulled a lacy handkerchief from her shoulder bag.

[201]

He took it from her held it to his nose. "Smells nice," he said. He tied it around the stick. He stuck the other end of the stick into the ground marking the spot.

They wound their way through the trees for a few minutes longer. Looking at a few of the other trails that had been made by children playing explorer. Trent finally decided there was nothing more to be seen. They went back to the car and drove to the winding driveway that led up to the big house.

Darcey got out of the car. She stopped dead still. Looking down at something lying in the grass. Sparkling in the sunlight.

"Trent," she called nervously. "Look at this."

Trent walked around to her side of the car. He saw the piece of jewelry that had attracted Darcey's attention.

"That's one of the ear rings I bought for Mom when we were in New Orleans." Darcey's voice was trembling.

Trent laid the ear ring on the sheriff's desk.

"What's that?" Blake asked.

"One of Mom's ear rings," Darcey answered. "I bought the pair for her in New Orleans last week."

"Where'd y'all find it?"

"In the grass a few feet from the front porch at the Pines," Trent replied. "We also found a place at the edge of the woods where it looks like someone laid behind a fallen tree and watched the house."

"How could my men have overlooked something like this?" Blake sputtered, slapping his hand on the desk.

"The ear ring is pretty small," Trent said. "It would be easy to miss in the grass. I didn't see it. Darcey was the one who found it."

"But this other thing with the log. You think someone laid out there in those woods watching the house," the sheriff summarized. "Then when he thought the time was right he sneaked up to the house, shot Beulah, somehow subdued Betty and carried her off back through the woods. Is that about it?"

"That's what I thought at first," Trent said. "It could have happened that way. But finding the ear ring in front of the porch doesn't exactly fit that theory. And don't forget that Johnny Blair said he was watching me, too. Watching me in New Orleans and here. He could have been the one lying behind the log. But it bears checking out. I marked the spot with Darcey's handkerchief on a stick."

Blake called his chief deputy. He told Lorca what Trent and Darcey had found. Lorca said he'd check it out.

"Nothing's ever simple with you, Trent," Blake said. "But never mind. The important thing now is to find Betty and get her back safely."

"How do we do it, Sheriff?" Darcey asked. "How do we get my mom back safely?"

Blake looked at her. Then down at his desk. He looked miserable.

"We wait," Trent answered for him.

"Wait?" Darcey shouted. "That's the best answer you have? We wait?"

"Look, Darcey," the sheriff said, coming to Trent's defense. "I'm sorry I don't have a better answer for you. But Trent is right. These people are interested in one thing. Gold. They think you know where it is. They're going to contact you. They'll do it soon. And they'll keep Betty alive as long as they consider her a bargaining chip for them."

"What do we do when they contact us?" Darcey continued.

"That depends on what they say," Trent said. "We'll make our plans according to that. Meanwhile, we remain calm. I know it's hard, Darcey. But we can't give in to panic."

"I've got every man in my department searching this parish," Blake reminded her. "We'll find her, Darcey."

Betty heard someone moving around in the other room. She pounded on the door. The movement stopped.

"I have to go to the bathroom," Betty shouted, pounding again. "Please let me go to the bathroom."

She heard what sounded liked footsteps moving toward her. The door opened by a man not much bigger than her. Thin light brown hair. Watery brown eyes. A slight pot belly. The man from the Treasury Department.

"The bathroom's over there," he said.

She moved quickly toward it. She moved through one big room. Two sets of bunk beds were set on the far side of the room. An old couch and recliner were arranged in front of an equally old television. There was a small, cheap dining table with four chairs in the center of the room to the right of what she took to be the entrance. A small kitchen between the bathroom and the front door.

"And don't bother trying the window," he said. "It's nailed shut."

While she was out of the room she had come to consider her cell she took the opportunity to wash. She didn't know exactly how long she had been there. She didn't have a wash cloth but there was soap. She washed her face and hands. Held her breath as she dried on the one dirty towel.

"I'm hungry," she told the man as she came back into the room. "Can I have something to eat?"

"No, you can't. Not now."

"Some water then. Could I please have some water?"

"Are you deaf, old woman?" the man shouted. "You ain't gettin' nothing." He took her by the upper arm and shoved her back into her cell.

She heard the click of the lock sliding into place. She had held herself together so far but now she was feeling low. As low as she ever remembered in her life. She could feel her courage slipping away. She stomped her foot. She would not let that happen. She remembered what her father had told her and his father had told him.

"Being brave doesn't mean you're not afraid. That's being stupid. Being brave is doing what you have to do when you're scared. Just don't let anyone see you scared."

Betty knew she didn't lack intelligence. She thought the man holding her prisoner did. She was afraid but she was determined this jerk wouldn't see it. She could do that.

She decided to look closely around her cell while there was still a little light. There wasn't much to see. Nothing that she could use as a weapon or a tool. Maybe she could take the table or chair apart. But both were made of light, weak sections of wood. Not much help.

She ran her hands under the work bench feeling for anything that might have been overlooked. Anything left behind. There was nothing.

There was what appeared to be a closet. But the door was locked. Neither the door nor the lock seemed especially firm but Betty wasn't strong enough to force it.

The cot was the only other object in the room. It was a thin mattress laid over a rectangular metal mattress frame. She stared it for a long time. She smiled. Betty was a fan of old movies. Especially the black and white film noir private eye movies made in the '40s and '50s. The song and dance man turned tough guy Dick Powell was her favorite.

It had been a long day. Jack Blake was tired. He had men searching every road in the parish for Betty Anderson. He had a state police helicopter flying overhead. He didn't know what more he could do. He knew if Trent and Darcey heard anything they would call him. He told the deputy on duty that he was going home. He said to call if they needed him.

When he walked into the house a few minutes later he could smell Jennifer's chili. His wife made the world's best chili. He stepped quietly into the kitchen. For a moment he stood in the doorway and watched her stirring the pot. Tasting. Adding spices. Oblivious to everything but the pot bubbling on the stove in front of her.

Jack walked up behind his wife. He put his arms around her. Kissed her neck. She was surprised. Pleasantly so. She turned in his arms and let him give her a proper kiss.

"Thirty five years later, Jennifer," Jack said, holding her, "and you're still the sexiest woman in the parish."

Jennifer laughed. "You're just too old to know better. You're home early."

"Yeah, I'm tired. There's been so much going on," he said. "But for now there's not a thing I can do. So I decided to spend a little extra time with you."

She kissed him again. "Well, I'm glad you did. Why don't you go get comfortable? The chili's ready. I'll whip up some cornbread. We can eat whenever you want to."

He swatted her on her still shapely bottom on his way out of the kitchen. In the bathroom he stripped down, laid his mobile phone on the counter, and got into the shower. The hot water felt good. He liked to shower when he got home in the evenings. Some details of his job weren't pleasant. He would stand under the stinging spray letting it wash away the nasty nature of the human race. The filth.

Washed and rinsed he turned off the shower. He slid back the glass door and reached for a towel. The end of the towel caught his phone. Before he could stop it, the phone was swept into the toilet. He watched in horror as it splashed into the water.

It was all he could do.

He reached into the toilet and retrieved the phone, which he now suspected was no longer workable. Wrapping a towel around his waist he ran for the kitchen, calling for Jennifer to get him a bag of raw rice.

"Rice? What for?" she asked as she reached for the rice.

"Dropped my phone in the toilet," he said. "Sometimes rice will draw out the water and save it."

She pulled the mattress off the frame and tossed it onto the floor. Just as she had hoped the frame was attached to the posts with heavy springs.

She guessed the tightly wound heavy metal springs were six or seven inches long. The springs looped through holes in the frame and the metal posts to hold the cot together. She didn't know if she had the strength to pull the frame forward enough to allow her to release the springs from the post.

It wasn't easy but not as hard as she had feared. Within twenty minutes she had been successful in removing two of the springs. They were heavy. She hoped they were heavy enough.

She hooked the two springs together. Without realizing it she had made a sort of nunchucks. She wasn't sure how such a weapon was used or if this was exactly what Dick Powell did. But he was her inspiration. At least she was doing something.

Her intent was to hold one of the springs and swing as hard as she could. She hoped she could put enough strength into it to hurl the second spring forward with sufficient energy to stun the man long enough for her to run.

She waited for dark. She thought her eyes would be adjusted to the dark. The man was in a lighted room. She would be able to see him better than he could see her. She wanted every advantage she could get.

Darkness overtook her cell. Still she waited. She saw the strip of light appear beneath the door as it began to get dark. She looked away from the slim sliver of light. She wouldn't look at it again.

She waited patiently until she thought her cell had been dark and the other room well lighted for long enough. She pounded on the door.

"Hey, I have to go to the bathroom again."

"You already went."

"That was hours ago. It's not a once a day kind of thing."

She could hear the man mumbling.

"Move away from the door," he ordered.

Betty made a noise she hoped sounded like she was moving away. She pressed herself tight against the wall beside the door.

She heard the click of the lock being disengaged. She raised her arm with the makeshift nunchucks. She was as ready as she could be.

The door opened. She could imagine the man standing a few feet back. She held her breath. Trying to be as quiet as possible.

"Come on out here," the man said.

Betty remained silent.

"Don't play games with me, old woman?" the man said, stepping forward.

As soon as he stepped into the door frame Betty swung her weapon as hard as she could. As she had hoped, the heavy spring swung forcefully into the man's face. The unattached hook at the end of the swinging heavy metal was sharp enough to gouge a long line starting at the left side of the man's forehead, across his left eye, burying itself in his nose. A copious flow of blood immediately poured down over his face effectively blinding him.

The man screamed, clutching at the metal dangling from his nose.

Betty wasted no time. She bolted past him. She shoved him into her cell and slammed the door shut, sliding the bolt of the lock home. She turned and ran for the door, stopping only to grab a bottle of water sitting on the table.

Once outside she ran to the woods on the far side of the driveway. Out of sight in the trees she took a moment to down half the bottle of water. Her thirst sated, she took a moment to look around. Tried to figure out where she was.

She had been right thinking she had heard water. Her prison was a small, rundown cabin on the lake. She could spot no landmarks. Nothing that would tell her where on the lake she was.

The driveway wasn't long. She would get out on the road and try to flag down a car. Someone would stop for her. She could be back at the Pines in minutes. Her spirits soaring for the first time since she awakened in the dark room, Betty stepped out of the trees. She walked up the driveway toward the road.

She should have stayed in the trees.

Neither Trent nor Darcey were hungry. They were far too concerned about Darcey's mother to think about food. But they ate. Trent insisted on it. He told Darcey that in times of crisis it was very important to make yourself do things you really didn't feel like doing. To make life as normal as possible though you felt as though the world was closing in on you. It was important to talk to people. To accept invitations. To eat.

They worked together in Betty's kitchen. Trent had picked up a couple of small New York strip steaks, a large potato and a couple of French rolls. They sliced the rolls lengthwise and toasted them. Trent cooked the steaks in an iron skillet while Darcey made French fries in her mother's deep fryer. Trent assembled steak sandwiches for them.

Darcey found Frank Sinatra on her cell phone music app. They listened to Sinatra. Ate steak sandwiches and fries. They could have been in a '50s steak house. The time travel was a brief relief from that which faced them in the here and now.

After dinner they sat on the porch. Trent opened a nice Merlot. They sipped the wine. They spoke very little.

Darcey walked to the edge of the porch. She looked out over the pasture. She could see the light markings of Prince George.

"Do you think Mom is still alive, Trent?" Darcey asked somberly.

Trent moved behind her. He put his arms around her. She let her head fall back onto his shoulder.

"I'm sure she is," Trent told her. "They need her to trade for what they want."

"But we don't have what they want. Then what?"

"Then it's up to us to figure out a strategy," Trent said. "We'll get her home."

"I wish I had your faith."

"Hey, Betty's no pushover," Trent reminded her. "Any woman who sleeps with a machete won't go down easy."

"Yeah, I guess you have a point there."

Betty was almost to the road when the car pulled into the driveway. She was framed in the headlights. The car stopped. The door opened. Betty made a try for the trees.

She heard the roar of the gun. The bullet hit just inches from her feet. Her ankles were peppered with gravel.

"Don't take another step," said the familiar voice. "This is a Bowen .50 caliber Special. It'll make a fairly small hole going in your back and a cavity big enough to put your foot through coming out your belly."

Betty stopped running. She stood still as the car's engine died and the headlights were turned off. She didn't move as she heard the footsteps in the gravel.

"Good evening, Betty," Valerie said. "Out for an evening stroll, are you?" The woman's laugh was unpleasant.

Back inside the small cabin Valerie ignored the cries coming from the back room. She made Betty sit in a chair. Laying the heavy revolver and her shoulder bag on the counter, she tied the older woman's hands to the chair with two lengths of cord.

Only then did she unlock the door to the back room. The man stumbled out. His face covered in blood. The bed spring still hanging from his nose. He was blubbering. Crying.

"Wayne, I didn't think you could get any dumber," she said. "But you managed to do it. You let an old woman almost kill you. Come here."

Wayne shuffled closer to her. Valerie reached up and jerked the sharp end of the bed spring out of his nose evoking another scream from the wretched man.

"Go to the bathroom and clean yourself up," she ordered.

Wayne hurried to obey.

"And try not to hurt yourself while you're in there," she called after him with a derisive laugh.

She turned back to Betty. "Now what are we going to do with you?" she said, menacingly. "Why can't you be just an old woman? Why must you try to escape?"

"Please," Betty said, "I'm so hungry. Please give me something to eat."

Valerie slapped Betty, her open hand leaving a red mark on the older woman's face.

"You get nothing. Do you hear me? Nothing," Valerie glared at her. "You get nothing to eat unless you earn it."

Valerie's tone of voice, the way she treated the man, the way she handled the high powered gun. All so frightening.

"What do you want me to do?" Betty asked nervously.

"I want you to make a phone call, Betty, and I'll tell you what you'll say. If you do as you're told you will be fed. If not…well, that's up to you. Wayne, get your sorry self out here."

The man stumbled out of the bathroom holding a bloody towel to his face. He lunged for the counter, reaching for something that looked like a gun but wasn't.

"Let me taser the old woman," he shouted. "Let me make her hurt."

"Shut up, Wayne. Put that thing down before you hurt yourself. That's why you can't have a gun. You don't have sense enough to use one. You're even a danger to yourself with a taser."

Wayne put the taser down without argument.

"There's a bucket of chicken in the car. Go get it."

Wayne left the room on unsteady legs.

"And don't get blood on the food, fool. If you do, then you don't eat."

Valerie picked up the heavy revolver and held it to Betty's head.

"I want that gold, old woman," she said. "Tell me where it is and you will live."

Betty closed her eyes. The pressure of the large bore barrel was chilling.

"I don't know where it is. We haven't found it. We don't even know if it's at the Pines."

"Don't lie to me, old woman. I'll kill you like you were a cockroach. Where's the gold?"

"I'm telling you I don't know."

Valerie cocked the revolver. With her other hand she turned Betty's head to face her. She forced the older woman's mouth open and pressed the thick barrel of the gun into her mouth.

"I'm going to ask you one more time. Nod your head if you're ready to tell me the truth. If I pull the trigger there won't be enough left of your head to identify. Now tell me where the gold is."

Betty didn't move. The taste of gun oil was near to making her gag. She didn't move her head.

"You're either telling the truth, you old witch, or you've got ice water in your veins. So now we'll see about making that phone call." Valerie removed the gun barrel from Betty's mouth.

Wayne returned with the bucket of chicken.

"You could take a lesson from this old woman, Wayne. She's got more guts than you do." She laughed. A belittling laugh.

Valerie reached into the bucket and got a drumstick. She took a bite of the drumstick, the heavy handgun in her other hand. The aroma of the chicken filled the room.

"Smells good, doesn't it?"

"It smells delicious," Betty said.

"Can I have some?" Wayne asked.

"Shut up, fool," Valerie replied. "You can eat later. We have business to take care of now."

Valerie finished the drumstick. She tossed the bone on the floor. Reaching into her bag she retrieved a mobile phone.

Darcey's phone rang. It came up as a blocked number. She answered, putting the phone on speaker.

"Darcey?"

"Mom? Are you all right?"

"Yes, I'm all right," Betty's voice sounded weak but not desperately so. "I need water and I'd like a bath. I feel oily. I even smell oily. But I'm all right."

"Is someone there with you?" Darcey asked.

"Yes. They've promised to give me water if I make this call and say what they tell me."

In the cabin Valerie poked Betty with the heavy revolver.

"They know you found my ear ring. They told me to tell you that if you don't turn the gold over to them within the next twenty four hours they will mail you the other one with my ear attached to it."

Darcey pressed her fist to her mouth. She wanted to scream. To cry. She knew she couldn't. She had to remain calm.

"Did you tell them we don't have the gold?"

"Yes. They don't believe me."

"Tell them if we had it we'd give it to them to get you back. You're far more valuable to us than gold. But we don't have it."

There was silence for several seconds. They had muted their phone.

"They said to tell you that you have twenty four hours to turn over the gold. If you don't have it you'd better find it. I have to hang up now. They promised me water. Plenty of water."

The line went dead.

"What are we going to do, Trent? They're going to cut off her ear. We can't find the gold in twenty four hours."

Trent started laughing.

Darcey couldn't believe he was laughing. "Stop it!" she demanded. "This isn't funny. This is my mother we're talking about."

"And your mother is a clever lady," Trent said. "Clever and gutsy. She told us where they're holding her."

"She did?"

"Sure. She referred to water four times in that short conversation. If all she wanted was the water they promised her in return for making the call she didn't have to mention it. But she did. Four times. And she said she feels 'oily.' Even smells oily. Water? Oil? Where is there water and oil? They're holding her in a camp somewhere on the lake."

Trent punched Jack Blake's number on his speed dial. He got voice mail. He left a message telling Jack they had heard from Betty and asking him to call as soon as he could.

Then he called Matt Lorca.

"Hey, Matt. You still have that beat up old bass boat?" Trent asked.

"That beat up old boat has caught us plenty of bass, buddy," Lorca laughed. "Yeah, I still got it."

"How about meeting us out at the lake? We might have a lead on where Betty's being held."

"Sure, buddy. Whatever you need," Lorca responded. "It'll take me a few minutes to get the trailer hooked up. I'll have to get gas. Might be an hour or a little more. Does that work?"

"It'll have to. Same launch we always used?"

"That's the one, buddy. See you there."

Trent and Darcey made preparations for what promised to be a long night on the water. Darcey got bottles of water for them while Trent made other preparations.

An hour and a half later they were sitting in the parking lot when Matt Lorca drove up. His old dually looked about as beat up as his bass boat. But knowing Matt, Trent was sure they were both in excellent running condition.

Matt expertly backed the boat trailer down the launch ramp, moving it slowly into the water. Trent held onto the line while Matt released the boat from the trailer. Climbing back into the truck Lorca pulled the trailer back up the ramp. He parked both in the empty parking lot.

Matt stowed a duffle bag under his seat in the stern. He held the boat steady while Trent climbed in first, then helped Darcey aboard. He and Darcey took the center seats. Matt would sit in the stern so he could control the boat. The bow seat they'd leave empty for the time being.

Matt pushed the boat off and leaped aboard. The motor started easily as Trent had known it would.

"Which way do you want to go, buddy?" Lorca asked.

"I guess south is as good a way as any."

Three miles down the shore line of the lake Betty sat again in her darkened cell.

After Betty made the phone call Valerie told Wayne to throw the prepaid cell phone into the lake. She made good on her promise of water and food if Betty made the phone call. The starving woman had been given two pieces of chicken, a biscuit and a bottle of water. Now she was locked up again. She had devoured the chicken in the dark and drank some of the water. She thought it wise to save some of it. She didn't know when she would get more.

With her belly full she lay down on the mattress. It was on the floor now but at least provided some small level of comfort. She fell asleep. There were voices speaking quietly. Doors opening and closing. The sound of vehicles that were probably on the road driving by. She was so drowsy. She thought she should be paying more attention. Nothing would wake her.

Until the door opened suddenly. Valerie strode into the room. It was obvious that she was angry. Dangerously so. She walked to Betty and slapped her again.

"You're too smart for your own good, old woman," Valerie raged at her. "But your cleverness will do you no good. You'll get no more food. No more water. I think it likely you'll never see anything outside this filthy room again."

Valerie grabbed the water bottle and left the room. The door slammed behind her. Betty could hear the click of the lock engaging. She sat quietly in the dark. Praying.

Matt guided the boat expertly along the shore line. Toledo Bend reservoir had been created by the construction of a dam on the Sabine River back in the '60s. It was the result of a unique partnership between the states of Louisiana and Texas. No federal funds were used in building the dam. A concept unheard of in later years.

Construction of the dam flooded thousands of acres of forest. Even decades later there were still stumps of trees protruding from the water here and there. Skeletal remains of trees once thick and green on the banks of the river. Potential misfortune to careless boaters and unaware fishermen.

"Do we know what we're looking for?" Matt asked.

"Not exactly," Trent replied.

"We could be out here a while. There are twelve hundred miles of shore line around this lake."

"Yeah, I know. I didn't say it was going to be easy."

Trent knew Matt was right. He didn't have any idea what to look for. The only clue Betty had been able to give them was that she was being held somewhere on the water.

They cruised slowly along. Most of the houses were dark. A few showed lights. They pulled closer to shore to examine those more thoroughly. One house was dark except for a light in an outbuilding.

Matt used the trolling motor to quietly bump the bow up onto land. Trent leaped onto the grass and ran stealthily up to the lighted room.

Pressed against the wall, he eased his head around to look through the window. Inside a middle aged, balding man was working on a partially disassembled outboard motor. His face was very close to the pieces he was working on. A requirement necessitated by the thick glasses perched on his nose. Feeling like a peeping Tom, which he was, Trent returned to the boat as quietly as he could.

The next hour seemed like six. The boat moved silently through the waters. Matt's intimate knowledge of the reservoir kept them from colliding with any of the old tree trunks standing like ghosts above water level. All three were thinking what none were willing to say. Even with the knowledge that Betty was being held on the lake they were embarked on an impossible task. There was no way they could find the right house in more than a thousand miles of shore line.

Trent finally said what no one wanted to hear.

"I think we're wasting our time."

"We can't give up, Trent," Darcey said anxiously. "Mom's in one of these houses. We have to find her."

"We're not giving up, Darcey. We just don't have enough information to figure out which of the hundreds of houses out here is the right one."

"He's right, Darcey," Matt said. "Your mother was very clever to give you the hints about being on the water and smelling oil. But that's just not enough information."

Trent maintained his poker face when he looked at Matt. He didn't want to believe he had heard what Matt said.

"How did you know Betty gave us those hints, Matt?" he asked.

Matt hesitated. "Jack told me, buddy. I talked to him just before I met y'all at the launch ramp."

"Jack wouldn't have told you that, Matt."

"I'm his chief deputy, buddy," Matt said, smiling. "He tells me everything."

"Jack can't tell you what he doesn't know, Matt. He doesn't know what Betty told us. I never talked to Jack after her phone call."

Matt said nothing.

"The kidnappers knew we found her ear ring. How did they know? I should have caught that one," Trent continued.

Silence

[214]

"You didn't burn your hand on your motor's cowling, did you, Matt? That's a burn caused by chloroform. The chloroform on the cloth you used to render Betty unconscious. I'll bet Betty has a similar burn mark around her nose and mouth. And that's why you wanted to take my car to the old warehouse. You were afraid we'd smell chloroform in your vehicle."

It was quiet on the boat. Matt looked out at the lake. Regret written on his face.

While Matt's face was turned away from them Trent shoved Darcey overboard. Without a word. He shoved her overboard.

Darcey was astounded to find herself underwater. She pulled herself back to the surface only to find Trent's hand on her head pushing her down. Was he trying to drown her? Why would he do that?

Matt turned back at the sound of the splash. Trent struggled to force Darcey to stay underwater. As her head popped above the surface again she saw Matt's arm swinging a hatchet. She saw him strike Trent's forehead with the blunt end of the small axe. Trent fell off the seat. Darcey hoped he was only unconscious.

Darcey sank below the surface. Arms pulling, legs kicking she swam deep. Underneath the boat. She swam hard away from the port side of the boat. She understood Trent had acted to save her. Now she had to get away. It was up to her to save him.

Lorca reached into the duffle bag and retrieved a small caliber rifle with a white extension on the barrel. He fired four times into the water on the port side. The suppressor he had made of a few inches of PVC, some steel wool, and wadded up newspaper with a few other odds and ends kept the sound of the shots to a minimum. Moving to the starboard side he fired three times more. He thought it was wasted effort but he might get lucky. Or Darcey might get unlucky.

Matt reloaded the small rifle. He immediately turned the boat and began searching for Darcey. He had to find her. If she was free none of them were free. He guided the boat toward shore. He would force her to stay in deep water. If he could do that for long enough she would drown. No one could tread water forever. If she tried to swim he would see the ripples in the water. He could track her down quickly.

Matt trolled along the shore for forty minutes. He saw nothing. He didn't see Darcey holding onto the skeletal framework of what was once a huge oak tree. She was underwater except from her nose up. When she saw Matt moving in her direction she would slowly, calmly lower her head beneath the water. There were no ripples. There was nothing to be seen.

She hoped he would give up soon and leave. She knew there were creatures in this lake. Alligators. Big ones. And snakes. There were snakes. Once she thought she felt something slither across her leg. She prayed it was a fish. A small fish.

She thought about the .38 that Trent had strapped to her ankle before they left The Pines. She knew the shells were sealed and would fire. Trent had told her the danger was water in the barrel and cylinders. She had to be sure all the water was drained out before she fired. Otherwise the gun could blow up in her face. But Matt was out of range of the small weapon. And she didn't trust her marksmanship against Matt's. He was a cop. She was an interior designer. It didn't seem a good match. She also didn't know how seriously Trent was hurt. And if it came to a shootout Matt could use him for a shield.

No, the smart thing was to avoid capture. Get away. Come back to fight again. She held onto the tree, her eyes barely above water. Watching.

Finally Matt decided it was useless to continue the search. Chances were Darcey had drowned. Even if she hadn't drowned she still didn't know where they were holding her mother. Moving slowly, quietly, with only the trolling motor to avoid attention he turned the boat back to the southerly route along the shoreline. He looked at Trent lying in the bottom of the boat. A trickle of blood stained his forehead. Matt hoped he hadn't hit him too hard. He didn't want Trent dead. He needed him alive.

After perhaps a quarter mile he turned the boat eastward around the end of a peninsula jutting into the lake. He disappeared from Darcey's view.

She thought it was probably three or four miles back to the launch ramp. She thought she could swim that in an hour and a half. She remembered that Trent had gone ashore to check out a house farther back along the shore. He had said there was a middle aged man working on a motor in the garage. She thought that was probably a mile from where she was now. She was sure she could swim that far in twenty minutes. Maybe half an hour. She quietly pushed herself back into deep water. Legs kicking. Arms moving rhythmically in a strong over hand. Her face turning up every third stroke to breathe.

Lorca beached the boat near his fish camp. He tied it off to a stump near the edge of the water. He quickly frisked Trent, finding the big 1911 semiautomatic. Sticking it in his own belt, he cuffed Trent's hands behind his back. Trent's phone was in his jeans pocket. Matt threw it into the lake. He lifted the unconscious man easily to his shoulder, picked up his rifle, and started up the slight incline to the front door of the cabin.

Lorca pushed through the entrance to find himself facing Valerie's .50 caliber revolver.

"Put that thing down, Valerie," he told her. Leaning the rifle against the wall, he gently laid the still unconscious Trent on the floor. He took no pleasure in hurting the man who had been his fishing buddy. It was something he had to do. It was just as simple as that.

Valerie's face lit up when she saw Matt. She ran to him. Raising herself up onto her toes she kissed his cheek.

"Hello, handsome," she said.

Matt looked at Wayne. Saw the blood still staining his face. Saw the misery in his eyes.

Lorca pushed her aside and walked past her. She laughed. He caught the subtle slow backward and forward rhythmic movement of her hips. He ignored her.

Matt looked at Trent. He looked out the window. His eyes were focused on something far away. He looked back at Trent.

"I'm sorry about this, buddy. I really am."

There was rum in the pantry. Ice and Coca Cola in the refrigerator. He mixed himself a drink. A stiff one. He didn't offer Valerie or her husband a drink. They were dangerous sober. He hated to think what they'd be like drunk. He didn't want to encourage her suggestive hip movements.

Twenty five minutes later Darcey wrapped her arms around another dead tree sticking up above the water. Her muscles ached. It had been a long time since she had swum such a distance. The .38 Trent had strapped to her ankle didn't weigh enough to slow her down significantly. When she was a competitive swimmer she had often trained with light weights strapped to her calves.

She thought the house where Trent had seen the man working on the motor had to be around here. She had no idea which of the two houses she could see was the right one. Both were dark. She knew it was late. She didn't know how late. Midnight maybe.

She pulled herself out of the water. Even though the evening was not cool she started shivering. She'd been in the water for more than an hour. While she was in the water she was warm enough. In the open air she was cold.

She reached the back door of the house she thought was the one she wanted. She knocked on the door. There was no answer. She knocked louder.

"Hello? Is anyone home? Please! I need help."

Silence.

She knocked again. Louder still. No response.

She turned and ran toward the second house. It, too, was dark. Reaching the door, she pounded as hard as she could.

"Hello! Is anyone home?" she shouted.

No response.

She knew that most of the houses along the lake were fish camps. A few retired people lived on the lake year round. Most people were only here on weekends and holidays. This was neither. It was Tuesday night. Or maybe Wednesday morning.

She pounded on the door one more time in desperation. Nothing.

She could run out to the highway and follow that back to the launch ramp. But she didn't know how much the road twisted and turned.

Swimming was more of a straight shot, she thought. She guessed it was no more than three miles by water to the ramp. Maybe less. She could do that in a little more than an hour. She could always come ashore again if she passed a house with a light on. And the water would be warmer. She was shivering uncontrollably now.

The water would be better. If Matt didn't come back to track her with his boat.

Matt sipped his drink as he watched Trent. He felt the alcohol warming his belly. He wasn't happy with the way this night had gone. He had made a stupid mistake. No one to blame but himself.

His bigger concern was the company he was keeping. He had partnered with a woman who had no moral center whatsoever. She would do whatever necessary to get what she wanted. No matter how cruel. No matter how bloody. The bloodier the better in her mind, he thought.

Her husband was not a factor. He did what she told him. When he wasn't carrying out her orders he stood around looking like he was about to cry.

He knew they would have to kill Trent and Betty now. He hated that. Betty Anderson was a good woman. He had known her for a long time. Trent was his fishing buddy. But now they were both as good as dead. All because he had made a stupid mistake. Because he had a bloodthirsty madwoman for a partner. Because Trent and Betty could identify Matt and his partners. He could feel his own moral center being dispelled.

He hoped the reward they got would make it feel better. He doubted it would. At least it would let him take off his deputy's uniform and spend the rest of his life drinking rum on a beach somewhere.

He took his time drinking the rum currently in his glass. He was in no hurry to face Trent. He would do what he had to do. But he was in no rush to get to it.

After half an hour Trent began to stir. Lorca sipped the last of his rum. He set the glass on the table. He laid Trent's handgun beside it.

Trent groaned. His head was aching. A pounding ache. He tried to move but could not. He discovered his hands were cuffed. His eyes opened. Closed again. The light in the room turned the pounding in his head into something much like an axe cleaving through his skull, which it very nearly had been.

Lorca stood and put his hands under Trent's arms. He lifted him into a chair. Trent's hands were still cuffed but at least Matt thought he owed him respect enough to get him up off the floor.

"What did you hit me with?" Trent asked, his voice sounding weak.

"A hatchet," Matt answered honestly.

"An axe? You hit me with an axe?"

"Just the blunt end of a small one," Lorca tried to justify himself. "And not hard. If I'd wanted you dead you'd be dead. You tossed me quite a curve, buddy, when you asked me to meet you at the launch with my boat."

"You didn't need gas, did you?"

"No. Sure didn't. You didn't know I picked up this old shack a couple of years ago. The boat was here. I had to get out here, get it trailered and get to the launch all without letting you see me. Had to make it look like I was coming from town."

"Sorry to cause you such inconvenience. Darcey?"

"Not sure. I fired a few shots but couldn't see anything. I might have got her. She might have drowned. She might have got away. But I'll get her sooner or later. I got no choice." Lorca hated saying that but it was the truth as he saw it.

"You always have a choice, Matt," Trent said.

"Not this time, buddy," Matt said, his voice sounding sad. "It's gone too far. It's out of control."

"You guys can have your bromance later," Valerie screeched. "Tell us about the gold. Where is the gold?"

It hurt when Trent turned his head to look at the woman. "I don't know where the gold is. I don't even know if there is any gold."

Valerie swung her big revolver in Trent's direction. "Don't lie to me. We know the gold is there. The old woman in New Orleans told us that much before she died."

"How did you know how to find Professor Richards?" Trent wondered.

Valerie laughed. "I followed you to the Mint. Twenty bucks to that kid Vinnie got us her address. He was easy."

Trent looked at Wayne. "Did you kill Professor Richards?"

Valerie laughed hysterically. "Him? Kill someone? He doesn't have the guts. I killed her. I slid that knife into her bony old back and watched the life go out of her eyes."

"If she told you the story of the missing gold was true she was telling you everything she knew."

"No," Valerie hissed. "No, she wasn't. I learned much more from Darcey. All about the train and your trip to Camp Moore. We were right behind you all the way."

"Why did you shoot at us in New Orleans?" Trent asked, more to keep her talking than for wanting the answer.

"We didn't shoot at you," she replied. "Why would we do that? I was trying as hard as I could to keep you alive. I hoped to follow you to where the gold is hidden. And that's what I've done. But it's time for the killing. If we don't get some answers now, more people are going to die."

Trent thought she was telling the truth about the shooting. The shots fired at them were from a small caliber weapon. The revolver Valerie was waving around was very large. Probably a .50 caliber.

"How did you get mixed up with these two, Matt?" Trent asked.

Lorca grimaced. "Well, I got a lot of information just working with you and the sheriff. Enough to make me believe the gold is somewhere out at the Pines. I got onto Valerie the same way you did. Found out she wasn't registered at the hotel. I just happened to see her go into the condo that old Wayne here had rented. Introduced myself. One thing led to another. Here we are. I don't mean to be pushy, buddy, but I want a piece of that gold, too."

"I wish I could help you," Trent said. "Believe me. You don't know how much I wish I could help you. But I don't know where the gold is."

"You're lying," Valerie hissed.

"I'm afraid I have to agree with my somewhat dramatic partner, buddy," Lorca said. "I think you know more than you're saying. I'd advise you to come clean. I can't promise to keep you and Betty safe if you don't."

"You can't keep us alive no matter what," Trent said, stating what they both knew was the truth.

Matt looked away from Trent.

"I'll do the best I can for you, buddy," he said softly. "I promise you that much."

"Why are you doing this, Matt?" Trent asked, genuinely puzzled to find his friend was a turncoat.

"Why? You want to know why?" Lorca asked, feeling the anger rising. "Because I'm tired of being poor. I grew up the poor Spanish kid in a white town, buddy. We were so poor there were nights when I went to bed hungry. I watched my dad work himself to death trying to feed his family. I watched him work for people in this parish for forty years. Then when he got old and couldn't work as hard or as fast as he once did they just kicked him into the ditch. He was loyal for all those years. In the end he got nothing for it."

"And you think I didn't have it hard?" Trent asked. "My folks weren't exactly well off. I know what it's like to be poor."

"Yeah, well, I didn't have a rich old aunt die and leave me a fortune."

"Maybe not," Trent said, "but you are chief deputy of this parish. That's a pretty good job. And you would have been a shoo-in to succeed Jack as sheriff when he retires."

"That old man will die in office and right now he looks pretty healthy."

"So it's just all about greed then," Trent said.

Lorca slammed his fist down on the table.

"Don't talk to me about greed," Lorca said. "After twenty years as a deputy, the last twelve as chief deputy, I have a crummy little house in town that still has fifteen years left on the mortgage, this shack of a fish camp that I also owe on, a beat up old bass boat, and a beat up old truck. I'm gettin' older, buddy, and things aren't gettin' better. This is a chance to get out of here and kick back in a part of the world where nobody knows me."

"I've heard that story before, Matt," Trent said. "It usually doesn't work out that way."

"I will tell you this, Trent," Matt said, leaning forward. He spoke softly and sincerely. "I'm sorry that someone has died. I truly am. I'll do my best to keep everyone alive now. But you got to come clean, buddy."

Trent looked into Matt's eyes. A long look. A deep look.

"I'm done with this," Valerie said impatiently. "Wayne, go bring that old woman out here. Her time has run out."

Valerie's husband obediently unlocked the door to the back room. He shuffled into the darkness and returned pushing Betty in front of him. She caught her breath when she saw Trent sitting in the chair, his hands cuffed behind him. She saw where the blood had trickled down his face from the blow from Lorca's hatchet.

"Trent, are you OK? Where's Darcey?"

"I'll live. Darcey got away."

"Thank God for that," Betty said. "But I'm sorry to see you here."

For the first time she noticed Lorca sitting at the table with Trent.

"Matt, you, too? Are you a prisoner, too?"

Lorca looked embarrassed.

"No, Betty, Matt's not a prisoner," Trent answered for him. "He's one of them."

"Matt Lorca, you should be ashamed of yourself," Betty said. "Your parents were good people. They raised you better than this."

"Yes, they did, Betty," Lorca replied, "and they died poor. Not even enough money for either one of them to have a decent funeral."

"You people are making me sick," Valerie spewed the words more than spoke them. "This is how it's going to work. You, old woman, get on your knees."

Betty raised her head and looked defiant.

Valerie wrapped her fingers in the older woman's hair and pulled her down to her knees. As she had done before, she grasped Betty's cheeks in her hand and forced her to open her mouth. She pressed the large bore barrel of her revolver into Betty's mouth.

"Get the idea, hot shot?" Valerie said to Trent. "You either start talking or I start shooting. This little cannon fires a .50 caliber round. If I pull the trigger this old woman's head is mush."

Trent looked at Matt. Matt looked away. It was silent in the room.

"What's it going to be, Mr. Big Shot," Valerie said. "I'm completely, totally out of patience."

"All right," Trent said. "I'll take you to where I think the gold is buried. Take the gun out of her mouth."

"Where you think it's buried?" Valerie shouted. "I'm not sure that's good enough."

"I can't do anything more," Trent said, trying to remain calm. He knew getting into a shouting match with Valerie would do nothing but get Betty killed. "I've figured out a few clues we've found. I think there's a logical place where it's buried. But I haven't had the time to dig for it. I'll take you there now."

Valerie looked at him. Her hand was tensing on the gun. Betty's eyes were closed. Trent and Matt both knew she was praying.

"I think that's the best the man can do, Valerie," Matt said. "What's the harm in taking a look? Killing Betty now isn't going to get us the gold any faster. What next? Kill Trent? He's the only one who might figure out whatever clues there are. Without him we have no chance at all."

Darcey moved like a machine now. Gliding smoothly through the water. Trying not to attract attention. Twice she heard loud splashes. Gators, she thought. She tried not to panic. Just keep moving she told herself. One hand over the other. Legs scissoring smoothly.

She reached the launch ramp exhausted. Pulling herself up until the water only reached her knees, Darcey laid her face on the wet concrete. Breathing heavily. Resting. Not for long. She didn't know when Matt might show up in the parking lot in front of her. Or something worse in the lake behind her. But she had to rest for a few minutes.

She raised herself to her feet and stumbled across the parking lot toward Trent's sleek black sedan. Just as she reached it she heard a noise. A noise coming from the lake. From the south. A boat.

She ran to the bushes edging the parking lot. Reaching for the .38 strapped to her ankle she turned the revolver toward the ground. Water ran from the barrel. It was clear of water within seconds. If she had to use the gun she could only pray that the seals on the bullets had kept the powder dry. She pressed herself into the ground, behind the bushes. Holding the revolver in both hands she waited.

In less than ten minutes Matt's boat came into view. He beached it to the right of the launch ramp, pulling it as far onto land as he could. He moved quickly to his old truck. There he unhitched the boat trailer. He was abandoning the boat and trailer. She didn't know what that meant for Trent and her mother.

Matt stopped and turned to look at Trent's car. Darcey tried to get deeper into the dirt and grass and bushes. He walked to the car. He ran his hand over the hood. She feared he was going to try do something to make the vehicle unusable. He didn't. He just caressed it. Admired it.

He turned back to his truck. He climbed inside and started the engine. Throwing it into gear he made a loop around the parking lot. His headlights went right over Darcey. He didn't see her. He drove to the parking lot entrance. It was near an intersection of Highway Six with a smaller road that ran along the lake. There was a blinking light over the intersection. Yellow on the highway. Red on the smaller road. Matt waited there. The lights illuminated him briefly as he sat in the truck's cab. Light. Dark. Light. Dark.

Darcey lay as still as she could. Barely breathing. The revolver held in front of her. As Trent had taught her, she kept her finger outside the trigger guard. If she needed to fire her finger had to move only a very short distance. Keeping it away from the trigger for the moment meant that a nervous twitch wouldn't fire an unintended shot. The last thing she wanted was Matt Lorca's attention.

It seemed like a very long time. It seemed like hours. It had been only fifteen minutes when a car approached the intersection from the south. There were four people in the car. A woman driving. A man sitting beside her in the front seat. A man and a woman in the back seat.

As the car slowed to make the turn to the east at the intersection the blinking lights showed Darcey that it was Valerie driving the car. She couldn't make out the others. The two in the back seat could be Trent and her mother. She wanted to think so.

As the car turned onto the highway Lorca pulled out of the parking lot and followed them. They quickly disappeared from Darcey's view. Still she waited. She didn't want to take a chance that one or the other would turn around to double check the parking lot.

After what she judged was probably five minutes she raised herself off the ground. She clawed her way out of the thick bushes into the parking lot. Staying as low as she could, Darcey ran to the right rear wheel well of Trent's car where she found the bundle attached to the metal frame with a magnet. Inside she found the spare remote for the car and a mobile phone.

Still watching the road to the east to be sure neither vehicle was returning, she touched Jack Blake's name in the contact list. The call went straight to voice mail. She told the sheriff that Valerie and her husband had both her mother and Trent as prisoners. With regret, Darcey told him that Matt Lorca had joined them as a co-conspirator. She told him that Valerie's car and Matt's truck were headed toward town from the lake with Trent and her mother. She said she intended to follow them. She asked him to please call her as soon as possible.

Darcey used the remote to unlock the door. Laying the phone in the console's cup holder and the revolver on her lap she started the big engine. She turned on the heat, setting it at eighty degrees. It wouldn't take long for warm air to fill the car. To take the chill from her skin. To dry her clothes.

Darcey wheeled the powerful sedan out of the parking lot and onto the highway. She was careful not to go too fast. She didn't want to get close enough for them to see her. She thought she didn't have to get close to them. She was sure she knew where they were going.

Just outside of town Matt pulled around Valerie's car to take the lead. He guided them along back streets through town. He led them through quiet residential neighborhoods. Past the even quieter old cemetery. They had to get back onto the highway at the east edge of town. He was careful to stay within the speed limit. He wasn't afraid of being ticketed. No cop in the parish would give the chief deputy a ticket. No cop in the state would give the chief deputy a ticket. He just didn't want a record of where he was at a particular time on a particular night.

He pulled up in front of the big house at the Pines. Valerie came to a stop behind him. Matt climbed down from his truck and walked back to the car. He opened the back door on Trent's side and helped the handcuffed man out. Valerie killed the engine and got out of the car to stand close to Matt. She looked up into his face. He felt her eyes on him. He moved a step away from her.

Meanwhile her husband was pulling Betty out of the car on the other side. He pulled her around the car to join the group.

"Where do we go from here, buddy?" Matt asked.

"There's an old wagon road that goes back up into those trees," Trent said, nodding toward the thicket at the edge of the pasture. "It's not much more than a trail. Your truck can probably handle it. I doubt if a car can make it."

"That's the trail we rode the horses on," Valerie said.

"That's right," Trent agreed. "Then you should remember the mound at the end of the trail."

"Yeah, there was a mound up there. Maybe he's telling the truth, Matt."

Matt nodded. He turned to Betty. "I'm sure you have a couple of shovels around here somewhere."

She looked at Trent. She figured he was stalling for time. She didn't know how to help him.

She said nothing.

"I'll check the barn," Matt said.

He lowered the truck's tailgate.

"All right. Everybody in the back of the truck," he ordered.

Valerie, Wayne and Betty all climbed up into the truck's bed. Trent sat on the tailgate and swung his legs up onto it.

"Turn around, Trent," Lorca ordered.

Trent did as he was told. Matt unlocked the cuff on his right hand. He slid it through a tie down at the corner of the bed and locked it again. He raised the tailgate and locked it into place.

Climbing back into the cab Matt drove down to the barn. He parked the truck at the large open door of the old building so that the headlights provided some illumination. Leaving the motor running while he went inside, he rummaged around until he found two shovels, which he tossed into the truck's bed.

"Point the way, buddy," he directed Trent.

"The trail enters the woods just to the left of that big hickory tree," Trent said.

Matt climbed back into the cab and backed it away from the barn. He shifted gears and steered toward the tree Marshall had pointed out. He drove slowly. The truck swayed as he drove across uneven ground.

Matt found the trail Trent had directed. He slowed even more as the truck entered the woods. Trent was right. This was an old wagon road. The truck bounced harder as he eased it along. The people riding in the bed held on.

They were deep in the woods when the trail ended. Matt killed the engine and walked around to the tailgate.

"All right, buddy, where is it?"

"I think it's buried in that mound there," Trent said, pointing to the spot. "I'm not sure. I told you that. But from all the clues I've been able to find that seems the most likely place."

"I sure hope you're right," Matt said with a look at Valerie. He unlocked the cuff that was attached to the tie down and replaced it on Trent's wrist. This time he cuffed Trent's hands in front.

"Come on down. Time for you to go to work," he ordered Trent as he lowered the tailgate. He handed Trent a shovel as the cuffed man jumped down from the truck.

Darcey slowed as she neared the Pines. She had stayed well back from the two vehicles for fear they would see her headlights and suspect someone was following them. As she approached the old warehouse she shut off the lights. She carefully threaded her way across the dirt clearing to pull the dark sedan as close to the trees as she could get it.

She checked the phone but there was no message from Jack Blake. Nothing. As much as she hated to do it, Darcey turned the phone off before putting it into her pocket. She didn't like being out of touch but the last thing she needed was to have the phone ring when she was within the hearing of Matt and Valerie.

She looked in the trunk to see if there was anything there she could use. Sure enough there was a heavy duty flash light. She wouldn't turn it on but it was a good thing to have if she needed it. She checked the revolver in her ankle holster, tipping the barrel again to be sure all the water had drained out. She took the time to pull the hammer to half cock and turn the cylinder to be sure all the water was drained from there as well. Just to be safe she replaced the wet cartridges with dry spares from her bag, which she had left in the car.

She felt her way through the trees in the dark. When she came to the rotting trunk of the fallen tree, she dropped down behind it. She watched as Lorca cuffed Trent to the tie down in the bed of the truck. As the other three climbed up with him and Lorca closed the tailgate. She watched as the truck bounced down to the barn. She saw Lorca go into the barn and come back with two shovels.

She wondered why the truck drove into the trees on the old wagon road. It could only be because Trent had suggested it. But why? Why would Trent take them down that trail? There was nothing there.

Nothing but the mound at the end of the trail. The mound they suspected held the bodies from the 1862 fight. Nothing but bones. No gold. Only bones.

Trent was stalling. Playing it one minute at a time. Hoping to find a way to save himself and her mother. He thought he didn't have any help. He didn't know he had her.

When the truck disappeared in the woods, Darcey rose from her hiding place and began jogging in that direction. She kept the big house between her and the trail just to be safe. She didn't know what Lorca had planned. He might drop them off in the woods and drive back out. If so, she didn't want him to see her until she was ready. When she was ready he would regret it. So would Valerie.

She reached the house. She stopped briefly to watch the trail. Seeing no sign of anyone coming back, she resumed jogging. This time she used Rube's cabin for cover.

Darcey repeated the process when she reached the cabin. She waited for a full minute. The next part was the riskiest. It was open ground for probably two hundred yards. No jogging this time. She ran at full speed.

It was uneventful. No one appeared from the trees. No lights. No shouts. No shots fired. She made it.

Ducking as noiselessly as possible into the cover of forest, Darcey allowed herself time to let her breathing return to normal. She looked back to where she had left the trees behind the house. She had swum four or five miles and run for maybe a quarter mile tonight. She felt like she had already done a mini-marathon with more yet to go.

She moved deeper into the trees. Staying parallel to the old wagon road. Shifting her position as quietly as she could. Soon she could hear voices. She could see lights. Remaining as low as possible she maneuvered closer.

She could see the truck. Lorca was leaning against it. He was holding what appeared to be a small rifle with some sort of white extension on the barrel. She thought she could see a semiautomatic hand gun stuck in his belt. It looked like Trent's Model 1911. The bright lights on the bull bar and cab of his truck lit up the entire clearing.

Valerie was standing in front of the truck. Darcey's mother was standing in front of her. Valerie was holding a very large revolver pointed at Betty. They were both watching Trent and another man digging in the mound at the end of the trail.

She realized Trent had convinced them the gold was buried in the mound. She had guessed right. He was stalling. Waiting for a break. Waiting for an opportunity. She would have to come up with some sort of diversion to give him that opportunity. She didn't know how to do that without getting them all killed.

Jack Blake snapped awake. He had fallen asleep in his recliner watching TV. He must have been more tired than he thought. It was late. Very late. He had slept for a long time. He was covered by a blanket. Jennifer covered him before she went to bed. She did that on nights when he fell asleep in the recliner. She didn't want to wake him. She wanted him to sleep. To rest. But of all nights this was not the one to let him sleep.

His phone! He remembered he had dropped his phone in the toilet. Probably ruined it. But he had put it in a bag of rice hoping to dry it out. He had called his office to tell them his mobile phone wasn't working. If anyone was looking for him they should call his home phone.

He went back into the kitchen where the phone rested in the rice. Extricating it from the bag, he could barely breathe as he turned it on. A miracle! The phone came on. It was working! And he had two voice mail messages.

His delight turned to terror when he listened first to the message from Trent and then the message from Darcey. A stupid accident on his part might result in three friends being murdered. And Lorca! Lorca! His right hand man. How could he have got himself mixed up in this mess?

Time to worry about all that later. He looked at the clock on the stove. It was just past two o'clock. He had to figure a strategy. And he had to do it now.

Matt leaned against his truck watching Trent and Wayne tossing shovelfuls of dirt from the mound into the trees behind them. He knew Trent and Betty had to die. Darcey, too, if he could find her. No, he had to find her. She had to die. He wasn't happy about it. He sincerely liked Trent. They had shared some good times together. Trent had never looked down on him like so many people in his life. The ones who were too eaten up with themselves to pay him any mind.

The ringing of his phone brought him out of the fog of past insults. He was surprised to see Jack Blake's name. Why would Jack be calling at this hour? On this night. This wasn't good.

"You're up awful late, Jack," Lorca said.

"Yeah, and I'm not happy about it," the sheriff said. It sounded like the phone connection was bad. Lorca could make out what his boss was saying but just barely. There was interference on the line.

"Got to be important to get you out of bed," Lorca tried to sound nonchalant. "What's up?"

"We have big trouble, Matt. Don't have time to discuss it now. My phone is about to die. I'm headed to the office. Meet me there as soon as you can."

"OK, boss. On my way."

Lorca didn't like this. It didn't fit the sheriff's pattern. In twenty years he had never had a call like this from Blake. Here he is watching a man who is about to die digging in the dirt for lost treasure and the sheriff calls. After two o'clock in the morning. Lorca didn't like this at all. Did Darcey survive and somehow get in touch with him? Didn't seem likely but maybe.

"We have a problem," he told Valerie. "The sheriff just called. Told me to meet him at the office."

"Do you think he's on to us?" she asked.

"No, I don't," he lied. "These kinds of things happen all the time. Just part of the job."

"Don't go," she urged.

"I have to go, Valerie. If I don't he will be on to us. Look, it's a minor complication. You and Wayne can keep things here under control. I shouldn't be gone long. Just keep these guys digging. The sooner we can find the gold and get it loaded up the sooner we can get out of the parish."

"OK," Valerie said, but she wasn't happy about it.

He handed Valerie a heavy duty flashlight.

"Genuine police issue," he said. "It'll keep this place lighted up until I get back."

Lorca started to get into his truck. He remembered something.

"Give me your car keys, Valerie. We left your car up by the house. We should have put it in the barn out of sight. I'll take care of it and leave the keys on the floorboard on the driver's side."

Valerie looked at him suspiciously.

"You'd better not run out on me," she warned.

"Why would I do that?" he responded. "If you get caught I'm in for it, too. I'm not dumb enough to think you won't take me down with you."

"You got that right," she said as she tossed him the keys. "Don't forget it."

Darcey pressed herself as deep into the dirt as she could get as Lorca backed his truck past her. She prayed the heavy brush would keep her from his view. She remembered Trent telling her that hiding in plain sight worked most every time. The theory was that if someone didn't expect to see you they wouldn't see you. Lorca didn't expect to see her. He didn't.

As he emerged from the trees and into open pasture Lorca headed the truck directly for the barn. This wasn't going to end well. He could sense it. There was no way he was going to meet the sheriff. He didn't know how Blake discovered that he was working with Valerie. But he did. The how didn't matter. The sheriff knew. Matt was sure of it. It was time for him to disappear. He needed a new vehicle. Valerie supplied it.

He drove his truck as deep into the barn as he could. With Trent's 1911 stuck in his belt and carrying his rifle, he walked up to the house where Valerie's car was parked.

When he reached the end of the drive he paused for a moment looking back at the Pines. He looked out at the woods where he knew he had left two people to die. Maybe four if Valerie and Wayne were caught and convicted. They could very well be sentenced to death.

He would not be. He was getting out now. He might get caught and convicted of something but it wouldn't be murder. The thought of going to prison for anything was chilling to him. He knew what happened to cops in prison.

It wasn't the time to worry about that. Tonight it was enough to figure out how to get as far away from here as he could. To the left Highway Six took him into town. To Jack Blake's office. To his chief deputy's office. Lorca turned right.

Darcey watched Trent and the other man dig. Watched Valerie pointing her revolver in Betty's direction. But she noticed that Valerie wasn't actually looking at her mother. Her attention was on the digging. She thought there could be an opportunity. She would have to be careful. She didn't want to do anything that would get her mother or Trent hurt. Or worse.

It occurred to her that if she noticed where Valerie's attention was focused Trent would notice it, too. She decided to wait to see what he did. She drew her revolver from the ankle holster. She didn't cock it for fear Valerie would hear the noise. But she held it ready.

Trent had already uncovered a few bones. Some fingers. One long bone he thought might have been someone's tibia. He didn't mention them to Wayne. He just covered them with dirt again and dug in another place. He had purposely suggested that Wayne dig in a place he thought less likely to uncover bones. Not that Wayne was putting much energy into the job. He doubted that Wayne put much energy into anything.

Trent's shovel struck something solid again. He carefully brushed the dirt away with the edge of his shovel. He saw exactly what he had been looking for.

"Got something here," Trent called out.

Valerie wanted to run up and see what he had found. She didn't want to give Betty the chance to escape.

"What is it? Is it gold?" she asked excitedly.

"Here, Wayne, check it out. See what you think," he said as he tossed the object to the man.

Wayne dropped his shovel and caught the object without thinking. The skull in his hands looked up at him with empty eye sockets. It grinned at him with ghastly teeth.

With a loud cry he dropped the skull at his feet, wiping his hands on his shirt.

It was the moment Trent had been waiting for. Hoping that Betty would react quickly, he swung his shovel as hard as he could at the horrified man. The heavy steel blade struck him squarely in the face. His already injured nose spouted blood like water through a fire hose as he dropped to his knees. He wailed as he held his face in his hands. The blood poured through his fingers.

Trent turned to Valerie. He was disappointed. Betty had tried to turn and run. Valerie was quicker. She grabbed the older woman by the hair and jerked her back. Betty was thrown off balance. She fell backwards. Valerie kept her hand wrapped in Betty's hair. She pulled Betty to her knees.

"You'll pay for this, Marshall," she hissed at Trent. "You'll pay dearly."

"Help me, Valerie," Wayne whimpered. "I'm dying."

"Shut up, wimp," she replied. "You're not dying but if you keep whining I might kill you myself."

She motioned with her revolver for Trent to come down from the mound and stand in front of her. He calmly did as she directed.

"I have such a hard decision to make," Valerie said dramatically. "Do I kill you first or the old lady here?"

Trent remained silent.

"I need you to keep digging," she continued with her soliloquy. "But Wayne can dig. He can't do much else but he can dig. So you're not completely indispensable."

She pressed the barrel of her high powered gun against Betty's head.

"I can kill the old lady first. Might be fun to make you watch her die knowing you caused her death."

She paused. Considering her options.

"Of course, she's a better bargaining chip than you if I have to negotiate my way out of here. No, I think it has to be you first. You're just going to cause more trouble if I let you live. You first then."

She aimed the revolver at his chest.

"How does it feel to know you're going to die, Trent Marshall?" she goaded him. "How does it feel to know that you have only seconds to live? That the last sight you see on this earth is the woman holding the gun that's going to kill you."

"Everybody dies, Valerie," Trent replied.

"You first," she said.

Trent heard the voice behind him.

"Eat dirt, Trent."

Trent dropped to the ground. Face down.

Valerie was caught utterly by surprise. The sight of Darcey standing behind Trent with her own revolver raised put Valerie off guard. For only a few seconds.

It was enough.

Darcey fired her revolver twice. She struck her target twice. Her first shot hit Valerie high in the shoulder breaking her clavicle. Darcey's second shot hit Valerie in the left thigh. It broke no bones but blood immediately gushed out of the hole.

Her arm useless, Valerie dropped her weapon when she was hit the first time. She fell to the ground with the second shot.

Trent quickly leaped to his feet to grab the .50 caliber revolver.

"Get down here, Wayne," Trent ordered harshly. "Come join your lovely wife."

The whimpering man climbed down from the mound. As he passed by Trent took the Taser from its holster.

"Betty, get up and come here," Trent. "Get away from them."

Betty stood on wobbly legs. She gave Valerie and Wayne plenty of room as she walked away from them.

Betty ran to throw her arms around Darcey. The daughter hugged her mother, one hand still holding the gun that had brought Valerie down.

"Are you OK, Mom?"

"I'm hungry and thirsty and mad but, yes, I'm OK," Betty said.

She walked back to where Valerie lay on the ground. She kicked her. Valerie screamed with pain.

"You nasty old woman, you'd kick a person who's down!" Valerie screeched.

"After what you put me through, you got that right," Betty said. She turned to Trent and Darcey, smiling. "Now I feel better."

Jack Blake's phone rang. He didn't recognize the number. He answered anyway. He felt relief wash over him when he heard Trent's voice.

"Are y'all ok? Where are you? What's going on?" The questions tumbled out of the sheriff's mouth.

"We're ok. We're in the woods on the far side of the pasture at the Pines. We have a couple of injured people so we need two ambulances."

"Who's hurt?" the sheriff asked, on the verge of panic.

"The bad guys, Jack," Trent said. "The good guys are all OK."

"Thank God," Jack said with obvious relief.

"Do you know where that old wagon road goes into the trees out here?" Trent asked.

"Yeah, I know it. Where's Matt?"

"He said he was going to meet you at your office. But my bet is he's getting as far from here as he can."

"Yeah, you're probably right. OK, we're on the way."

The sheriff arrived first followed by three of his deputies in separate vehicles. He left one of the deputies at the house. The others he stationed where the wagon road entered the trees. He drove his own SUV down the trail until his headlights revealed a dramatic sight.

Wayne Erickson was sitting on the ground. His bloody hands pressed to his face. Rocking back and forth. Moaning.

Valerie Martin Erickson laid on her back. Darcey had used pressure to slow the bleeding from the wound in Valerie's leg. They both needed medical care.

Trent was leaning against a tree holding a heavy duty flashlight in one hand and a large caliber revolver in the other.

Betty sat on the ground near Trent holding a smaller caliber revolver uncomfortably in both hands.

It was a quite a sight.

Jack used his key to unlock the cuffs on Trent's hands.

By the time Trent finished briefing the sheriff on the night's activities the ambulances had arrived. Blake personally advised Wayne and Valerie they were under arrest and read them their rights. His deputies guarded them while the EMT teams tended their wounds. They were loaded into separate ambulances. Each was cuffed to a gurney.

"So, Darcey, you used your grandfather's 'eat dirt' trick on Valerie," Jack laughed. "I've heard that old story all my life. Never thought I'd see it done. I'd give a lot to have seen the look on that woman's face when Trent dropped to the ground and she saw you standing behind him."

"My face was in the dirt, Jack, but it must have been a sight to see," Trent, a look of delight on his face.

Trent, Darcey and Betty rode in Jack's SUV to the barn. Trent didn't think they would find Valerie's car there. He was right.

In his anger the sheriff kicked the side of Lorca's truck. It would be hard to prove that the resulting dent in the door matched the size of Blake's boot.

"Ungrateful is what I call it," Blake said. "I gave him the only chance he ever had in this parish. He could have been sheriff when I step down."

"Matt was impatient, Jack. He thought you were living too long."

"The way he's headed I'll outlive him for sure."

Betty and Darcey were walking up to the house. They could have waited to ride with the sheriff but they were both anxious to shower and find something to eat. Trent waited to ride with Jack.

The sheriff called his Criminal Investigation Unit to go over the truck. He didn't think they would find much but he had to try. He directed two of his deputies to put up crime scene tape around the half dug out mound and to cover it with a tarp to protect whatever was buried there.

"I'll call LSU about the bones y'all dug up. Not sure who to talk to but they'll send archeologists or historians or somebody out to finish the dig y'all started," Jack said as they drove up to the house.

"By the way, Jack, what happened with your phone? Darcey and I both tried to reach you but got voice mail."

The sheriff mumbled something.

[235]

"What?" Trent asked. "I didn't hear you."

Jack didn't respond. He looked out the window. He looked back at Trent.

"I dropped in the toilet," he said, quietly.

Trent stared at him with dubiety. "You did what?"

"I dropped my phone in the toilet, OK?" Jack said, staring straight ahead. "Had to put it in a bag of rice for several hours to dry it out."

Trent roared with laughter. After the danger and drama of the night it was comic relief. Trent laughed so hard the muscles in his belly started to hurt.

"All right," Blake sputtered. "You've had your laugh. But, Trent, if you tell anyone about this...if I hear one word about it...if I hear one snicker when I walk down the hall so help me I'll find something to charge you with and I'll keep you locked up until you're so demented you can't remember why you're there."

Trent wiped his eyes with his sleeve. "OK, Jack. Don't worry. I wouldn't want you to lose the next election because of your toilet." He started laughing again.

Jack stopped the SUV. He crossed his arms over the steering wheel. The look of disgust on his face was directed out the windshield.

"I'm not kidding, Trent. Get it out of your system now. Because I don't ever want to hear about this again."

Trent got his laughter under control.

"All right, Jack. Your secret is safe with me."

"I appreciate that." He turned to look at Trent. "And just so you know, when I got it dried out and heard the messages y'all left I was scared. It's not a feeling I'm used to. I kept thinking my clumsiness might have got y'all killed. I couldn't live with that."

WEDNESDAY, MAY 13TH

Daylight was peaking over the horizon when they finally got to bed. Trent slept past noon. He awoke to the smell of frying bacon and coffee. He leaped out of bed. It took only minutes to shower, shave and get dressed. He came bounding down the stairs to find Darcey and her mother busy in the kitchen.

Darcey handed him a cup of steaming coffee as he walked into the kitchen.

"One teaspoonful of sugar, right?" she smiled.

"Perfect," he said, leaning to give her a kiss. Not a peck on the cheek. A real kiss. Darcey was pleasantly surprised. Her mother pretended she hadn't seen it. "Smells mighty good in here, Betty."

"I was hungry last night but too tired to eat more than a bite. We're going to make up for it today," she promised. "Starting with bacon and eggs and fried potatoes and biscuits."

"You're a remarkable woman, Betty," Trent said as he sat at the table, sipping his coffee. "There's not many women who could go through what you've been through in the last couple of days and carry on like nothing ever happened."

"I come from strong stock, Trent," she explained. "The Belmonts have always been tough. You know that machete I keep around? My snake killer?"

"Yeah, and old Wayne was lucky you didn't have that thing with you. You nearly killed him with a couple of bed springs," Trent laughed.

"Let me tell you where that machete came from. My grandfather Belmont owned a saw mill at one time. One day something went wrong. One of those big blades got overheated or something. It came flying off the frame and stuck in the wall just a few inches from Grandpa Belmont's head. Everyone in the mill ducked for cover. But not Grandpa. He never flinched. He just started giving orders. He shut the mill down and got his men to work replacing the broken saw. They were so impressed with how cool he was they had the machete made for him from the steel of that busted blade."

"Yeah, Wayne was lucky. Where'd you get the idea for the bed springs?"

Betty laughed. "Saw something like it in an old Dick Powell tough guy movie."

"Darcey, remind me never to get your mother mad at me," Trent said.

Jack Blake called in mid-afternoon. Wayne and Valerie, he said, were under guard in the hospital. Wayne was still whining. Valerie was growling at everyone who came near her. Both would recover from their injuries.

"Have they done any talking?" Trent asked.

"Wayne is way beyond talking," Jack laughed. "He's singing like a canary now that he's separated from Valerie and under guard. I think he feels safe for the first time since he married her."

Trent chuckled. "How about Valerie? She told us that she killed Professor Richards. But that might be inadmissible in court as hearsay."

"Maybe," Jack said. "But Wayne was an eyewitness. He told us all about it. By the way, we got the tests back on Johnny Blair's knife. Traces of your DNA and his mother's. That's all. We found a blood-stained knife out at Matt's camp. Chances are good it'll have Professor Richards' DNA and Valerie's fingerprints. Meanwhile Valerie says she won't say a word without the three of you present."

"Us? Why would she want us there? That's weird."

"I couldn't tell you," Jack said, honestly. "And weird isn't the word for that woman. She's pure meanness."

"Yeah, I won't argue with you there," Trent agreed. "OK then. We'll head into town."

"Thanks. Meet me in the hospital lobby."

"In the lobby? What's the matter, Jack?" Trent teased the sheriff. "You afraid to be in the room alone with her?"

Jack laughed, taking the teasing in good nature. "Nobody with good sense would want to be alone with that woman."

The deputy guarding Valerie's room opened the door. Valerie lay in the hospital bed with her eyes closed. Her shoulder was bandaged. Her arm immobilized in a sling. Her good arm was cuffed to the rail of the hospital bed. She opened her eyes when she heard them come in.

Blake reminded her that she was entitled to have an attorney present.

"I don't think it matters. I'm sure my loving husband has told you all about my many sins," she laughed.

She looked at Betty and Darcey. "So the mighty Belmonts have come to call," she said, her voice dripping with sarcasm. "Are we having a veillee? Isn't that what we call it down here? When all the quality folk get together."

"It's an occasion when friends get together," Trent said. "The word doesn't apply today."

"Maybe we should call it a family reunion then," Valerie said, with a wicked smile. "Three cousins in the same room for the first time."

Betty and Darcey looked at each other.

"I'm afraid we don't know what you're talking about," Darcey said.

"Really, dear cousin? You didn't know that we're all family?"

"You'd better explain what you're talking about, Mrs. Erickson," the sheriff intervened. "I have questions of my own for you and I don't intend to stand around here playing word games."

"Of course, Sheriff," Valerie said. "Back in the days when the Belmonts were first sitting on all that stolen government gold there was another branch of the family tree taking root out in Colorado. But while the Louisiana Belmonts prospered the Colorado Belmonts never had anything. We got not a single crumb from our wealthy southern cousins. This fine family down here never even acknowledged our existence."

"I don't know what you're talking about," Betty said. "I never knew I had family in Colorado."

"Of course you didn't, Cousin Betty," Valerie said. "The family has always been proud of the Belmont brothers who wore Confederate gray. Richard and Henry. Pride of the family. But there was another Belmont who was brother to Richard and Henry."

"Benjamin," Betty said, suddenly realizing to whom Valerie was referring. "The youngest brother. He left home while he was still very young. None of the family here ever heard from him again. I think I recall hearing that his parents tried to find him but weren't successful."

"Probably because they didn't look in the right jails," Valerie said, laughing. "Oh, we have our family stories, too. Benjamin didn't much like to work. He drifted around. Gambling. Stealing when he could get away with it. They say he killed two men. One in Arizona. Another in New Mexico. He wound up in Colorado. His only accomplishment there was getting a girl pregnant.

"He knew what his family down here was up to though. He knew about the gold. That happened before he ran off. His daddy tried to keep it secret from him but he figured it out. He didn't know what happened to it but figured his family kept it. According to our family stories he always said he was going back to the Pines to get his share. Unfortunately he died before he got around to it. Some disagreement over a card game as it was told to me. He never even saw his son.

"I grew up hearing about how we were cheated out of our rightful share of stolen gold. My father came down here years ago to see what he could find out. His last name was Martin so you guys didn't know you were related. He even got a job working at the Pines for a while. He poked around the place whenever he had the chance but couldn't find any clues. Then your husband fired him, Cousin Betty. So he came home empty handed."

"I remember him," Betty said. "He was prickly. Took offense at anything we said to him. Not much of a worker. You're right. My husband did fire him. He caught him sneaking around at night. We didn't know then what he was looking for but my husband kicked him off the farm."

"Yeah, he wasn't too bright. I decided to be smarter about it. I spent years doing research. I even moved to San Francisco for a while. I know where you live, Cousin Darcey. I followed you many times. I even got to be friends with one of your employees. I won't mention which one. I'm sure you'll understand.

"By the way, Trent, you'll be interested to know that she lives a remarkably boring life in San Francisco. She works long days. Has hardly any social life that I could see. Her best friends are a woman from Boston who is a lawyer and her executive assistant who is gay. As far as I know she could even be a virgin," Valerie laughed.

Darcey blushed. She couldn't look at Trent.

"After Wayne, my poor, incompetent husband who excels only in his remarkable lack of common sense, failed to frighten your mother, Darcey, into revealing any family secrets, I found out through my friend in your company that you were going to New Orleans. I even knew you would be staying at the Monteleone. It was no coincidence that I was on the levee the night that nutcase tried to knife you, Trent. I warned you because I needed you both alive. You two were my best hope of getting my hands on that gold."

"Wayne did frighten me," Betty said, "but I couldn't have revealed any information about the gold. I don't know where it is."

Valerie laughed. "You're either lying or your family spent it all years ago," she snarled.

"Did you fire two shots at Trent and Darcey?" Blake asked.

"No. Why would I do that? I already told you I wanted them alive. They were no good to me dead."

"Do you have anything else to say?" the sheriff asked. "Are you ready to sign a statement admitting to the murder of Ellen Richards?"

"I surely am not," Valerie said. "Do you take me for such a fool?"

"It doesn't really matter," the sheriff told her. "I have enough evidence to get a first degree murder conviction."

"And I suppose my dear husband will be saving his own worthless self by putting me on death row."

"That's about the size of it," the sheriff said. "You might not like it but it seems fair to Ellen Richards."

Darcey turned back as the group left the hospital room.

"Why did you kill Ellen Richards?"

Valerie laughed. "Why not? She told us all she knew. We didn't need her."

Darcey joined the group as they walked the short distance to the sheriff's office.

"That is one cold blooded woman," Jack said. "When her time comes she'll spit in the eye of whoever puts the needle in her arm."

"Jack, how about touching base with your contacts in Colorado again," Trent requested. "We should find out if she has any family left out there."

"Yeah, good idea," Blake agreed. He typed a quick e-mail and sent it off to Colorado. "Now we have to find Matt Lorca. I'm not going to let him get away."

"Any idea where he might be?"

Blake handed Trent a slip of paper with a phone number and the name Erin Walker written on it.

"His truck was clean. This is the only thing we found. It had fallen down beside the driver's seat. Looks like it'd been there for a while."

"Erin Walker. Do you know her?" Trent asked.

"Yeah. She's a nice person. Had a tough break. Her husband was killed in Afghanistan a few years ago. She works as a cook at one of the catfish places out by the lake. She has a young son so she works days. She should be home by now. I have her address. Want to go with me to talk to her?"

"Wouldn't miss it for the world," Trent said, "if you can give me a ride to the Pines."

Blake stopped the big SUV in the driveway of an older house on the east side of town. It was a brick house with a screened porch on the front. Trent guessed it was built in the first half of the last century. Darcey could tell him what year if she was here. Maybe even what month. The house was well maintained. Grass freshly mowed. Not a mansion but a respectable home.

Erin Walker answered the door after the first ring. She was expecting them. Her brown hair was cut short. Easier for a single working mother that way. She was a pretty woman. Trent thought she was in her early thirties. She looked weary. That made her look older than she was. Weariness and grief.

She invited them in. It was as neat and tidy inside as out. There were a few child's toys arranged against the wall near the television, well out of the way. She was a woman who took pride in her home.

The sheriff introduced Trent. She invited them to sit down and asked if she could get them coffee or a coke. They both declined the offer.

"Thank you for seeing us, Mrs. Walker," Blake said. "I apologize for invading your privacy. I'll do my best to see you're not involved publicly. But anything you can tell us about Matt Lorca could be very helpful."

"Thank you for your thoughtfulness, Sheriff. Is he in trouble?"

"Yes," Blake said firmly. "I'm sorry to say he's in the worst kind of trouble. It's my job to bring him in for trial. I don't like it. But it's my job."

She looked out the kitchen window to watch her son playing on a swing set in the back yard. He looked to be six or seven years old. "This is a small town. You know how small towns talk. Timmy was only a baby when Bryce was killed in Afghanistan. I thought this was the best place for us. Bryce and I both grew up in this area. Both sets of grandparents are here."

"We found your name and phone number in Matt's truck, Mrs. Walker. Did you have a relationship with him?"

"I wouldn't call it a relationship, Sheriff," she replied. "Some mutual friends introduced us at a barbeque. I hadn't dated anyone since Bryce's death. I guess I was starting to feel lonely. Matt can be very charming. And he was your chief deputy. I thought he would be safe. A good companion. I wasn't looking to fall in love or anything like that. Just someone to go to a movie or dinner with. It didn't last long. Matt turned out to be less than he seemed."

"How so? Was he abusive, Mrs. Walker?" the sheriff asked.

"No, not really abusive. Just, well, strange."

"Strange in what way? Can you give us an example?"

"Well, one night I made us dinner at his house. After we ate he turned on TV and started watching a basketball game. I cleaned up the kitchen and put the leftovers in the refrigerator. But I'm not really much of a basketball fan. I asked him if he would take me home.

"He looked puzzled. Then he gave me that big grin and said sure, he'd take me home. He told me to go to the garage and get in the truck. He'd be right there he said. But he never came. I waited for a while then I went back in the house. I thought maybe he had a phone call or something. But he was just sitting there watching the game. He told me to go back to the garage. I did but I called my dad and asked him to come get me. He was there in about ten minutes. I went out the garage door and left."

"Did you see Matt again after that," the sheriff asked.

"No. He called a couple of times but I didn't answer. He came to the restaurant but I wouldn't come out of the kitchen. And my boss wouldn't let him go back there. I guess Matt decided he didn't want to make a scene with him being your chief deputy and all. I never heard from him after that."

"Did he ever mention any names to you? Friends? Relatives?"

"No, he didn't talk much about himself. I think he has some cousins somewhere south of here. I did hear he has a girlfriend who lives in the next parish. I think her name is Rhonda something. She has an unusual last name. Two words. Like some kind of European royalty."

"Was it Van Fleet perhaps?" Blake asked. "Rhonda Van Fleet?"

"Yes, I think that's it. But I don't know where she lives."

"That's OK. I can find her."

"Rhonda Van Fleet. That's quite a name," Trent said as Jack drove toward the Pines.

"Her real name is Rhonda Korman," Blake said. "Guess she didn't think that was fancy enough."

"You know her?

"Oh yes, I know her" Jack laughed. "And I know where Matt met her."

"Well? Where?"

"In my jail," Blake said. "She's been an occasional guest. Never anything big enough to get her hard time. Hot checks. Smoking a little dope. Never enough to charge her with dealing. Prostitution a couple times. All those little things where judges tend to send 'em home with a stern warning or give 'em probation."

"Why would Matt get involved with a woman like that?"

"Well, with all her faults Rhonda's several steps over Valerie Erickson."

"You have a point there," Trent agreed. "I guess I didn't know Matt as well as I thought I did."

"You didn't? Huh!" the sheriff said morosely. "The man was my chief deputy for twelve years. I fully intended to see that he was elected to succeed me when I retire. He had me fooled. I'm starting to doubt my judge of character."

"Don't go there, Jack," Trent encouraged. "There's nothing wrong with your judgment. The man who helped me get through a hard time wasn't all bad. I don't think he meant to fool anyone in the beginning. When he became chief deputy he thought the leading citizens in the parish would finally accept him as an equal. But they didn't. He was still just a poor Spanish kid as far as they were concerned. At least that's the way he saw it. As the years dragged on I think it just ate at him. A thing like that can change people."

Jack dropped Trent at the Pines but didn't get out himself. Jennifer was expecting him for dinner. They agreed to see if they could find Rhonda Van Fleet the next morning.

Trent started to walk up to the porch. Before Jack could wheel around and head back to the highway Trent turned back to him. "Hey, Jack, do you have one of those portable bubble gum lights?"

"Yeah. It's pretty slick. Plug it into the cigarette lighter. Sits on the dash. Even has a siren that goes with it."

"Why don't you bring that tomorrow morning and let's take my car."

"I guess I could," the sheriff said. "But why?"

"Because the engineers who built Trent's car say it'll do two hundred miles an hour," Darcey answered, "but so far it's only been tested out at one eighty nine." She had come out onto the porch carrying two rum and cokes.

Jack laughed. "Well, I have to admit if we get into a chase Trent's car would do better than this big old rig. I'll bring the portable. See you in the morning." He waved as he drove down the drive.

"It's going to be a warm evening," she said. "I thought this might be more refreshing than bourbon."

Trent accepted the drink gratefully. They sat on the porch watching the horses as the light began to fade. Betty came out to join them.

"Betty, for a teetotaler you sure are developing a well-stocked bar," Trent grinned.

"Trent, hanging out with you makes me need one," she responded.

THURSDAY, MAY 14TH

It took Jack a couple of hours to find the judge and get a warrant for the arrest of Matt Lorca. He would need that since he would be out of his jurisdiction. Maybe out of his state. He got a search warrant for Rhonda Korman, aka Rhonda Van Fleet. It was almost eleven o'clock by the time he got to the Pines.

They got the portable light and siren set up in the CTS-V. Trent retrieved his back up hand gun from the trunk. A Walther PPK. The small semiautomatic's magazine held six .380 rounds. Trent had two extra magazines.

"Are you kidding me?" the sheriff laughed. "A Walther PPK? You going through a James Bond stage?"

"I crave a martini every time I shoot it," Trent said. "But it's a fine weapon. Small enough to be easily concealed. It won't bring down an elephant but it'll sure put the hurt on a bad guy. It's enough."

"Huh. I'll show you what's enough," Jack said as he pulled a rifle from his SUV that looked like something the Navy Seals would use. It was something the Navy Seals would use. "An M4A1 assault rifle. Air cooled. Gas operated. Fires a 5.56 millimeter cartridge with a 30 round magazine. 14 and a half inch barrel. And it has an adapter that converts it to a grenade launcher."

"Where did you get that?" Trent asked, not believing what he was seeing.

"Homeland security grant."

"You really have a grenade launcher?"

"Uh, no. They wouldn't let me have that," Jack grinned, sheepishly. Trent laughed.

"Did you get those for all your guys?"

"Nope. Just for the sheriff," Jack said. "And I have two extra magazines. You have 18 rounds. I got 90. Let's go huntin'."

Trent steered the powerful black sedan down the drive toward the highway.

"We're only going after one man, Jack."

"You never know."

Jack had called Clint Wells, sheriff of neighboring Natchitoches Parish, to ask his assistance in serving the warrant on Rhonda. Wells told him to call when they got to Natchitoches and he would meet them at her house.

Sure to his word, Wells was leaning against his car when they got there. Rhonda's house was the opposite in appearance from Erin Walker's. Where the Walker yard was neat and well-tended, Rhonda's front yard was a mess. Overgrown with weeds. Grass growing through empty beer cans in a lawn that hadn't been mowed in a year or more. A large trash can overflowing with garbage sat at the corner of the house. A dull gray sedan sat in the driveway.

Sheriff Wells pushed the doorbell. There was no ring to it. He knocked on the door. They heard movement inside but no answer. He knocked again.

"Go away." The voice was female. Not clear. Not friendly.

"It's Sheriff Wells, Rhonda. Open up. We need to talk to you. We have a warrant. Don't make us serve it."

The door opened a crack. Just enough for them to see part of a face.

"Wha d'ya want? I ain't done nothin'."

"I didn't say you did, Rhonda," Sheriff Wells said. "These gentlemen just need to talk to you. You might be able to help them."

"More cops? I ain't helping no cops."

"I might remember it favorably some day when you need a friend," Wells said.

There was a pause. The door opened. There was no telling what the original color of the woman's hair was. It was a yellowish-platinum now. The bruise under her eye was a reddish-purple. Her swollen lip was just red. Her nose was at a strange angle. Broken.

"Looks like you could use a friend now, Rhonda."

"Yeah, I know," she mumbled. "I'm pretty, ain't I? Y'all might as well come on in."

The inside looked like the outside. Empty beer cans littered the floor in the small living room and the kitchen counter. Dirty dishes were stacked in the sink. A pizza box still holding one shriveled slice sat on the small dining table.

"Who did this to you, Rhonda?" Sheriff Wells asked.

"Ask him," she said nodding her head toward Jack Blake. "He ought to know."

"Was it Matt Lorca, Rhonda?" Blake asked.

"Yeah, Mr. high and mighty Matt Lorca. Your chief deputy."

"Tell us what happened, Rhonda," Wells said.

"He showed up here in the middle of the night. Got everything he wanted. First I heated up a can of chili for him. Then he had a little piece of me. After that he went to sleep. Told me to wake him up in two hours. When he got up he said he was taking all the cash I had and my car. I told him he couldn't have my car. My mustang. The only thing I ever had worth anything. That's when he went to work on me. Said he had to change my mind. He did."

"I figured that was Valerie's rental car in the driveway," Trent said.

"Any idea where he might be headed, Rhonda?" Jack asked.

"Yeah. His cousins have a camp down on the Atchafalaya River near Butte La Rose."

"Do you know how to get there?" Jack continued.

"He took me there a couple of times. It's on the road north of town. Can't tell you more than that."

"Thanks, Rhonda. You've been a lot of help," Sheriff Wells said.

"We have to take that car out there, Rhonda," Jack told her. "It's evidence."

"That's just great," she cried. "That's what I get for helping? What am I supposed to do now? No car. No money. Face all busted up. How am I supposed to get by?"

"First thing is we get you to a doctor," Wells said. "As for the rest of it, we'll just take it one step at a time."

"We'll get your car back for you, Rhonda," Trent promised.

Jack called his counterpart in St. Martin Parish. He was out of town and wouldn't be back for four days. He told Jack to serve his warrant. He said he'd let his chief deputy know what was going on. If Jack needed help, he said, the deputy would provide back up. Jack said he thought they could handle it. But they wouldn't hesitate to call if they got into trouble.

They drove the one hundred sixty five miles to Butte La Rose in an hour and thirty nine minutes. They could have made it in less time, Trent said, but he had to slow down when they passed through Opelousas and Lafayette. Not that between the two of them they couldn't have talked themselves out of a ticket. They just couldn't afford the time it would take to do it.

Jack looked at him like he was loony.

Butte La Rose is a very small town. The Butte part of its name came from its location on relatively high ground for a part of the country where the land is mostly low lying marsh. The La Rose, Trent had been told, resulted from the French Revolution. Several Royalists escaping the guillotine moved to the area. The rose was the symbol of their lost society.

Many of the houses in the village aren't permanent residences but camps. The owners come down for hunting and fishing. For late night poker games. For fish fries and beer and bourbon. It was one of those camps they had to find.

Trent pulled into the only gas station and grocery store in town. Trent started the pump to fill the car with gas. Jack went into the grocery store.

Blake was talking to the clerk when Trent came in. The clerk was saying that the fishing had been slow. It was a ritual. Jack was a stranger asking about the fishing. The clerk was a local who had his own favorite fishing holes. He wasn't about to share them with some guy who just wandered into town.

The clerk was wearing a Saints tee shirt.

"Who dat?" Trent said.

The Cajun clerk grinned. "Who dat gonna beat dem Saints? You with him?"

"Yeah. I keep trying to get away from him but he keeps tracking me down."

The clerk thought that was hilarious.

"You want a fountain coke?"

"Sure," Jack said.

"Your friend got a Dr. Pepper. What kind you want?"

"I'll have a Coca Cola."

The clerk filled a cup halfway with ice. He set it under the lever marked Coca Cola and filled the cup. Trent paid for both drinks. He told the clerk to keep the change. The clerk decided these two were all right. He resumed the fishing conversation with Jack.

"Well, if you go about a mile down past Bayou La Rose the river makes a gentle curve to the south. That's a good spot. Get on the inside of that curve up near the bank. There was some erosion and a big tree fell into the river. Made sort of a pool behind it. Fish like pools like that."

"Yeah, pools like that are good. Thanks, man. We'll look for it," Jack said.

"With the water temperature where it is now largemouth bass and spotted bass should both be biting."

"Oh man, that sounds good," Jack said, one fisherman to another. "Say, we have some friends who have a camp down here. Haven't seen 'em in a while. Thought we might try to look 'em up. You might know 'em. Their name is Lorca."

The clerk went cold. "Yeah, I know the Lorcas. You friends of theirs?"

Blake caught the instant change in attitude when he mentioned the Lorcas.

"Well, not really friends. I used to work with one of 'em. Didn't really know him well. I just remember he said his family had a camp somewhere around here."

"Yeah, they have a camp here."

"Know where it is?"

Trent stayed quiet, drinking his coke. Outside a pickup truck sitting high on oversized tires pulled up to the pump.

"Go about three miles north up the Atchafalaya River Highway. That's this road right out here," he made plain, pointing. "Keep your eyes on the river side. You're gonna pass some real nice places. Then you're gonna come to one that looks like a shack. Trashy. Neighbors don't much like how bad it looks. But nobody wants to talk to the Lorcas about it. They're not the friendliest folks around. The neighbors are scared of 'em."

"Thanks for the information, friend. Maybe I should just take a pass on trying to find 'em. It's not like we were really friends."

"That's what I'd do, me," the clerk said.

The silence outside was shattered by the sound of rubber squealing on concrete. All three men looked outside as the pickup truck with oversized tires suddenly accelerated. It turned left from Herman Dupuis Road onto the River Highway.

"There's one of 'em now. Don't know what got into whichever one it was to make him take off like that."

"Thanks, friend. Appreciate your help," Jack called over his shoulder as he and Trent made a run for the car.

The clerk stood in the doorway watching as the black Cadillac's wheels scattered gravel across the lot. He jumped, startled, when Jack turned on the flashing lights and hit the siren.

"Say, I don't think y'all are fishermen at all," he said. "You ain't even got a boat."

The black truck rapidly fading from sight looked like a toy atop the huge tires. A cross between a pickup truck and a swamp buggy.

"How do you even get into a thing like that? The tires are taller than me," Jack said as he tightened his seat belt.

Trent let the 640 horses under the hood run full out. The truck that had been moving quickly away from them seemed to now be driving in reverse. They were rapidly gaining on it.

"Don't tell me how fast we're going. I don't wanna know. Just get me in front of that truck," Jack shouted as he reached for the M4 lying in the backseat.

The black sedan caught up to the pickup like it was standing still. Trent was soon on the truck's tail. Close enough that he could see Matt's face in the rear view mirror. Matt looked staggered when Trent pulled up alongside the truck. Trent urged more power from the racing engine and easily passed the pickup.

The look on Matt's face turned to shock when Jack leaned out the window with the frightening weapon in his hands. The sheriff had switched the firing mechanism to full automatic. He fired a series of three round bursts, all of them aimed at the front of the truck's engine. Jack had been a lawman long enough to know that the fastest way to stop a vehicle was to ignore the tires and go for the engine. There were numerous hit points in the engine that would stop a vehicle quickly. Starting with the radiator.

Sure enough thick waves of smoke began breaking from the engine.

"Ha. Got him," Jack said smugly. "His engine's done for."

Trent didn't feel so smug.

They passed the shack that the clerk had described as the Lorca camp. Immediately past it the truck turned sharply to the right. Matt was steering directly into the woods alongside the road. The pickup bounced dangerously on its huge tires but stayed upright. Black smoke was now roiling over the vehicle's cab.

"How can he see where he's going with all that smoke?" Jack questioned.

"He doesn't have to see," Trent said as he slammed on the brakes. "He knows exactly where he's going."

They had been going so fast it took several hundred feet for Trent to bring the sedan to a stop. He made a U-turn and headed back to the spot where Matt had left the road, pulling onto the shoulder and killing the engine.

On foot Trent and Jack followed the clear trail the truck had made as it crashed through the brush and damp land beneath it. Jack held his powerful M4 in ready position. Trent drew his semiautomatic hand gun.

The truck hadn't made it far off the road. But far enough. They approached the pickup from both sides. Black smoke swirled around the cab. It was impossible to see inside.

"Matt, if you're in there come out with your hands empty and in plain sight," Jack ordered. "Do it now!"

There was no response. Trent eased around the passenger's side. The smoke cleared enough to let him see through the window.

"He's not in there, Jack," Trent said. "He's headed for the river. A boat."

It was easy to see where Matt had run through the brush. Trent followed the trail on a dead run. Jack ran behind him. Much slower.

"I'm getting too old for this," the sheriff muttered.

Trent broke out of the brush into a clearing no more than twenty yards behind Matt.

"Freeze, Matt," Trent called out. "Don't make this any worse than it is."

Matt turned back toward Trent. "How could it get any worse, buddy?" he shouted.

Trent barely heard the sound. "Pffffhht." He felt the bullet whiz by his ear. He hit the ground when he realized the white tube on the end of the rifle in Matt's hands was a sound suppressor. He shouted a warning to Jack just as Matt fired again. "Pffffhht." "Pffffhht." Trent again heard the small caliber bullets as they passed over his head. He heard a grunt from Jack. Trent fired off three rounds in response. But Matt was already running. He was too far away and moving too erratically for Trent's hand gun to have an impact.

Trent looked back to see Jack holding his left bicep.

"How bad are you hit?" Trent asked.

"Not bad," Jack said through gritted teeth. "Caught one in muscle. Don't think anything's broken. Go get him."

Jack was already taking off his belt to fashion a makeshift tourniquet. Trent went after Lorca.

By the time he got halfway across the clearing he heard the boat motor come to life. Matt was up to speed and nearing the middle of the river by the time Trent made it to the small dock. He held the Walther PPK in both hands and took his time. Aimed carefully. Fired twice. Both shots were ineffective. Matt was out of range.

Trent turned and looked across the clearing to the rickety house. The Lorca camp. A bright red Mustang sat in the driveway. Trent turned and trotted back to where Jack laid against a tree. He took a look at the sheriff's arm. Jack had already managed to slow the bleeding.

"I think you're going to live, Jack," Trent assured the older man. "But we better get you to a doctor. Can you walk back to the car?"

"Yeah, I can walk," the sheriff said, grumpy. "Small caliber. Hardly lost any blood. I never heard any shots. What's he got? A suppressor?"

"Looks like a homemade one."

"He's starting to really irritate me. Can't believe we let him get away again."

"The chase isn't over, Jack."

The doctor at the closest hospital confirmed the sheriff's self-diagnosis. It wasn't a serious wound. But it was a wound requiring minor surgery. When the bullet had been removed the young doctor informed the sheriff that he would be spending the night in the hospital.

"I don't think so," Jack said. "It's hardly more than a scratch. I've got work to do."

"So do I," the doctor said. "My job was to take a bullet…"

"A small bullet," the bad-tempered sheriff interrupted.

The doctor continued patiently. "…out of your arm. I did that. My job then was to sew up the hole it made. I did that. And now my job is to keep you here over night to make sure there are no complications. And, sir, I will do that also."

"Young man, do you know who I am?" Jack fumed.

"Yes. You're the man who's spending the night in my hospital." With that the doctor left the room.

Jack looked at Trent. "Well, couldn't you at least say something?" he sputtered.

Trent had been looking at the bullet the doctor had removed from Jack's arm.

"The doctor's right, Jack. You need to take it easy tonight. .22 long rifle. Hang on to it," he added, passing the small piece of lead to the sheriff. "I think it'll match the one that killed your deputy at the Pines."

"Yeah, I do, too," the sheriff agreed. "Small caliber bullet to the brain at close range. Homemade sound suppressor. Matt sounds more like a professional hit man than a cop."

"I guess you learn a few things if you hang around jails long enough," Trent observed.

"What are you going to be doing while I'm taking it easy?"

"I'm going to get Matt Lorca."

Jack's face turned so red Trent considered calling the doctor back. "I can't believe you'd do that without me!"

"Sorry, Jack. But what's more important? Catching Matt or you being there when he's caught?"

Jack stared at Trent. He didn't like it.

"Yeah, we got to get him," he said finally. "How you gonna do it?"

"I'm going to the Lorca camp. He'll come back tonight."

"Why would he come back?" the sheriff questioned.

"He had to leave in a hurry with nothing but the clothes he was wearing and the small caliber rifle he had in the truck. I think he'll come back for clothes. Maybe food. Maybe money. And for my Model 1911, which, by the way, you should be glad he didn't have on him. A .45 would have made a much bigger hole in you."

"Maybe I should get some deputies out there with you."

"No, Jack, that won't work. Matt's no moron. He's been a lawman for a long time. He'll be on the lookout for cops. My car's black. Easy to hide at night. I'll just find a good place to hunker down and wait to see what happens."

"What about back up?" the sheriff asked.

"We can work it like we did before. When you get a call from me on your new phone," Trent said, "send the troops in fast. If I call but don't say anything send in more troops faster."

Trent stayed in the shadows as he slinked back to the Lorca camp. It was full dark. Close to nine o'clock. He thought Matt would wait until late to return. He would wait until there was no traffic. Until people at their camps were in bed or at least settled in for the night. That's when he would come back.

He stopped and dropped to a knee when he came within sight of the Lorca camp. There were no lights on. There was no boat tied up at the dock. The red Mustang was still there. It was quiet. He stayed still for another five minutes. Watching.

Satisfied that no one was around he moved slowly into the woods. He found what he was looking for at the edge of the trees closest to the river. A large hackberry tree surrounded by a growth of dwarf palmettos. His black shirt would be hard to make out at night. The palmettos would obscure Matt's vision. He lowered himself to the ground, trying to burrow into the moist dirt as much as he could.

The damp ground made Trent's position uncomfortable. It also kept him awake. He was tired. He could easily fall asleep. But not with the moisture seeping into his clothes. Sleeping in wet clothes wasn't going to happen. He was miserable. But awake.

It was after eleven o'clock when he heard the motor. It was somewhere out on the river. It could be someone doing some night fishing or maybe a neighbor coming home. He expected to hear the sound pass on by. It didn't. The motor was killed. The river was silent.

He didn't move. Not so much as a twitch. He was barely breathing.

At first there was nothing. Then he heard the sound he was expecting. The quiet electric motor. The trolling motor. Barely audible. He could just make out the ghostly image of the boat out in the river. It glided slowly by the Lorca dock and out of sight. It could have been someone doing a little night fishing after all.

The sound receded. Then became louder again as the boat passed the dock once more. The pattern repeated for half an hour. Trent's muscles were beginning to cramp from staying still for so long.

Trent saw the boat emerge into sight as Matt used the near silent trolling motor to guide it to the landing. He quickly, quietly, tied the boat to the dock. He stepped onto the wooden planking, the rifle with the white suppressor in his hands. Trent had no doubt there was a shell in the chamber.

Once on the dock Matt was every bit as cautious approaching the house as Trent had been. Followed the same procedure. He knelt in the shadows of the small landing for a full five minutes. He knew there would be no light. He was looking for movement. For anything that might give away the presence of someone waiting for him. Matt was an experienced cop. Trent knew he would wonder why there were no cops there. But he needed something from the house. He might need the Mustang.

Finally satisfied that he was alone, Matt rose and began walking toward the house. He held the light rifle with the homemade suppressor in ready position. The rifle had the advantage of silence. It was good for close range assassination. But it fired a very small bullet. In a shootout at close range Trent had the advantage in firepower.

The rifle, Trent guessed, probably held ten rounds in its magazine. The Walther held six. Advantage Matt. But maybe not. They had each fired three rounds earlier in the day. Trent had reloaded. He had a full magazine. He didn't know if Matt had any spare cartridges with him. If he hadn't reloaded he would be left with seven rounds. Close to even.

Trent watched, barely breathing, as Matt walked slowly, quietly across the clearing. He followed with the barrel of the Walther as well as with his eyes.

It was a contest in patience. Matt moved slowly. Carefully.

Trent waited for him to get halfway between the boat and car. He wanted to be able to cut him off if he bolted in either direction.

Just a few more feet. A few more. There! Trent's prey was in the exact position the hunter wanted.

"Stand where you are, Matt. Drop the rifle," Trent called out.

Matt stopped dead still.

"Should have known it would be you, buddy," he said. Trent knew Matt was smiling. He saw nothing to smile about. "Anybody with you?"

"Drop the rifle, Matt," Trent said again.

"Don't think I can do that, buddy," Matt said. He quickly turned and fired two rounds in the direction of Trent's voice. Firing blindly as he ran for the same trees that were concealing Trent.

Trent fired three rounds at the running man. Matt moaned as he fell into the brush.

Trent couldn't see Matt. He couldn't be more than thirty feet away. Moving as quietly as he could, he turned slightly to face the spot where he thought Matt would be. He heard no movement from that direction. He reached for his phone. Holding it tight to his ear he hit the speed dial that would ring Jack Blake. When Jack answered Trent said nothing. He laid the phone on the ground. Jack would hear everything. He would say nothing.

"You hit, buddy?" Matt called out.

"No. You?"

"Yeah, you got me good, buddy," Matt said. "In the side. I'm bleeding something awful. You call for back up?" Trent could hear the pain in Matt's voice.

"Yeah."

"Can't let'em take me, buddy," the chief deputy said.

"Why not, Matt?" Trent pleaded. "This is all crazy, man. You're gonna wind up dead."

"Prison would be the same thing for me," Matt laughed. "You know what they do to cops in prison. I'd rather get it over with fast. I'm truly sorry about all this, Trent. I just wanted respect."

"That's bull, Matt," Trent said.

"What would you know about it?" was the angry response.

"I know today you shot the man who was going to make you sheriff when he retired. You assassinated a colleague who respected you. And you were willing to let Darcey, Betty, and me die. You're ready to kill me tonight. That's all I need to know. You're just a cop gone bad, Matt. That all there is to it."

In the distance they could hear sirens.

"Got to get this over before those boys get here," Matt said, sounding weak,

"Don't do this, Matt," Trent pleaded. "Don't make me kill you."

"It's not your decision, buddy," Matt said. "I have to get back to the river, which means I have to kill you. If you want to stop me, you have to kill me. I'm not going to prison. It's either you or me now."

Trent saw Matt rise from the brush he had been using for cover. He stepped into the open and immediately began running toward Trent, firing the rifle as he ran. Trent held the Walther in both hands. The sights were steady in the middle of the running man's chest.

Matt fired five times. Trent fired twice. He heard all five of Matt's shots zing through the palmettos over his head. He heard the thud of his bullets striking solid flesh. He watched Matt fall to his knees, the rifle dropping from his hands.

Matt looked down. He saw the blood spurting from two new holes in his chest. More blood flowed from the earlier round he'd taken lower on his right side. He looked up. Stared directly into Trent's eyes. He grinned as he toppled over. Trent shivered at the horrifying sight.

The first vehicle from the St. Martin Sheriff's Department slid to a stop behind the Mustang just as Matt begin firing. Two deputies climbed out. Weapons drawn they crouched behind the open doors.

"Are you all right, Mr. Marshall?" one of the deputies asked.

"I'm good, deputy," Trent responded.

A second car with lights flashing rolled to a stop. Trent was surprised to see Jack Blake get out. His arm was immobilized in a sling but other than that he looked fine.

The deputies cautiously moved closer to the man lying, bleeding, on the ground. Jack followed them.

One of the deputies knelt down by the dying man. He tossed the rifle aside. Jack stood behind him, looking down at the man who had once been his chief deputy. Trent raised himself up from the wet ground. He approached the man who lay bleeding. He knelt by Matt's side.

"We heard the whole thing on my phone, Trent," Jack said.

"He didn't give you any choice," one of the deputies said. "It was like he wanted to die. Suicide by cop, we call it."

"No, not by cop," Matt said, his voice weak. Barely audible. "By friend. Thanks, Buddy."

Matt smiled. Trent watched as the light went out of his eyes.

Jack realized what Matt had done to Trent. It was like that night ten years ago out on the lake. Trent had just taken another blow to the soul. Jack looked down at the man who had been his chief deputy. He was disgusted.

"You're worthless trash, Lorca," he said to the dead man. "And I hope you can hear me on your way to hell."

FRIDAY, MAY 15TH

Jack and Trent checked into a motel for a few hours of sleep. Trent's clothes were wet and filthy. He showered, then cleaned them as best he could. He laid them out to dry while he slept.

Later in the day they drove to the St. Martin Parish Sheriff's Office. Given the circumstances they were told that they were free to go. If there was to be an inquest and if the district attorney wanted either of them to testify they would be notified.

Trent's Model 1911 semiautomatic, which had been found in the Lorca shack, was returned to him. They were also given permission to return Rhonda's Mustang to her.

Jack Drove the Mustang. He insisted that Trent stay behind him. He wasn't about to try to keep up with the black CTS-V. In fact, he had no intention of getting into any vehicle with Trent behind the wheel ever again.

They dropped the Mustang off at Rhonda's house. She expressed her gratitude. She tried to sound sultry when she said if there was ever anything she could do to return the favor all they had to do was knock on her door. Any time. Night or day. They left quickly. Jack even forgot his recently sworn oath to never again ride in a car that Trent was driving.

Trent was quiet on the drive from Natchitoches to Jack's house. Jack knew what was going through his mind.

"Trent, this wasn't your fault," Jack said as he opened the door. "Matt was determined to die before going to prison. In some sort of weird way I can understand that. He was a rat to make you be the one to take him out. But it didn't have anything to do with you. You just happened to be there with a gun."

"He could have waited a few minutes," Trent said. "He heard the sirens."

"Yeah, and that's what makes him a rat," Jack said. "You have nothing to feel sorry for, Trent. Nothing at all."

Trent looked at Jack. He nodded. Then looked away. Jack climbed out of the car and closed the door. He stood looking after the sleek black sedan as it drove away.

"How awful for you, Trent," Darcey said. "How completely unfair."

They were sitting on the porch. Darcey had a bottle of Merlot ready for his return. She had poured each of them a glass.

He had just told her everything that had happened since he saw her last. He spoke in a monotone. He didn't look at her. He stared into the darkness of the night.

Reaching for the bottle, she refilled their glasses. Setting the bottle aside, she put her arm around Trent's shoulders. She leaned down and kissed him.

Trent didn't respond to the kiss. He felt dead inside. Cold.

Darcey was surprised at his lack of response to her touch. Her kiss. But she knew she couldn't push him. He had to deal with this in his own way. She sat again in her chair, one leg curled beneath her.

"I'm so sorry, Trent. I know how terrible for you to have to go through this again. It's not your fault, you know. You did what you had to do. Matt forced you to do it."

"Maybe so. But I did it. I was the one who did it."

"This time isn't like before, Trent," Darcey said. "I'm here to support you. You won't be left alone this time."

"I wasn't left alone ten years ago, Darcey."

"But Ivy said your wife..."

"Ivy sees it the way she wants to see it. Kate is a good woman. She didn't desert me. I deserted her. I was dead broke. I'd been drunk for three months. She wanted to support me, too. But I told her to get away from me. I made her leave me alone. She begged me to let her stay and take care of me. I pushed her out the door and slammed it behind her.

"When I got my life straightened out I called her. She wouldn't take the call. I don't blame her. I made her hate me. I'll do the same to you, Darcey."

Darcey was quiet. She didn't know what to say.

"I'll be leaving in the morning," Trent said after a long silence.

She nodded, turning her head away slightly so he wouldn't see the tears.

MONDAY, MAY 18TH

Ivy sent Trent upstairs to shower and get into some fresh clothes. And, she told him, he should shave while he was up there.

He looked pathetic when she and Walter arrived in the late afternoon. Walter was out in the courtyard. Weeding. Cleaning. Taking care of the plants that were like his children.

Ivy was in the kitchen. She cooked down some okra to get the gumminess out of it. She added some chopped onion, minced garlic and chunks of ham.

She and Betty agreed they would not interfere in Trent and Darcey's lives. But that was before Trent showed up at the Coffee Pot for Sunday breakfast looking like he'd slept in a culvert. She called Betty.

Betty told her everything that had happened. The murder of Johnny Blair's mother by her son. His subsequent arrest. The kidnappings. The arrest of Valerie and Wayne Erickson. The death of Matt Lorca. Ivy knew what that meant. For the second time in his life Trent was staggering under the weight of guilt. Undeserved. Unearned. Unfair. Unbearable. Guilt.

She knew what he was doing. Why he looked so bad. Sure enough when she let herself into the house she found him asleep on the couch. An empty wine bottle lay on the floor beside him. There were three days' worth of empties in the overflowing kitchen trash. It was time to shake him up.

She was adding lima beans, corn and chopped tomatoes to the pot when Trent came in. He was freshly shaved, his hair washed and brushed, wearing a fresh tee shirt and jeans.

[261]

"Now that's the Trent I remember," Ivy said. "Come here and give me a hug."

Trent smiled as he hugged her, giving her a bonus kiss on the cheek.

"Smells good in here," he said. He poured himself a cup of coffee from the pot Ivy had made. Adding a little sugar, he sat on one of the stools at the kitchen island.

"Succotash," Ivy said. "Made southern style with okra and ham."

Ivy was adding seasonings as she talked. She tasted it. She was satisfied.

"Now, son, we need to have a talk," she said. "Tell me all about it."

"I don't want to talk about it."

"You got to talk about it, Trent," Ivy insisted. "Listen to me, son. I went through this with you ten years ago. You didn't do anything wrong then. You haven't done anything wrong now. You can't let yourself get eaten up with guilt. It'll destroy you."

"Maybe that's what I deserve."

"You hush your mouth," Ivy said, indignant. "You don't deserve no such thing."

"I was responsible for the deaths of two friends."

"I swear I don't know what I'm gonna do with you," she said. "You had something to do with a criminal going to jail. That's true. And you shot another criminal who was trying to kill you. That's true. Neither one of those events had anything to do with friendship. Neither of those men were your friends."

"I don't know, Ivy. I think it's something to do with me. I tried to be a good son. Both my mom and dad died young. I tried to be a good friend to Josh and to Matt. Looked what happened there. I think people would be better off staying away from me."

"I'm not gonna put up with that from you, Trent," Ivy said, firmly. "What you're doing now is plain, old feeling sorry for yourself.

"You were a good son. The best. Your momma and daddy loved you. Their dying had to do with their health. Nothing to do with you.

"You've got friends who would take a bullet for you. As a matter of fact, Jack Blake did take a bullet for you a few nights ago. Jordan would do the same.

"You've got Walter and me," she continued, her voice getting a little softer. "We never had any children. But we've got you.

"And no matter whether you want to see it or not you got that young woman waiting up there at her momma's house who's just flat out crazy about you. If you had any sense at all, you'd know that you feel the same about her.

"It's time to let go all that bad stuff, Trent. You're feeling sorry for yourself. And if you don't stop it I'm gonna come over there and slap the sorry right out of you."

Trent laughed. For the first time in several days he laughed. He gave Ivy another hug.

Later that night he punched a number on his speed dial list. She answered on the fourth ring.

"Hey," Trent said. "Are you still at the Pines?"

"Yes. For another week."

"Would it be ok if I drive back up there tomorrow and hang out for a few days before you leave?"

"I'd like that," Darcey said.

TUESDAY, MAY 19TH

He was on I-49 north of Lafayette when his phone rang. Jack Blake was calling.

"Hey, Jack," he answered the call. "What's up?"

"Where are you?" Jack said. He didn't sound happy.

"Headed your way. Just passed through Lafayette. What's up?"

"The worst thing I can think of," the sheriff said. "Johnny Blair escaped from the mental institution yesterday."

"He what? How could that happen? I thought he was being restrained."

"I did, too. I told those doctors he was dangerous. Come on to my office when you get to town. We got to catch this guy or there's going to be more killing."

"I'll be there in less than two hours." Trent pressed the accelerator to the floor. He thought the CTS-V would do 200 mph. The portable lights and siren were still connected. He turned them on.

Johnny Blair was lying behind the log at the edge of the woods watching the big house at the Pines. The same vantage point he had used before. He felt a lot better this time. The knife that turned on him was gone. The sheriff kept it. He was glad. The knife was driving him insane.

Now he was sane again. In control. He had a new knife. A large chef's knife he'd taken from the kitchen at the hospital on his way out. It was just a knife. A tool. It wasn't trying to control him.

He thought he'd been lying there for about an hour when he saw movement. The old woman came out of the house. She stopped and spoke to someone inside but he couldn't make out her words. She got in her car and drove away.

Trent Marshall's car wasn't there. That probably meant he wasn't there. That left only one person. The blonde. Trent's girlfriend. Johnny giggled quietly. Oh, this was too perfect. He would have Trent's girlfriend. Sooner or later Trent would show up. He would make Trent watch him slit his girlfriend's throat. Then he would kill Trent. This was so much better than before. He was so much smarter than the crazy knife that tried to control him.

"So how did he manage it?" Trent asked. They were sitting in Jack's office at the parish courthouse.

"About as sickening as when he killed his mother. He had an appointment with a therapist. The therapist told the guard to wait outside. Since Johnny's right arm was broken and in a cast the therapist didn't think he had to be cuffed. His good arm should have been cuffed to the chair but it wasn't. The therapist was sure Johnny would open up if they were alone. He opened up all right. Grabbed a sharp pencil from the therapist's desk and pushed it through his eye. The guard heard the commotion and went charging in. He got the pencil through a carotid artery.

"Before anyone else could get there Johnny locked the office door. He took all the money both men had and the therapist's clothes and car. A dark, late model Toyota."

"Any idea which way he headed?"

"Which way do you think, Trent?" Blake thundered. "How many times do we have to catch this guy?"

Jack had deputies combing all roads coming into the parish. He suggested that Trent should go to the Pines in case Johnny showed up there.

Darcey was in the den looking through old photograph albums. She liked to do that when she was home. She loved the pictures of her father. Her father and mother together. Her as a little girl on a horse being led by her mother. Her grandfather Belmont walking by her side to catch her if she fell.

She heard the front door open and close. She thought her mother had forgotten something she needed for her Ladies' Club meeting.

"Mom? Is that you?" she called.

There was no answer. She thought that strange.

She laid the album aside and went to the door. As she stepped into the hall someone grabbed her from behind. A sharp blade was pressed to her throat. She didn't make a move. Didn't make a sound.

"Hello, Trent's girlfriend," the young man said. He giggled as he talked. "Bet you never expected to see me here."

Darcey risked speaking.

"Why are you here?"

"Why am I here?" the man laughed. "Trent Marshall killed my father. I'm going to kill him. But first I'm going to make him watch me kill you. That's sort of a bonus." He laughed again.

Trent had a hunch. Before he reached the lane leading up to the big house at the Pines he turned into the yard of the old warehouse. He was right. A late model Toyota had been backed into the warehouse. He went through the car but found nothing. Johnny didn't have anything to leave behind. The one thing he was sure to have would be with him. He was sure to have a knife.

Trent eased quietly down the trail to the fallen tree where Johnny had lain to watch the house. He had been there again. Fast food containers were lying on the ground near the old tree. He ate a burger and drank a coke while he watched.

Trent knelt behind the log and watched the house. Betty's car was gone. He didn't know if Darcey was with her or if she had stayed behind. If she was with Betty there was no hurry. If she was in the house he knew he didn't have much time. He thought Johnny would keep Darcey alive until he showed up. But Johnny was insane. There was no way to predict what he would do. He rose and threaded his way back through the woods to the warehouse.

Minutes later the sleek black sedan turned off the highway and drove up to the big house at the Pines. He took a deep breath. Calm, he told himself. Stay calm. He went up the steps and onto the porch. He opened the front door and stepped into a horror show.

Darcey stood at the end of the hall. A strip of cloth was tied around her mouth as a gag. It looked like her hands were tied behind her back.

Johnny Blair stood behind her. His left hand was on her forehead holding her head back. Though his broken arm had been put into a cast he could still use his hand. It held a large knife to Darcey's throat.

"Hello, Uncle Trent," he laughed. "Bet you never expected to see me again."

"Hello, Johnny."

"Those idiots in Shreveport couldn't keep me," Johnny laughed. "They didn't know how smart I am. But you do, don't you, Uncle Trent?"

"Yes, Johnny, I know how smart you are."

"And you know I'm smart enough to know you have that big gun with you. Put it on this table here."

Trent pulled the Model 1911 from where he had shoved it into his belt next to his stomach. He very carefully laid it on the table to Johnny's left. That brought him closer to Johnny.

Johnny released Darcey's forehead to reach for the gun but kept the knife pressed tightly against her throat. He stuck the gun in his own belt.

"I don't like guns but I know you do. That was just so you don't get any ideas."

Trent remained silent.

"Do you remember when I was a little boy, Uncle Trent, and we used to play games?"

"Yes, I remember that. Those were good times."

"Yes, they were," Johnny said, smiling.

The smile disappeared.

"They were good times until you ruined them by killing my daddy," Johnny shouted.

Trent said nothing. Johnny smiled again.

"We're going to play a game today. I made up all the rules while I was waiting for you to get here," he said, proud of himself. "This is the way the game is played. I have your girlfriend here. Her hands are tied so she can't hurt me. But I can hurt her. And I'm going to hurt her. I'm going to kill her. But I'm going to do it very slowly. I'm going to draw my knife across her throat. And you're going to stand there and watch her die."

"Not a chance," Trent said. "No way I'll stand here and watch you murder her."

"Oh, but you will," Johnny laughed. "Remember I've got your gun. If you come at me I'll shoot you. Oh, but I won't kill you. I'll shoot you in the knee. It'll hurt really bad. You won't be able to walk. Yes. That would be so good. Why don't you do that? I'm changing the rules to let you do that."

Trent didn't say a word. He walked firmly toward the two people at the end of the hall. His eyes locked on Johnny's. He watched Johnny's eyes grow wide. Johnny never expected Trent would actually take the initiative. He was rattled. He let go of Darcey's forehead. He pulled Trent's big Model 1911 from his belt. He aimed it at Trent. Pulled the trigger. The only sound was an empty click.

Johnny's surprise that the gun was empty jolted his confidence. He was distracted for seconds. Only seconds. But enough time for Darcey to hurled herself backwards against him. The action created a space between her neck and the blade.

"I've got you," he screamed as he tried to drop the gun and wrap his hand in her hair. "You're dead now!"

Trent reached behind him for the Walther PPK. He aimed. Fired.

A round red hole appeared in Johnny's forehead. The knife fell from his hand. There was a look of surprise on his face as he dropped to the floor. The back of his head was gone. Most of it splattered on the walls and door behind him.

He would not escape again.

SUNDAY, MAY 24TH

Trent had booked them two suites at the hotel on the lake. None of them wanted to stay at the Pines until it could be cleaned and painted. Jack put them in touch with a company that specialized in cleaning crime scenes. Trent made the arrangements. All signs of the terrifying experience would be eradicated by today.

They had spent the time resting. Recovering. They ordered room service meals. They were all suffering from adrenaline let down. On Saturday he talked Darcey into a round of golf. It was the first time she ever played. For a beginner she was pretty good. They enjoyed the uninterrupted time together. She thought she'd look into lessons when she got home.

Sunday morning he called Darcey to remind her it was his day to breakfast at the Coffee Pot. They couldn't do that but at least they could breakfast together in the hotel restaurant. As he walked by their suite Darcey came bounding out of the door to leap into his arms. He held her close. Kissed her. A deep kiss. They stood for a few moments with his arms around her, her head on his chest.

"I told myself to play it cool," Darcey said, pressing herself into him. "I told myself to let you take the first step. But after what happened Thursday I can't do it. I'm so glad we're both still alive."

"Me, too, Darcey. That last parley with Johnny cut it a little close."

"Are we going to have a shoot out every time you're at the Pines, Trent?" Betty's voice came from the door behind them."

"I sure hope not, Betty. I'm getting tired." Trent laughed, as he gave her a hug. She surprised him with a kiss on the cheek.

They were back at the Pines by shortly after noon. Jack Blake showed up not much later. He said he was driving by and thought he'd check

[269]

on them. He also wanted to be sure the cleaning job had been done efficiently. Betty assured him it looked like nothing had ever happened in the hallway.

They sat in the living room. Jack's arm was no longer immobilized with a sling. Trent's arm was healing. It wasn't the physical scars that lingered after the trauma the four of them had suffered. They would fade and be forgotten. The internal scars were more worrisome. They were still talking through the mystery that brought them together. It was the way to minimize hidden internal scars.

"There's one thing I don't understand about Rube's story," Jack said. "Why didn't General Taylor or General Lovell send more troops after the gold?"

"I don't think General Taylor ever knew about it," Trent said. "Taylor was considered a military genius and an outstanding leader. But he suffered from crippling arthritis. He would be in his tent unable to command for weeks at a time. I suspect Rube showed up when the general was incapacitated. Bohmer probably never gave him the message."

"What about Lovell?" Jack asked.

"Lovell was also a good general. He made the right decision to withdraw from New Orleans. He knew he couldn't protect the city with the ragtag collection of farmers he had been given as an army. He knew if he tried to put up a fight the city would be leveled. But the politicians in Richmond destroyed his reputation to hide their own culpability in losing the city. He was justifiably bitter and probably not inclined to help the Confederate government recover a fortune, most of which he suspected would probably wind up lining the pockets of Richmond politicians."

"It's too bad we haven't found the gold," Jack said. "It's awfully frustrating to know it's here but not know where."

"I guess you're right, Jack," Betty agreed. "It's too bad we couldn't find the gold and put all the rumors to rest forever. But we always knew we were looking for a needle in a haystack."

"Who said we haven't found the gold?" Trent asked with a smile.

They all three stared at him in disbelief.

"You know where the gold is?" Jack sputtered.

"Yep. Sure do."

Betty and Darcey sat in stunned silence. Jack not so much. He leaped to his feet, flinching as the sudden movement sent a bolt of pain through his injured arm.

"Well, do you think it would kill you to let the rest of us in on your little secret?" he almost shouted.

Trent laughed as he stood up. "It would be my pleasure, Sheriff. Would you and the ladies take a little walk with me?"

They followed him along the path leading to the family cemetery. They stood in front of the weathered tombstones.

"I don't know why this didn't occur to me earlier. Keep in mind that the plant down by Rube's cabin is called by many names."

"Most people around here call it a Spanish dagger," Jack said.

"True, but it's also known as the Lord's Candelabra," Trent pointed out, "because of the spray of white flowers it produces. That's what Blanche Belmont called it. She saw the flowers as a memorial to her sons. The son who died following orders and the son who disappeared."

"Yes, Rube wrote about that in his journal," Darcey recalled.

"And he gave us the clue we needed in that journal also," Trent said. "Take a look at Henry's tombstone. Notice his middle name."

"Adam," Betty said. "Henry Adam Belmont."

"In his journal Rube referred to the plant beside his cabin by another of its names. Adam's needle."

"Adam's needle!" Jack said. "The needle we've been looking for. The plant marks the location of the storm shelter."

"Rube said in his journal they filled in the old storm shelter," Betty recalled.

"No," Darcey contradicted her. "He didn't say they 'filled it in.' He said they 'covered it over.'"

"What's the difference?" the sheriff asked.

"Remember that Andrew Belmont was insistent that a cabin be built on that spot and that Rube would live in it for the rest of his life. Andrew and Rube took special care to build a sturdy cabin. One that would last for a century or more."

"They built the cabin over the old storm shelter!" Jack exclaimed.

They made a brief stop by the vehicles where both Jack and Trent retrieved powerful flashlights. All four then walked down the ridge to the old cabin. Stepping inside Trent had the same feeling as the first time he had visited. As though someone, or something, was leading him on. As though whatever it was wanted him to reveal its secret.

Trent looked around the cabin. His eyes locked onto the pantry. He opened it. While Jack aimed the light into the pantry Trent felt around the sides. He pulled on the single shelf and found it slid easily out.

Laying it aside he felt around the bottom. His hand stopped on what felt like a piece of circular metal.

He looked back at the others with a smile as he slipped his finger into the metal ring and raised the bottom of the pantry. In the light of Jack's flashlight they saw the ladder-like steps leading to a room below the cabin.

"Keep that light aimed down there, Jack," Trent said, as he turned on his own light. He started down the steps.

"Be careful, Trent," Darcey said. "Those steps haven't been used in more than a hundred years."

Trent tested each step before putting his full weight on it. Each step was still sturdy. The air was musty. Expected in a room closed for a century and a half. He brushed away a tangle of spider webs guarding the steps.

Reaching the dirt floor he moved his light around the room. There were shelves where once old jars would have been stacked in place. Food that generations of Belmont women had put up for winter.

Jack looked at the shelf against the back wall of the room. It looked somehow different. He flashed his light along the shelf at the ceiling. Again along the floor. There were semicircular scrapes in both places. Very faint. A squad of Union shoulders stripping food from the shelves wouldn't have bothered to look.

Following the direction the marks on the floor and ceiling, he pulled on the right side of the shelving. It gave way. Not much. But there was definite movement.

"Jack, give Darcey your light and come give me a hand," he called up.

The sheriff climbed carefully down the stairs, aided by the light Darcey kept on him.

Between the two of them Trent and Jack were able to turn the shelving until it opened like a door. Behind it was another small room. The secret room Andrew Belmont had dug out in the event the family needed a place to hide from marauders. A dozen wooden boxes were stacked in the small space. All but one were intact. A handful of gold coins had spilled out of the one box that had begun to rot.

"Is it there?" Betty asked anxiously. "Can you see it?"

Trent stepped back into the light Darcey was still aiming down into the hole. He held up his hand.

"Betty, what does this look like to you?"

Betty reached down and took the object from his hand.

"Oh my," she said. "So this is what all the fuss has been about?"

From below they could hear the sheriff, amazement in his voice.

"A twenty dollar gold double eagle," Jack said from below. "And there are 20,000 more in these boxes."

Jack had a heavy lock placed on the entrance to the underground room to which he held the only key. He posted two heavily armed deputies to guard the cabin. He would keep guards at the cabin and at the entrance to the Pines around the clock until arrangements could be made to remove the cache.

Betty was upstairs in her room. Trent and Darcey walked hand in hand up the stairs. They stopped at the door to her room. Trent took her in his arms. Kissed her. She pressed herself against him. She could feel him stirring. She could feel his hands moving lower. Pulling her even tighter against him.

Then she felt him freeze. She felt the disappointment rushing through her. It wasn't going to happen tonight.

"I....uh...I'm sorry, Darcey," Trent stammered. "I...uh...Well, your mother's right here....And the deputies..."

"My mother would be delighted to find you in my bed tomorrow morning, Trent," Darcey said. "Don't blame this on her. And those deputies aren't here to watch us."

"I'm sorry," he said again. He turned and walked down the hall to the room that had become known as his room.

Darcey watched him go. She went into her bedroom alone.

"A gentleman," she muttered. "I'm starting to dislike gentlemen."

In his bedroom, Trent stared out the window. Wondering what was wrong with him.

SUNDAY, JUNE 24TH

Trent seldom invited anyone to join him for his ritual Sunday morning breakfasts at the Coffee Pot. This Sunday Jordan Baron was with him. The detective had been busy with a series of mundane crimes for the past few days. He was anxious to hear everything that had happened.

Jordan had put away a plate of blintzes filled with cream and mascarpone made in house, topped with sour cream.

Trent had a taste for crab. He ordered Crab Cake Jonathan. Topped with grilled shrimp, tomato and poached eggs, drizzled with hollandaise.

Ivy ignored Jordan's protests when she set a calas swimming in maple syrup in front of each.

"You're going to have me on a sugar high that'll last for days," he said.

"Go for a run down the levee," Ivy said, as she walked away.

Trent had filled Jordan in on the whole story from beginning to end.

"I think I'm glad y'all left New Orleans when you did," Jordan said. "That woman who was flirting with me at Arnaud's turned out to be a cold blooded killer."

"Yeah, you're lucky you didn't hook up with her," Trent said. "I might be dining alone this morning."

"And the guy with the knife on the Moonwalk was Josh Blair's son who wanted revenge against you. He didn't have anything to do with the gold."

"Not a thing," Trent said. "A very sad case. A young boy whose life was destroyed through no fault of his own. He couldn't deal with his father being a criminal and dying in prison. He was completely insane. Had he lived he would have spent the rest of his life in a mental institution."

"And Jack's chief deputy joined up with them," Jordan said. "That one's hard to believe."

"He wasn't the man we thought he was, Jordan," Trent said. "He tried to make me believe it was all because he was discriminated against because he was poor and Spanish. The truth is he was just as greedy as the rest of the bunch. It was all about the gold."

"The only loose end is who shot at you and Darcey. They all denied doing it."

"Well, Matt didn't deny it. Never had a chance to confront him with it," Trent said. "But I don't think he had motive. He was like Valerie. He wanted me alive."

"So who fired those shots?"

"I don't know for sure but I have an idea. Are you willing to go out on a bit of a limb?"

"Why not? Nothing exciting has happened down here since you left town."

It was nine o'clock. Trent was watching another old western movie on television in his office. His feet up on the desk. The glass of Merlot in his hand.

Jordan called to say he was coming in. Trent went to the kitchen for another wine glass and to open a second bottle. When Jordan came into the library Trent muted the television and motioned Jordan to the chair near the desk. A glass of Merlot was waiting for him.

"Bon temps," Trent said, the traditional New Orleans toast as he held up his glass. "Good times."

"Bon temps," Jordan returned the greeting.

"Turns out your hunch was right," Jordan said. "The bullets we dug out of your door were .32s. Steve Burgess still carries the old .38 service revolver."

"And his hideout?"

"A snub nose .32."

"The ballistics test?"

"The .32 was a perfect match. It was definitely Burgess who shot at you."

"But why?"

"He still blames you for his career dead ending. I think when y'all got at each other few weeks ago here at your house, well, it sent him over the edge. He thought you humiliated him in front of me. It was more than he could take. I sent two uniforms to arrest him. Unfortunately he saw it coming and sneaked out. But we'll get him. And he can explain it all to a judge."

"You had men blanketing this neighborhood within minutes of the shooting. How did he get away that day?"

"He didn't. Two of my men found him in a bar right down the street. Drunk. He was still on duty. They felt sorry for him. They didn't mention him in their report. They get to explain that to me."

JULY

The Treasury Department managed to bring the boxes of gold coins up from the hidden room beneath Rube's cabin without damaging the old building. The precious metal was now in the hands of its legal owners after a century and a half.

Archaeologists completed the dig at the mound in the woods. After they removed all the human remains and artifacts they filled in the hole with dirt. They planted wild grasses, flowers and saplings indigenous to the area. Within a few years no one could tell there had ever been anything unusual buried there.

Darcey had gone back to San Francisco. She had been away from her business for too long. A few days before she got back to her office her receptionist, who handled many of her travel arrangements, didn't show up for work. Darcey had already figured out she was the woman Valerie befriended. The woman who kept Valerie informed on Darcey's activities. Her disappearance saved Darcey the trouble of firing her.

A package arrived for her not long after she returned to San Francisco. Inside was a gold double eagle and a note from Trent

Dear Darcey,

We got to know your ancestors, Andrew and Blanche Belmont, and their friend, Rube Jackson, though they've been gone for a century and more. I am in awe of them. They had the strength of character to take with them to their graves the secret of where a fortune in gold was hidden. They did that because they believed it the right thing to do. It's unfortunate that our world today has too few with their integrity.

Speaking of that I wasn't exactly honest with the federal government when I told them all the double eagles were still there. I held out four. I think Jack, Betty, you and I deserve a remembrance of the adventure we experienced together.
Trent

Jack and Betty each received similar notes and packages.

Trent and Darcey talked on the phone often. At first they talked once a week. Then two or three times a week. Before long they talked every night.

She told him she missed him.

He told her he missed her.

She asked him if he might want to visit San Francisco.

He said he would like to do that.

Some day.

Darcey was still thinking about her last conversation with Trent. She was not happy with his continued hesitation. But she hadn't decided what, if anything, she should do about it.

She and her executive assistant, Miles Diaz-Douglas, were in her kitchen making dinner. Darcey was busy making pork fried rice. Miles was making a shrimp salad. They both worked efficiently with the confidence of people comfortable in the kitchen.

Scott Douglas, Miles' husband since same sex marriage had been declared legal, and Darcey's best friend, Mandy, were sitting on stools at the kitchen island watching the action. Scott, a soft spoken middle aged venture capitalist, and Mandy were both self-described non cooks. They were both very good at ordering delivery or drinking wine while watching others cook.

"You're still hung up on that man in New Orleans, aren't you?" Mandy questioned.

"You know me too well," Darcey said. "I guess I am. It's so frustrating. I know he feels the same about me as I do about him. But he doesn't seem to be able to let himself go. He's struggling with a burden of guilt most of us can't even imagine. This latest adventure turned out well but it added one more layer of remorse to an already heavy load. I'm trying to be patient but I really don't know how much longer I can go on with the way things are."

"Girl, you need to go down there and get that man," Miles said, as he used two wooden spoons to toss the salad with dramatic flair. "I have told you a million times that you can have any man you want. This Trent is no different from any other man."

"You also think you can have any man you want, Miles," Scott said, laughing.

"And don't you think for a minute that I can't," Miles bantered back. "I just don't want any other man."

Scott rolled his eyes but smiled, pleased with Miles' response.

"Actually Miles might be right," Mandy said.

"You're not serious?" Darcey said, surprised at Mandy's comment. "I can't just go to New Orleans and drag him back here

"Why not?" Mandy responded. "It's a matter of strategy, Darcey. I recall you telling me that you began to make progress in solving the mystery of the empty Mint when Trent turned the tables on the bad guys. They had been controlling events. When you took control away from them things started happening."

"True," Darcey said, "though some of those things almost ended with all of us dead."

"But that didn't happen," Mandy said. "What did happen was you forced your antagonists out into the open where you could see them. Once you did that you had a fight on your hands for sure. But it was a fight you could win. And you did."

"Maybe you're right," Darcey said, thoughtfully.

"I know I'm right," Mandy said, reaching for the wine and refilling their glasses. "The one who determines the battle field wins. It's a strategy taught at military academies and law schools."

"And in business schools," Scott added.

"You see?" Mandy said. "Scott agrees and he's the most conservative man I know."

"You get yourself back down to New Orleans, girl, and bring that man home," Miles said, holding his glass up to toast what he considered the final decision.

With a pensive look on her face, Darcey clinked her glass with her friends. Taking control of events. It's all about controlling events. She remembered Trent saying the same thing.

Three days later Jordan hosted Trent to dinner to celebrate solving the mystery of the empty Mint. Trent had decided the Lord's Candelabra was the name he liked best for the plant of many names. He asked Walter to plant one in the courtyard in memory of Andrew, Blanche, Henry and Rube.

It was a pleasant evening. Jordan left his car in the courtyard and they walked to the restaurant. Trent was surprised when Jordan led him to Antoine's. At more than one hundred seventy five years, Antoine's is one of the oldest restaurants in the country. It's also one of the most expensive. Not a place Jordan could often afford on a cop's salary. He said it was a special occasion.

They toasted the event with glasses of excellent Prosecco.

They dined on Oysters Rockefeller, an Antoine's original creation, and grilled pompano. After dinner Jordan suggested they adjourn to the restaurant's bar for a Sazerac.

The detective was in an unusually talkative mood. He told story after story of life in New Orleans. He even described in detail the debate regarding the origin of the Sazerac. One theory was that the original Antoine himself had created it at his apothecary before he became a restaurateur. He talked about how the word cocktail might have come from American mispronunciation of the French word coquetier. He checked his watch often.

At nine o'clock Jordan said he had an early day coming up. It was time to go. Back in the courtyard, Trent thanked Jordan for a great evening. He watched the cop drive through the faded green gate. He waited to see that the gate closed securely.

He locked up the house. He went into the library to look once again at the Colt Dragoon, the LeMat and the matched pair of Philadelphia Deringers. Betty had insisted that he have them. He tried to refuse the gift, pointing out the value of the weapons. But Betty wouldn't relent.

He had commissioned construction of a special humidity-controlled case in which to display them. They were priceless. The gold double eagle surrounded by the weapons was priceless, too. But in a personal way.

He thought he might put on the pajama bottoms and tee shirt in which he usually slept. A glass of Merlot, an old movie or a good book sounded like the perfect ending to what had been a pleasant though somewhat puzzling evening.

He walked slowly up the stairs. The hallway light was still on when he opened his bedroom door. Strange, he thought, that the door was closed. He seldom closed it. He stopped dead still in the doorway.

There were candles burning on the nightstands on either side of the bed. Someone was sitting in his bed. The bed clothes pulled up to her chin. She held a silver plated small caliber revolver with polished walnut grips in her hand. It was cocked. It was pointed directly at his chest.

"I was beginning to wonder if Jordan was going to keep you out all night," Darcey said.

Trent didn't know what to say. Didn't know what to do. He said nothing. Did nothing.

"I'm tired of waiting, Trent Marshall," the woman with the gun said. "If you don't get your clothes off and join me I swear I will shoot you."

"Nothing gets your attention like a beautiful woman in your bed with a gun," he said, slipping his arms out of the sport coat he'd worn to Antoine's and tossing it aside. He began to unbutton his shirt.

Darcey let the covers fall to her waist revealing her magnificent breasts.

"And you'd better have plenty of beads," she said, releasing the hammer and laying the revolver on the nightstand.

Trent stared at her breasts. He was right. D cup. Definitely a D cup.

Two hours later he went downstairs for a bottle of chilled Prosecco.

Two glasses.

More beads.

www.ingramcontent.com/pod-product-compliance
Lightning Source LLC
Chambersburg PA
CBHW051536260626
47170CB00003B/963